To Marilyn,

I hope you enjoy the photos!

Merry Christmas

The Trials of Innocence

The Trials of Innocence

Book Two
of
A Prisoner's Welcome
Author Version

SHANE MOORE

Wandering Sage Publications

The Trials of Innocence: A Novel © 2008 Shane Moore
All rights reserved. Printed in the United States of America. No part of this book may be used or reproduced in any manner whatsoever without written permission except in the case of brief quotations embodied in critical articles and reviews. For information address Wandering Sage Publications, 3224-1 Rue Royal, St. Charles, MO 63301

Wandering Sage Publications is a division of Wandering Sage Bookstore & More, LLC.

First Edition.

Genre: Fantasy / Series

ISBN: 1-933300-56-6– perfect bound 6x9, 404 pgs.

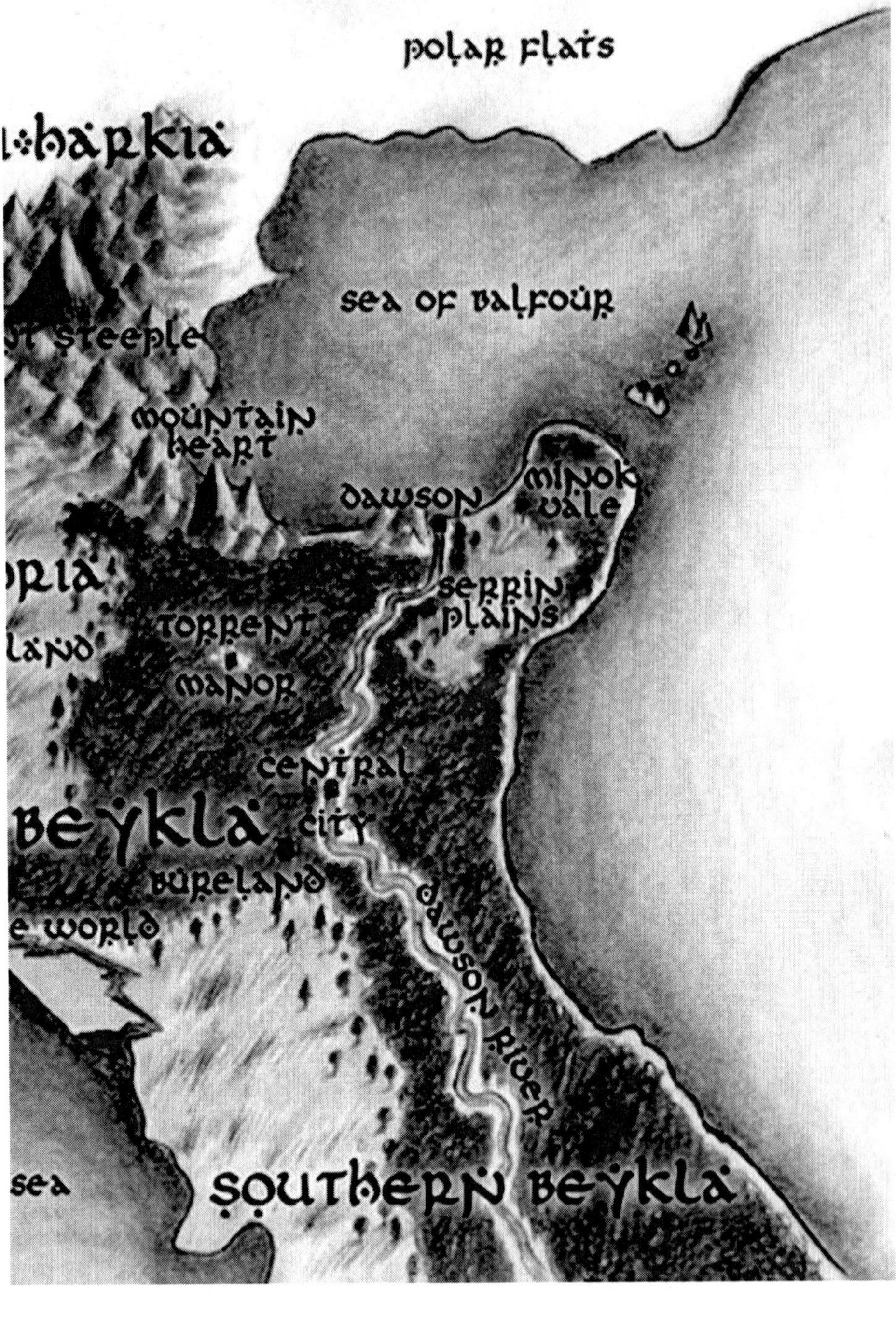
Polar Flats
Sea of Balfour
Mountain Heart
Dawson
Minok Vale
Serrin Plains
Torrent Manor
Central City
Beykla
Bureland
Dawson River
Sea
Southern Beykla

Table of Contents

Chapter One………………………. 1

Chapter Two………………………. 37

Chapter Three……………………. 98

Chapter Four……………………… 141

Chapter Five……………………… 167

Chapter Six………………………. 213

Chapter Seven……………………. 237

Chapter Eight……………………. 267

Chapter Nine……………………… 306

Chapter Ten………………………. 346

Glossary…………………………. 381

Chapter One
Darrion-Quieness

*H*e awoke from his deep slumber and his thick pale lids fluttered slowly revealing his vivid green eyes. Darrion-Quieness, the great white dragon, licked the outside of his giant toothed filled maw and yawned. The ancient beast stretched his limbs and rolled over on his giant pile of gold and jewels. His pointed nostrils sniffed the frigid air and detected some intruders in his cave. They were at the entrance of his lair and he lazily decided he had a while to wake up before he devoured them. Darrion-Quieness was a white dragon, one of the weaker of the dragon races, but he had survived a millennia and grown to mammoth proportions. He was three hundred feet from head to tail his scales had changed from gleaming white at birth to a pale murky opaque. His dark black claws were long and hooked, protruding several feet from his scaled toes. His thick oversized head was well armored and he had a single spine with a sail crest that angled back toward his body. His long white leathery wings permitted flight, but he certainly was not the most agile creature in the air.

Darrion-Quieness stood and glanced around his ice-covered lair. Their were many frost giants frozen in solid ice that littered his cave. They were his favorite food, and they were in abundance in the tallest peaks of the mountains. Darrion-Quieness had the ability to control the weather and he elected to make it a perpetual winter around his small mountain home. The cold weather attracted many colder clime creatures such as frost giants and other beings in which Darrion-Quieness was more than happy to feed on. Occasionally adventurers or other humans would wander his way, but most intelligent beings stayed far clear of his mountain home. Sometimes some foolish hero, usually a human, would try to rid the world of the horrible evil named Darrion-Quieness, and the dragon usually toyed with the foolish morsel before he ate him.

      But something was different about this group today. The giant dragon could smell many humans and he didn't detect any weapon oil or armored men. This troubled the great white. If they did not have swords and armor, they were probably spell casters, and wizards posed the largest threat to the dragon. He hated fighting wizards because he had difficulty discerning how powerful they were. Darrion-Quieness sighed as he silently positioned his back to wall of his sleeping chamber. He wasn't about to provoke the mages, so he would have to barter with them rather than battle today. He would rather battle, but he didn't get this old by foolishly fighting the spell casters.

      The ancient dragon sat on his pile of gold and jewels and waited for the intruders to show themselves. They sheepishly rounded the corner to the main cavern. He counted seven in all. They wore long black robes and bore the mark of Nalir. Darrion-Quieness smiled a pearl toothed grin. Though he wasn't going to eat today, he was going to get many diamonds as payment. The old dragon loved diamonds more than anything else. He scanned the humans for several seconds, trying to see the pouch where the diamonds were kept, but he could not see it. He decided that the humans were crafty for hiding the treasure because he was known to just take the diamonds and eat the people rather than speak to them. The dragon thought he might just decide to test their might and get both dinner and diamonds.

One of the humans stepped forward. Darrion-Quieness could smell many magical enchantments about him. He was small for a human and kind of old.

"Darrion-Quieness, it is I, Soran, that calls your name today. We have sought you out so that you might aid us. We have brought the usual payment. It will be delivered upon receiving answers to the questions we seek." Soran said. His voice quivered with fear from the mere sight of the powerful beast. Soran had cast spells to protect him and the other mages from the dragons aura of fear. Yet, he could still feel the great white's powerful magic prying at his mind's defenses.

Darrion-Quieness didn't respond. He ignored whatever the human was saying and thought about the wonderful diamonds he would receive from the day's transaction. Soran took the dragons silence as permission to continue.

"Before, we came to you and asked about the prophecy. You told us that a man was born that would crush the kingdom of Nalir. You said he was an orphan with the surname Ecnal. We have slain every Ecnal in the land of Beykla, where the orphans have such a surname. What..." Soran was cut off by the dragon.

"How many beautiful shinning diamonds did you bring?" Darrion-Quieness asked, picking his teeth with his giant black talon.

Soran stammered. "Y-you will be p-paid when our question has been answered and we are safe from your lair."

The dragon frowned. His glaring emerald visage made all of the mages gulp with fear. He stared at the small group of wizards and watched sweat drip from the brow of many of them. He was sure his cave was cold, and if they were sweating it was surely out of fear. With amazing speed the giant creature zipped forward. He inhaled deeply and his throat swelled as he lowered his head. A giant cone of blue air rushed from his mouth and covered the seven wizards. The dragon swept his head from side to side as he exhaled the cone of frigid breath. The dragon paused and raised a wicked claw to smite any of the mages that were still alive. To his pleasure, only Soran had survived his horrible breath. The wizard was pinned in a coffin of ice. Only his head and one of his arms were free. Soran tried to speak but could not. He fought for consciousness as his traumatized body slowed from being half frozen. He stared helplessly at the terrible beast that stood before him.

"Hector!" The dragon called out. " I know you can hear me. I can sense your weak scrying. How dare you send your goons to disturb my sleep and have the gall not to send any diamonds. I know of your talents, king. I demand payment now! "

A strange blue light formed and an image of Hector De Scoran appeared. The king was adorned in black and silver plate armor. The armor had intricate designs of scorpions on the shoulders and their tails stretched down the king's arms.

"Fitting that you show an weak image instead of coming yourself. Afraid you will suffer the same fate as your lackeys?" The dragon taunted.

"Do not tempt me beast, I have allowed you to make a home on my land. The only time I will come to your lair will be to claim your hide as my trophy."

Darrion-Quieness spread his wings and roared. The cave shook and small rocks and debris fell from the thunderous sound. He despised the human king and he despised being taunted even less.

"But for now, you are useful to me. I have brought your diamonds and I offer these men as tender morsels to placate your perpetual hunger."

Soran gasped. He didn't understand why his master would do this to him. Kalen, he, and his colleges had done as the king had asked. They had deciphered the prophecy, they had...deciphered the prophecy. It made perfect sense to the doomed wizard. His group was no longer useful and the knowledge they had of the prophecy made them a liability to the wicked king. The trapped mage struggled against frozen prison, but he could not move.

The image of Hector produced a large bag of diamonds and dropped it to the floor of the cave. The bag slowly transformed from a glowing image to a tangible bag. The dragon reached out and tore open the bag with a single claw. He purred in delight at the hundreds of diamonds that spilled out.

"Ask your questions, Hector, and then be gone." The great dragon said as he plopped down on the icy cavern floor in delight.

Hector De Scoran smiled and paced the cavern floor. "Did we succeed in slaying all of the Ecnals in Beykla?"

The dragon laid on the cavern floor slowly counting his wonderful diamonds.

"No."

"How many did we miss?" Hector asked.

"One."

"Where is he at?"

The dragon stopped counting for a moment. " You waste your time, Hector. The more you seek to invalidate this prophecy the more you will enforce validity."

"So it can be changed." Hector asked eagerly.

Darrion-Quieness exhaled and resumed counting. "All prophecies can be changed, but they always seem to have a strange way of fulfilling themselves."

Hector pondered the dragon's words. " Where is this, Ecnal?"

"He is in the Beykla, in Central City."

"What is he doing there?" Hector asked eagerly.

"One hundred thirty seven."

Hector frowned. "What?"

"One hundred thirty seven. That is how many

diamonds you have given me."

"What does that have do with anything? That is more than enough payment for these simple questions."

"Good bye, Hector. Do not disturb me again for One hundred thirty seven days, or I will fly to your castle and test your boasts of power." The dragon waved his hand and the image of Hector was gone. The mammoth beast walked over and looked down at the terrified wizard.

"What is your name?" He asked the imprisoned man.

"S-S-Soran." The man stuttered from both fear and from the temperature of his rapidly freezing body.

The dragon shook his head. "No, your name is lunch." The dragon said as his massive jaws snapped on Soran's half frozen body. The dragon crunched and chewed the wizard as he climbed back on his mound of gold and jewels. After his nap he was going to have to take a trip near Beykla. He wanted to see what was so special about the son of a fallen goddess. He swallowed the small meal and drifted back into his deep sleep.

    *   *   *

"Damn that lizard!" Hector screamed as he tried to re-establish the link that took him to the dragon's lair. He focused his mind and channeled many powerful weaves into the spell. After several unsuccessful attempts, he turned his attention to what he learned. The king recalled the dragon said that the Ecnal was in Central City, so that is where he would start looking.

"Guard. Send for a sage or one of the wizards." Hector commanded. The guard nodded and left the king's chambers.

Hector thought about his many agents he had in Beykla. His favorite was the wererat guild that was ran by Pav-co. Perhaps he would see if the fat thief might know of the Ecnal's whereabouts.

A few minutes later a young sage rushed into the room. "Yes, my lord. You sent for me?" The man stammered, falling to the feet of the imposing king.

Hector looked down at the kneeling sage with an arched eyebrow of superiority.

"Spencer, is it?"

"Y-yes, my lord." The sage whispered.

"I recall you have always served me well." Hector said with an evil grin.

Spencer thought to mention when he failed to answer a question Hector had asked him, but he didn't want to bring up the fact, if Hector didn't remember it. The king had threatened to kill Spencer on a later day for not knowing the answer. Certainly Spencer didn't want his king to remember his promise of death. That was the only promise the king always seemed to keep.

"I always serve with my all, my lord." Spencer said as a trickle of nervous sweat ran down the side of his face.

"Well Spencer, I have a minor task for you." The king said haughtily.

"Yes, my lord?" Spencer asked as he scooted on the floor closer to Hector's feet.

"It is an easy task. Perform it expeditiously and I will forget I planned to kill you."

"Yes, my lord. Name it and it will be done." Spencer said as his voice cracked with fear.

"I want you to go to the library and tell my first wizard, Kalen, that I need to get a message to Pav-co." Hector said as he stroked the blade of a curved silver dagger. " Tell Pav-co that I want him to find the Ecnal and kill him. He is to return the Necromidus to me as proof of the deed."

"Yes, my lord." Spencer said and the sage scurried from the room.

Hector sat back in his throne and smiled, pondering the Ecnal's death as Spencer hurried from the chamber. Regardless of what the dragon said about the prophecy, the Ecnal could not harm him, or his kingdom, if he was dead.

*   *   *

Spencer rushed into the king's bathhouse. Hector laid comfortably in a steaming bath. He rested his feet up on the end of the emerald colored marble and sipped wine from a golden goblet that rested on the rail near his head. There were many attendants helping with his bath, including many scantily clad women.

Spencer quickly kneeled down at the base of the tub. "You sent for me, my lord?" The messenger asked eagerly.

Hector took a long sip from his goblet before answering. " Yes, Spencer, I did. I need for you to go find out how the tasks fare that I asked Kalen to do."

Spencer gulped hard. He hated Kalen. The evil mage always tormented him whenever he went to his chambers. Spencer wanted to tell the king all the horrible things Kalen said about him, but Spencer feared that Hector might become at angry at him for some reason, so the meek sage turned messenger, kept the comments to himself. It had been a few days since he had to go to the gray elf's chambers, but he vividly remembered the last unpleasant encounter and he wasn't eager to repeat it. "My lord, I am sure that elf has done as you wished. He is very competent at what he does."

Did you tell him my instructions?" Hector asked as he sat up suddenly in his tub. Water from the over filled vat spilled out and splashed on Spencer's arm.

"Yes, well, kind of. He took it from my mind. I hate it when he does that." Spencer said as he wiped some of the sudsy water from his sleeve.

"He read your mind?" Hector asked, more elated than surprised. "Good, his studies are paying off. He is progressing faster than anyone I have ever known. He will be a powerful ally one day."

Spencer winced. He knew that Kalen had no intention of being Hector's ally. He decided that he must tell his king of the mage's backstabbing intentions.

"My lord, I do not wish to bring bad news, but for my lord's sake I think you should know." Spencer said with a cracking voice as sweat began drip from his forehead.

Hector chuckled at his young sage's anxiety. "And what devastating tale will you spin for me today, my faithful servant?"

Spencer wrung his hands before he started. "My lord, the mage had intentions of taking over Nalir when you die. He told me so. He said you were weak and he..." Spencer was cut off by Hector's booming laughter.

"Spencer, my most loyal servant. Do you presume to think that I do not know my allies intentions? I know all of them. Of course he desires my kingdom. If he did not, he would not useful to me at all." Hector bellowed.

"But, my lord, I don't understand. I thought..."

"Do not think, my faithful servant. You do not have the mind power to understand the tasks of running an empire. But alas, you are very loyal. Mark my words, dear Spencer, one day I will make you more powerful than Kalen ever will be. Until then however, you will serve me here. Now go and find what I asked."

Spencer nodded and slowly backed out of Hector's chambers. He closed the door and ran as fast as he could to the mage tower. His mind raced as he contemplated what kind of power would Hector give him? Would Kalen still be around? Spencer hoped he would be so he could use some magic of his own against the tormenting mage. What a glorious day it would be.

Spencer reached the chamber door of the mage tower. He opened it and barged right in. He knew there would be a horrible consequence for intruding without knocking, but it was ok, because he knew that one day he would return the pain tenfold to the tormenting mage.

"Who dares disturb my work?" Kalen growled as he lost his concentration and the sparkling drops of magical energy that floated in front of him spiraled out of control before popping into nothingness.

"I bring message from the king, mage." Spencer said confidently.

Kalen studied the messenger very close. Never had he seen the messenger so confident. The meek slave would expect a horrible thrashing for such an intrusion, yet there he stood as if he were telling a sibling that he had work to do. Kalen slowly walked from around his desk. He cast a few quick spells to see if it was the king disguised in some magical illusion, but as far as he could tell it was the foolish sage. Kalen probed Spencer's mind for a few moments before he realized that it was indeed the sage that had rudely intruded on his studies.

"Fool." Kalen said calmly as he waved his hand and began a spell. "You will pay for this intrusion."

Spencer stuck out his chest defiantly. "Do your worst, wizard. King Hector told me one day he will make me more powerful than you will ever be, and you had better be long gone or I'll make you suffer for whatever you..." Spencer stopped his sentence short. He looked down in horror at the strange bumps that were beginning to grow on his hand.

"What are you doing to me?" He asked as pain ripped through his side forcing him to his hands and knees.

"Just making you into a little more appealing." Kalen chuckled.

Spencer stared in horror as his fingers turned green. They then curled up into the palm of his hands and fell off. He slapped his knobby hands at the severed digits, trying in vain to pick them up. His skin stretched and pulled taught over his face as his eyes bulged and moved farther apart. He cried out in pain and anger at the smiling face of the gray elf. He tried to lunge forward but he could no longer feel his legs. He tried to look down at them but was having difficulty moving his neck. Spencer's mind was nearly torn in two from intense searing pain. It felt as if his body was being ripped and stretched from the inside out. In a few seconds the once sage lay on the ground of the mage chamber. His once soft skin had been replaced by hard scales. His eyes had shifted to each side of his narrow head. His arms had shifted and withdrew into large fins and his legs merged forming a webbed tail. The pain had finally ended. Spencer tried to speak, but he could not. He couldn't stand or move his arms. He just felt his body involuntarily flopping on the hard stone floor. Terror gripped the sage. He couldn't breath. He struggled for breath but he could not get one. He felt himself slowly losing consciousness.

 Kalen smiled in glee at the large fish that flopped on the stone floor of his chambers. He watched with a morbid pleasure as the once sage, now fish, struggled to breath the air of the room. The elf walked over to the mirror that he used to communicate with the fat thief from Central City. With a wave of his hand he activated the two way mirror. In a few moments the magical energies took hold and the chambers of the guild leader shone from the other side. What he saw did not bode well. The entire chambers was in shambles and there were many half dressed women that were laying in twisted disgusting positions. They appeared as if they had been raped many times and their bodies bore wounds that would have taken a few hours to kill them. The gray elf scryed the area, searching for a conscious mind to detect, but all he felt was death. The elf dismissed the mirror and turned to the fish that lay still on his floor. There was a fluttering gill every few seconds or so. Kalen pondered the sage a few moments. The walk to the kings chambers was so far, and he hated climbing the stairs. With a heavy sigh he waved his hand and dismissed the magic that had transformed the sage from man to fish. In a few seconds Spencer lay on the ground gasping for air.

"You are lucky today, sage, for I need to relay a message back our king. Go and tell him Pav-co's guildhall has been sacked. I do not know by whom or why. Tell him I am awaiting his wishes on how to follow up on our tasks that we incurred prior to this event."

Spencer nodded quietly and stumbled from the room. His arms and legs were sluggish from the transformation.

"Where is your bravery now, sage?" Kalen mocked.

Spencer collapsed outside the closed door of the mage tower and wept. He didn't weep out of pain or fear. He wept out of complete and total despair at the evil that surrounded him. It was at that moment that he knew that Kalen would kill him at his first opportunity and Hector would do nothing to prevent it.

Spencer took along walk that day to Hector's chambers. He had never thought the elf's powers could do something like that. He didn't even think Hector could do that. No, he struggled with the realization that perhaps the elf would someday soon make good on his boasts for taking over the kingdom. Spencer shuddered at the thought of answering to vile wizard.

After a long walk to the king's chambers, he decided that no matter what happened, if he could escape Nalir, he would.

Spencer knocked on the king's chamber door. He pushed the large heavy wooden door open and slowly plodded down the slick marble floor. He walked past the intricately carved throne of gold and onto the stone balcony. Hector sat in his leisure chair and gazed off into the horizon of the vast swamp.

"My lord, I bear message from Kalen." Spencer said solemnly.

Hector turned and looked at the sage that stood before him. He was usually wracked with fear, bowing and trembling. Now he stood apathetic before him.

"What news Spencer?"

"My lord, Kalen reports that the guild hall in Central City has been destroyed. He says he doesn't know how or by who." Spencer said as he stared blankly at the swamp that was a few hundred feet below him. The forlorn sage thought about jumping. He doubted he would survive the fall, which was precisely what he was hoping for. He fantasized about the peace of death, about not having fear or pain anymore. He had no ambition no desire to see another day. Spencer knew he was nothing more than a tool to be discarded when he was no longer useful.

Hector could detect the sullenness in Spencer's voice. He didn't know what to make of it, but in truth he didn't care. He had many more important matters to attend to that the everyday ramblings of a depressed servant.

"Good job, Spencer. You may take your leave for the rest of the day."

Spencer paused for a moment, taking one final glimpse of freedom that was a few hundred feet below, before he turned and left the chamber.

Hector sipped wine from his goblet as he gazed over his kingdom. It was mostly swampland with a few patches of fertile ground. These patches were densely occupied by small cities that grew crops and mined resources for the small kingdom. Though Nalir was small in land area, it was one of the most populated and had vast resources to fuel his army.

Hector rose from his leisure chair and walked into the throne room. " Guard." he called out.

A man wearing scale mail armor and wielding a wicked falchion rushed over. "Yes, my lord." the guard said with a deep bow.

Hector paused for a moment with a stern look of abstention on his ageing face. "Go and fetch the priests, I have need of them. Tell them to meet me at the alter."

The guard nodded and rushed out of the chamber.

Hector strode to the far end of his throne room and slid one of the heavy tapestries back that hung from the ceiling to the floor. He stepped behind the arduous curtain and walked to an iron door that was in the middle of the stone wall. The door was small but was covered in strange divine runes that ran in three circles. He traced his armored finger along the dark symbols that were etched in the door. They were put in place to keep creatures that were pure of heart from entering and it kept creatures from the abyss from escaping. Some of the runes had rare crystals and gems placed into them with minor arcane enchantments. The whole concept was a little confusing for Hector. While he was an accomplished wizard, he had little understanding of divine magic. What amazed him more, was how the priests used arcane and divine magic together to bind the creatures they summoned to the room.

Hector removed his gauntlet and traced his bare finger over the encrusted symbols again. He smiled as his skin tasted the warm heat the gems emitted.

"You sent for us, my lord?" Came a raspy voice from behind the king.

Hector turned to see four of his priests entering his throne room. The lead priest was adorned in a deep violet, almost black, robe with bright red symbols on the back and around the cuffs. The others were similarly dressed, but did not wear as ornate robes. Hector outstretched his arms at the sight of the priests. Hector worshipped Rha-Cordan, the god of death. Though the god himself wasn't inherently evil, many of his followers were. Rha-Cordan determined where all souls went when they died. Hector, understanding all men die, ascertained that the god of death had the ultimate power of soul decision. Although Hector didn't understand the details that the other gods had influencing Rha-Cordan, he new that ultimately the god of death had the final decision.

"Resin Darkhand, good to see you, my friend." Hector said as he bowed low.

The priest said nothing in return, but bowed much lower than his king. "Why have you summoned us, my king?" Resin asked.

"We must summon the arch demon Bykalicus once more." Hector said nonchalantly.

Resin shook his head and sighed. "My lord, Bykalicus is no lesser fiend. He is a mighty demon and has a kingdom himself in the deep abyss. He will not take this summoning lightly."

"But you can keep him in the summoning ring by the will of Rha-Cordan?" Hector asked.

Resin nodded his head slowly. "Yes, that is correct but there is much more to it than that. If he were ever to escape the abyss and come to our plane of existence, he would wreak havoc on his enemies. If you continue to summon him, taking him away from his duties against his will, he will undoubtedly call you his prevailing foe."

Hector chuckled. "He cannot come to our plane of existence unless he is invited or brought, correct."

"Yes, my king. but..."

"And the only way he can move or perform on this plane by his own free will, is to kill his summoner?"

"Yes, my lord, but you are not understanding." Resin pleaded.

"Can any mortal scry on the mind of a demon and his power?" Hector asked with his hands on his hips.

"None that I am aware of, but..."

"And would a demon allow any other mortal, or fiend, to get revenge on those he hates?" Hector asked, folding his arms under his chest.

"No, he would not, but you do not understand. Demons with his power are resourceful beyond our comprehension."

Hector waved his hand in dismissal. "I understand completely. No fool that has the power to summon a demon, will allow himself to be slain, just to gain revenge against me. And no demon will reveal his enemies to any other creature. So we are perfectly safe.

Plus Rha-Cordan guides our souls after death. And since we are in his divine favor, there is nothing to worry about." Hector rationalized.

"As you wish, my king." Resin said in defeat.

The group of priests walked into the summoning chamber. It's four walls were made of solid stone. There were no windows or furnishings of any kind. In the center of the floor was a circle that was fifteen feet in diameter that was composed of large runes much similar to the ones that surrounded the door, except they were on a much grander scale. The stone floor was made of rough stone, not like the smooth stone of the rest of the castle. The runes were deeply carved into the hard stone and were covered in strange red dust and dried blood.

Hector went and stood by at the far end of the room and prepared some of his basic spells. His priests encircled the runes and began chanting. They raised and lowered their arms several times, citing the greatness of Rha-Cordan. Hector finished his protection spells that shielded his mind from scrying, from magical fear, from charms, and other spells that would render him helpless. Demons were more skilled than powerful human wizards and arch demons were more powerful than most.

The priests finished their chanting and dances. The four stood , arms outstretched with their heads tilted back. A frigid wind ripped through the chamber blowing their robes up around them. The runes began to glow red hot as a bright scarlet light appeared in the center of the summoning circle. The light rapidly stretched and grew, forming a vertical ring. In the center of the ring, Hector cold see the infinite wasteland known as the deep abyss. Small demons scattered from the portal dragging half eaten bodies of men and women that screamed for help that would not, nor had come, for an eternity.

"Bykalicus." The priests whispered in unison. The demons on the other side hissed and growled at the announcement of the fabled abyssal king.

"Bykalicus." The priest said slightly louder than before. The wind picked up in the room and it made a shrill howling sound as it tore around the priests.

"Bykalicus." The priests said louder, their voices echoing throughout the entire abyss as dark sulfurous clouds started churning.

"Bykalicus!" They screamed reaching up the ceiling with their outstretched arms. The wind in the abyss howled and the sulfurous clouds bubbled and frothed within themselves in an excited storm of hellish fury. Then as suddenly as the storm began, it stopped.

The priests looked into the shining crimson portal they had formed. There was nothing on the other side, save for the barren wasteland of the abyss. The priests began chanting again, very softly.

A large muscular clawed foot stepped through the portal. It was dark red and covered in protruding veins and sinew. It had thick black claws that erupted from scaled toes and a large black horn that protruded from knee. As the imposing figure stepped all the way trough the portal, the priests gasped aloud. The demon stood well over fifteen feet tall. His dark red skin had flames trickling all over his incredibly burly body. He had giant bat wings that were tucked back behind him and wielded a giant great sword that was aflame with blue fire. The demon's eyes were bright yellow and had an aura that extended horizontally past his face. He had two giant goat horns that protruded from his head and curved over his back and his large canine maw dripped an acidic drool that burned and singed the stone floor were it landed. The powerful demon slowly stretched his neck and looked from side to side chuckling.

"Sloof uoy ot htaed." The demon growled, then paused and watched the foolish mortal's as they struggled to understand the abyssal tongue.

Resin waved his hand and chanted, sending waves of divine energy around the demon to convert his language to one they could understand.

Bykalicus smiled, knowing the humans would have to create a magical weave for them to understand him. In doing so, he could determine their power with the arcane arts, but to his surprise, the humans wielded divine magic. The power of Rha-Cordan. Bykalicus grumbled, knowing he couldn't cross the mighty god of death, or his disciples while still partway in he abyss. He took a deep breath and decided to see what these fools wanted. Perhaps he might trick them into releasing him on the prime material plane. He would love to crush a few human kingdoms. It had been over ten thousand years since he was last able to do that." This is the third time you have summoned me with your puny mortal magic." Bykalicus said as he stared down at the intricately crafted protection runes around the circle.

"If they are so puny, demon, then sever the bonds that hold you and kill us." Hector taunted.

The priests all turned in astonishment at their king. "My lord, you should..." Resin was cut off by the booming voice of Bykalicus.

The demon's fists were clenched and his rippling muscles went taught with fury. "Do you think that death is what you have to fear from me?" Bykalicus asked.

Hector shook his head from side to side. "I fear nothing from you slave, you will serve me as commanded and then return to serve your dark gods."

Bykalicus tucked his head back and outstretched his arms. His arms extended out, wide from his body, and his fists tightened. The arch demon's body quivered as he roared in such a fury that the chamber walls shook, knocking the priests from their feet. The flames that danced across his body flared up to white hot fire, forcing Hector and the priests to shield their face from the intense heat. Bykalicus glared at the pathetic human that stood before him. The massive flames that sprouted up around his body subsided back to the small wisps that were there before, but they danced more rapidly across his body now. He smiled at the image of the number of foolish mortals that thought they were intelligent, wise, or powerful enough to taunt him, but in the end, he always feasted on their souls, as he would feast on these morsels, in due time.

"Where is the Ecnal?" Hector asked confidently.

"You presume I know much, fool." Bykalicus retorted.

Hector narrowed his eyes. "I command you to answer, demon. Where is the Ecnal?"

Bykalicus smiled, his face distorted unnaturally into a sinister guise of wickedness. "He stands atop a cliff looking out on your vast swamp filled kingdom. Behind him stands an army that defies Rha-Cordan as a storm of vengeance brews behind him. I can hear the thunder of his voice and feel the reign of his power. Though Rha-Cordan screams for his army's soul, they refuse him, as he offers the souls of your soldiers instead. The Ecnal stands poised full of a hate-filled power that you could never dream of. He plans to kill you, and it would prove an easy task for him. But I assure you, Hector De Scoran, you will not succumb to his power."

"Power? Is this the son of the mother of mercy?" Hector asked in disbelief.

Bykalicus chuckled. "You see me as I am standing before you, mortal, yet you are as a blind man. You are responsible of the slaying of thousands of innocents on a whim that one might be the son of the departed mother of mercy. Yet, you knew not, who she was. For the purposeless slaughter to further yourself, your power, a deed of complete vileness, I will answer but one more question."

Hector was silent in thought. It was the Ecnal that

was prophesized to destroy his kingdom. Was the identity of the orphan's mother important? He suspected the Ecnal might the son of the mother of mercy. If she was indeed dead, she posed no trouble to the living. Hector lifted his head. "How do I defeat the Ecnal?"

Bykalicus grabbed his belly with his clawed hands, bellowing so deeply, mortar from the bricks in the summoning room fell to the floor in large chunks. "Find his father's body, and have your priests perform the DeNaucght."

The demon turned and stepped back through the portal. Many lesser demons that had gathered near the portal gate, fled in terror at the site of Bykalicus. They bounded over the

dark desolate land, kicking up small rocks under their clawed feet as they clambered away. Once the demon stepped through the portal, the top of it narrowed as the bottom raised up to the top, until a small scarlet horizontal line floated about three feet off of the

stone floor. The line then collapsed within itself until a small red dot remained suspended in the air. Then the sparkling crimson spec of magical energy popped into nothingness, and the portal was no more.

"My lord, I tried to warn you." Resin said as he picked the many ice crystals out of his hair that had formed from the frigid air of the abyss.

"Warn me from what?" Hector asked. "The demon has said nothing that I have not heard before, except the DeNaucght. What is that?"

The priests looked at each other worriedly. Resin straightened his robe and knocked some of the ice crystals from his hair. "We know not what the DeNaucght is, my lord, but be rest assured, we will research the matter thoroughly. But my lord, I feel I must caution you to angering the demon lord so. It can bring nothing but ill events for us."

Hector waved his hand in dismissal. "I know what is

needed to get onto this realm. The foul beast is well kept in the abyss. And after I die, Rha-Cordan will keep my soul from such tyrants as he, because I have served the god of death so well." Hector said as he walked from the room, undaunted as drops of melting ice dripped from his hair and onto his shoulders and face.

"My lord, shall we work on interpreting what the demon said?" Resin called out as he and his acolytes walked from the summoning chamber.

Hector shook his head and waved his hand in release. "There is nothing to interpret. The demon said it clearly. Obviously he was speaking of the future. The Ecnal can not kill me. Though we must perform much research on the fate of my kingdom."

"As you wish, my lord. What of the DeNaucght?" Resin asked.

"I will expect you to find how to perform as soon as possible." Hector commanded.

"As you wish, my king." Resin said, as he bowed out of the throne room.

Hector walked back out onto his lofty balcony. He sat in his plush velvety chair and placed his weary feet up on the stone rail. The cool autumn wind washed over his wet face as the king gazed out on his land. He imagined the Raynard cliffs that separated his boundaries from the fertile lands of the elven kingdom of Vidora. He supposed the Ecnal would look off of those cliffs. Hector tried to imagine how Ecnal's army would deny Rha-Cordan, the god of death. He wasn't sure how anyone could deny the dark reaper their souls. The weary king mulled over the demon's words as he drifted off into deep sleep.

   *   *   *

The great dragon, Darrion-Quieness, soared high above the fertile kingdom of Vidora, known as the land of the elves. He gazed at the sparse cloud cover that floated well below him like hundreds of giant balls of cotton. He didn't dare soar much lower than he was flying. Though the powerful wind currents made flying more tiresome at this height, the elves didn't take too kindly to white dragons taking perch on their lands. Though he could easily wipeout any elven village he encountered, Darrion-Quieness knew that attracting the attention of the elven nation was not wise decision. The elven heroes and powerful mages, often crusaded for hundreds of miles, to rid the world of those who threatened their lands. He knew of a great green named Yohr-Acht. The ancient green dragon had decided to make a lair on the fertile lands of Vidora. The damnable elves marched against him and nearly slain the green as they drove him out. He wasn't sure exactly where Yohr-Acht had moved too, but the great white thought it was somewhere near the Vidorian border. Darrion-Quieness decided that too, was not a good place to land. He feared the power of the green dragon. Greens were more powerful than whites, and Darrion-Quieness despised the odor of their nasty chlorine gas breath weapon. It took days to rid his hide of the awful smell. In fact, even if he stumbled upon a much weaker green dragon, he tried to avoid the encounter because of his dislike for their breath attack. He had endured the taunts of many greens that survived the encounter with him only because of his dislike for the chlorine. Had the dragon any pride, he might have killed the weaker greens for their insolence, but Darrion-Quieness had learned long ago that pride often coincided with death.

  The great white flew for several days until he found a fairly large mountain range that was in the middle of the Vidorian kingdom. The range was not a tall range, and it seemed to be only a few hundred miles long, as opposed to the many other ranges on Terrigan that were usually twice as tall and long. He slowly circled down, carefully searching for signs of any elven villages. When he was satisfied that there were none, Darrion-Quieness landed atop the largest snow-covered peak. The mountain top had pierced the cloud veil and was covered with many layers of snow and ice. Though the weary dragon couldn't find a cave at the mountain's peak, he was more than camouflaged in the deep snow he had landed in.

Like a cat stretching before he went to sleep on a soft pillow, the great white made a bed in the giant snow drift. He folded his wings around him, creating a buffer from the wind, and tucked his long thick tail around his muscular body. He closed his deep green eyes and summoned the innate power to control the weather. The great dragon imagined thick clouds forming above him and then a great snow. He concentrated on the large snowflakes that cascaded down from the billowing cloud cover that hovered above him. In a few minutes, a storm had formed just above the mountain peak and a heavy snow began to fall, just as the beast had imagined. The summoned storm did not move with the wind or dissipate until Darrion-Quieness dismissed it. Soon the dragon was enveloped in a soft white blanket of cool refreshing snow that covered him just like the many large rocks that rested a top the great peak. The dragon snuggled under the comforting layer of snow and he quickly slipped into a deep sleep.

Darrion-Quieness awoke from his long peaceful rest. He poked his head out from under the snow that had fallen over his body. The large brick of crumbling white snow that had formed on his wide scaled head while he slept, tumbled and fell into pieces causing his bright emerald eyes to flutter until the snow had all fallen away. The peak had sustained just about it's limit for snowfall and the dragon surmised he had been asleep for a couple of days. The great white climbed from under the icy white blanket and slowly stretched his ancient muscles. He hadn't eaten in about a week and his stomach was protesting angrily. He stretched his fantastically immense bat like wings wide and stuck out his thick scaled covered barreled chest as he gazed over the great peak. With a mighty leap the dragon launched from the face of the mountain sending large icy boulders cascading down it's side as he began to soar toward the valleys below, searching for something to eat. He preferred the taste of frost giants, but the great white wasn't sure if there were any of their kind living in this mountain range. The dragon hated frost giants, unless he was eating them of course, and he scanned the area for any sign that the gray skinned giant race may have made a home here. The wicked race of giant kin often killed or enslaved younger white dragons to use as food or made to serve as mounts. Darrion-Quieness often went hundreds of miles in search of the cursed giants to line his lair with them as frozen tasty snacks.

    After a few hours of searching, he spotted some movement in the snow near the base of one of the valleys. Using the low flying mountain clouds as camouflage, the unnaturally stealthy beast glided within a few hundred yards undetected. He gazed down at what he hoped to be a frost giant hunting party. But to his dismay, he saw seven large humanoids that only stood about eight feet tall and had blue skin, rather than gray. They were very muscular and wore only large loin cloths made of animal hides. Their blue skin was calloused and their heads were bald with strange tribal tattoos on their face, chest and arms. Their foreheads were sloped back and they had wide plump lipped mouths with yellow flat teeth, save for two large canine teeth that they probably used for cutting flesh. They were all male and wielded either a great stone axe or large tree trunks they used as clubs. The largest one, that seemed to lead the group, appeared to be the chief. Directly behind him were two smaller ones that drug the bodies of two armored men, an armored elf, and a tied up halfling.

    Darrion-Quieness smiled as he soared undetected

above the blue skinned giant kin. He wasn't overly fond of mountain ogres, but they were distant kin to the frost giants and were kind of tasty if they were frozen solid enough. The great white guessed the ogres had caught some unwary adventurers and planned to eat them. Darrion-Quieness smiled wide as he pondered the irony of the situation and started his descent from the clouds.

He tucked his powerful wings close to his body and laid his arms and legs back toward his tail. He straightened his long neck and plummeted at unearthly speeds toward the unsuspecting ogres. The wind rushed past the colossal beast as his decent increased rapidly. His bright green eyes watered from the rush of the wind, and the dragon smiled just before impact. He decided he hated frost ogres too.

*   *   *

Stieny Gittledorph was quite possibly having the worst day of his life. And by the looks of things around the little thief, the day was most likely to be the last day of his life. The tiny halfling had made quite a name for himself in the elven village of Navlashier. He had lived comfortably for some time by lifting unguarded jewels and other trinkets from unsuspecting adventures. He was even a skilled cutpurse and had made quite a fair sum at that trade as well. The thief thought about the events that led up to his current predicament, rethinking the encounter with a few 'ifs' and several 'maybcs.'

All was going well until those darned adventures got a little testy when he took a jewel from them. Granted it was the largest emerald the little thief had ever seen, but it was still just a rock. If they didn't want him to steal it, they wouldn't have left it so unguarded. They had left the magnificent crystal hidden in a secret pouch at the bottom of a small silk bag that they kept under their pillow when they slept. That was mediocre security as far as Stieny was concerned, but they had only placed three magical wards on the door and four simple locks. Any self-respecting thief could do no less than lift jewel with such poor security. The irresponsible adventures had never thought to check the ceilings for hidden doors, or they would have discovered Stieny's favorite method of relieving local adventurers of valuables. The halfling had a network of tunnels in the ceilings in every inn in town and frequently helped himself to whatever valuables the newcomers had. This group had to have some kind of expert tracker with them, Stieny figured as much. With his luck their was always something bad.

He had fled the town to lie low in his little cave hideout when the troublesome adventures appeared in the mountains. Stieny fled out the back through a secret door, but that darned elf in the group spotted it right away. The halfling was just about to make his escape when he was ambushed by a large group of mountain ogres. He would have escaped too, but he dropped the jewel in the deep mountain snow. While the adventures were fighting the ogres, something hit him in the head and knocked him unconscious. When he came too, he was tied up from head to toe and was being drug through the cold icy snow behind the disgusting mountain ogres. Stieny noticed the adventures had met a gruesome fate, at least they looked dead to the little thief, but what troubled him the most was he noticed that the huge emerald was missing from his pouch. They nerve of those disgusting ogres. It was one thing to capture him and take him home to be eaten, but the little thief drew the line at being stolen from.

"Stupid thieving ogres." The little thief said under his breath as he struggled to look around. He was tied up by thick waxed rope that held his hands at his sides and wrapped around his thin little body. Halflings were not a normal commodity for ogres, so he guessed he had been captured by the adventures before the ogres had captured them. Stieny had managed to free his right arm and could wriggle out in a few seconds, but the halfling knew he could not outrun the fiendish beasts, so he elected to wait for a more opportune time to escape.

"Well, at least it can't get any worse." Stieny mumbled under his breath, sure to not to let the ogres know that he was awake.

As the halfling lay on his back being drug through the snow, he spied a large pale white object shooting from the sky. The object was coming in so fast Stieny almost didn't recognize it's reptilian features.

"Me and my big mouth." he said to himself. "Me and my big mouth."

      *   *   *

Darrion-Quieness tucked his giant wings tight against his body and dove down in blinding speed. He could feel the wind rushing past his scale encrusted face causing his bright green eyes to water as he watched the snow covered gully rush up to meet him. When he was about a hundred feet from the lead ogre, Darrion-Quieness shifted his massive body back and extended his giant wings. The dragon's massive leathery wings caught air and slowed his plummet as he stretched his claws and prepared to tear into the flesh of the lead ogre. The dragon's sword like talons ripped into the dark blue hide of the unsuspecting ogre and as the force from the blow shattered the beast's bones. There was a great explosion of snow and ice as the dragon's body crashed into the earth. The other ogres covered their faces and heads as the thick pieces of snow and dirt fell onto them. They slowly lowered their arms and peered at a massive crater that had suddenly appeared before them. The blue skinned ogres growled back and forth between themselves trying to determine who should investigate the crater when a giant pale white scaled hand with long black talons crunched into the hard snow. The ogres looked at each other hesitantly and started backing away, ignoring the halfling and the dead adventure's bodies.

Darrion-Quieness slowly raised his thick head until his bright green eyes barely broke the edge of the crater. He smiled a wide toothed grin as the ogres turned and fled with their arms raised in terror.

Darrion-Quieness climbed halfway out of the hole and sucked in a deep breath. His long neck swelled and his head reared back. After a few moments, the colossal beast violently threw his head forward and thrust his wings wide as he expelled his glacier breath attack.

A cone of blue air erupted from his mouth and spread over the terrified ogres as they howled in pain. The dragon swept his head from side to side completely covering all of the giant kin with his icy breath. The two remaining ogres ran away in terror as they tried to crawl up the side of the deep ravine. Their skin was more of a violet hue than the original blue and they had difficulty moving their arms and legs from the exposure of the abyssal cold. Their skin was cracked and blistered and bled everywhere it had to stretch to move. One of the ogres rubbed and clawed at his face and eyes as he stumbled around blindly in the snowy valley.

The dragon flexed his powerful legs and leapt over to the top of the ridge just as the pair of fleeing ogres reached the peak. Snow and ice from the top of the ridge cracked and tumbled away from the giant dragon's weight as the beast smiled an evil grin, bearing his long sword like teeth. The two mountain ogres fell backward and tumbled down into the snow. Darrion-Quieness shot out a clawed hand and snatched one of the falling ogres by it's blistered leg. As the ogre tried in vain to break free of the dragon's iron grasp, the dragon hopped down from the ledge in pursuit of the remaining ogre, crushing the one he had in his claw under his tremendous weight as he landed on the frozen tundra. The ogre's body made a sickening pop and went limp as the great beast crushed the life from it.

    The last ogre fled as fast as he could screaming in terror down the middle of the ravine. He kicked up large chunks of packed snow from under his fur covered boots as he fled. Darrion-Quieness paused to take a bite out of the ogre he had pinned to the ground while waiting for the last one to get far enough away so he could lash out at it with his heavy tail. The heavy scaled tail shot out like a giant whip, catching the ogre in the midsection. The force of the blow knocked him from the trail and his body hit the side of the rocky ravine. The ogre fell limp and was quickly covered by a pile of snow that fell from the top of the small overhang.

    Darrion-Quieness paused and scanned the area for more enemies. After a few minutes he was certain that there were none and he began to pile up the ogre's bodies. The dragon packed them in the deep snow drifts to freeze them for later and he quickly ate the ones that were frozen solid by his frigid breath weapon. After the dragon finished eating, he began to pile up the gear of the ogres and the dead adventures that they seemed to have caught. He counted the gold coins each had and wished he had time to fly back to his lair to save the loot. But the great beast knew he did not have time for such endeavors, so he resounded to burying the fair amount of gold coins in the snow bank, then he froze it solid with his icy breath. He was just about to take flight and begin the three day journey out of Vidora, when he noticed a single set of tiny footprints in the snow leading away from the battle, over the ravine, and down the steep hill on the other side. Darrion-Quieness narrowed his eyes as he thought for a moment, trying to figure out who had been watching him. After a few minutes, he noticed the dead halfling that was tied up and drug behind the ogres was missing. He contemplated just leaving the pathetic creature to his own devices in the frozen mountain wasteland, but the dragon imagined a legion of great elven wizards that were friends to the halfling coming to hunt the dragon for treating their little friend so poorly. The dragon shook his head from side to side sending spittle flying from his mouth as he snapped from the daydream of battling scores of elves. Though the prospect of a small war was somewhat inviting, the great white had a mission and battling leagues of elves was not in it. So he elected to hunt down the little bug, before he became a problem.

With a mighty leap the great beast was in the air soaring east above the tracks that lead down toward the base of the mountain.

*   *   *

Stieny's large round eyes had spotted the dragon only an instant before the gigantic creature crashed into the lead ogre, crushing the monster instantly under it's tremendous weight, sending up a shroud of snow and ice from the force of the impact. The earth shook under the blow and the other ogres were knocked from their feet while rocks and other small debris fell from the tops of the ravine. The ogres scrambled to their feet as a giant cloud of snow and ice drifted down in front of them, obscuring their vision.

Stieny, however, worked feverishly at freeing his other arm and cutting the thick course rope that bound him. In seconds, the tiny halfling was free from his bonds and running as fast as his little legs would carry him. He plodded through the deep snow, scurrying toward an alcove in the side of the rocky ravine the ogres had been traveling in. Though it wasn't one hundred percent protection, he hoped it would be enough to survive the horrible breath of the ice beast that would surely come at any minute. As he trudged through the waist deep snow, he could hear the familiar sound of a great breath being taken in. The little halfling winced as he felt the air beginning to tighten and expand from the wicked force of the expulsion from the dragon's icy breath. He squeezed as much of his little body behind a small rocky outcropping as the abyssal cone of cold ripped past, freezing even the very air it rode upon. The wind howled and screamed and he could feel the horrible coldness that was just a few inches away. His back furry tunic that was exposed to the valley air began to harden and crack. The thin leather straps that held his knives and his short sword cracked and froze and his hair hardened and broke apart in the abyssal wind. Stieny could feel the bone chilling cold rippling behind him, coating the rocks near his face turning them into a dullish blue-gray and a thin layer of ice made popping and cracking sounds as it formed all around him.

    When the air began to turn back to normal temperature, the chilled halfling turned to inspect the effects of the great dragon's breath. To Stieny's bewilderment, the soft white fluffy snow had frozen solid. It was no longer compiled of a thousand tiny flakes of ice, but a sheer sheet of white frozen terrain. Every rock, tree, and bush sagged under the weight of inches of ice, that clung to their surfaces and branches. It seemed as if the very air itself had frozen around everything that had been in the path of the great white's breath. There was a deadly calm and a great fog that floated softly over the newly frozen ravine that slowly began to dissipate before the halfling's eyes. Stieny was terrified to venture out, but he knew that if he remained where he was at, it was only a matter of time before the dragon would find him. Just when he had mustered the courage to try to make a run for it, Stieny's sharp little ears heard the sound of the ogres slipping and sliding on the icy ravine floor. They were screaming in fear and fleeing for their lives. The tiny halfling poked his red chubby face from around the corner of he rocky alcove. His rosy cheeks were blistered and red and he had small icicle hanging from his brown curly hair. He witnessed two of the ogres trying to climb the ravine wall to escape the wrath of the voracious beast. Their skin was blistered and cracked and it appeared as if they did not have much use of their fingers and their arms. Stieny gasped, clutching his neck with his thin little fingers as he looked at the great white dragon. It was the largest beast he had ever seen. It was at least a hundred yards long from the tip of it's massive head and the end of it's spine riddled tail. It's large white scales were a murky white at the apex and a light blue just near the base. He could see many gold coins and other precious metals and gems that were embedded in between the scales near the dragon's underbelly from spending hundreds of years laying on a horde of treasure. The dragon's head was covered in a large white bony sheath that seemed almost as if his skull was just under the scales. He had a great ebony spine that splayed back from the top of his head, toward the base of his skull, and over the back of his neck. There was a large flap of thin white skin affixed to that spine forming a small sail. The dragon's eyes were an effervescent green that seemed to pierce into the halfling's soul as they evilly watched the ogres futilely climbing the ravine wall.

 Stieny watched the colossal beast for a few more seconds before he noticed he had started running down the other side of the ravine as fast as his short little legs could carry him. As Stieny reached the bottom of the slope, he stopped and glanced around. He had no recollection of climbing out of the ravine or even running this far. He had no idea what

 direction he was facing and he wasn't overly sure where the ravine he ran from actually was.

 The young thief dabbed the sweat from his forehead and slowed to a walk, pondering the event. He had heard that the most powerful dragons emitted some kind of a fear aura. He surmised that he must have somehow fallen prey to it. The cries of the helpless ogres echoed across the valley and Stieny knew he had not run far. He reached back and grabbed his ice covered hood, pulling it over his head the best he could. As he pulled the cover up, to protect his head from the cold wind, the frozen leather shroud shattered in his finger tips. The confused halfling studied remains of the hood in his hand. The leather was dry and cracked and covered in a thin layer of ice. The little thief knew he didn't have much time to find somewhere to hide. Stieny hoped the dragon wouldn't miss him, but he knew that the giant lizards were quite gifted in the powers of recollection when dealing with numbers. The fiendish beast's often sat and counted their millions of coins every day, never counting the same coin twice.

Stieny struggled through the deep snow and as he rounded a rocky outcropping on the trail he had been drug down when the adventurers captured him. He turned up the tiny rabbit trail that lead to a small cave at the base of the rocky extension. Huddled in the dark, the cold scared halfling sat and waited.

*   *   *

Darrion-Quieness glided down the trail following the tracks of the tiny halfling. The dragon had a full belly and was really wanting to relax on the mountain peak before he flew off toward Beykla instead of chasing the worthless halfling worm. But the dragon knew he couldn't let the halfling wander into town, he might alert someone to his presence and the dragon hated having enemies following him. And if there were enemies that the dragon didn't want, it was enemies from Vidora. The damnable elves would seek to vanquish him for no other reason than he was a white dragon, the racist pointy eared hellions, and they called *him* evil.

He tracked the halfling a while longer when he came upon a small rocky outcropping that the tracks led into. The dragon looked around the other side and saw that there was not another exit from the cave. The beast scratched away at the base of the boulders and was delighted to find that they sat on the surface, rather than extended into it. That told the dragon that the cave didn't extended into the earth, merely a few feet under the rocks. He decided that one quick burst of his frigid breath into the hole and he could be assured that the halfling would be no more.

Just as he started to suck in air, he heard the squeak of the little voice.

"Please, great dragon, don't kill me. Perhaps I could be of some use to you." Stieny said knowing that the beast was probably full from eating the ogres, and hoping it could speak common, the generic language of surface dwellers.

Darrion-Quieness cocked his head to the side and marveled at the stupidity of the foolish creature. "Don't you know you have nothing to offer me, save for some diamonds, but if you had any, I'd just kill you and take them anyway." the dragon said as he noticed the halfling's cloak had been frozen from his breath.

Stieny gulped and re-adjusted his collar. "Well, I am sure there is something I could do for you, great and majestic beast."

Darrion-Quieness sat on his haunches and scratched at his chin while he pondered the thought for a moment. Eventually he was going to have to find some humanoid to infiltrate Beykla and find the Ecnal. He figured since this halfling was already afraid of him and not from the city, the halfling could not summon any powerful friends to save him. All he had to do was fly him there and he was set.

The dragon unconsciously dug at his underbelly with one of his sharp claws, knocking a few coins and jewels into the soft snow. "I noticed you have been mildly exposed to the power of my breath attack."

Stieny didn't reply, he just sat motionless in fear.

The dragon pulled a bright gem away from his under belly and lightly breathed on it. Stieny could see the very air around the gem harden and grow heavy as great particles of ice fell around it like a miniature snow storm. The beast then showed the gem to the halfling and dismissed the fear aura that surrounded him, knowing the halfling would no longer be affected by his magical fear.

"I have trapped your soul in this gem, little one." the dragon lied as he held the large emerald before the halfling's little face. "Notice that you no longer have that gnawing fear pulling at your insides?"

Stieny nearly burst into tears. All he wanted was to not lose his life, instead he had now lost his soul. He knew it was so, because he could indeed no longer feel the presence of that gnawing fear.

"I will return your soul to you in good time, little one. But first, you will accompany me to Beykla, I will explain more later. But know if you ever flee I will find you, and if for some reason I cannot, I will crush the gem, thus destroying you and your soul." the great white said, lowering his shoulders and motioning for the halfling to climb onto his back.

Stieny merely nodded weakly and climbed aboard the great beast. He marveled at how soft the dragon's smooth white scales were. Then in an instant, the giant beast exploded into the air and for the first time in his life, Stieny was flying.

" Ultimate despair. A point in which a being can no longer descend. A shallow where they can only stay on

the same level or begin an ascension. I believe every great man or woman that has ever lived has suffered from this plight at one point in their lives. Some may have had reached it as a child, others not until the day of their deaths, but all have some form of ultimate despair. What makes the person great though, is not merely reaching this point, but reaching it and going beyond. It is understanding oneself and developing a kind of reprise that can never be challenged.

*   Too often men are fooled by vengeance or love and think they have this reprise, but they have yet to begin to achieve the self-actualization that is necessary to gain this higher being. It is difficult to explain how the transformation comes about, and impossible to describe. It cannot be purposefully sought and cannot be artificially created. It alone is more powerful than all the magic of all the gods in Merioulus combined. Once attained, this personal state of well being can never be stolen, crushed or changed, it will always remain unchallenged Even in death, it is the single most powerful core of existence. Unfortunately, all to often, a person is lost before they come to this higher being.*

*   The transition of ones soul is never immediate. Frequently one begins the journey to this higher being, only to die long before reaching it. Only the greatest of all beings complete the cycle. However once completed, the person knows they have reached a pinnacle in their lives, reached an apex of their soul that cannot ever be bound, broken or destroyed. It is a feeling of such euphoric proportions that there is not a combination of words in all the languages of existence combined, that can describe it. I simply refer to it as a true birth."*

-Lancalion Levendis Lampara-

Chapter Two
Plight of the Stormhammers

*A*merix awoke face down on the shore of the sandy beachhead and stared at the fine granules for a few moments before raising his sun scorched head. He rolled over on his back and weakly stretched his stiff muscles. He looked down at his many wounds that covered his old withered body. The wounds were covered with many small thin yellow spores. "Damn flies." The dwarf said to himself as he began the arduous task of sweeping the larvae eggs from his infected wounds. When he was sure he had gotten them all, the old dwarf gingerly rose to his feet. He coughed up some muddy brown water and didn't bother to wipe the soupy concoction from his long silver streaked beard as he plodded to the edge of the river. In front of him, the cold Dawson River curved around the beach he was on, and splashed against a large rocky cliff on the other side. The cliff was covered in thick leafy green vines in some areas and many birds of prey nested and perched on the vast rocky ledges. There was a large stork-looking bird that prodded dagger like beak into the shallow water near the edge of the river, pulling out a long slender fish it had speared. The bird didn't seem to mind the large dwarf as he kneeled down at the water's edge and sipped.

Amerix paused for a moment and stared at the reflection of the old dwarf that gazed back at him from the water. The old dwarf looked into the eyes of his father, his father's father, and beyond, yet he only saw grief and hardship. Try as he might, Amerix could not locate any real success. There were countless victories in battle, but each of his ancestors had died in battle. The glorious mail of Stormhammer was then passed on to the first born son. This tradition had survived tens of thousands of years, but no longer. It had ended when Amerix's only son fell to an illness that could have been cured, had it not been for the politics of the Beyklans. Suddenly the old face had returned. He finally recognized the dwarf that was staring back from the water. Though it seemed still distant, he recognized the burning hate for the Beyklans. His mind quickly shifted into the thought of their screams and his sadistic pleasure at the emotion he felt when his wicked axe sliced deep into the flesh of one of the Beyklans. Ah his axe, what a fine weapon he possessed. The weapon was forged by some distant father, probably twenty times removed, and it had been passed down to each son until it was given to him by his father.

  Amerix reached down to feel the enchanted weapon, but he grasped only the dry leather sheath that once held the pommel of the ancient blade. Despair again washed over the ancient general. He had nothing. He had squandered everything his fathers had passed onto him. He had lost clan Stormhammer to a white dragon and an army of dark dwarves, he had lost his armor, his axe, and his great helm. He couldn't even protect his only son when the boy needed him most. And now, he sat defeated on the shore of some unnamed beach, crushed and broken. The powerful dwarven general, probably the greatest dwarven warrior to have ever lived, dropped his forehead on the sandy beach and wept. He wept from the bowels of his soul. The wailing was so intense, every bird, every frog, every insect; even the plants shifted their leaves to alleviate themselves from the sound of ultimate suffering; the sound that now came from the belly of the old defeated dwarf. The wailing drifted from the valley into the forest, it echoed far across the land and into the twilight of the day. And as the sun set on Amerix Alistair

Stormhammer, it set on the great general, father, and king. Once the red sun of the day that was vanishing into the dark horizon of the western sky, had set, all that was left was an empty hollow of a dwarf that could never be filled. The great warrior lay defeated on the sandy beach. Not defeated by any enemy he had ever faced, but defeated by the blinding hatred that had nearly consumed him from the inside.

As the waning light of the day shifted into darkness, the dwarf cried himself to sleep. He slept only because, try as he might, Amerix could not will himself to die.

*   *   *

He was lead down the unlit passage, back into the under dark. The group of dwarven miners took him to a small cavern with a single pool and tossed him in. The young red haired dwarf tumbled down the rocky slope about thirty feet and came to rest at the base of a small pool. Therrig Alistair Delastan sat up and glared at the Stoneheart dwarven miners that collapsed the tunnel behind him. He was exiled in the small underground cavern, bound, bleeding, and with no food, weapons, or armor.

The wounded dwarf examined his clothing. He still wore the padded undergarments that he wore under his thick plate mail to soften the burden of the heavy steel. The padding was worn, but it still would function as some sort of protection, should he meet some underground beasts. Therrig wiped the small trickle of blood from a gash that had opened above his left eye when he had been tossed into the cave. The small cut above his eye continued to bleed despite Therrig's continual attempts to staunch it. After his shirt sleeve was soaked with blood, he managed to stop the bleeding and rose to his weary feet. Therrig didn't bother trying to climb back to the passage the miners had collapsed. He knew quite well the prowess of the Stoneheart miners and that if they sealed the passage, it was indeed sealed. The outcast slowly walked over to the pool and knelt. He cupped the crystal clear water with his hands and began to wipe his face and arms, being careful not to get the cut over his eye wet. He had grown accustom to being clean over the years and being dirty was aggravating to him. After he washed his face and hands, he sat at the base of the pool and chuckled to himself. He knew better than to chuckle out loud, there were many monsters in the under dark that would love to find an unarmed dwarf and have a nice little lunch. Yet, the irony of the situation wasn't lost on him. He had been a faithful follower of Amerix, and even followed his orders to the letter, yet it was his own kin, Amerix, that had ordered him banished, not the good loving Stoneheart clan. But whom was responsible, meant little to him. He would have his revenge on the entire clan. Clan Stormhammer was no more, and if he had any say in the matter, Clan Stoneheart was soon to follow.

Therrig was sitting on the shore eating some beovi that he had caught in the small pool, when his keen hearing detected two pair of footsteps coming from a passage that was on the north side of the cavern. Therrig tossed the remnants of the white pale fish into the water. He knew the splash would attract the attention of the pair while he rushed over to a dark alcove and awaited for the trail blazers to show themselves.

Two well armed dwarves emerged from the north passage. The passage was higher than the cavern floor and had a small ledge that led down to the pool. The dwarves were wearing thin chain shirts and bore large hammers that they carried with both hands. Their skin was a dull gray and their eyes were murky white and they had thin gray beards that barely touched their chests.

The pair looked over the ledge down at the pool and

scanned the cavern for the source of the splash. " You sees anything, Artone?" The other dark dwarf asked while he shook his head. He scanned the cavern floor for signs of life but located none. His murky white eyes that were designed to see only the infrared light spectrum picked up on a warm spot on the rocky floor next to the pool. He pointed to the warm area.

"You sees the body mark?" Artone asked while his pupil-less eyes scanned the cavern looking for the humanoid that made it.

"Yea, I sees it. Kalistirsts?"

"Nopes, not none of dems. Theys don't sits on the shore. Theys get dems fish and eats em elsewheres." Artone said. "Plus theys don't travel by demselves. Theys always go wit dems friends."

The other dwarf nodded in agreement and looked to Artone. The older dark dwarf shrugged his muscular shoulders and started down the slope.

"Whats ever is, ain't no big. We's can go kills it."

Therrig hugged the wall of the alcove keeping his body behind the large boulder as the pair of dark dwarves walked by. He didn't hear all of the conversation, but he knew the dark dwarves were coming to find him. Therrig hated dark dwarves more than anything. It was their kind that attacked and wiped out Clan Stormhammer with the aid of a white dragon named Darrion-Quieness. Therrig was not sure why the dark dwarves or the dragon were interested in Clan Stormhammer, but he had vowed to kill either whenever he saw them again.

Therrig gathered a small rock and placed it in the palm of his hand, stepped out from the alcove and cleared his throat. The dark dwarves, who were just reaching the cavern floor stopped in surprise, and whirled round to see the dwarf that stood behind them.

"Who be's yee?" Artone asked nervously.

Therrig stepped forward with the palmed rock facing behind him. " I am Therrig Alistair Bigbody. My clan is just a click away." Therrig said as he pointed back behind him, continuing to approach the two dark dwarves.

Artone examined the clothing that Therrig wore, though he could not see anything but the heat spectrum, the dark dwarves were adapt at identifying the slightest variations of it. He noticed that Therrig wore no armor and no weapons. As Therrig came within a few steps of him he spoke again.

"If yous from Bigbodys, why yous got no armor or weapons?" Artone asked.

Therrig smiled wickedly. "I have a weapon. It's right here!" Therrig said as he lunged forward and swung the rock down, catching Artone in the face. Blood shot out from the gruesome wound and the older dark dwarf fell to the ground clutching his broken nose. The other dark dwarf swung his heavy hammer at Therrig, but the cumbersome weapon was too slow. Therrig ducked the clumsy strike, grabbing the hammer Artone had dropped and leaped into the icy water. He splashed into the pool and stood chest deep in the frigid subterranean pond.

Artone winced as he held his hand against his bleeding nose. "He's gots me sledge fool, goes and gets it!"

"But he's in the pool." the younger dwarf protested.

Artone growled in response, and the younger dark dwarf sighed as he began to slowly wade into the icy water. Artone picked up the rock and heaved it at Therrig. Therrig just submerged as the rock splashed harmlessly on the surface where he had been standing. He resurfaced a second later smiling confidently.

"You throw like a kalistirsts." Therrig taunted.

Artone screamed in rage. "I'sa kill yous, Bigbody!" the dark dwarf screamed. His voice echoing off of the cavern walls.

Therrig chuckled in return and submerged again.

"He's gone and wents under again." The younger dark dwarf said, looking back at Artone.

"Don't tells me, fool! Finds em!" Artone screamed, shaking his fists violently in the air. The younger dwarf turned back around as Therrig erupted from the pool behind him. He hooked the handle of the sledge behind the dark dwarf with his powerful arms and pulled back, forcing the cold steel shaft into the dark dwarf's throat and cutting off his air. The dark dwarf struggled against the weapon and managed to slip his hand between the hammer and his neck.

"Helps me, Artone!" The dark dwarf grunted as he struggled to free himself from the hammer.

Artone rushed forward into the pool, but only waded in ankle-deep. "Come ons fool!" Artone shouted. " Gets loose and splits his skull!"

Therrig could hear the splashes of Artone in the water. He shoved forward, forcing the dark dwarf under the surface. The icy water rushed around Therrig's face and head. He knew he couldn't spend too much time in the water or the cold would dull his movements. He pulled with all his might at the hammer forcing the final breaths from the lungs of the dark dwarf he held. When he felt the dark dwarf's muscles relax, he released the dead dwarf and emerged from under the surface.

Artone held the other dwarf's hammer in his hands and growled. "Yous killed me scout. Nows I'sa going to kills yous!" Artone screamed as he rushed in with the dead dark dwarf's hammer.

Therrig waited for the charging dwarf to close. Artone's hammer came down in an over hand strike. Therrig side stepped the heavy hammer as it slammed into the shallow pool. It made a loud clap and water splashed away from the hammers stone head. Therrig held his hands far apart and brought the together as he swung. The hammer came down rapidly and struck the dark dwarf in the knee. A resounding snap echoed off the cavern walls followed by a shrill scream as Artone's knee shattered. The wounded dark dwarf fell in the knee deep water clutching his morbidly broken leg. He tried to stand on the broken leg but it twisted and bent under the weight of his body. Therrig chuckled and circled Artone. The wounded dark dwarf shifted his weight to face Therrig, much to Therrig's delight. Each time Artone had to move to face Therrig, he had to hop and briefly put weight on his broken leg. He would involuntarily yelp in pain as he shifted.

"Comes on dog." Artone taunted, hoping Therrig would rush him. His mind was going numb from the pain, and he wasn't sure how much longer he could stand on the broken leg, but to his dismay, Therrig said nothing. He just continued with his sinister smile and stayed true to his circle.

Therrig circled the dwarf for almost an hour, taunting him and giggling with sadistic glee as Artone tried to remain on his feet. Eventually, Artone couldn't tolerate the horrific pain and he collapsed. Therrig walked over and looked down at the grimaced face of Artone, the deep dwarf.

"This is for Clan Stormhammer!" he shouted as he brought the heavy hammer down on the unprotected head of Artone. The dark dwarf's skull shattered, killing him instantly. Therrig pounded the lifeless body for twenty minutes until splattered blood dotted his face like a hive and blood ran from Artone's pulpy body like a tiny crimson river on it's exodus to the sea.

Therrig removed the undamaged armor from the drowned dark dwarf and placed it on. The armor was tight, since dark dwarves weren't as strong as normal dwarven kin, but it was better than the rags he had been wearing. He meticulously hooked each leather strap and hoisted the stone hammer over his shoulder as he walked north through the passage from the pool. He had gathered a few supplies and made a few coins from the kill. Therrig hummed to himself a dwarven battle tune and hoped he might come across some more dark dwarves. He had a lot of rage to vent.

    *   *   *

 Amerix awoke on the sandy beach again. He spit out a few large green beetles that had crawled in his mouth while he was asleep. The surprised beetles scampered away from there warm hiding spot as the old dwarf sat on his but and stared at the tranquil river scene that lay before him. The sun was high in the sky and it hurt his eyes, but he made no attempt to shield them from it. He was barely conscious of the plethora of insects that landed on the back of neck and arms to feast. The old dwarf just sat and thought of nothing, and everything, at the same time. He stared at his thoughts that seemed to visualize on the rocky cliff that stood before him. He counted the cracks, the number of vines, how many sticks floated past. He watched the birds of prey dive in and out of the water, snatching fish and other aquatic animals. He watched a large line of ants march over his thigh and continue across the beach. Amerix sat all day and well into the evening, though to him it seemed as he merely blinked a couple of times and it was dark. He glanced down at his red blistered skin that had been scorched from the sun, but ignored the painful rash and laid back down. He closed his eyes and thought about his wife and son, praying to Durion to send an army to slay him. Yet as the night progressed, only the birds and crickets seemed to answer his silent prayers. Amerix laid on his back, unaware of the hundreds of dwarven bodies that began floating past his sandy bed. He soon drifted off into deep sleep and was happy to know peace there.

    *   *   *

 "These are the heroes that helped hold the bridge." A

militia sergeant said as he pointed to Lance, Jude, Ryshander, Kaisha, and an unconscious Apollisian that was being tended to by the surgeons. Lance started to protest, but got a quick elbow in the ribs from Kaisha. He looked at her with a frown that quickly melted away against her wry smile.

"He was the true hero." Kaisha said as she pointed to the ground where Apollisian lay with his head propped under a soft pillow.

"Is he dead?" The militia sergeant asked as he motioned to a powerful looking armored man and a group of similarly dressed soldiers. The front man wore a great helm with black hawk wings that were outstretched as a bird in flight. His armor was thick and he wore a long red silk cape with the banner of Beykla draped down his back. The men behind him wore bright brass colored scale mail of the Beyklan high guard, with similar silk capes, and red tunics.

"No, he is just wounded and exhausted, but if he doesn't see a healer soon, he might be." Kaisha said.

Ryshander shifted forward adjusting his tattered clothing. " We all could use a good healer. We have gold to pay for services."

Lance winced. He and Jude had little gold left. He thought about sneaking off and checking the dwarven bodies, but Jude had explained that soldiers don't usually carry gold with them into battle.

"There is no need to pay. You have already paid with blood." the man with the hawk helmet said.

Jude nodded. "Thank you sir, my companions and I are grateful. Where might we seek these healers of yours?"

Lance fumed, he despised Beyklan's, let alone be grateful. He tried to save some innocents, not preserve their morbid sovereignty. Had he gave it more thought, he wouldn't have tried to rescue the stupid girl behind the bar. All that got him was a severely wounded shoulder.

Ryshander seemed to be having equal difficulty with Jude's words. He despised the local magistrate as much as Lance despised the country. He didn't intervene to save any innocents, just to make Kaisha happy. Plus, he was no companion to the barbaric swordsman or his slick mage. Yet the armored man seemed oblivious to Lance's and Ryshander's contempt. "There is no need to seek them out, noble hero. I have already arranged for them to come here. After I heard the tales of how you rallied the soldiers and made a stand on the bridge, I ordered the clerics to come here after they tended to their own church."

Lance frowned. "You ordered? Who are you?"

The man chuckled and feigned a slight bow. "Why I am Duke Dolan Blackhawk." The man announced. "And who might I be speaking with?"

All four of the heroes stammered in surprise. "I am Lance Ecnal. This is my friend, Jude." Lance said. Jude bowed low and saluted with his massive two-handed sword. Lance pointed to Ryshander and Kaisha. " And they..." he was cut off by Ryshander.

"I am Ryshander and this is Kaisha." the wererat interjected as his lower lip began to quiver and twitch from anger. Kaisha bowed low, but Ryshander held his gaze.

"And who is that noble hero?" The duke asked, as he motioned to the downed paladin. Seemingly oblivious to the wererat's glare.

"We know not his name, my lord." Kaisha said.

Ryshander glared at her. How dare she refer to the man that had killed or imprisoned their fellow guild members as lord?

"Well citizens, we will learn his name when he awakens. After you receive your healing, I request your audience in city hall. That way we can prepare the ceremony for your medals." With that announcement the Duke turned and started back toward the large city hall building. It had suffered some scorching, but it was no worse for the wear.

"We need to leave." Ryshander said as he grimaced from the pain that came from his many wounds when he tried to sit on the burnt porch of the Blue Dragon Inn.

" Why should we leave, my love?" Kaisha asked as she kneeled and grasped his gloved hands." We could rebuild, start a new home, or maybe Pav-co will return."

Ryshander shook his head. " That fat thief will not return, at least not for a long while, and I do not wish to do all the work of rebuilding just so he can return one day and reclaim it for himself."

Kaisha nodded her head in defeat. " Then where will go, my love? Dawson?"

Ryshander often thought about going to the great city that was at the base of the Dawson River, hence name sake. But the city was full of dangers that just didn't exist in Central City. There were many guilds larger than Lostos ever could have been, but the price for failure was death. " I do not know, Kaisha. I just want to be rid of this place. I nearly lost you several times in the last two days. I just want to go away where I can never fear of losing you again." Ryshander answered truthfully. He surprised himself at his honesty and then felt foolish for sharing his emotions in front of the others. He stared down at the earth in attempt to hide his embarrassment from the woman he loved. He felt warm soft hands grasp his face and lift his head. He raised his chin and stared deep into the beautiful brown eyes of his one true love. She smiled at him in such a way that seemed to melt away his anger and fear. Her smile sang a thousand word song that made it okay for him to say what he felt and not be ashamed for it.

" I love you." she whispered and gently kissed his lips. He returned her kiss and weakly hugged her.

*   *   *

"When they come to get their medals, kill them." the duke said as he marched down the marbled corridor of the city hall. The clacking of his metal plates echoed down the singed corridor.

"But sir, I thought you said..." a robed cleric began to protest. "It is not just."

The duke whirled around. His long red cloak spun around him. "You want justice?" the duke asked. Jabbing his index finger into the face of the violet robed cleric. "Fine. Ryshander and his girlfriend, Kaisha, are thieves of the guild Lostos. They are wanted on too many charges to mention. I am sorry if you were planning to make a grand ceremony for five heroes. You will just have to have it for three." the duke said as he turned from the hallway and entered his stateroom.

The cleric lowered his head and nodded. "Yes, my lord." he said as he turned and made for the door of the burned office.

"Also..." the duke called out. The cleric paused as duke Blackhawk finished his order.

"Find that viper, Ganover, his pride nearly cost me my city. Put him chains and bring him to me for trial. He must pay for denying the paladin." the duke commanded as he sat on a partially burned oak desk.

"Yes, my lord, I will make it so." the Cleric said as he bowed low and backed out of the duke's office.

* * *

She awoke to find herself being dragged on her back down a moss covered stone corridor. Both of her eyes were swollen shut and she could not see. The deep slash wounds she had, ached and she could feel the taught ropes tied around her body, arms and legs. She noticed there was a horrible pungent smell accompanied with the wet moss that seemed to come from her left. It was then that

Alexis Overmoon deducted that she was in the sewers of Central City.

Alexis pretended to be unconscious as the dwarves dragged her further down into the sewer. She expected she was being taken to general Amerix for execution or some kind of trial for trumped up war crimes. She didn't dare tug at her bonds, at least not yet. She didn't want to risk the dwarves realizing she was conscious. If she were going to somehow escape she needed to learn more about her captors, her surroundings, and she needed to try and get her eyes to open.

She was dragged for another ten or so minutes when the dwarves stopped. They roughly dropped her feet that was tied to the lead rope. Alexis strained her ears to listen to what the dwarves were saying through the constant ringing that echoed in her head from the many blows she took that rendered her unconscious in the alley.

"We need to take her to the rallying point." One dwarf argued.

"No, we need to take her to Commander Fehzban. It makes no sense to go to the rallying point with a prisoner." the other retorted.

Alexis listened intently to the two dwarves arguing and lightly struggled against her bonds. She surmised that as long as they argued she might get a chance to test the ropes that bound her, hoping they would be too engrossed in their disagreement to take notice. Alexis knew it was risky, but she figured she would have little opportunities before there were many eyes upon her.

Alexis first lightly pulled against the ropes that bound her hands and discovered she had no extra movement. In fact she noticed that the ropes were slowly cutting off her circulation. She could just begin to feel the tell tale tingling in her finger tips, but when she checked her legs, she found that the ropes were quite loose from her being dragged. Given the right opportunity, she would be able to stand and run, though unless she figured out how to get her eyes open, she knew she wouldn't get far. Alexis heard the dwarves were reaching a conclusion so she relaxed and waited for another opportunity to test her ropes.

"Fine, we will take her to Commander Fehzban, but I'll have you know, it will be your beard in the shaving chair if Amerix gets mad, not mine."

The other dwarf smiled at the small victory and roughly jerked up on the rope holding Alexis' legs. " And I'll have you know that when Commander Fehzban hands out praises like dolgo seeds it will be me standing with my hands out."

Both dwarves paused as they looked at each other. "Boy a good handful of dolgo seeds would sure hit the spot."

The other dwarf merely nodded as he imagined roasting the mountain nut over a slow fire. Both dwarves seemed to have similar fantasies for a moment, and then they smiled, shaking their heads as they started back down the moss-strewn corridor.

"I can't wait until this war business is over with. I have been having forge withdrawals." The dwarf chuckled.

The other nodded and smiled. "I hear that. I would have never thought I would miss working. But as they say; the grass is always greener, but it still has mites."

Alexis noticed the closer the pair got to the familiar areas of the sewers the more light hearted they became. She was drug another thirty minutes down the moss covered corridor, then they stopped.

"Go and fetch the commander, I'll wait here." one dwarf said. The other nodded in delight as he imagined the comforts of home that he hoped were only a few weeks away.

Alexis tugged at her bonds once again, though she did so with care. She didn't notice any new weak spots from the trip, much to her dismay, and she still couldn't get either eye open and her hands were close to being numb from poor circulation caused by the tight knots. She resounded to wait. Getting killed here in the sewers would help nothing and she hoped she might be able to reason with this Commander Fehzban. She was glad at least they weren't taking her to Amerix. Alexis was sure that demon would remember her well placed arrows and she recalled Apollisian talking about how the dwarves themselves were not evil, though he was sure their were a few among them that were. She hoped that Apollisian was right about the majority of them. She also hoped that the Commander could recognize her royalty and that she might use it to gain favor with him. But the general pessimistic side of her figured he would have some kind of personal grudge with her family. That was just how her luck seemed to go of late.

*   *   *

"What do you mean you can't find Amerix?" Commander Fehzban yelled to the haggard messenger. His armor was bloodied and dirty and he walked with an obvious limp.

" We can't find him. He was last seen near the bridge when the re-enforcements came from the east. Our lines were scattered and many of the men fear he is dead. Our entire eastern front has been decimated and the rest of the army is fleeing to the rallying point, near the entrance back into the underdark."

The battle was a huge success for the dwarves. They had split the humans defenses, they had pushed to the bridge, allowing the weaker groups to flee to the west and slowly crushed the strongest group that was making a stand on the bridge over the Dawson river. They had set ablaze buildings of strategic position or buildings that would hurt the humans moral if they had been burned. It seemed as if the battle was going to be another easy victory. Amerix led the charge on the final push when he learned that the human champion from the Torrent Manor was alive and leading the resistance, and that was when things began to fall apart. The humans had a wizard, a giant of a man, two swordsman that seemed impervious to attacks, and there was the champion from Torrent, holding the bridge. Amerix ordered the majority of the front into battle and the humans had hidden horsemen on the other side. The heavy lancers charged across the bridge and in seconds wiped out the eastern front the dwarves had established. Behind the thunderous hooves, were a flood of pikemen that hit the fleeing dwarves in the backside. Commander Fehzban still didn't understand why the humans had such a force on the eastern side of the city, but that didn't matter now. The battle had been lost and Fehzban was waiting for a word from Amerix before he sounded the full scale retreat to Mountain Heart, their home city in the Pyberian mountains.

"Sir, with all due respect, Amerix is dead, or captured at least. Let us flee to our homes and prepare for the human's counter strike. We can make it home in a week or so. I'm sure the king will be glad to hear of our victories." The messenger pleaded.

Fehzban stroked his long beard. " So be it. Sound the retreat. We will make haste back to Mountain Heart and plan our defenses there. The Beyklans have learned we can strike anywhere. Perhaps their people will fear our might and force their leaders to leave Clan Stoneheart to their own devices."

The messenger's face cracked into a huge smile. "Yes sir! I will make it so." he shouted as he eagerly ran from the command chamber.

Fehzban gathered his gear and looped his thick leather backpack over his left shoulder. He rolled the maps and battle plans onto the wooden table and piled them up. Fehzban reached into his pack and removed a small wooden flask. He placed the brown cork in his mouth and pulled until the wooden flask popped open. After pouring the thick syrupy brown liquid on the parchments and the table, he set them on fire. The commander stared quietly at the small fire as it spread to the table and slowly engulfed it. He worried that this was merely the first defeat in a series of defeats that eventually led the demise of clan Stoneheart. Fehzban stood mesmerized by the fire for many minutes until the table was nothing more than a pile of smoldering ashes, then he turned from the chamber and started down the corridor.

As he rounded the corner of the command room he heard his name being shouted by a dwarf that was dressed in chain armor and wielded an axe. The same armor the front linesmen wore when they were sent into battle on the eastern front. Fehzban's spirits soared at the possibility that he had news of Amerix.

"Commander Fehzban!" The dwarf shouted as he ran up to the commander.

" What news do you bring of the front lines?" Fehzban asked eagerly. "What of Amerix?"

The dwarf seemed confused. "What do you mean; *of* Amerix? I am sure he has a fine grasp on the bridge and is preparing to burn the city down around the foul human scum. We have returned because we have captured a prisoner." the dwarf said happily.

Fehzban became enraged. The stupid front liner had no idea the battle status and he left the battle because he caught a prisoner. "I hope you are trying to make me laugh front liner, and that I am just in a foul mood, because I am becoming angered that you have left the battle because you caught a damned prisoner." Fehzban shouted with his fists tightly clenched at his sides, his unfastened helmet straps shaking as he spoke.

The dwarf took a step back as all the color drained from his face. "Not just any prisoner sir, but the elven archer from the Torrent Manor. And sir, we were ordered to bring her back." the dwarf more pleaded than announced.

Commander Fehzban shuddered. He remembered Amerix speaking of the elven archer back at the Torrent Manor. The commander feared that she was royalty or someone of significance. Rarely did elves travel with humans, unless one or both, were someone of great importance. The thought of angering an elven nation on top of the humans gave the old commander a shiver.

"Bring her to me and be gone. Go to the rallying point and meet up with the remainder of the army, we are heading home." Fehzban said.

The dwarf was visibly shocked. He had no idea why they were heading home so soon. Surely the razing of the city could not have been completed so soon. Fearing the worst and feeling defeated, he did as ordered. He turned and slowly plodded back down the sewer corridor, to his companion.

"I can see by the long face, we should have went to the rallying point." the dwarf chuckled in victory as he clapped his friend on his shoulder.

The dwarf merely shook his head from side to side. "We have lost the battle I believe. We are to meet at the rallying point as soon as we deliver the prisoner to Commander Fehzban."

The other dwarf's face turned sour. "What do you mean we lost? How can that be? We had them pushed back to the bridge?" he argued.

The other dwarf just shrugged his shoulders. "Perhaps we didn't lose, perhaps Amerix feels that we need to leave soon. All I know is that Commander Fehzban gave us orders to meet the rest of the army at the rallying point."

"Was he mad at us for coming here?"

The dwarf shook his head. "No, he was pleased at our captive, I think. He just seemed defeated to me."

Neither dwarf said anything else. They bent down

and picked up the rope that held the feet of the elf and started to drag her down the corridor.

    Alexis was elated at the news she heard from the dwarves. If in fact the dwarves had been routed it was a mammoth victory. She couldn't imagine how Apollisian and Victor had succeeded but she found herself surprised at how she was uplifted when she imagined the paladin alive. She was happy for Victor too, but not like the strange feeling she had when she thought of the paladin. She dismissed the jumbled mass of emotions when she felt her feet being roughly thrown down.

    "Here she is, commander." the dwarf said sullenly. Fehzban nodded and dismissed the pair with a wave. They silently turned and hurried down the corridor to the rallying point as ordered. Fehzban paused until he was sure the pair had left. When he was satisfied they were gone, he leaned down and whispered to Alexis.

    "Stay still if you can hear me, elf. I mean you no harm." Fehzban wasn't sure his grasp on the elven language was firm so he repeated the phrase in dwarven, just in case she was conscious and could speak both languages. He paused for a moment and watched the elf. She was bound tightly by the rope and wrapped from neck to ankles. Her feet were a little loose, but the ropes around her wrists were extremely tight. Her face was purple and swollen from being beat and he doubted that if she were conscious that she would be able to see out of her eyes.

    Alexis didn't know what to think of the dwarf. He spoke a little elven but she wasn't sure exactly what he meant. She thought he mentioned something about going to harm her, but it was not in the tone or the context she would have expected. She wasn't sure how she would defend herself if he was going to harm her, all she could move was her legs and she could only thrash them about at best. She listened instead, but heard no one else but the dwarf that had spoke. Her keen hearing scanned the passages for footsteps, weapons being drawn, but she heard nothing but the rhythmic breathing of her and the dwarf that stood before her.

Fehzban kneeled down before the elf and placed his hands on her face. He closed his eyes and began chanting softly to himself. " I call forth the power of Leska and in her divine might, that she cast out the pain and heal the injuries that have befallen the child that lays before me."

After his chanting, his stubby hairy hand turned warm and began a soft white glow. Magical energy erupted from his hand and flooded into Alexis. She wanted to cry out, but the warm energy was soothing to her battered face. In a few moments the pain was gone and she opened her eyes, staring at the bearded face of Fehzban. He was an older dwarf and his beard extended just above his waistline and was braided in three braids that hung down. The ends of them were decorated with bright green wraps that held the braids to keep them from unraveling. He wore a small metal helm that was open faced revealing a bright smile and deep blue eyes. He wore thick plate armor that bore a large dent in the center that seemed to have been made recently. Alexis said nothing to him. She just started intently at the face of her rescuer or her executioner, though she doubted the latter.

Fehzban smiled at the elf. She was beautiful, even for an elf, and he noticed a mark of superiority from her. It was subtle at best, but he could detect it nonetheless. Even bound, gagged, and beaten she emitted an air of superiority that could come only with nobility. Most dwarves lacked the wisdom to discern the difference between elven commoners and nobility. It wasn't an easy task for any dwarf. Elves were so lucid that it was nearly impossible to discern their hierarchy, but Fehzban had dealt with elven nobility in the orc wars and had learned the difference through many embarrassing trial and errors. The old commander stared down at his elven captive. Her blonde braided hair was long and stained with blood, though her wounds were all healed. She stared at him with her beautiful brown eyes that seemed to sooth him. He reached down and cut the ropes that bound her.

Alexis rubbed her hands together vigorously, trying to get blood flowing in them as quickly as possible. She was certain the dwarf that stood before her was not an enemy, at least not at the present moment. He was obviously a cleric of some kind. She stared at the dwarf again, but this time without blurry vision. He was adorned in full plate armor that bore a great dent in the chest. His armor was dull and grimy, but appeared as if he kept it polished and clean under normal circumstances. He wore a small helm that had an open face, but she noticed, through her clear vision, that the helm bore a few scars from untold battles. Under his armor he wore a finely woven green tunic that was held together by gold colored seams. His short cape was made of green silk and depicted the gold emblem of Leska on the rear of it. He wore thick metal plates that extended from just below his knees to the tops of his heavy walking boots. He was a formable looking adversary to say the least, but Alexis detected a glint of deep rooted passion in his steel blue eyes that was not characteristic to the blood thirsty dwarves that she seen ravage the Central City and the Torrent Manor. She noticed a gleam of empathy and caring that she had not seen in the diminutive people.

"Well are you going to just sit there or are you going to introduce yourself, elf?" Fehzban said in his native dwarven tongue. He was not sure how well she understood his elven, but by her reaction from the first time he spoke it she seemed quite confused.

Alexis slowly rose on unsteady feet and dusted herself off. Though she was covered in the grime from the sewer, Fehzban was amazed at how much dignity she managed to restore to her stature by the simple motion. "I am Alexis Alexandria Overmoon. First daughter of King Christopher Calamon Overmoon of Minok forest." she said as she raised her chin in the air with pride at the announcement of her titles. Though revealing her first name was not a custom any non-elf unless they were good friends, she felt it was fitting to show exactly who this dwarf was speaking to.

Fehzban seemed unimpressed at her titles, but he was astonished at her ability to speak dwarven. He kept his tone soft and soothing. "Your equipment is there." he said as he pointed to a dirty sack that was laying next to the wall. Her sleek white ash bow poked out from the sack that was full of her chain armor and other equipment. "You need to take your leave, as I am taking mine. You are not an enemy of Stoneheart or any other dwarf kin. My deepest apologies for any wrongs you have suffered. I would like to extend to you some sort of retribution for all that you have suffered by the hands of my men, but alas, I do not have the means at this time. Someday *Alexis Alexandria Overmoon*, I shall compensate you." Fehzban said, over pronouncing her name. He turned and quickly hurried down the corridor. His back hid the deep smile he wore from speaking her full name. His heavy plate armor jingled and rattled as he ran, but he didn't seem to mind as he disappeared into the darkness.

If Amerix has deserted, or has been slain, who will answer for this? He thought to himself. The dwarf took a deep breath as he continued down the passage. Following the general's orders may very well be the last action he does as a free dwarf.

Alexis fumed. How dare that dwarf call her by her full name. Alexis started to protest, but she had little time to don her gear and she was afraid she might be caught unaware in the dark sewers and she needed to get back to Apollisian as quickly as possible. She opened the dirty bag, placed on her thin chain armor, grabbed her long sword and composite long bow, and darted down the sewer corridor.

*   *   *

Amerix awoke face down in the crusty sand for the fourth consecutive day. He opened his heavy eyelids and gazed cross eyed and expressionless at the many fine granules of sand that rested before him. There were a few dark colored grains, but most were light brown or tan. The old dwarf stared, fixated on the tiny rocks, until a small ant wandered by. It zigzagged way across the rough terrain, pausing to hold on whenever Amerix exhaled. The small black insect didn't seem daunted by Amerix's breath that acted like a frequent windstorm that ravaged the land around it. Whenever the wind stopped, it paused a while longer to make sure it was safe, then it would start again, only to be blown away by an unsuspecting breath a few moments later. Amerix closed his eyes after the ant was blown away, seeing nothing else worth staring at, but not tired enough to sleep. The intense hunger he felt the first and second day had given way to a general cramp that constantly gnawed at him, but his great despair seemed to shield his mind from any pain or hunger he might have normally felt. The old dwarf laid face down in on the beach for a many hours before forcing himself upright. His once powerful arms were weak from starvation and shook with fatigue when he used them to prop himself up. The dwarf seemed undaunted at his own weakness and even cracked a small smile at the thought of himself wasting away. His head was light from malnutrition and he felt sick to his stomach. He was covered in a thousand tiny insect bites and the renegade general was sure he had many mites that had made a home in his hair and beard. Amerix chuckled at the thought of how a week ago he would have never allowed himself to be so dirty, even if he was a dwarf, but now. Now he wasn't even sure if he wanted to be a dwarf anymore. He was pretty sure he didn't want to be alive, despite the fantastic hallucination he had had under the river. He knew it was just that, a hallucination. Amerix placed no weight in what was said to him, knowing that it came from deep in his own mind and not from the lips of his departed wife and son.

As he sat in the sandy beach with his legs out stretched in front of him, Amerix occasionally wiggled his toes to ward off flies as he watched the many beautiful birds that hunted and swam in the river bottoms. Amerix was in no fear of being attacked by anything, though he would likely not care if he were, it would end the dilemma of life for him. He didn't fear attack because the Dawson River was so ancient it had carved a deep crevice in the earth over the last ten thousand or so years. The small beachhead he was on was rare in the great river bottoms. Usually the only dry spot was a large rock that had fallen from the cliff and jutted up from under the river's edge. And as it was, the rocky cliff on the eastern side of the cavern, was only a few hundred feet away, so Amerix was quite secluded in his tiny world.

The renegade general sat on the beach most of the day baking in the warm autumn sun. His light skin became blistered and red, but as the days wore on, it was replaced by a golden bronze. His body soon depleted the fat reserves he had built up, and his once somewhat flabby arms, wore away to a tight iron like sinew. Amerix repeated this process day in and day out, occasionally munching on a large beetle when the hunger pains seemed to rouse his brain from desolation, but he did little else.

*   *   *

Therrig cautiously navigated down the gloomy tunnel that the dark dwarves came from. It was a small passage that appeared to have been a string of limestone at one time, that had all but been wore away over time from a small trickle of water than ran down the center. The stream slowly filtered by like the dawdling drain of a sewer that was about one foot wide and no more than a few inches deep. The walls of this particular passage were made of thick clay, with small patches of limestone. Therrig followed the passage for a few hours when he noticed the ceiling was expanding. The renegade paused and ran his hard-calloused finger over the stone surface of the passage. He detected many unnatural grooves and nicks that made him suspect that the corridor had been widened unnaturally. Therrig paused and studied the walls and rocky crevices that extended several feet in front of him where the ceiling jumped from seven feet to thirty. He noticed several small ledges that seemed just the right height to conceal a sentry and just low enough to allow an attack on any unwary passer-bys. Under the largest ledge, bright yellow mineral deposits marked a small trickle of water coming out of the wall that formed the tiny stream that ran down the passage he just came up.

    Therrig slowly made his way under the rocky ledge and focused his ears trying to hear the faintest sound, but he heard nothing. After a few moments he was satisfied that there were no enemies about, Therrig continued on into the large corridor. In the distance Therrig could see the passage turned to the right and still continued to enlarge. It was readily apparent now that the passage was not natural and he even noticed a crude pick axe that was resting against the wall near the end of the corridor. The pick axe was not crafted well and the head was made out of some kind of dark metal. The shaft was also made from the same metal, but was very thin, making the tool unbalanced. Therrig smiled a yellow toothed grin. He knew the pick axe was made by the dark dwarves. The inferior race usually didn't have access to the finer ores, and their weapons and tools, if made from metal, were usually weak and dark colored. The shaft was made of the same metal, because the dark dwarves didn't have access to wood to have any wooden shafts in their tools or weapons. So the dark dwarves made their shafts of the same ore they made the tool heads. In order to make the weapons or tools practical, they had to make the shafts thin and narrow in order to keep the weight down. This thin shaft often made the weapon awkward and unbalanced.

    Therrig slowly walked up to the crudely made pick axe that was resting against the wall of the cave. He carefully placed each foot softly in front of the other. The young dwarf wasn't a master at moving silently, but on the smooth stone of the passage, he was confident at his ability to do so. As he reached the pile of tools, he looked down and examined the thin metal handle. He could detect slight variations in temperature on the handle where it had been held recently. Therrig reached down and felt the narrow shaft. It was impossible for him to feel the temperature difference, but he could plainly see it the distinct lines between shades of blue.

    As he looked down the ever expanding cave corridor, Therrig noticed it's ceiling rose to sixty feet. At the top he saw many long stalactites hanging down, indicating that it was a natural corridor. The young dwarf paused and leaned against the cold stone wall, pressing his back against it in attempt to hide. Therrig slowed his breathing as he tried to detect any would be enemies that might be making their way down the large passage. To his surprise, he could hear many voices coming from around the corner in the corridor. Therrig stalked forward, keeping his back against the wall, and his eyes ever scanning forward. As he rounded the corner, the corridor opened up into a huge expansive cavern. There was a passage that zigzagged down the ledge that he was standing on. At the bottom of the ledge were thousands of stone dwellings that had been crafted in a marvelous underground city. He could see many giant towers that were hundreds of feet tall erupting from the stone dwellings, that at their peaks, had stone bridges that led into passages that were carved into gigantic stalactites that were hanging from the ceiling. The huge stalactites had many windows and other constructs in them. To the far north of the immense city, there were large mushroom fields that were being tended by scores of goblins that were often beaten with whips by dark dwarves. There was a great river that ran down the center of the city and it came from the wall on the north side of the cavern and exited on the south side of the city into a deep tunnel. There were beautiful bridges that spanned the river in several points. It was uncommon for dark dwarves to build anything that even remotely resembled a work of art. Disregarding the immaculately ornate buildings and structure, Therrig took a deep breath and moved closer to the edge of the rocky outcropping that over looked the city. His eyes darted over the streets and alleys searching for a secluded spot to make his descent into the large city. Everywhere he looked, Therrig saw dark dwarves. He noticed temples that were constructed in the honor of Durion, the mountain god. The same god that the Stormhammers had worshipped. Though the dark dwarves were often at war or at least at odds with the Stormhammer clan, Therrig found the thought of revenge much greater than the irony of working with the race that wiped out his friends and family hundreds of years ago.

The crazed dwarf known as Therrig Alistair Delastan began his descent into the city of the dark dwarves. Hoping to either forge a new alliance and have revenge against clan Stoneheart, or kill as many of the light skinned dwarves as mortally possible.

The passage into the dark city was narrow and steep. Large boulders covered in small cracks lined the edges the path and small rocks skittered under Therrig's feet threatening to topple him. He steadied himself and slowly made his way to the bottom of the passage seemingly undetected. As he neared the base of the trail, he could hear steel ringing against rock from behind a large stone wall that divided the trail and the a small courtyard. The wall was finely crafted, but age and wear had rounded off it's fine points. Therrig quietly walked along the base of the wall listening to the ringing steel, taking steps with each ring. The wall was made of large stone bricks that were covered in a dark green moss. The moss was overlaid by thick black vines that grew from the base wall and rose up and over the top of the stone structure. The vines had many small white flowers that budded, but Therrig was unable to discern the color with his infravision. Infravision, the ability to see in complete darkness by the use of the heat spectrum, prevented the dwarf from seeing colors, unless they were in conjunction with a heat source.

    Therrig ignored the flowered vine and circled around the far side of the wall. Once he rounded the corner, the wall was tiered, becoming smaller the further he went and he soon could see glance over the top with little climbing. Therrig lightly rubbed his hands together and pulled himself up ten or so feet, to the top of the stone wall. He could see about thirty small humanoids breaking rocks with large hammers. The humanoids were about three feet tall and had long pointed noses and ears. Their heads were scaly and riddled with small bumps. They had dark beady eyes that could see as well as any creature that lived in the under dark. Their skin was green and they had only four fingers on each hand. The creatures, Therrig recognized as goblins, hammered at the rocks as four dark dwarves drove them on with the threat of a whip strike. The four taskmasters were wearing chain armor and no helm, showing their pale, thin, ugly faces and small beard. The dark dwarves wore dark black tunics that appeared to be made out of some kind of leather. They had large black whips in their hands and bulky metal hammers hooked to their sides through a thick leather loop. Occasionally one of them would strike out and lash a goblin for no apparent reason other than their own sick entertainment. They all four would laugh when the goblin cried out and worked furiously for an hour or so, thinking he might avoid another lashing if he worked harder.

Behind the four dark dwarves was a large stone building that was protected by the wall. There was a great doorway that extended beyond Therrig's ability to see in the dark. The frame was ornate and covered in intricately carved stones. The structures looked very familiar to Therrig, but he couldn't place his finger on it. The roof of the building was made of stone also, but it was constructed in thin rock like slabs, much like the humans wooden shingles, to displace any water that may drip from the giant stalactites that hung from overhead. The buildings were amazingly crafted and there was not a single square inch of them that had not been carved by an artesian.

Therrig paused at the thought of how long it would take to carve such designs on an entire building. Many of the designs were worn or damaged and it was obvious that the dark dwarves had nothing to do with the art work of the city. He surmised that this was probably the home of some other dwarven clan that the despicable dark dwarves had conquered. Therrig fought the strong urge to leap the wall and cut down the dark dwarves where they stood, but he knew that would solve nothing, except alert the masses to his arrival before he could make his way into the heart of the city. Therrig wasn't exactly sure how he would enact his plan, but he knew that the dark dwarf leadership was set upon the "might is right" principle. He hoped that he could somehow over throw the current leader and take charge of the city. Quite a difficult task, he reminded himself and decided that getting accepted in the general culture would be his first agenda.

Therrig slowly climbed down from the wall and made his way along the southern part of the city. Everywhere he went there were amazing crafted buildings and structures. He saw countless praises to Durion, the dwarven mountain god, and even a few alters. Therrig struggled to understand why the dark dwarves would have alters to the mountain god. Dark dwarves usually worshipped sinister gods, like Kobli or Rha-Cordan, not a surface dwelling dwarven god. But as Therrig passed by countless alters to the mountain god, it was undeniable to him that his dark cousins had taken a liking to Durion.

Therrig was almost halfway around the southern tip of the city when he say it. It was as if he had been stabbed through the heart with molten hot stake. Standing before him was the depiction of a great dwarf. The statue was almost forty feet tall, though it had been severely damaged and defaced, there was no mistaking it. The figure wore a great helm that had horns jutting out from either side. It was an open faced helm that revealed the steady face of a proven warrior, yet the gentle, kind-hearted eyes of a father. The dwarf's thick beard was long and unbraided extending well below his belt line. He wore a glorious suit of finely crafted plate armor that bore many nicks and scratches in it from the dark dwarves trying to deface the imposing figure. The legs were severely damaged with most of the stone around them knocked away revealing a solid core of trinium, the strongest known metal. The base of the statue was torn away revealing the thick trinium core that extended below the surface, keeping the statue from being knocked down. The figure held a great hammer that housed a huge blue jewel on each side of head. The jewel still shined brightly, illuminating the area with a soft azure hue in all directions. Therrig stood before the awe inspiring statue of Midagord Milence Stormhammer. First king, and founder, of clan Stormhammer. Suddenly a torrid of emotions ripped through the renegade dwarf. He recalled playing around the statue when he was a small boy after he and some of his friends had completed their lessons for the day. He chased his friends, and they chased him, in a never ending game of tag. Therrig remembered sitting at the base of the statue when he first heard the screams. His family ran around their buildings franticly trying to hide, while his father rushed out of the house in his armor and he held the family hammer. It was a brilliant war hammer that glowed scarlet at the head. Therrig could taste the danger, and ducked behind the base of the great statue. The statue of the king always made him feel safe.

Therrig could see thousands of figures erupting from the north passage followed by a great beast. The creature had a long serpentine head and had great wings that were twice as long as body. The heat spectrum of breath was so cold that it was black. It was so black it seemed to draw in all the light from around it. Therrig had never seem such cold in his young life. He remembered the sound of steel ringing against steel and the anguish cries of women and children as the dark invaders swept from house to house killing all of the inhabitants. Yet, Therrig remained hidden on the southern most part of town, behind the feet of the great king and warrior, Midagord. He watched as a small faction of his kin formed a line of defense atop the hill on the west end. They were out numbered one hundred to one, but they fought valiantly. For every one that fell, fifty of the enemy fell, but soon, they were forced to withdraw further south. It was as if the plague of dark dwarves, led by the white dragon methodically purged the city of his kin from north to south. Yet, Therrig hid undetected under the watchful stare of his king. The young dwarf saw the last of his brethren fall at the western front that had held for so long. He saw hundreds of dark dwarves rushing down the eastern trail toward his house. Therrig stared in utter fear at the horrific beast that unleashed a breath attack that was so cold it was as if the abyss itself was opened up and began to swallow the buildings and towers of his home city. Yet he hid, cowering under the feet of his king. Therrig knew that his king would save them. He would stride up confidently and challenge the evil beast, just as he had done in the past to invaders. Therrig had no doubt his king would slay the white lizard with a single blow and then glare at the dark dwarves so menacingly that they would either throw down there weapons and flee in terror, or the would weep and cower, begging for forgiveness for their evil deeds, but the king did not come, yet still, he waited.

The sound of fighting grew ever so near, so close the copper smell of death assailed his nose as it floated past him, and still he waited. He could see the dark dwarves as they kicked in the door to his home and entered. He heard the screams of his mother and sisters as they were cut down, and he watched in horror as the dark fiends erupted from his home with his mothers head on a pike. He watched as they laughed and kicked his sisters' heads around on the ground for sport.

Therrig buried his face in his hands, not able to bear the sight of what he was witnessing. The young dwarf's spirits were lifted somewhat when he saw his father run to him from the west trail. His father was covered in blood and bore wounds in many places. There were seven other dwarves with him, including the King and his son, Prince Amerix Alistair Stormhammer. He wanted to say to his father that he had been brave, but he had not. He wanted to say to his father that he tried to stop them from killing his ma' and his sisters, but he had not. He tried to speak but all that came out of his mouth was a pitiful cry of defeat. Tears streamed down his bare face and soaked his shirt as he moaned in agony at the horror he had endured. His father grabbed him firmly by his shoulders and looked him straight in the eyes. Therrig could hear his father as if he were there again. His father's voice was as angelic as a choir of angels to the renegade dwarf.

"Son, always know that I love thee. Go with Amerix and the others. Yer ma' and sisters have been wronged. The King and I cannot let that crime go unanswered. We will catch up as soon as we are done." his father said as he drew his hammer and started off to his house with the King. Therrig remembered seeing the king wearing little armor but he wielded the mighty hammer he was known for. Therrig recalled nodding his head slowly and he reluctantly began walking to the others. They roughly pulled him into a small boat and frantically started rowing into the southern cave of the river that ran through his home city. He remembered looking back the whole way, desperately searching for his father, that Therrig would never see again.

Therrig came to his senses as wet tears ran down his dirty blood stained face. He glanced around again and realized where he was at. He was cowering under the base of the statue again, only this time, the statute's legs were smashed and damaged. The beautiful golden plaque had been ripped off and defaced, but the hammer still shined bright as it did when he was a boy. Therrig wanted to cry, to hide, to run away again, but he glanced down at the stone hammer that was in his hands. He looked at his once weak and boyish arms that were now strong and powerful. Hate filled his heart. He stood fully erect and stepped out from behind the stone statue and started at the house that was his as a boy. As he placed one foot in front of the other and could hear again the screams of his mother and his sisters. Therrig took deep breaths as he walked up the door way. The portal had never been repaired. He could still see dried blood on the inside of the walls when he walked in. The renegade dwarf's knuckles turned white from gripping the stone hammer so tightly. He could see a female dark dwarf standing in the kitchen area where his mother once stood. She was singing while he could hear two small children playing in the other room.

"I'sa gots a pie for yous, my dear, my dear.
I'sa cooks it hots for yous, my dear, my dear.
and evens thoughs hots, hots
and the stoves I'sa foughts n' foughts
I'sa do for yous, my dear."

The singing was cut short by a wicked slice from Therrig's stone hammer. The heavy weapon hit the woman in the back of the head, splattering blood all over the wall and sending her lifeless body headlong onto the counter. The renegade dwarf smiled in satisfaction at the twitching body of the female dark dwarf convulsed and fell onto the floor. He quickly stepped to the side of the doorway and placed his back to the wall that led to the living area of the home. He recalled walking into the kitchen from that area as a small boy to ask his ma' what she was cooking for dinner. She would shoo him out with a laugh.

    A small boy walked from around the corner. He looked like any other small dwarf, except his skin was a pale gray and his eyes were without pupils, designed to see only in infravision. The boy started to cry out at the sight of his mother on the floor bleeding, but Therrig's hammer silenced him before he could utter a single sound.

    Therrig roughly kicked the body of the small boy next to woman and it thudded sickly on the stone floor as he headed into the living area. The room was nothing like he remembered, except for the design. The once grand stone furniture was worn to indiscernible shapes, and there were no tapestries hanging on the walls like when he lived there. He could hear a young girl singing in the far room that was his as a child. A sense of jealousy, pervaded him and baleful revenge wafted over the renegade dwarf. He stepped into his old room and silenced the little girl as she played with a wooden doll, oblivious to the murder she was about to be victim to.

    Therrig carried the body of the small girl into the kitchen by her hair and tossed her lifeless form to the floor. He imagined if his mother and sisters were piled in a similar way when the dark dwarves killed them. Therrig stepped over the dead and placed the heavy stone hammer on the counter and removed a sharp dagger from the drawer next to the wash basin. He turned to the bodies in remembrance of the fate his mother and sisters suffered, though he was sure to have more sport than they did.

* * *

Lance shook Ryshander's hand firmly. "Well if you must be off my friend, it was a great pleasure meeting you. Had it not been for you and Kaisha, I might not have survived the battle with Grascon."

Ryshander nodded his head slowly. He was a little uneasy at being called anyone's friend. "I am sure you had the battle well in hand, my young mage. All we did was help tie a few loose ends for you." he said as he motioned over to Kaisha who was taking a deep draw from her flagon of cider. "She promised to decipher some elven for you. We cannot stay here any longer, but we are heading south, towards the southern part of Beykla. It seems they feel the way the king had dealt with the dwarves has been wrong and they blame him for the war. Whether it is true or not is no concern of mine, but I tend to agree with them. We will spend a few days in each town, until we reach a small settlement north of the great mine. It is called Terrace Folly. Have you heard of it?"

Lance frowned and turned to Jude. The big swordsman shrugged his shoulders and waved his large hand, trying to get the bar maids attention to refill his mug.

"Well, I guess we haven't, but as soon as we are done here, I hope to look you up." Lance said as he placed his right hand on Ryshander's shoulder. He hadn't received any clerical healing on his left arm yet, but the clerics were supposed to be at the Blue Dragon Inn soon. The Inn hadn't suffered much damage, and the Inn Keeper, who never missed an opportunity, set up shop, hired new bar maids right away, and began to get as much of the Westvons' gold as possible.

Ryshander uneasily accepted Lance's hand and stood up from the charred table. The wererat thief gave a farewell wave, then he and Kaisha departed out the front door of the charred common room.

"Strange pair." Jude said as he took a sip from his newly filled mug.

Lance turned his chair and faced his large friend. "Yea, you would think they were related, with that same nervous face twitch."

Jude took another large draw from the mug and shook his head, spilling some of he contents from the corner of his mouth. He wiped the froth away from his chin with his sleeve and smiled. "Nah, I was talking about the way they fought. They weren't that good of sword fighters, but they were seldom wounded from the dwarves' weapons. In fact, I think Ryshander hadn't been hurt at all until he fought that big dwarf next to the bridge. Ya know, the one Kaisha tumped over the edge." Jude said as he made a heaving motion.

Lance frowned and rubbed his forehead with his good hand. He was tired from the fighting and some of the militia reported that there were still dwarves barricaded up in some of the eastern buildings near the coliseum. The whole event was very taxing on the young mage.

Jude sensed his friends exhaustion which made the large swordsman more aware of his own. He leaned back in his chair and propped his feet up on the charred table, causing dark soot to crunch under the weight of his boot. "Ya know, my friend, I don't care if they were parishioners of the dark gods themselves. They helped us out of a tight spot and even saved that knightly fellow. In my book, face twitching or not, they are all right." Jude said as he took a final draw from his third mug of ale. He hammered the flagon down with a smile and let out a light belch.

Lance nodded distantly. "But don't you think it was kind of strange that they seemed to appear at the most opportune times?"

Jude shrugged his thick muscled shoulders as he held his mug aloft for the serving wench to refill. "You mean stranger than a thousand dwarves spilling from the sewers of a Beyklan city and killing hundreds of townsfolk?" Jude asked cynically.

Lance chuckled, but didn't reply as he rubbed his aching shoulder. What Jude said ringed true, it just seemed as if the pair were following them, but Lance could not figure why.

Jude leaned forward after the serving wench refilled his mug. "Look Lance, I find this whole stinking city strange and twisted. I want to leave as soon as possible and return home. We are lucky we didn't get ourselves killed with this fool adventure."

"You're right, my friend. I no longer have the money to pay your wages. You are free to go home to the squalor you were living in." Lance replied bitterly.

Jude frowned and slammed his mug down on the table, sloshing ale on the charred table and the floor. He raised his large hand and shook his thick index finger at Lance. "You damnable ass! I didn't come on this little trip because of your gold. I came because I knew you would go on this fool journey with or without me, and I knew someone was going to have to save your puny neck and I'm quite pleased at the many times I have successfully done so." Jude growled.

Lance was surprised at Jude's anger. He didn't mean it the way it came out and offending his lifetime and only friend was not what he intended. "Look Jude..." Lance offered softly.

"I didn't mean to insult you. I..."

Jude cut in and held his hand up to stifle any response from Lance. "Say no more, my friend. I was needing a little adventure in my life, whether I was willing to admit it or not, and I would be glad to travel with you and save your neck as many times as need be. All in the name of friendship." Jude said as he leaned back, placing his feet back on the old burned table.

Lance smiled wryly. "You mean like the time

Grascon came into the room and you were laying on the floor while my superior skill and power overwhelmed the enemy that felled you?" Lance said with a chuckle.

Jude frowned at first, but could not contain a chuckle himself, and soon both had a hearty laugh."Don't get me started." Jude gurgled and raised his mug in the air. "A toast to friendship." .

"To family." Lance corrected.

Jude nodded. "To family."

The pair finished their mugs and sat in content in the burned out common room of the Blue Dragon Inn when three men in brass colored scale mail armor and long red silk capes came in. They had long swords that hung confidently at their sides and their helms were opened faced with chain bishop collars around their necks. Three men strode in behind the armored soldiers wearing thick violet robes with bright orange fringes and cuffs. The robed men each displayed a holy symbol depicting golden balancing scale crossed by a gavel and they were in their early to late twenties. Another man stepped into the room behind the others wearing a green silk tunic and breeches. He held a scroll case in one hand and a strange looking rod in the other.

"I am looking for Lance, Jude, Ryshander and Kaisha." he said.

Lance raised his good arm and winced as the movement hurt his injured shoulder. "I am Lance." he said, then motioned to Jude who was soliciting the serving wench for another mug of ale. "And this is Jude."

Jude nodded his head as he took a drink from his flagon.

"What can we do for you?" Lance asked.

"The Duke sends his regards and offers healing services from the church of Stephanis. Where are your companions?" the man asked.

Lance sat forward in his chair. "They left already. Said something about going to Westvon, why do you ask?"

The man in the green tunic displayed a look of anger and disappointment that didn't seem to coincide with his response. "They were to receive accommodation for their bravery."

Lance nodded hesitantly, but Jude studied the armed men. They began a sweep of the common room and then started up the charred wooden stairs to the inn's rooms. Jude motioned to Lance and twitched his head at the men as they started up the stairs as the priests laid their hands on them. They could feel the bizarre warm sensation as their wounds were magically healed, and Jude focused on the armed men as they disappeared from sight.

"Where are they going?" Lance asked as he marveled at the complex weaves of magical energy that the priest used to heal him. What fascinated Lance the most, was that the priest didn't seem to guide the weaves at all, they seemed to move on their own, as if they understood the command and where simply following a routine order. All of Lance's spells he had to guide each individual strand.

The man in the green tunic shifted uneasily. "They are checking to see if there are any dwarves left in the building. Just a common procedure that you needn't concern yourself with."

Lance shrugged his shoulders, but Jude kept his muscles tense, prepared to draw his great sword if needed.

Soon the priests were done healing them and the three armed guards came back down the stairs. "If you see Ryshander or Kaisha, send them to city hall so they can pick up their reward." The man in the green tunic said as the group turned and exited the charred common room.

Jude shook his head as he held his mug aloft for yet another refill. "Those men were not looking for dwarves and I seriously doubt they were hoping to give Ryshander and Kaisha any kind of a reward that they might have wanted."

Lance nodded. "I figured that group had a different agenda. That's why I told them they were heading to Westvon, though I doubt they believed me."

Jude shook his head in agreement. "No matter. Lets get out of this Rha forsaken town. I don't care where we go, as long as it is away from here."

Lance pondered the encounter for a moment. "Why didn't that group question where that knightly fellow was?" Lance asked.

Jude smiled as the serving wench refilled his mug. He took a long deep draw and wiped his mouth with his dirty sleeve. "I don't know, maybe he was part of the city's fighters and they already took care of him." Jude more asked then said.

Lance stared at the black charred table in thought. "Maybe, but I doubt it. This whole city has a hidden agenda if you asked me, but I don't really care. So long as it doesn't involve us."

Jude nodded.

"That's no way for a group of brave freedom fighters to talk." came a voice from the door way of the common room. Lance and Jude turned to see the knightly figure that battled the dwarf on the bridge. He stood a full six foot two inches tall and was adorned in his plate armor. The slash wounds were repaired and the dents had been pounded out. The armor was polished bright and he wore a vivid violet cape with the symbol of the scales and the gavel, like the robed men wore that just spoke with them. His short sword was in scabbard that was lashed tightly against his leg and an empty scabbard for a long sword hung at his side.

Lance smiled and stood up extending his hand to the imposing man. "Finally I get to learn the name of the mysterious champion that battled the dwarven nightmare."

The armored man took Lance's hand and shook it. "I am Apollisian Bargoe of Westvon and champion of justice." Apollisian said with an iron smile.

"I am Lance Ecnal and this is my friend, Jude." Lance said as he pulled out a charred chair and bid Apollisian to sit.

The paladin sat down and placed his armored hands on the burnt table. "I wish I could visit and trade tales, but I am looking for a friend of mine, that I fear may have perished in the fight. Her name is Overmoon. She is an elven archer and I hoped you may have seen her."

Jude said nothing and took another drink from his flagon. When he finished he sat up in his chair and puffed out his chest, obviously intimidated by the imposing figure that sat at their table.

Lance tapped his head as he replayed the events of the battle over and over in his mind. "I don't think I recall any archers during the battle, let alone an elven archer." Lance said remorsefully. He could see the disappointment in Apollisian's face.

" I'm sorry." Lance said.

Jude cleared his throat."What about the woman that was on top of the Inn when we were fleeing. She was very small and was using a bow."

Apollisian nearly knocked the table over as he leaped to his feet. His chair tumbled behind him. "Yes! She was on top of the Inn laying cover fire for me and Victor. Where did she go?" Apollisian pleaded.

Jude leaned back in his chair to distance himself from the excited paladin. "I don't know where she went. We saw the fires in the west and decided that east was best way to flee town. So Lance and I darted back down the stairs."

"How do you get to the roof from here?" Apollisian asked.

Jude motioned to the stairs and before he could say anything else, Apollisian was in a full run. When he bounded up the stairs Jude shook his head and took another drink. " That fellow gets excited easily."

Lance nodded. " But surely you would be excited too had we been separated in a terrible battle."

Jude shook his head as he finished the mug of ale and plopped it down on the table.

"Nah, I would be counting my blessings to be rid of the bane known as, Ecnal." Jude said with a chuckle. Lance flicked a piece of burnt wood at his friend and they shared an enthusiastic laugh.

*   *   *

Amerix awoke to another bright shinning day in the hot sun. The weather was progressively turning cold and the trees near the edge of the river seemed to have lost a third of their leaves in the last few days that Amerix had laid on the small sandy beach. He rubbed his dry calloused hands over his cold bare arms. The old dwarf was for the most part, a victim to the elements without his clothing. He glanced over to the blood stained leather tunic and breeches that lay in a heap where he left them when he emerged from the cold swift river. He considered placing the ragged clothing back on, but it was as if he was donning a former skin of his old self. Amerix found it odd, but he had no desire to even resemble that creature that was formally called Amerix Alistair Stormhammer.

The renegade dwarf stared off into blank nothingness as he recalled the day his home city was attacked by the dark dwarves and the white dragon. The invaders erupted from the northern river cave that cut the large dwarven city in half. He had been at the palace when they hit, training with his axe and a hammer. While his father rushed out to meet the invaders, young Amerix was sent to oversee the evacuation of the women and children. His father's commands had infuriated him. He had just graduated from the academy in top honors and no dwarf in all of Dregan City, save for his father and some of the top military commanders, could best him in combat, yet he was sent to do a whelps job. Looking back, Amerix had the wisdom to see it was a father looking after his only son, but at the time, Amerix saw it as if his father lacked any faith in his battle prowess. Amerix realized later that if he had fought in the horrible battle, he would have surely died. Every dwarf that fought on the front lines died, save for his father. The King of clan Stormhammer battled all the way to the final dwarf at the southern end of city. Amerix recalled back at when they reached the southern river cave, they spied a young whelp cowering under his father's statue. One of the master-at-arms, Vrescan Alistair Delastan, Amerix's older cousin, cried out that the whelp was his son. King Midagord and Vrescan exited the boat, scooping up the boy and placed the whelp in the boat. They then went off to fight side by side against the dark invaders. Amerix pleaded for his father to flee with them, but the old king smiled sadly into his son's eyes and said he could not. Amerix recalled his father's voice on that frightful day all to clear.

"Their is a duty that I must do, my son. A duty that you are just beginning to remotely fathom. The mantle of a king is a heavy mantle indeed. Vrescan's family has been slain, as has our own. Take the boat and sail south. The river will open up into a valley near the human kingdom of Adoria." Midagord said as he hastily removed his plate armor. The old king placed them at the feet of his only son and fought back tears of pride as he recalled when his father had given him the very same honor by bequeathing him the family's breast plate and helm.

As he stared up into the cold blue eyes of his father, Amerix knew at that moment he would never see him again. He started to protest, but he was silenced by his father's stern raised hand.

"Take this wisdom with you as you take the armor of Stormhammer, my son. For one day, you may be a king. Always know that any man can wear a crown, but know that only a king can hold his head up high when the fates of his people are his to bear." Midagord said as he grasped his son by each shoulder sternly. After a long pause of staring into the young blue eyes of Amerix, Midagord turned and purposefully marched past the great statue that was erected to depict his strength and honor.

    Amerix watched helplessly as his mentor, his king, his father, charged into a battle that could not be won with the cry of vengeance on his lips.

    Amerix did as he was told. He sailed south into the valley and eventually settled with a clan of dwarves in the Pyberian Mountains called Stoneheart. He married and had a son. Amerix had never forgot what his father said to him, even though he had changed in ways his father would never understand. The world was different now then it had been when he was a whelp. The renegade general stared for a few more fleeting thoughts, then glanced down at the pile of rags that was once a fine set of padded armor that he had wore the day he sailed out of Dregan City. He found it fitting that they now laid soiled and dirty on the shore of a nameless beach of the Dawson River. Amerix had spent all of his adult life trying to seek personal atonement through battle for the loss of his entire way of life. The old dwarf chuckled when he realized that only in defeat had he achieved atonement. Amerix cracked his first genuine smile in so long he couldn't recall the last one he had. He had managed to find reprieve in the knowledge that his soul was not determined by the battles he won, not by the enemies he slew, or the great armies he crushed. He realized that his soul was determined by no one other than himself. The ancient dwarf rubbed his arms in attempt to warm them in the cool autumn morning.

    "I'll come home to you soon father." be whispered to the wind. "But first, their are two enemies I need to slay."

    *   *   *

Tharxton sat on his magnificently crafted throne in the grand palace ballroom that was located in the middle of the fabled dwarven city of Mountain Heart. In front of him, the polished marble floor was filled to the brim with politicians and other influential persons of clan Stoneheart. The young king rested his weary head on his ceremonial armored hand as he listened to the ramblings of three thin astute looking dwarves dressed in fine blue tunics. His other hand methodically twisted and pulled on the end of the braids of his thick red beard. The face the young king wore was one of great sadness and vicious contempt. He had returned to his home to find that the renegade general had led his army further south and into a second battle with the humans. The old dwarf had met defeat and had most likely been slain. The remainder of the army returned to Mountain Heart at the instruction of their commanders and now faced trail under treason and desertion. the king had weathered the other trials with patience and sullenness, but now, he had reached the commanders of the army. They were second only o Amerix himself. The voices of the pleading barristers that surged in the commander's behalf echoed on his unconsciousness as they announced the last commander to be tried. Tharxton forced his weary mind back into the chamber and clear from his intermittent doldrums.

"My king, Commander Fehzban was to follow all of Amerix's orders. Amerix was the first general, and the commander had no other recourse except follow the general's commands." The thin dwarf said as he paced back and forth before the chained commander who merely stood in silence in the great hall with his greasy, dirty hair covering his face as he stared at the polished floor. Behind them hundreds of dwarven officials and cabinet heads listened on intently, occasionally muttering to themselves about well placed strategic arguments from both sides. Tharxton had spent the last few weeks listening to the pleas of the army's officials. He had ordered only a few executions of soldiers that he was sure beyond a reasonable doubt, had committed atrocities in the eyes of Leska. The young king had the aid of his clerics and priests in the trials, but he issued at least some kind of punishment to each and every dwarf that had participated in the battles. Some ranged from dismissal from the service and the loss of weapon privileges, to banishment. A few not only were banished, their names were stricken from the clan's records as if they had never existed.

Tharxton had worked his way from lowest in command to the highest, next to general Amerix Alistair Stormhammer, who was considered dead. That only left commander Fehzban to stand before him and be judged. The young king asked for personal accounts from other officers and soldiers alike. He used the magic of his priests to ensure the truth was being told and had executed any who tried to lie during the proceedings. It was soon not necessary to use any truth spells when the soldiers witnessed the result of lying, but the King did so anyway. He wanted no doubt as to the accuracy of his verdict. Tharxton became enraged when he learned that the paladin Apollisian, the elf, Alexis Overmoon, and the paladin's squire Victor, had blood shed by his troops for a second time. He was even more outraged at the retelling of the story when the elf was brought before commander Fehzban. Tharxton cursed aloud in the presence of the clergy and threw his goblet of wine in the face of the commander. Fehzban merely closed his eyes and accepted the taint of wine as Tharxton announced his judgment.

"If the damned general would have ordered ye to leap into a pit of vipers, methinks you would have smiled as ye fell." Tharxton screamed as he rammed his fist into his hand. Fehzban shook his head slowly from side to side and started to respond, but when his ashamed eyes met his king's, he silenced himself in shame and hung his head low and stared at the floor once again.

The weary king shook his head and began again more slowly and solemnly. "The most grave punishment will befall you, Commander Fehzban. For your sins against clan Stoneheart, you are herby banished. Your name will be blotted out of every book, every tablet, every plate that exists in clan Stoneheart's archives. Your family will be mandated to move from your home and it will be destroyed. They will destroy everything they own from this day and before. They are not to have one single token of your existence. You are to leave Mountain Heart never to return under penalty of death." Tharxton commanded as he looked over the astonished crowd that had jammed into the room of the palace. "And further, if the name Fehzban ever escapes the lips of any person, regardless of age, race, or clan, in our great city of Mountain Heart, from this moment to the end of time, their fate will mimic his. So teach you children well, and make them mind the law, for I will not be lenient to any violators."

The onlookers and other dwarves in the hall all mumbled and gasped in shock. They obviously felt the punishment was grave and not befitting the crime. Though Tharxton was not issuing the sentence based off of the crime Fehzban committed. He issued the order based off of the result that was sure to come from the crimes that were committed, undeniable war with the humans. "The law shall remain until our grand children's grandchildren cannot recall the horrors that Commander Fehzban has committed in this clan's name." the king turned his head and regarded the teary eyes of his once faithful commander and spoke much softer. "There is a price to pay be a leader of our brethren, Commander. I pay this price now, as do you."

Fehzban lowered his head and wept as the king finished his sentence. His tears ran down his dirty face and soaked into the filthy gray prison rags he had wore since his return to Mountain Heart weeks prior. Fehzban knew he would face grave charges, but he felt he had no other recourse but to follow the orders of Amerix during the mandate of war. Though looking back, he realized that his actions would probably lead the Beyklans to make war with clan Stoneheart until the clan was no more, yet Fehzban kept his head lowered, unable to look at a single face that bore down on him as Tharxton finished his declaration of castigation.

"Fehzban Algor Stoneheart, you are hereby denounced from clan Stoneheart, and denounced from the dwarven race for crimes against Leska's divine teachings, and crimes against the morality of good. You will be forever known as the nameless and you will be stripped of everything that was before today. Your hair and beard will be burned off with acid, never to be grown again. You will be branded iniquity so that where ever you go, those that have reason will see your mark. May Leska send your soul to the dark clutches of Kobli for the damnation you have wrought on us all." Tharxton announced as he slammed his gavel down on the arm of his throne and stood erect, eying the cowering weeping Fehzban. The crowd stood up, quietly mumbling as Tharxton slowly rose from his desk and walked past Fehzban toward the door of the palace throne room.

Fehzban wanted to look at the face of his king one last time, but he could not. Instead he stared at the hardened boots of a king that was no longer his.

Fehzban was roughly pulled down a dark corridor from the throne room. The passage wreaked of feces and urine and Fehzban could hear the moans and shouts of prisoners that littered it's halls. He was blindfolded and shackled, not even allowed to look upon the walls of his once loved city's dungeons. The ringing of his short shackled steps echoed in his mind, oblivious to where he was being taken. He felt himself being led into a small room that smelled of a strange pungent odor. He was roughly forced backward into a greasy wooden chair as large metal clasps were locked around his legs, arms, and waist. He felt no panic, no fear, no remorse and Fehzban cared not if he lived or died. Though he was saddened to a state of shock, he could sense the movement around him and could hear the pop of several corked bottles. When the dwarven sentries removed his blindfold, the dirty rag fell around his neck and Fehzban looked around. He was in a small room that had no doors or windows. The walls were stained with dried blood and had small patches of dark green moss that grew on them. The ceiling was bricked stone, just like the walls, but there was no moss or dried blood on it. There was a large wooden table at the far end that contained many small leather cases with large metal instruments sticking out and one bulls eye lantern with it's shield facing out from the room, making the light reflect off of the walls, giving the room an eerie kind of glow. Some of the instruments on the table had sharp, knife-like edges and some were serrated like a tree saw, but each leather container holding them was covered in blood stains. Next to the leather instrument packages were three small dark glass vials. Their corks had been removed and placed on the table. The bottom of the corks were more sponge like than cork like. Fehzban's chair was against the wall near the only entrance into the room and was made with a strong sturdy wood and the metal shackles that were affixed to it, must have been bolted in the back, because Fehzban couldn't so much as budge them.

    The door opened up and a squat looking dwarf came in. He was an old dwarf and had white hair and beard. He was bald on the top of his head and his beard was long, but thin and hung loosely from his chin and it bobbed when he spoke. Fehzban focused more on his rotten yellow teeth and his pungent breath, than what he said.

    "Ye has been bad boy? Yes?" the old squat dwarf said with a wicked smile.

Fehzban scrunched his nose at the foul odor that came from the old dwarf's mouth.

"Yes, ye had been bad. What's yer name, bad boy?" the old dwarf asked with a wicked smile.

Fehzban said nothing. He was more fixated at the dream like events that were unfolding before him.

The squat dwarf tightened his fist and struck Fehzban in the face. Pain erupted from Fehzban's mouth as his tongue swished his broken front teeth amid a mouthful of blood and saliva. The once proud commander's eyes went wide as if the punch had ripped him from his minds secure hiding place. The phalluses that he clung to, hoping against hope that he was dreaming, came to an abrupt end. He smelt the strong acrid odor from the three vials on the table. He noticed the thick layers of dried blood that lined the walls of Fraitizu's workshop. Fraitizu, the name echoed through the corners of his mind. The old dwarf was the clan's interrogator of prisoner's that were sentenced to die. If the clan cared little what happened to the prisoners they sent them here. A profound sadness swept over him as he knew no dwarf had ever been sent to Fraitizu's lair. The place was reserved for orcs, goblins and other wicked creatures. Fehzban quickly pushed the thought from his mind. It had to be a trick or some kind of mind torture. Surely he wasn't really be meant to be here.

Another nefarious punch landed against Fehzban's right eye. A plethora of lights erupted in Fehzban's mind as his head snapped back from the blow and crashed into the hard wood back board of the lockdown chair. Hot sticky blood dripped from a small cut under his right eye and thin runny blood poured from his mouth and ran down his chin, before dripping on the dirty gray prison tunic he had worn for weeks.

"I asked ye a question you stupid orc lover. But by all means, keep quiet, I heard what ye did, and I hope to beat ye until ye die. Know I asked ye, what yer name is."

Fehzban looked at the squat dwarf. His skin was pale and he wore a pair of thin spectacles. He had a strange red spot on the top of his head, where he probably once had hair when he was younger. Fehzban became so angry he wanted to leap from the chair and beat the treacherous little fiend.
    Another punch struck Fehzban in the chin. He felt a large pop as his jaw was rammed hard into the back of his head. Shooting pain ripped through his jaw as he lost muscle control in the lower part of his face. His front teeth slid out of his mouth in a tiny stream of blood and spit. Fehzban vomited from the severe throbbing that was erupting from his broken jaw and swooned. His vision became fuzzy and he could hear a steady ringing in his ears.
    Fraitizu frowned. "Ah no ye don't. Ye ain't leaving my party so soon." the squat dwarf turned and went to the bench and retrieved a small white vial that was sitting behind the three dark black ones. He picked up the vial and uncorked it. He placed a small dirty rag over the top and briefly turned it upside down, soaking the rag with it's contents. As he walked back over to Fehzban he spoke to the guards. "Ye can leave if ye want to. I'm about to get into me work."
    The guards nodded and eagerly departed from the small stone room as Fraitizu waddled up to Fehzban, placing the soaked rag under the commander's nose. Fehzban tried to turn his head away from the foul smelling concoction, but he was held steady in place. To the commander's surprise, the concoction cleared his head, but the intense pain still remained. It then became clear to him that Fraitizu wanted him awake for whatever plans he had in store. Fehzban felt more hate rip through his body. He quickly dismissed it though and rationalized that many thousands had sat in the chair before him, and surely hate had helped none of them.
    Fraitizu grabbed a fistful of Fehzban's hair and

jerked him close to his pale wrinkly face. "I am only going to ask ye one more time, then if ye doesn't answer I am going to break out my squealers." Fraitizu said as he motioned to the table containing over ten small blood soaked leather pouches. "What is yer name?"

Fehzban wanted to spit in his face, too break the bonds that held him, reach out and crush the throat of the old evil dwarf that stood before him. But he knew he could not. So the only recourse was to placate the squat little demon until he was free.

" Ma name ith Fethsban Algo thonhar." Fehzban tried to say through his slack broken jaw."

Fraitizu sighed and shook his head. " I figured ye to be smarter than that." He said with mock sadness that was replaced by a wicked grin. "Didn't ye hear the king say that it was a crime to say that name. Now I am going to have to punish you."

Fehzban glared as menacingly as possible for a dwarf that had a right eye that was bleeding and swollen shut, that was tied down in chair completely immobile, and that was missing his front teeth with a steady stream of drool and blood pouring from his mouth.

Fraitizu turned and walked over to the wooden table containing the many leather pouches. He mulled over them for a few moments then made a happy sigh when he located the one he wanted to use. The interrogator meticulously opened the pouch ever so slowly and procured a long cork screw looking wire that was about an inch in diameter. The end had a flat horizontal wooden handle and the tip was serrated like a saw. He returned and stepped in front of Fehzban.

"Open yer hand and flatten it over the end of the chair." Fraitizu said with an eerie calm.

"You ticked ma." Fehzban muttered in response.

Fraitizu said nothing. He reached down and tried to move Fehzban's hand where he wanted it. Fehzban jerked his wrist and grabbed the small frail hand of Fraitizu.

Fehzban squeezed with all his might. Fraitizu shrieked in pain as the bones in his hand popped and snapped. The interrogator dropped to his knees and fumbled at his belt. Tears welled in his eyes from the iron grip of his captive that shook his hand and arm. Fraitizu fumbled at his belt, removing a small hammer from his waist and struck Fehzban in the wrist. Fehzban involuntarily let go of the wicked dwarf and cried out at the pain that shot up from his newly shattered wrist. Fraitizu rubbed his limp broken hand and glared at Fehzban.

"Ye stupid ox. Now I am going to make ye wish ye were dead!" Fraitizu growled as he brought the steel hammer down time and time again on the commander's hand. Bones splintered and poked through the top of his wrist and hand as blood dripped down the chair like a water root that had been severed by a miners pick axe. When Fraitizu finished the vicious attack he huffed and wiped sweat from his brow as he stared at Fehzban's viciously mutilated wrist and hand. He tossed the hammer onto the table with a disgusted look on his face. The small iron tool clanged and bounced around on the wooden table coming to rest near the wall. The old interrogator retrieved the cork screw looking tool and placed the tip on the back of Fehzban's broken hand. He slowly twisted the screw and watched in cruel satisfaction as the serrated head of the tool slowly burrowed way into the back of Fehzban's hand. Fehzban screamed in severe pain as the wicked tool burrowed into his flesh. Fehzban vomited a second time when the tip of the screw pushed against the skin on the palm of his hand. He felt his skin stretch, resisting the screw until it could hold no longer, and the tool ripped through the palm of his hand with a sickening pop.

"Ye like that, bitch?" Fraitizu asked as he spit at the feet of Fehzban.

The pain riddled dwarf tried to answer, but his tongue only let out a pitiful moan of pain and despair.

Fehzban tried to formulate a spell in his mind, but he couldn't focus through the pain. He tried to laugh defiantly, or make some other sound that was more attune to triumph or at least a sound that would make him feel like he had some form of conquest in face of his wicked captor, but he found he could only cry.

"Yea, ye likes it." Fraitizu said with an evil grin. "I've got some more toys for ye. Don't go no where little traitor. I'll be right back." the interrogator chuckled as he turned to the wooden table loaded with the leather pouches of torturing tools leaving the drill securely in the commander's hand. Fraitizu rubbed his chin with his good hand as he mulled over which pouch he wanted to select next. Each time he started to get one, he shook his head and looked at a different one. He suddenly smiled as an idea entered his mind and he knelt down in front of the table and opened the cabinet that was below it. He pulled out a large rusty looking iron device. It was larger than a man's head and had knobs and screws at several joints. There was a large bar that rested horizontally under the main chassis and many leather straps ending with thick buckles on the back. The inside of the iron contraption had hundreds of tiny iron spikes that had long since rusted. Each spike was affixed to a screw and had a tiny barb on the end. Fraitizu hefted the bulky device over to Fehzban and placed it on the ground in front of him. He weakly flexed his broken hand, seemingly relishing the pain that erupted from the motion and he gazed at his captive that was helplessly strapped into the chair.

Fehzban didn't stare at the device in terror like most of the victims he used it on. Although every person he used it on, man or beast, shrieked in terror when they saw it for the second time. Fraitizu knew he could not use it a second time because that usually meant death, so he was going to make the first usage last. He hoisted the heavy iron device up and placed it around Fehzban's head. Fraitizu strapped the thick leather laces in the back and pulled them tight until he could see the skin discolor from lack of blood. The wicked interrogator liked it that way, because when he screwed the spikes in, the blood often popped out like the insides of slug when stepped on. When he fastened the long iron bar just under the commander's chin, Fraitizu strapped it into place. He adjusted the screw on the bottom until the thick iron bar rested tight under Fehzban's chin. He then went to the back of the iron contraption and fastened it to latches located on the back of the chair like he had done countless times before. Fraitizu hummed a little tune and smiled as he tightened everything down and made sure the head piece was securely affixed to the thick wooden chair.

Fehzban's mind raced despite the numbing pain from his hand. He closed his eyes and began a prayer to Leska. "Oh great mother of mothers, keeper of the mountains, tender of the greatest trees, honor be thy oath and deed. I ask you..."

Fraitizu frowned at the prayer and quickly screwed a tiny screw into Fehzban's face. Blood spurted form the wound and ran down his prisoners cheek, but the prisoner continued his prayer undaunted.

" ...For strength to sever these bonds in thy glory..."

Fraitizu's eyes went wide and his jaw hung open. He quickly rushed to the front of the mask and tightened the screw that was under the iron bar resting against Fehzban's chin. The bar made it impossible for the captive dwarf to speak. Fehzban continued the prayer in his mind, though he was unsure if the spell would work, since he could not speak.

"Though you cannot hear my speech from my throat, I know that you see that which is hidden and my faith is resolute. I thank you, mother of earth for setting me free." Fehzban whispered in his head. He then opened his eyes and grinned at the nervous Fraitizu as he quickly screwed in a fourth screw into Fehzban's face. Fehzban slowly flexed his powerful arms and raised them against the thick iron shackles that held him. He felt the shackles give slightly and he increased the pressure. His smile of hope quickly transformed into a torrent of despair. As the once proud dwarven commander struggled to force the shackles open and tried to rip free of his evil captor, but he could not. It was in the next instant he felt the touch of Leska leave him. She had turned on him just as the multitude of his people had. He had nothing, had no one, and was completely alone. Suddenly all the pain from his body returned. He felt each tiny barbed prod that had been jabbed into his face. He felt the hot sticky spurts of blood shoot down his cheek when a new barb was slowly stabbed into his flesh. He simply wanted to die.

"Kill me, you coward." Fehzban tried to say, but the iron bar under his chin kept his mouth closed exceptionally tight.

Fraitizu walked to the front of his prisoner and gazed at his handy work. The iron mask-like structure, called a "Bordeck", was perfectly in place and needle like iron barbs were all deep into Fehzban's face. Many tiny streams of blood streaked down his prisoner's cheeks and soaked into his dirty prison rags. Fraitizu snickered evilly as he watched his prisoner struggle with the obvious revulsion of his fate. The wicked captor stepped closer and reached under Fehzban's chin and began to slowly tighten the screw. The old bordeck squeaked as the iron bar under Fehzban's chin began to slowly tighten. Fehzban struggled against the pain in his jaw. He tried to shift his weight, or move his head in a futile attempt to alleviate the ever growing pain, but he could not. Fraitizu chuckled when he heard a muffled pop as one of Fehzban's teeth shattered as his bottom jaw was forced into his top by the crushing bar. Fehzban's muffled screams of pain seemed to drive the sadistic dwarf faster as he continued to screw the bar tighter and tighter. In mere moments, all of Fehzban's teeth were shattered and he began to choke on the blood that was rapidly rushing down the back of his throat. Fraitizu fearing the death of his playmate, quickly loosened the bar and watched in horrific satisfaction at Fehzban's mutilated face. He removed the bordeck from his prisoner, ripping the deep rooted barbs out as he pulled it off. The barbs left deep lacerations in Fehzban's face from the iron mask shifting when it was tightened down. Fraitizu gently placed the iron contraption on the table and slowly picked the large pieces of flesh from the hundreds of barbs that clung to them like a hooked fish. He hummed a tune to himself that seemed to coincide with the intelligible moans from Fehzban.

"Tomorrow my pet, we will work on yer other hand. Ye see, ye are scheduled to be with me for some time. The king has stated that I can do as I wish with you, as long as I do not harm your ears. I asked If I could remove your eyes and he nodded. I asked if I could rip out your tongue a little each day, and again he nodded." Fraitizu said as he walked over and grabbed Fehzban's face in his unbroken hand and roughly pulled it close to his.

Fehzban's eyes rolled around in their sockets. He was seemingly oblivious to his horrid captor that spoke to him. "I asked the king; Why can I do all of those things to the rest of him, but not to his ears? Do you know what the king said, my little traitor? He said; Because I want the filthy murderer of women and children to hear the screams of every man woman and child that comes in sight of his hideous shell. He said he wants the sound of their terrified voices to echo in his beautiful ears for all of eternity. The king said he hoped that the horrid deformities that I leave with are so severe that you are forced to live alone and in hiding from all that you may find any solace in. That you may die alone, wounded and lost, just as you have left clan Stoneheart." Fraitizu finished as he spit in Fehzban's face. Fehzban was unconscious to the spit that ran down his cheek. He did he take any notice of wicked Fraitizu as he blew out the lantern and left the room, locking it behind him as he went. Had Fehzban been conscious he might have felt some kind of comfort in the darkness, but instead is mind was far away, being saved from the horrible torture his body was enduring.

" Unconditional love. Women and men alike seek this out. They believe this supposed emotion that can heal all wounds, win all wars, and defeat all enemies. They think the emotion has the ring of a euphoric power, though I learned long ago, lacks any foundation more solid than the breath it takes to say it. Though many will disagree with me, there is only one setting in which unconditional love exists. That is the bond from mother to child. Notice I do not say, mother and child, for the child, if horrible wronged or abused by the mother, can withdraw their love. Yet a mother, regardless of the evils done to her by that child, can no easier cease to love him or her, than she could make the sun to cease to shine. All other kinds of love are most certainly conditional. Some more than others of course, but when measured, all are conditional.

I hate the phrase; " blood is thicker than water." It is the sound of a fool trying to spout wisdom. In my life, as well as others, a friend is easily more trustworthy than any family member. Family members too often fall back on the adage, whatever I do, he will always be my brother. I can think of no other friendship, other than a family member, that takes the plutonic love for granted. It is true when I say; One family member can do more harm to you than a thousand enemies. Believe me, it is a fact. You see it is not the dagger that an enemy slashes at your chest that utterly defeats you. You anticipate such an attack from an enemy. There is no betrayal, no sadness; it is in a way, expected. It is the dagger that is plunged deep into your back that can wound you to your core existence. Though pain from the stab into the back is undoubtedly severe, it is the horrible pain of the ultimate betrayal that can crush your soul.

Yes, in my life I could have counted all of my friends on each hand, and they were willing, and sometimes did, give their life for mine. Though I would have given mine for theirs, I was so unfortunate to never *have had that opportunity. Yes, you see true friendship is like a soft ember glow from a campfire. It is seen best only when it is surrounded by darkness."*

-Lancalion Levendis Lampara-

Chapter Three
A Champion's Plea

Alexis slowly climbed from the open sewer grate that led to a dark alley between two large stone buildings. The buildings were made of light brown stone that lined the foundation. The walls were made of thick wooden planks that bore many burnt patches from the battle. The alley was littered with bodies of dwarves and humans alike. Alexis stepped alongside the wooden walls of the alley and crept toward the bright street. The sun was in mid-morning and it lit the cobblestone boulevard well. The elf drew her long sword, slowly making her way to the edge of street and peered out into the cobblestone by-way from the dark alley. She saw human patrols marching through the streets calling out to any citizens that seemed to be alive. There were other groups of militiamen picking up bodies and throwing them onto hefty wooden carts. She noticed that the carts were either exclusively for dwarven bodies or for human bodies and were thick, sturdy and made of wood. The cart's wheels squeaked as they were drawn down the road by a single horse. The horse was in poor condition and appeared old, but it was suitable for the task they had chosen for it. The humans seemed diligent in their duties, and somewhat cheerful, despite their onerous task picking up the victims of the tragic attack.

Alexis quietly sheathed her sword, pulled her cloak over head and slipped into the street. She walked quickly with her head down and made her way east, away from the human patrols. The further east she went the more sporadic the damage was. Some areas were barely damaged, and the citizens were out in force repairing their own dwellings. Other areas were so badly damaged that the duke's men were pulling any standing structure down with thick war horses and strong iron chains. Few tried to hail her and when they did she pretended not to hear. The militia that survived the battle were too busy with the task of cleaning up the city that they paid her little more than an after thought.

 Alexis rounded the corner by the city hall when she came to a large structure that was badly burned on the outside. walls were severely scorched and had gaping holes in them in other places. She recognized the damaged building immediately. The Blue Dragon Inn had suffered a lot of fire damage. Structurally it appeared as if it would stand, but it had been rigorously burned. She walked to the front and saw three figures in the brass colored scale mail armor and red silk capes of the Beyklan high guard. Behind them were three men in brightly colored robes. The robes were thick and looked as if they kept the wearer warm in the harsh autumn winds. The robes were a deep violet and bore many strange swirling patterns on the sleeves and the cuffs of the neck, near the collar. They bore religious symbols that Alexis did not recognize while in the front of the group a small thin man wearing a silk green tunic walked purposefully across the street and led his unique looking entourage toward city hall.

 Alexis avoided making eye contact with the many militia soldiers that roamed the streets outside the inn and gripped her cloak tight about her face while she ducked into the common room of the Blue Dragon Inn. The common room was not as she remembered it. The once bright and vibrant room, was now black and charred. All the tables and chairs were covered in a thick layer of charred wood and soot. Large tapestries that once hung from the walls, were piled up in the corner, burned almost beyond recognition. There were only two patrons in the area. They were sitting at a table at the far end of the room. One had his massive feet propped on the burned table that they were sitting at holding his mug aloft for the serving wench to fill, while the other sat across from him sipping a flagon of his own. The pair appeared deep in thought and seemed oblivious to her presence. She started to turn to the bar keeper, who was eyeing her suspiciously, when she noticed that the man sitting across from the large swordsman was the man she had seen a few days earlier in the Cadacka. Alexis could feel the instant rage beginning to build in her. She placed her hand under her cloak, readied her sword and walked over to the pair. The large one had a great sword strapped to his back and wore a thin suit of chain armor that bore many thin cuts in it. One of his muscular arms rested at his side, and his weapon arm was held aloft in attempt to fetch the serving wench. The man in the cloak didn't seem to be armed and looked up at her over the brim of his mug as he sipped. She paused involuntarily when her eyes swept across his. She was held by his gaze taking a long look into the man's deep green eyes. She was shocked at the inner fire that danced in his emerald orbs. It was if the human that sat before her, with the chiseled child like face, had an indwelt fire that he did not know he possessed. His boyish features hid the wisdom and strength that an eternity of challenges and struggles could only create. She recalled seeing the same indwelt strength in her grandfather's eyes before he passed, but to her dismay, she recalled her grandfather having only a fraction of the power that she saw in the eyes of this boy. Alexis held her hand on her sword, not drawing the blade and striking down the human as she had originally planned. Instead she just stared as if in a daze at his sparkling emerald eyes.

    Lance shifted uncomfortably as the short woman

stood before him. She was certainly attractive perhaps a few years older than he. She had long blonde hair that was pulled back and hidden under the hood of her green cloak. Her eyes were an almond brown that flickered back and forth across his face rapidly. She was maybe five foot tall and her slender green cloak was draped loosely around her body. She held one hand inside, and the other was in at her side. Lance stared at her uneasily for a few moments when Jude spit out a mouthful of ale on the table. Lance jumped from his chair and looked angrily at his friend. Jude leapt up from his chair, knocking it over backwards behind and drew his sword.

"Lance, step away from her, she is armed!" Jude yelled kicking over the charred table. Lance backed away slowly and readied a spell in his mind, though he doubted she was any threat.

Jude stepped in between her and Lance. "Take your hands slowly from your cloak madam, or I will cut you down where you stand." Jude commanded.

The woman didn't reply. She just followed Lance with her eyes where ever he went. Alexis's jaw did not close nor did she blink as she watched Lance.

Jude nervously stepped toward the small woman. He cursed himself silently for not noticing her weapon hand under her cloak earlier. Her small stature and the way she deftly moved across the room should have alerted him that she may be hiding some kind of a sword. He could tell from her stance that she was no dunce with a blade.

"I have warned you, my lady. Now step away and show your hands or you will be cut down from where you stand."

Alexis did not move. She was barely conscious of the large man that stood next to her. She did not notice if he was armed, and she didn't care. She wrestled with the voices she could barely hear that were seemingly emitted from Lance's eyes. Sounds she had never heard before.

Sounds that were older than time. Sounds that were so muffled to her soul that she could not discern if they were sounds of laughter or horrifying screams. She stood transfixed on those dazzling emerald orbs.

    Jude did not know what to do. It was obvious this woman was a threat to Lance. The swordsman was certain by the way she stood, that she was indeed a danger to anyone she attacked. Jude knew if he allowed her to draw the blade he could not see, but was surely hidden under her cloak, she could be a deadly opponent. He could wait no longer. Jude flexed all the muscles in his powerful arms. They propelled his great sword on deadly arc toward the unyielding woman that stood before him with blinding speed. Jude watched as he struck at her waiting for her to even slightly shift her wait in an offensive manner, but she did not. His sword whistled harmless passed. The mighty swordsman could not bring himself to strike down a helpless woman regardless of what imaginary threat she posed. He waited for her to react to his strike and slip a blade into his unprotected ribs, but she did not move. Jude quickly regained his stance and stood amazed that the woman did not even flinch as his great sword whistled inches from her head.

    "Lance, did you cast a spell on her?" Jude asked in a confused manner.

    Lance shook his head. "She seems spell bound, but not by my hand." Lance said as he walked up to the strange woman. He bent down and looked into her eyes.

    Alexis gazed into Lances brilliant emerald orbs. She ignored the sword that whistled by her head, though every instinct that dwelt within her screamed to parry the strike, she could not. Now the boy stood before her, staring intently into her eyes. The voices were becoming more audible. They were sounds of millions of souls crying infinitely for mercy that they would never receive. It seemed as if all the souls suffering from eternal damnation in the deep bottomless abyss, cried out from his beautiful, but sinister, eyes.

"Overmoon!" Apollisian shouted as he jumped the bottom four stairs and ran to her. She turned her head slowly and blinked her stinging eyes repeatedly.

Apollisian ran up to her and grabbed her by both cheeks. "I thought you lost! What happened? Why didn't you come to the bridge like we planned?"

"I... I..." She stammered, trying to recall the exact events that just took place. "I was captured by dwarves." she managed to say.

Apollisian shook his head in disbelief. "How did you escape? Were you harmed? Where did they go?" Apollisian asked excitedly.

Alexis placed her delicate finger over his lips before he could go any further. "I am ok. They did not harm me past enduring. Their leader named Fehzban, freed me as they were marching back into the under dark. I think they do not know where Amerix is." Alexis said calmly.

Apollisian glanced around the room and peeked suspiciously at the table that was flipped over. He eyed Jude's great sword that was loosed from sheath.

"What is going on here?" Apollisian asked accusingly.

Jude stumbled over his own tongue. "Uh... we uh... she had a sword..."

Alexis cut in. "They thought me a threat, but no more. Tell me of Amerix. Is he indeed dead?" The elf asked, trying to distance herself from the boy.

Apollisian eyed Jude a second longer before he answered as if to convey to the giant man that if he tried to harm Alexis he would defend her with his life. " He is indeed dead. Thanks to this man." He said as he motioned to Jude with an obvious grimace on his face. "And a woman named Kaisha. They forced him over the bridge into the icy waters of the Dawson River."

Alexis turned to Jude and looked at him as if it were for the first time. "I thank you swordsman for your bravery."

Jude flushed at the praise from the beautiful woman. He motioned to Lance. "If it was not for him, I would not have been able to aid Apollisian."

Apollisian recalled the aid Jude gave him when he battled Amerix before the bridge and how Jude had saved him there. He relaxed his glare, but he still kept a leery eye on the pair as he righted the table and pulled over two slightly burned chairs for him and Alexis.

Alexis sat in the burned chair and looked around the room. "Where is Victor?"

Apollisian glanced down and paused before answering. "Amerix killed him. He tried to aid me, even when I told him not too. I knew Amerix was too skilled for him, but he would not listen. His body is buried in the cemetery." Apollisian said remorsefully. He closed his eyes and whispered a quiet prayer. "Stephanis guide his soul to Yahna. Let him frolic in your glory and may justice prove his heart through out."

Alexis placed her hand on the armored shoulder of the paladin. "My friend, we must talk about matters that are private."

Apollisian nodded and stood from the table. They walked up the charred stairs to the room they once rented.

When they were gone Lance turned to Jude. "I thought you were going to kill her. Why did you swing your sword at her?"

Jude exhaled deeply as if some profound weight was lifted from his shoulders by the pair leaving the room. "She was poised to strike at you quickly. She had a sword under her cloak and she was almost ready to use it." Jude said as he tried to dry the wet spot from his ale that spilled when he kicked the table over.

"Why would she try to kill me?" Lance asked doubtfully.

Jude shrugged his shoulders. I don't know. Why not. There are a lot of crazy people in this town. Look at that assassin. What was his name? Grascon, I think. Why would he want to kill us?"

Lance cringed. He had not told Jude that Grascon was the thief he had doubled crossed to get the papers he had that were in elven. "Well, my friend." Lance stammered. "You see, the papers I have...they are stolen."

Jude shook his head slowly from side to side. "Figures you would keep something like that from me. Anything else I need to know about?"

Lance shook his head as Jude held his mug aloft for the serving wench to fill. "Anyway, it seems strange for someone to try to kill you over some stupid papers. I wonder what makes them so important?" Jude asked.

Lance shrugged. "I'm not sure. I thought they were some kind of execution order or some other connection to my parent's death. But now, I have learned they aren't even written in Nalirian, they are written in elven. I have to wait to travel south to Terrace Folly, to meet up with Kaisha and Ryshander, before I can even read them."

Jude sighed and placed his heavy hand on his friend's shoulder. "Patience, my friend. We will find someone who can read them, rest assured."

*   *   *

Alexis and Apollisian stood in the dark burned out stairwell that led to the many rooms of the Blue Dragon Inn.

"We have to go back to see my father. I think he might be connected to the Abyss Walker. I have seen it in his eyes!" Alexis pleaded.

Apollisian motioned her to calm down. "Quiet. Do you want them to hear? Who is this Abyss Walker?" he asked.

Alexis took a deep breath. "I do not know. I remember my father mentioning it when I was much younger."

Apollisian ran his hand through his long golden hair. "Alexis, we have to travel to Dawson City and avert a human counter assault against the dwarves. They will be undoubtedly prepared and the Beyklans have seriously underestimated their number. It is obvious that the dwarves can strike any Beyklan city if given enough time. The south, who is not in favor with the King's decision's about the civil war in Andoria and not in favor with his treatment of the dwarves, is growing restless. The rumors of a coup are gaining ground so we need to travel to Dawson and plead to the king to swallow his pride and let the dwarves be. If he presses an attack and another Beyklan city is assaulted, I feel the south might act against his throne."

Alexis's face flushed. "You humans and your ignorant priorities! I am talking about all races of the realms being slain by the Abyss Walker, and you assume that a stupid human kingdom that has stirred up a bees nest more important. If this man is the Abyss Walker, he is prophesized to single handily annihilate half of the world and all of the heavens. It is written that he will bring about plagues as never seen before the beginning of time. Surely that has to rate somewhere in that moronic paladin code of yours."

Apollisian took a deep breath and closed his eyes briefly. He fought the urge to lash out at Alexis's attack on his faith. Instead he calmed himself and spoke softly. " For someone as old as you are, you act as though you were some ridiculous child who needs a good paddling. I understand that you believe in this Abyss Talker..."

"Abyss Walker." Alexis corrected with a stern glare.

"Whatever. You have no proof other than some feeling you got when you looked in his eyes. You want me to risk the lives of hundreds and thousands of people because you say you saw something in an orphan's eye. That is ridiculous. You give me one shred of hard evidence and I will consider speaking with the Minok

Nation."

Alexis started to respond only to cut herself off. "I don't have any proof and I don't remember the text that my father talked about word for word, but I know there is something strange about him and I believe that he is the Abyss Walker. He wears an elven Cadacka for Leska's sake."

Apollisian exhaled slowly. "I recognize their is something strange about him, but he is no threat. I searched his soul several times. There is no evil there. He is quite selfish, but nothing evil. Nor his large friend. The fact he wears a ceremonial elven mourning cloak is no proof that he is in bed with Rha-Cordan himself."

Alexis nodded reluctantly. She did not like conceding to Apollisian. It wasn't so much that he was a human. She had gotten used to the fact that he possessed wisdom that even some of the elven elders did not have. A trait that was quite exceptional for any human. It was more the fact that he was a man. She had a strange rancor towards men. They were rash and bold, often suffering or acting of their own pride rather than of their intelligence, yet more often than not, they ruled over women. She fought the urge to shout at the paladin and instead took a deep breath to strengthen her resolve. "Ok. Let us go and plead the dwarven case to the king, but after that, I insist we travel to Minok and speak with my father, but lets ask them to accompany us so I can keep an eye on him."

"We will not waste a single moment from now until then." Apollisian said, smiling. When they walked out from the stairwell, Jude was standing facing Lance. The two were an odd pair to say the least.

Apollisian extended his armored hand in front of them. "Lance and Jude. I am needed to speak with the king on some urgent matters. Myself and Overmoon..." he motioned to the elf that was standing next to him with an aggravated look on her face. She still wore her cloak up, hiding her pointed ears under thin silk folds. " We would like it if you accompanied us. The king no doubt would like to hear other first hand accounts, and I am sure the High King of the Elven nation would like to know the pair that had helped battle the dwarven onslaught that had nearly killed his daughter."

Lance nearly swooned. Apollisian wanted to take them to see the king? The king of Beykla? The thoughts of the grand castle began to flood through his head and he was completely oblivious to the mention of the elven king.

Jude however was not overly impressed with the mention of kings and found it strange they had helped an elf in the battle against the dwarves.

"Are you suggesting that Overmoon is an elf?" Jude asked skeptically.

Alexis slowly removed the hood of her thin green cloak. Her long blonde braid spilled out and fell across her chest, exposing her narrow pointed ears. Lance nearly had to catch his jaw to keep it from hitting the floor. He couldn't believe he was standing in front of a real live elf. Elves rarely ever spoke to humans, let alone allow two to travel with her. Lance made no attempt to hide his excitement, but Jude nonetheless was more than suspicious.

"Why is an elf fighting a battle that concerns the lives of only humans?" Jude asked skeptically.

Apollisian started to answer but Alexis cut him off. "My father is High King of the elven nation and has asked his personal friend here." She motioned to Apollisian. "To teach me the ways of Stephanis, that I might learn the rigors of true justice."

Jude was reserved, but could not deny the elf's beauty. She was small in stature, but she held herself with such an air of superiority that he did not doubt her claim of royalty.

Lance stood wide eyed in disbelief. He wanted to rip the pages from his pack and hand them to her, hoping she would read them on the spot, but something inside of him stayed his hand. He wasn't sure what it was, but there was something she was hiding from them. Jude looked at Lance. "Well Lance, what do you say? We were getting ready to move on."

Alexis cut in. "Where were you going?"

"Back home to Bureland." Lance replied. "My father is surely worried about me. I have been gone a long time."

Apollisian nodded. But Alexis prodded further. "We could send a messenger to your father that you are safe, and that you will return home as soon as you can. I can even arrange for some monetary compensation for him if you wish. Call it a reward for helping us in the battle." Alexis offered.

Lance nodded eagerly. He longed to travel with her and the paladin. She could decipher his letters after a few days after they got to know one another, and his father could surely use any money he could get. "What do you think, Jude?" Lance asked.

Jude looked at him and then at Apollisian and Alexis. The elf was surely beautiful, but there was something hidden that he could not put his finger on. Jude could see the eagerness on Lance's face and he reluctantly agreed.

"Ok Lance, I'm with you where ever you need me, but I am not sure any king will find us as complimentary dinner guests."

"It is settled then." Alexis said. " We will depart early in the morning. Do you have any horses?"

"We had two." Lance said. "But I am not sure where they are at or if the stables were damaged."

"The stables were unharmed. We will meet you there tomorrow at dawn. Good day." Apollisian said as he and Alexis made their way out of the common room and into the street.

Lance sat back down at the burned table. Jude sat

down also and rubbed his tired brow.

"What adventure are we headed for now?" Jude asked wearily.

Lance seemed ignorant to his friend's exhaustion. "I hope you are hungry, Jude, because we are about to dine with kings."

*   *   *

They had flown for a few weeks, occasionally stopping to rest on top of large mountain peaks along the way. Stieny had survived on what little game he could catch with the dragon never letting him wander far. The halfling had no intention of trying to escape as long as the dragon held his soul in that cursed jewel. They had finally landed on a large mountain peak in the Pyberian range. Stieny was sure the peak had a name, but he had never been to this area of the world. The halfling stood on the edge of a steep cliff looking out over a vast sea that stretched out to his north and gazed at the water that glittered like a myriad of shining specks of light that were reflected from the rapidly waning sun. The red globe, that was halved by the watery horizon, set the twilight sky aflame with deep reds and yellowish hues. The thin clouds that streaked across the sky were colored purple in the pneumatic evening canvas.

Stieny sat on the rocky face and let out a resounding sigh. The air was much crisper in Beykla than it had been in Vidora. The trees that were below him all shined amber and crimson hues from their autumn leaves. Checking his gear, Stieny removed a piton from his pack and hammered it into the side of the rocky face. Small pieces of stone splintered away from the thin crack as the metal teeth bit into the cliff. The halfling laced a thin waxed rope through the eye, around his torso harness, and wrapped it around a thin metal clip that was hanging from the back of the canvass harness next two his other coiled length of rope, while letting the long thin waxed rope fall from behind him after he had secured a tight lashing in the piton. The rope skittered and tumbled down the cliff and jerked violently when it reached the end of length. The halfling slowly began the arduous task of repelling down the steep cliff. It wasn't that the rock face was too difficult for the nimble halfling to climb down, it was the knowledge that if he fell, he would surely perish from the plunge.

    Stieny reached the end of his rope and stared up at the distance he had descended. The snow covered peak was well over three hundred feet above him and the wax line he descended down, wavering and bouncing along the side of the cliff as a light breeze blew by. The halfling hammered in a second piton and repeated the process, descending down another three hundred feet before stopping, removing the harness and climbed down the remaining forty feet.

    When he reached the ground he tossed the leather pack containing the small metal hammer and the pitons behind one of the many large boulders that rested at the foot of the steep cliff. He had no problem finding one, as some were larger than the mountain ogres that had captured him. The ground descended rapidly from the cliff but Stieny deftly maneuvered his way between the giant boulders and thin evergreen trees that littered the side of the mountain. The halfling hiked for most of the night, stopping for only brief rests, then pushing forward. When the night sky turned into an deep azure hue, he stopped and made camp. Robins and other song birds began their songs of the day, while Stieny unpacked his bed roll. He wearily tossed the bedroll open and plopped down on it, not having the energy to crawl inside, despite the chilly autumn wind that whipped through the thick trees of the mountain plains. The little halfling closed his exhausted eyes and in seconds was fast asleep.

* * *

Apollisian slowly chewed his eggs and tapped his cracked wooden fork on the thick oaken plate that sat before him. He had purified the food before Lance and Jude came down, in case of poison. It was not uncommon for evil denizens to try to poison the champion of justice whenever they got the chance. Alexis stared quietly at her breakfast, humbled by the feeling of tremendous peril, when she looked into the Lance's eyes. However Lance and Jude conversed eagerly as they enjoyed the fine breakfast that the paladin had purchased for them. Their money situation had become bleak, and they were eating left-over from the specials of the day.

"Overmoon, did you send that the messenger to Master Ecnal in Bureland?" Apollisian asked as he ate another small bite of eggs.

The elf nodded, averting her eyes from Lance. "Yes, the messenger was sent out this morning. He was pleased to be traveling south, away from the conflict. I believe he was equally happy to be delivering a message that was not military in nature."

Apollisian nodded in approval and glanced at Lance and Jude. Jude was sizing up the bar wench and paused, staring blatantly at her. She had long black hair that was pinned behind her head and wore a heavy overcoat that seemed an odd attire for a serving wench. When she finished serving, the serving wench awkwardly left the dining area and went into the kitchen when she noticed she was being watched.

"You fancy the serving wench, Jude?" Apollisian asked.

Jude turned back and picked through his eggs slowly as if searching for something. "No, not exactly. Lance and I have stayed here since we arrived in Central City. I don't ever recall seeing her, and I noticed she had a long thin dagger under her tunic, strapped tightly under her arm, as if she was trying to conceal it. It was much in the shape of an assassins dagger. I am sure I would have remembered her long black hair." Jude replied.

Apollisian said nothing in return. He merely closed his eyes and hummed softly to himself. Alexis got up from the table and made her way to the door of the kitchen. She positioned herself on the hinge side, so if the door opened up, she would be behind the potential enemy.

Lance noticed Apollisian and the elf's actions and readied a spell in his mind. Jude went to the front door of the common room and scanned for potential enemies outside. After a few brief seconds, Apollisian stood up from his chair and drew his sword.

"There is evil afoot in the kitchen." Apollisian proclaimed.

Alexis drew her bow and kicked the thin wooden door in. She leveled the narrow shaft around the room. It was a long room with a long flat cooking surface that lined the south wall. The cooking surface was littered with kitchen pots and pans, and on the far end were many vegetables that were being prepared for the lunch meal. There were many large wooden cabinets that rested above the counter and a large stand up closet that stood at the end of the room that probably housed aprons and other cooking apparel. There were some scattered dishes on the floor and a trail of spilled ale that led out the east door into the scullery. A figure shot out from behind a large cabinet and rushed for the door. Alexis raised her bow and fired two arrows in a blink of the eye. The slender shafts whistled toward their target at blinding speed. One of the shafts hit the figure in the side just under her armpit, The green fletching barely protruded after the shaft had sunk almost completely in. The other shaft lodged deep into the figures hip, making a sickening thud sound as it pierced bone. The figure let out a feminine cry and stumbled into the scullery room.

"Intruder in the kitchen!" Alexis shouted as she

hurried to the door the figure had darted into.

Apollisian charged forward, lowered his shoulder, and knocked the thin wooden door from hinges as he burst into the kitchen. Small pieces of splintered wood erupted in the air as he emerged into the room. He saw Alexis rushing through the east door with her bow drawn and an arrow notched.

Jude was standing in the doorway when he heard Alexis shout from within. He heard the paladin's heavy footfalls rushing toward the kitchen so he bolted out the common room door and ran around into the alley way on the east side of the inn. His boots crunched under charred wood from the fires that had not been cleared from the alleys yet. Lance hurried behind his large friend, trying to keep up with his huge strides.

Alexis burst into the scullery with her bow drawn and up. She slowly stepped forward scanning the dark room with her infravision. She didn't see anything but steadily advanced. The room was dirty and smelled of mildew. Hundreds of dirty dishes were piled up in a large wooden tub that was filled with brown stagnant water. The tub was sturdy and re-enforced with large iron bands that ran horizontally around it to keep it water tight. The water filled tub rested against the east wall, next to wooden door that was cracked open. Light seeped in from the door making it difficult for Alexis to use her infravision. There was a thin wall that didn't connect to either side of the room, but acted as a partition, dividing the one room into two. There was a large counter with clean towels neatly folded next to hundreds more clean dishes that were efficiently stacked on the large counter.

Apollisian focused on his inner thoughts and hummed lightly again. He felt his soul floating from his own body and drift around the room briefly, it swooped and glided around the large room and came to rest on the black vileness of evil. He recoiled from cold touch and his face grimaced as he came out of his succinct trance.

He pointed to the south east corner of the room with his sword. Alexis nodded and advanced around the large tubs of dishes on the east side, and the paladin advanced around the piles on the west.

Jude rushed down the alley and slowed when he neared the south eastern corner. He leaned against the charred building and strained to listen as Lance came panting up next to him and placed his hand over his mouth to try to quiet his breathing in response to Jude's angry glare. Jude looked down the alleys in all directions. The Blue Dragon Inn towered above the other buildings, but they were still two stories each. The alleys were dark, even in the day, and it reeked with the smell of rotting flesh. Jude spied a couple of dwarven bodies that were lying face down in a puddle of water. The bodies were bloated and swollen and many large late season blow flies crawled on their rotting faces. Jude ignored the repulsive sight and focused on the back door. He kept his weapon raised, and turned the weapon sideways to bring the flat of the blade down. He intended to take this person alive. This was the second unexplained attack on him and Lance, and the swordsman wanted answers.

Alexis rounded the corner and saw the serving wench huddled in a corner. She was shivering with pain, but she was not bleeding. The only part of either arrow that could be seen was the bright green fletching that was hanging out of each wound. The wench sat with her eyes closed panting with quick short breaths as beads of sweat lined her forehead. Apollisian rounded the other corner and sheathed his short sword. He took out a fine set of polished steel manacles and placed them on the woman's wrists. She seemed oblivious to The elf or the paladin's presence.

"Why is she not dead?" Alexis asked. "The first arrow has pierced her heart and both lungs. The other arrow perfectly stuck into her hip socket freezing the movement of her leg, yet she lives, and look, she doesn't even bleed. What manner of wicked creature is she?"

Apollisian frowned. "I know not, Overmoon, but she surely intended our deaths." he said as he removed a thin glass vile from her small belt pack. He smelled the liquid and quickly replaced the cork. "Surely some kind of poison."

Alexis kept an arrow notched incase the woman rose up, but the captive merely panted and sweated, with an occasional face and nose twitch. Apollisian searched her person and found a long thin dagger, neatly tucked under her arm near her side. He pulled the thin blade from sheath and examined it. There was a small wooden plunger at the pommel of it and the bade had a hollow recess at the end. There were three thin red lines on the hilt with a heart in the background.

"She is an assassin." Apollisian growled.

Alexis nodded, never taking her eyes from the strange woman. "It seems she was up to no good, but how can you be sure she is an assassin?"

Apollisian stepped away from the woman and held the dagger up so Alexis could see it. He pressed the wooden plunger on the pommel and dark blue liquid dripped from the hollow area near the end of the blade.

"What is it?" Alexis asked.

Apollisian kneeled down and took the sheath from the woman's side and placed the dagger in it, then stuck it in his belt line. "It's called a venom dagger. A very dangerous weapon used by skilled assassins. Rarely can a single person afford one. They are usually owned by guilds and loaned to assassins when they are assigned a job. There is a crest on this one, though I do not recognize who it belongs to. I'm sure the local magistrate will be able to tell me where it is from.

Jude could hear the elf and the paladin inside talking and motioned Lance to enter. They pushed through the back door of the scullery and Lance crunched his nose at the odor of mildew in the room. Alexis spun around quickly, but relaxed when she saw who it was.

"We were waiting in the alley in case she tried to run out the back." Jude said as he pointed to the back door.

Apollisian nodded. "Thank you, I am glad to see you have some combat sense about you. It will surely be a benefit to have you along on the journey."

Jude nodded in thanks, sheathed his great sword, and looked at the small woman that was in shackles. Lance stared at her intently, trying to recognize her face, but he could not.

"Who is she?" Lance asked.

"An assassin of considerable skill. In fact, had I not called on Stephanis to neutralize poison this morning before we ate, we would undoubtedly be dead." he said. "I tend to attract many enemies due to my plight to seek out justice and serve it where it is needed, but rarely have a made an enemy in which I have not known. And I do not recognize the guild insignia."

Jude frowned at the mention of another assassin and looked at Lance. Lance returned his look and shrugged his shoulders, then looked back at the assassin and watched as her face twitched.

"Her face just twitched!" Lance exclaimed.

Apollisian looked at the woman and back at Lance in confusion. "So?"

"She is a wererat." Jude said, remembering The way Grascon's face twitched when they battled him in their room.

Lance cringed at the thought of a second wererat assassin that was sent against him, not the paladin.

Apollisian nodded his head in recognition at the mention of the wererat and rubbed his chin.

"That explains the lack of blood from her wounds." Alexis said. "Had I not hit the mark exactly she would have shrugged off my arrows and escaped."

"Good. That means all I have to do is remove the

arrows and her unnatural healing abilities will take over, correct?" Apollisian asked.

"I think so. That is what happened to the last one that attacked me." Jude said, wincing before he finished.

"What do you mean the last one that attacked you?" Apollisian asked.

Jude kicked at the ground nervously under the angry gaze of Lance and the paladin. Lance spoke up before Jude could respond. "We were attacked by one of the rat people in our room one night. Jude and I fought him, before we killed him. Kaisha and Ryshander said he used to be a member of the thieves guild here in Central City years ago. We are not sure why he attacked us." Lance lied. He knew he had double crossed the thief in Bureland, but he had only double crossed one thief. Why was this one here trying to kill him?

Alexis frowned. "Assassins don't randomly kill or rob people. They are paid to kill, they kill for a reason."

Apollisian nodded. " Overmoon is correct. They don't choose their targets randomly. I will remove the arrows and use the zone of truth to interrogate her. She cannot lie, nor refuse to answer my questions. We will get to the bottom of this."

Lance shivered nervously. What if she was in leagues with Grascon? Blast! Lance had never thought of the thief having a partner. Lance cursed himself for not thinking of every possible outcome.

The paladin tugged and pulled at the arrow that had pierced the woman under her arm. She writhed in pain and hissed as he slowly pulled the white ash shaft from her body and marveled at the gleaming shaft, devoid of any blood. Apollisian closed his eyes and chanted. " Oh Stephanis, champion of justice, I ask that thee take away the shield of deceit that lie in this room. I ask that ye open the grasp of justice and compel this being of the dark to answer my queries true as if she were filled with righteousness. In thy light I thrive."

When Apollisian finished his chant, Lance could feel the air thicken around him, giving him goose bumps and making the hair on the back of his neck stand on end. He glanced at Jude, who seemed oblivious to the magical change in the air around them. Lance could see millions of tiny specks of energy floating around in the air from the corner of his eyes, but whenever he tried to look directly at them they were gone. The woman quickly came too and opened her eyes glaring at her captors.

"Who are you?" Apollisian asked.

The woman hissed and laughed mockingly at him. "I am...I..." the assassins eyes went wide with disbelief as she struggled against the magic that compelled her to speak. "I am Kellacun." she said finally as if the struggle against the magic was exhausting.

"Why did you try to kill me and Alexis?"

The assassin grinned. "I was not trying to kill you, fool!" Kellacun said.

"You lie dog!" Alexis growled with rage as she rushed the assassin.

Apollisian held his hand up, motioning for her to stop. Alexis held herself but gave the assassin a threatening glare.

"She is bound by the magic of Stephanis." Apollisian said. "However difficult for us to understand, her responses are truthful."

Apollisian turned and began again. "Who where you trying to kill?"

Kellacun struggled a few seconds against the magic that surrounded her, but her strength quickly waned. "The Ecnal." she said.

Lance swallowed hard and Jude angrily fought the urge to draw his word and cleave her head from her shoulders.

"Who is the Ecnal?" Apollisian asked.

Kellacun pointed a slender finger at Lance. "He is."

Apollisian turned and looked at Lance, then turned

back to the assassin. "Why did you want to kill the him?"

" Because I was paid."

Lance relaxed a bit. He was comfortable in the fact he doubted Grascon would have paid anyone to help him, but then the dreaded feeling of who else might want him dead replaced his previous fear.

"Who paid you?" Apollisian asked. "Was it Grascon?"

Kellacun wrinkled her nose at the mention of the exiled thief. "No, had I seen him, I would have likely killed him first, just for fun. I was paid by my guild master, Pav-co."

"Why would Pav-co want the him dead?" Apollisian asked.

Kellacun shrugged her shoulders. "I'm not sure, but I think the King of Nalir was paying well over a thousand gold crowns for his head."

Lance balked. Who was the King of Nalir? He had thought he had papers from Nalir, but they turned out to be elven. Perhaps Nalir was connected to his parents death after all. Perhaps it was Nalir that had ordered his whole family killed, but he had escaped. Now eleven years later, they were trying to finish the job. But why? The questions rocketed around in Lances mind.

"Why would the King of Nalir want him dead?" Apollisian asked.

"I don't know. He probably found out that he was one of, if not the last, Ecnal alive. Since he paid us, and everyone else under the sun, huge sums of money to kill them all years ago."

Lance felt his knees waver and he had to sit down. Jude placed a reassuring hand on his friend's shoulder.

Apollisian rose, dismissed the zone of truth, and turned to Lance. "I am sorry to hear that you are an Ecnal." he said somberly. "I hope that your parent's passing has been eased by the hand of time."

Lance took a deep breath. "It has been very difficult

for me. My mother and father were murdered when I was but twelve cycles old, or six years to you northerners." Apollisian nodded in recognition to southern Beyklan ways to measure years by the two moon cycles that take place every four seasons. Lance continued. "I managed to escape the house out the back. I ran and ran until a woodcutter named Davohn took me in. I had a sufficient life, but I am here in this city searching for answers to their deaths." Lance said, leaving out the papers he has and the fact the were cut down by men in Beyklan high guard uniforms.

Well, when we travel to Dawson, perhaps the king's records can shed some light on the Ecnal murders. I was but a squire when they were happening, but I remember them as if they were yesterday. Perhaps the king's investigations can shed some light on them, and perhaps allow your grief to finally rest."

Lance nodded. "My thanks to you already, Apollisian."

"Mine too." Jude said. "Lance has been my friend since he came to live in Bureland. He is a good man."

"Well it seems are departure has been postponed a few hours. Alexis and I will take this prisoner here to the magistrate for trial. We will return shortly and begin our journey." Apollisian and Alexis walked back through the kitchen, into the common room, and out into the street. Lance and Jude plopped down in the chairs they had been eating at. They looked at their plates and then at each other. At the same time they got up and sat done at a different table.

   *   *   *

Amerix walked around the edge of the small sandy beach. He followed the sandy shore as it curved around the undersized river flat he had been living on and he smiled as the warm sand crunched between his toes and the tepid autumn air gently warmed him between cold breezes. The old dwarf came to a place where the river flat ended and the cliff face began. It was a tall cliff probably some two hundred feet up, but the climb was not sheer and there were many hand holds in which he could use to pull himself up. He checked around the ground to find a good place to start his ascent, when he spied one of the dwarven bodies that had been tossed over the cliff and into the river. It had been swept down current and became lodged in a group of logs and rocks in an eddy created in the bend of the river.

    Amerix rubbed his cold arms as he stared longingly at the thin chain armor and the heavy leather padding that the dwarf had been wearing underneath. Most dwarves were poor swimmers, and Amerix wasn't exactly skilled at it either. He argued with himself for several minutes on whether or not to retrieve the body. The chain armor was rusted from being submerged for so long. It wasn't until the body had become bloated that it had risen from the river bottom to the top. And even then, the chain armor seemed to keep the body from fully reaching the surface. The body floated just under the top of the water as it bounced back and forth against the rocky shore from the river current. Amerix made his way over the precarious rocks and laid on his belly. He grunted as he reached down and hoisted the wet, bloated body of one of his kin from the river. Amerix ignored the horrid look of death from the body as he dragged it to shore. To his surprise when he got it to the sandy beach, he noticed the body had a long sword in a fine leather sheath that hung from it's back. Amerix recognized the damnable blade immediately. He grabbed the long sword by the pommel, drew it and hoisted it over his head. He drew back as to hurl the cursed weapon back into the river when he paused. He had carried the damned sword since the battle of the Torrent manor, and the sword never ceased unbearable shrill noise. Yet as he held it aloft, staring at beautiful craftsmanship, water glistening on perfect, flawless blade, the sword made no noise whatsoever. Amerix pulled the sword close and examined it. He cautiously turned it over awaiting the damnable shrill to begin at any minute, but it did not. Amerix shook the sword angrily. " Come on ye damn sword. What's the matter with ye? Why ain't ye screaming?" Amerix said as he stared at the wet blade as if it would respond, but instead only the chirping of birds and the constant trickle of water running in between the large rocks that lined the edge of the river flat and the cliff wall answered.

"Well if ye ain't gonna hum, then I'll carry ya. I could use a good blade." Amerix said as he piled up the leather clothing and the rusted chain armor. After scrubbing the filthy clothing in the edge of the river to get as much of the stench off as possible, the old dwarf put the suit of padded leather armor on. He the slipped the rusted chain shirt over his head and strapped the leather scabbard to his back that held the sword he had gotten from the paladin at the battle of the Torrent Manor.

Amerix spit on his hands and wiped them in the rocky dust near the base of the cliff. The chalky sand like dust from the broken stones that fell to the river flat acted like a gripping agent for the dwarf. Once he was satisfied he had as much grip as he could, he began to climb the sheer rocky wall.

It took him almost two hours. The climb wasn't overly treacherous, but Amerix was not a skilled climber and he often had to stop and ponder where he wanted to place his next handhold. Once he reached the top, he pulled himself over and lay on his back breathing heavily. His malnourished body was weak and the climb had exhausted him. He lay panting for many minutes and finally sat up. The trees at the top of the cliff where beautiful. They were cloaked in many colorful orange, red and yellows from the autumn season. Squirrels and other tree creatures skittered about the tops of the tress, sounding alarms announcing the appearance of danger on the forest floor.

Amerix dusted the chalky residue from the cliffs, off of his pants and shirt and began his trek into the forest. The dead dwarf's clothing was too small for him and it chaffed his under arms and the inside of his legs when he walked. The boots were impossible to force on, so Amerix walked barefoot. He winced occasionally when he stepped on a sharp rock, or when he walked to close to a bramble patch. Amerix knew little of the surface animals or plants. He had no idea which ones were poisonous and which ones were not. When he was a member of clan Stoneheart, they had hunters and gatherers that did that sort of task. When he was younger and lived underground, before the attack, he seldom, if ever, ventured to the surface.

The old tired renegade general walked south, knowing that the war was north and southern Beykla was sympathetic to the dwarven plight. Amerix walked for the rest of the day, taking frequent breaks and chewing on an occasional piece of bark, or a beetle when he found one. The old general wasn't exactly sure where he was going, but he knew he was walking in the right direction.

*   *   *

It had been a few hours since Apollisian and the elf had left the burned out inn. Jude had spoke to the barkeep, Fifvel, about hiring assassins jokingly and the barkeep nervously laughed with the large swordsman. Fifvel's strong man, Glaszric the half-orc, had not been seen since the fighting and the barkeep feared him dead. Lance and Jude recommended that he speak with the militia guardsmen that were assigned to retrieving the dead, thinking that they would remember picking up something as unique as a half-orc's body. Fifvel agreed and offered Lance and Jude free drinks for the afternoon. The pair sat at the bar, as a merchant and four of his workers began unloading new tables and chairs into the common room, when the paladin and the elf walked in.

"Good news and bad news." Apollisian said as he marched into the room, giving the workers ample space to unload their wares. Alexis slipped past and walked near Lance but she did not look at his face.

"What's the good news?" Jude asked as he sipped his flagon of ale with his left elbow leaning back against the bar.

Apollisian patiently waited for the men to put down a new table, then walked over to Lance and Jude. "The king is now on his way here to see the damage first hand, so we do not need to travel to Dawson after all."

Lance said nothing and stood emotionless trying to discern why the elf acted so strange when she was near him.

"What's the bad news?" Jude asked as he suspiciously looked over the rim of his ale filled mug.

Alexis piped up as she stared at the floor near Lance's feet. "You will not have a journey in which to accompany us on. That means no gold."

Jude spit out his mouthful of ale and sat forward trying to keep the liquid from dripping from his chin to his tunic. "You mean you were going to pay us in gold?" Jude asked with a hint of disappointment in his voice.

Lance looked at Jude and smiled. Despite what his hulking friend might say, he loved gold. He would save his mother from a rampaging orc if he had too, but he would allow himself to be paid if someone offered it.

"How much gold?" Jude asked as he wiped his mouth with his sleeve and took another deep draw from his mug.

"Ten gold crowns per day." Alexis responded flatly, as if the sum was nothing that an alley man couldn't get begging.

Jude spit out a second mouthful at the

announcement of the fee he and Lance would have received.

Alexis fought to keep from grinning at the large swordsman's greed for the coin. Lance looked at Apollisian, but the holy warrior said nothing when it came to the pay and seemed unaffected at the announcement.

Alexis paused for Jude to wipe his mouth a second time. "But after we speak with the king, we are headed to Minok, the capitol city of my great people and we could use your escort on our way there."

Lance eyed the elf suspiciously. He didn't trust her. It seemed as if she had an agenda of her own. The paladin seemed uninterested either way, but the elf lingered on Jude's response.

"Thanks but no thanks." Lance said, and watched in satisfaction as the elf's smile changed into a scowl.

However, Jude started a scowl of his own. "Lance! Are you crazy?" Jude said getting up and pulling Lance to the side part of the bar, away from the paladin's and elf's ears.

"Ten crowns a day? That is a lifetime of pay we could make in a single day. More than our fathers will probably ever see, and you want to turn it down?" Jude asked incredulously.

Apollisian turned and started toward the door. "You work out the details with them Overmoon. I am heading to city hall."

Alexis suddenly stiffened. "You want me to stay alone? With him?" she asked as she motioned to Lance.

Lance frowned and looked at Jude. The large swordsman shrugged his shoulders as the elf turned back to them.

"You work it out. We can negotiate pay later." Alexis said as she hurried out of the Inn.

"Negotiate?" Jude asked rhetorically. "We could get even more money each day?"

Lance frowned. "She is up to something. And what

do you think she meant when she said she didn't want to be alone with me? What was that about?"

Jude laughed. "You just don't know women. They are always up to something, and as for her not wanting to be left alone with you, I figured you would be used to that response by now."

Lance punched Jude in the arm. "Ha-ha. Very funny. I had better not forget this day."

Jude stopped chuckling. "Why is that?"

Lance gave a wry smile. "Because it will probably be the only day in our lives when you say something witty."

"Have your laughs." Jude said, finishing his mug of ale. Even Fifvel was chuckling at the pair's verbal sparring.

Lance walked over and grabbed their packs. He tossed Jude his dirty leather pack and placed his on his shoulder. "We had better decide how much gold we want to extort from the royal elven coffers, but I think regardless of what she pays us, it is we, that will be extorted."

*   *   *

Alexis ran and caught up with Apollisian. "Why did you leave me in there with him?" she asked.

"I do not approve of your deceitful tactics of encouraging them to accompany us to Minok." The paladin said flatly as he strode down the road.

"What is deceitful about it?" Alexis asked. "I have offered them pay to travel with us. Does a merchant that charges twice as much for an item than he paid for, deceitful?"

Apollisian said nothing as he walked. Alexis continued. "I can't very well say; Hey, I think you might be than man prophesized to bring doom on the world. He might not even be the Abyss Walker, but my father's elders need to at least see him."

Apollisian stopped and turned to face Alexis. He started to chastise her for rationalizing an act that was certainly not the way Stephanis wanted tasks performed, but he was stopped dead in his tracks when he looked into her beautiful almond eyes. Her hair was braided back from the top of her head and it's tail hung loosely across her chest, fluttering in the soft autumn breeze. How could he be angry at such beauty? "I am sorry, Overmoon. I just think it is deceitful that's all. There is no need to get defensive. I wasn't naming you the heiress of Rha. I just disagree. OK?"

Alexis nodded. "I will be honest in every question they ask."

"I would hope so." Apollisian said as he draped his arm over Alexis's shoulder. She started to protest but it felt nice to have a friendly arm around her. "The Duke awaits." Apollisian announced as the pair turned and marched down the dirt road toward the large stone building that was city hall.

Apollisian and Alexis walked down the marbled corridors of city hall. The debris from the attack had all but been removed and there were little, if any, signs that a battle ever took place inside. Apollisian rounded the corner and stood tall and proud in the doorway of Duke Dolan Blackhawk's chambers.

The Duke glanced up from his desk. "Apollisian and..." the Duke drummed his fingers on his heavily bearded chin. "...Overmoon, is it?"

"Yes, my lord." Alexis said giving a shallow bow.

"What can I do for you?" the Duke asked as he quickly slid some parchments into his desk drawer.

"We are to speak with the king when he arrives." Apollisian said in a commanding tone. "I will not be denied."

"I see that you will, paladin. The king is due in sometime this afternoon. Shall I send a messenger for you or..."

Apollisian interrupted. "We will wait here for his arrival."

"So you shall." the Duke said as he narrowed his eyes. Duke Blackhawk was a proud leader and he despised the way the king allowed holy champions of justice to walk around as if they were born noble because the fools owned neither claim to land or titles. "You may leave my office now."

Apollisian narrowed his eyes in return. "So we shall." he said as he and the elf left the Duke's office.

The pair walked down the corridor and turned into a small room. It had a man behind a single desk. He was about thirty years old and his fat belly was smashed against his desk as he leaned forward to write on the parchments that sat before him. He looked up at the paladin and the elf. The fat man glanced back and forth quickly sizing them up. When his eyes rested on the holy crest on Apollisian's shoulder plate, he jumped.

"You need a room, my lord? He asked as he quickly pulled out a small wooden box containing many keys. "We have a few left."

"Yes sir, but we need them for only a few hours, at least until the king arrives." Apollisian responded politely.

The man blushed at being called sir. He started to make a joke about Apollisian and the elf only needing it for an hour, but quickly changed his mind. He handed Apollisian a small brass colored key. "It is just down the hall." He said pointing to a door that was behind his desk.

Apollisian and Alexis walked through the hall and checked each door until the number scrolled on it matched the key. The paladin unlocked the room and they entered. It was a small room, but was nicely furnished and smelled of rose petals. He sat down on the bed and began removing his armor.

"What was that about?" Alexis asked as she placed

her back to the door, folding her arms under her breasts.

"Large cities have rooms for politicians to stay in if they do not want to stay at an inn. Sometimes..."

Alexis cut in. "Not that. The Duke and you. I thought you two were going to draw blades."

Apollisian smiled as he hefted his heavy breast plate over his head and let it clang to the floor. He mussed his blond hair with his hand and wiped it backwards out of his face." I despise men of his nature. They are in power only because they were born into it. They too often feel the people exist to glorify their position. When in truth, his position exists to glorify them."

Alexis stared into Apollisian's deep blue eyes. She marveled at the unyielding sense of morality that danced within them. Her father had indeed chosen a remarkable man for her to travel with. "But why shouldn't he be glorified by his people if they love him?" she asked.

Apollisian nodded solemnly. "I do not say Duke Blackhawk is an unjust man, but I say he has many moral short-comings that prevent him from being a great leader."

"But can everyone be great? If that were true, no one would be great. Everyone would be ordinary, despite how smart or wise they were." Alexis chided as she stepped closer to the bed. Apollisian stood and started unbuckling the straps to the heavy metal plates that protected his arms.

"Not true." Apollisian responded as he stared into Alexis's beautiful almond eyes. He almost stuttered in his response. "Every leader should be great. They should be the greatest person of the group they lead. That is why..." he paused. He became lost in her beauty. He longed to lean forward and kiss her soft supple lips.

Alexis didn't seem to notice that he didn't finish his sentence. She was staring up at him. Her eyes danced across his chiseled features. His mussed blonde hair dangled about his face in long heavy streaks. His skin glistened and his deep blue eyes seemed to sparkle more vibrantly as she became lost in them. She leaned closer, longing for his embrace. She had never felt this way in all her years in Minok. She had always found males to be ignorant and petty, often boasting of their own conquests than speaking of anything intelligent.

    Apollisian leaned closer to her until he could feel her hot breath against his face. It seemed the closer he got to her the more perfect her features had become. He had traveled with her only a short time, but during that span it seemed as if he had known her for a life time. Cold shivers erupted down his spine, never had he longed for someone the way he longed for her. He stared into those beautiful brown eyes as she stared into his. Just as they both abandoned cultural boundaries and leaned forward to embrace in a kiss, there was a loud knock at the door.

    "My lord, the king arrives!" the fat man that they had met from behind the desk announced from the other side of the door.

    "Uh...Thank you sir, I will be right out." Apollisian said as he awkwardly stepped back and began placing his armor back on.

    Alexis too walked in a circle confused and flushed. "Uh...shall I go with you?"

    "No, it isn't necessary. My meeting will be brief. Go and secure our escorts if you like. I shan't be long."

    Alexis nodded and picked up her pack. She opened the door and turned back looking at the handsome man she had traveled with. She wanted to rush into his arms and kiss his face for eternity. She wanted to wrap her arms around his thick chest and never let go, but instead she smiled and walked from the quaint little room.

    Apollisian ran to the water basin and splashed water on his face and began wiping some of the grime away with a towel. He took a brick of lye that was sitting in a dish and wiped his under arms with it, then rinsing with a wet corner of the towel. He wished he had time to actually bathe, but he had to have first audience with the king.

After he wiped himself down, he took the wet towel and wiped the inside of his armor clean. Then he quickly slipped the heavy plate over his head. He swiftly fastened the side straps, grabbed his sword belt and rushed from the room.

Once the door closed Alexis exhaled deeply and went back inside of the room. She sat on the edge of the soft bed and let herself fall back.

"What am I doing?" she thought to herself. "He is a stinking human for Leska's sake. He will die in about forty years or so. I wont even be out of my centennials. Plus he will be as old as an elder in twenty years." Alexis thought as her mind drifted back to his chiseled smile and his steel blue eyes. "But he is so handsome, and how can he be so wise for so young? But stubborn. Way too damn stubborn." she thought.

Alexis lay on the bed thinking of a hundred reasons why she shouldn't have feelings for the paladin, but despite every one of those reasons, she could no more deny her feeling for him, than she could deny her heart to beat. In a few minutes she was fast asleep.

Apollisian took a deep breath as he darted down the hallway to the central corridor. He chastised himself under his breath for getting so close to the elf. Not only would she live five or six times longer than he, her father, King of the Minok nation, would order his head on a plate if he became involved with his daughter. Plus, he had taken a vow of celibacy when he became a paladin of this church. He was wed to Stephanis in a matter of sorts. If he wedded as a mortal, he would lose the ability to wield his god's divine power.

Stephanis would not grant him the divine protection that was necessary to hunt down and smite those who were unjust Apollisian rushed into the corridor and witnessed chaos. Men were rushing around with stacks of papers while others were trying to tidy up. Apollisian navigated past them as best he could. Occasionally he bumped into one, but the frenzied man didn't even seem to notice. When he got outside it was a spectacle to see. Apollisian had met the king only once in his life, when he was squire. His paladin went before the king to address the remnant fighting of what was left of the orc wars that were occurring at the time. Now the grown paladin marveled at the sight as if it were his first time again. Fifty men with shining red lances held high rode in the front. They were adorned in brass colored plate armor that gleamed in the autumn sun like sparkling flecks of gold under a trickling fresh spring brook. They wore red silk tunics under their mail that glistened as if they were wet and they wore full faced helms that had a bright red plume that draped along their back. The thick plumes bounced and waved as they rode while each lancer held a shield in their off hand that was painted with the Beyklan crest. The long narrow shields were made of thick steel and reflected the sun as brilliantly as the plate mail. The lancers held the reins of their war horses proudly and the horses pranced with their heads held high. The horses were large thick chested creatures with legs that were powerful, but slender, and their coats were dark, sleek, and trim. The horses were covered in thick barding that matched the mail of the lancers and the heavy metal plates that covered the animals head, neck, chest, and flanks was equally adorned. Behind the lancers were four carriages that were surrounded by men wearing the same armor as the lancers except these men bore finely crafted long swords that gleamed like polished chrome. The carriages were so adorned that they seemed to be made of pure gold and they sparkled like a jeweled ring on a bride's wedding day. Huge patches of brass colored metal held a thousand rubies that were in the shape of the Beyklan crest, a crown tilted on it's axis with a long sword through the middle of it. The carriages wheels were made of wood that was painted red with many thin spokes that were red and yellow, alternately, and lined with various jewels.

As the carriages rolled down the street, Apollisian could see there were fifty lancers, dressed the same as the front lancers, that covered the rear of the entourage. The carriages slowed and stopped in front of the steps that were before Apollisian's feet. There were many city officials that were eagerly awaiting the king's arrival and they danced nervously in one place as if they were trying to warm themselves on the cusp of a great blizzard.

The royal guardsmen that were armed with the long swords, dismounted and opened the carriage doors. Many servants and noble women stepped from the carriages but he did not see any man that was wearing a crown. The many silk clad perfumed men and women walked past Apollisian as he looked back and forth wondering if he had missed the Beyklan king.

After the ladies had exited the carriage, the front lancer dismounted and removed his thick armored helm. His long brown hair spilled out from under the visage revealing a middle-aged clean-shaven face. He handed the reins of his warhorse to the man behind and tucked the red velvet lined helm under his left arm, as Duke Black hawk bowed before the man.

"My king, I have eagerly awaited your arrival." the duke said without looking up.

"I doubt that you have, Dolin. We have matters to discuss in reference to your replacement while you were away. I am displeased with his handling of the dwarven attack. Which means I am displeased with you." the king said as he scanned the crowd standing atop the marble stairs in front of the city hall building.

"My king..." the duke began without lifting his head, or rising from his kneeling position. "...I must apologize for..."

The king interrupted the duke when his eyes met Apollisian's. "Go to your quarters Dolin. We will address you apology there." the king said, never taking his eyes from the paladin.

"Yes, my lord." the duke replied as he hurried up the stairs never looking back.

Apollisian wanted to look away from the king. Never had he met such a penetrating gaze. The king's dark eyes seemed to invade, judge, and protect all at the same time. Apollisian swallowed hard as the king approached slowly with an aura of superiority. The paladin could feel his nose tingling from anticipation and he was sure his feet had left the ground. The tyrant that stood before seemed to emit an awe-inspiring power that he had never been witness to. The paladin waited at the top of the smooth marble stairs.

When the king reached the top he paused and looked Apollisian up and down and Apollisian never released his gaze. The king was a large man, probably a few inches taller than Apollisian. He wore the full plate of the Beyklan high guard, just as the other lancers, but his seemed to shine more brilliantly. He was no smaller than six foot five inches tall and was thick chested, holding himself with his shoulders back and his chin out. His mere posture screamed royalty louder than any crown ever could have. Neither of the two men bowed. Apollisian prayed his memory of ceremonies was well intact from the church. He was about to perform one of the most important of all.

"You dare not bow to a king?" the king asked, arching an eyebrow.

Apollisian held that iron stare. "I bow to only one king." he said unyielding.

"And who is this king who is mightier than the king that stands before you? How dare you make such a claim?" the king replied with an angry tone. The crowd seemed to gasp and mumble amongst themselves.

"I make no such claim. He can never be claimed by one man. His power is supreme and unforgiving. The wrath of his greatness can only be served by him and him alone." Apollisian replied without pause.

"Then why serve him at all? How can he protect you?" the king asked as he drew his sword and stepped back in a defensive posture.

Apollisian kneeled as he spoke. "He cannot protect me, nor will he. He is not about protecting any one man. He is the unyielding right to justice that no man can take away, nor any man hide from." Apollisian said as he outstretched his arms and placed his empty hands up toward the sky. He leaned his head back, exposing his neck and he closed his eyes as he continued. "His sword is mightier than all the swords combined, and his wrath is as a wave of cleansing water, washing away the taints of those who have been wronged. Those who would wrong me, shall drown in an endless sea of despair for an eternity."

The king placed the tip of his sword at the feet of Apollisian and he leaned on it as he kneeled with the paladin. "Then let us thank this king for his wisdom, and hope that he shall guide our hearts to carry out that which those who have been wronged cannot." The king said as he bowed his head before the paladin. Apollisian placed his armored hand on the head of the king and they prayed. After a short while Apollisian stood while the king still kneeled at his feet. The crowed gasped aloud. The king's guards held their stances eyeing the crowd suspiciously. They had heard of the ceremony though they feared the crowd might of not.

Apollisian ignored them and placed his hand on the king's head a second time. "Then rise brother, and bask in the light of justice knowing that Stephanis shall watch over you and yours."

The king rose and smiled. Apollisian visibly relaxed as the king spoke. " It is good to see you again Apollisian. I haven't had the pleasure of meeting you since you were anointed."

"The pleasure is all mine, though I must admit being able to recall the formal greeting between you and a champion of the faith, knowing I never have to perform it again for some time is no pleasure."

"Is Victor not following along in his studies as well as you liked." the king asked as he glanced around with a frown.

Apollisian lowered his head. "I'm afraid Victor was slain during the battle trying to hold the east bridge."

The king shook his head from side to side. "We lost too many good men in that battle. I understand the Duke's lackey, Mortan Ganover, had resisted your call for the militia."

"He didn't resist per say, my liege. The law alloys him until sunset to relinquish command. It is just that the dwarves attacked just before sunset." Apollisian said.

"We will address the Duke's inability to appoint proper leadership later. You have my ear paladin. Is their anything you have witnessed about the dwarves. I trust your judgment over all else. I did not decree such authority over champions of Stephanis to ignore them."

"Well, my liege,..."

The king interrupted. "Their is no reason to call me liege, Apollisian. We both serve the same king. We are brothers. You may refer to me in familiar as Thortan Theobold."

"Thortan..." Apollisian paused adjusting to referring to the king in familiar. "...My revelations in regard to the matter of the dwarven conflict are not necessarily what you may want to hear. They are unbiased, however, and offer, what I believe to be a great political insight to other area that are of interest to you."

King Theobold did not respond as he awaited for Apollisian to continue.

"You see my...er....Thortan, I believe that Stephanis has disagreed with the sanctions in regards to the Adorian civil war. The dwarves have suffered by the taxation our kingdom inflicts and we have obviously suffered under their attacks. The south, who are rumored to not hold you in high favor are threatening a revolt, and it will be difficult to say the least, to stave off a revolt and a dwarven nation that has numbers in the tens of thousands. I think in order to have true justice for both sides, we need to lift the sanction and never tax the dwarves again. They, in turn will de-escalate the war and cease to attack. This leaves your kingdom to concentrate on the revolt and quell it before it grows, thus giving justice to a people, that I believe have been wronged, and keeping this great nation intact at the same time."

    The crowd mumble amongst themselves at the boldness of Apollisian. King Theobold raised his hands and hushed them. They immediately fell silent.

    "Your wisdom is above reproach, my young paladin. I shall do as you suggest. I will send message to the king of clan Stoneheart and I have already dispatched a legion of royal soldiers to keep order in the south. You made your case well, young paladin. I thank you for your time. You are free to seek out justice where it eludes others." King Theobold said as he simply walked away and entered the civic building.

    Apollisian sighed in relief and slowly made his way back to Alexis. They were setting out on their journey to the Minok nation this afternoon, and it was not a small one.

" Leadership. Many men have been leaders, but few have truly possessed leadership. Kings, generals, chiefs, and any other title given by men to other men are just that, titles. They have no bearing on man's ability and offer him or her nothing more than a burden. People do not actually seek out leaders. They seek out security. The masses, in their own ignorance, do not look for the greatest person or the best leader. They look for someone that has the same ideals or beliefs as they do. Too often the masses ask a question, not seeking the correct answer, but merely any answer, as long as it is feasible and provided. Any one person could spout lies and foolish banter as long as the people he or she speaks it to have no knowledge of what he is speaking of. Rarely does one person stand up and challenge the masses and their ignorance.

I have noticed that crowds are fickle creatures. A single person can rise up and coerce the masses with little more than a random direction, and that crowd will blindly charge into the fray without thought of the danger or whom they are following. Some would argue that the masses followed the leader because he had leadership ability. I disagree. I say that a true leader doesn't give speeches, he doesn't inspire fear or awe in order to get the masses to follow him. A true leader simple does what he or she feels is the right thing to do. It is the masses that then follow suit behind him. It is not the fact they are looking for an idea or that he or she rose from the depths of a crowd and shouted passionate commands. He simply and quietly chose a path. The crowd merely recognized the path and chose to follow. Those types are great leaders. These "True" leaders will never be abandoned by those that follow them, and they will never be victims of a coup against them. They may lead the masses for a short time however, because true leadership is not the same as a title longevity. As I have said before, the masses are fickle and ignorant. If his followers somehow abandon a true leader, it will be because he simply decided to go another direction. Their rejection will mean nothing to him, because he was not intending to lead them in the first place, he was merely traveling down the road he believed was correct. Alas, I feel a there is no such thing as a "True Leader" merely true followers."

-Lancalion Levendis Lampara-

Chapter Four
Children of the Forest

Kellacun was roughly thrown into a dark dirty cell. The sable haired woman skidded along the bare stone floor that was covered in filth and a dark green slimy residue that wreaked of feces and urine. Many rusted iron shackles hung from bulky steel hooks that were about ten feet up on the far wall. There were a few bleached white skeletal arms that hung from the shackles and dangled directly above several piles of moldy bones. Rats and other vermin had long ago eaten the flesh from the skeletons that were piled up in gruesome heaps of decaying frames. There was a single window that was set about thirty feet up the moss covered wall. The small portal was riddled with thick iron bars that appeared to be well maintained. The rusted chains holding the dangling shackles were attached to small pulleys that were secured just a few inches below the bottom of the window.

Kellacun felt her arms being grabbed by rough powerful hands and hoisted up. "Up we go, you dirty little bitch." the coarse voice whispered in her ear. She could smell the fetid odor of ale and rotted onions that wafted from his breath. Kellacun did not resist the man as her wrists were roughly shackled. She had been severely beaten and clung to consciousness like an insect on a log in a gale wind. The assassin was barely aware that the skin of her wrist had been pinched in the shackles when it was closed. A small amount of blood dripped from her fresh wound as she felt herself being lifted to her feet. Out of the corner of her eye she could see the guard. Her vision was a little blurry after her beating, but he appeared to be a burly, obese man. He was wearing a dark brown sleeveless leather tunic that was soiled with grease and sweat near the arm pits and just under his chin. Rings of dirt that had collected in the wrinkles of his arms and legs covered his fat body. He had long dark greasy hair that clung to his sweaty face and neck in clammy strings. His plump arms jiggled as he quickly pulled the rusted chain taught, hand over hand, hoisting Kellacun to her feet. The guard slowed and then strained as her body weight pulled against the chain. When he hoisted her a few inches above the ground, the guard hooked one of the chain links around a smaller iron hook that protruded from the wall.

    Kellacun winced in pain as she tried to cling to the ground with the tip of her toes, but soon her entire body weight rested on her frail thin wrists. The fat guard chuckled as he finished securing the rusty chain that held her aloft. Kellacun kept her eyes closed, trying to ignore the growing pain as the shackles ripped open the delicate skin of her wrists. Though the wounds would soon heal, the wererat still felt the stinging pain. The guard waddled over to the thick wooden door of the cell and fumbled through his pockets. A few seconds later he procured a set of brass keys on a large steel ring. The guard locked the heavy cell door from the inside and placed the keys back in his pocket with his thick fingers.

    Kellacun gripped the rusted chain just above the shackles and pulled, relieving some of the pressure that was on her arms. She had not recovered the strength to hold herself long, but the pain in her wrists was becoming unbearable. The fat guard chuckled again and wiped his dirty arms across his mouth as he waddled toward her. He waited for a few moments and Kellacun could no longer hold herself up. Her muscles went slack and she yelped in pain as her wrists supported her entire body weight again.

"Hurt?" the guard asked with a rotten yellow toothed smile. He didn't seem much interested in her reply, it was more a question of stupidity than of merit. When Kellacun didn't answer he looked her up and down. She was strung up by her wrists with her head hung low. The fat jailor knew she was due to be executed in the morning for attempted murder and a plethora of other charges that occurred over a seven year period. His sick brown eyes took in the prisoner that hung helpless before him. She wore a light brown prison tunic that was too big for her small frame. The oversized neck hole hung down in front of her exposing her deep pale cleavage. Her breeches were loose and slack, made for a male prisoner, and clung to her shapely hips by a thin twine that had been crudely wrapped around to act as a belt. Her face was bruised from the beating she took and her long black hair hung down in front of her chest.

The fat guard loosed her breeches and rubbed his hands together in anticipation as the filthy garment fell around her ankles. He bent down and eagerly removed the wide legged pants and tossed them behind him. Her sleek sallow legs shined in the pale light that fell in from the tall window. The fat guard began to unfastened his own breeches in such a haste that he more ripped the leather belt loose, than unfastened it. Looking back at the locked wooden door to ensure he was not to be disturbed, he spread Kellacun's legs and stepped between them. She cried out in pain from the shackles but seemed oblivious to the corpulent guard that groped her buttocks.

"You be a good girl and I'll finish quickly." the portly jailor said as he licked his three fingers and ran them up and down between her legs as his fat coarse digits slightly penetrated her.

Kellacun was vaguely aware of what was going on. She had been in and out of consciousness since her beating, but she was being rapidly brought back to awareness by the corpulent guard's molestations. After he finished wetting her, the guard lifted her up by her buttocks and drew her hips near to him. He guided himself in easily and vigorously ravaged her.

Kellacun began to rush back to her cognizant mind. Something was not right. She was in pain, but it was not like the ache she had prepared for. Something was wrong, different. She struggled to speak and mumbled a jumble of incomprehensive words. The fat guard seemed to be excited with her mumbling, mistaking it for moans of pleasure, and continued his vigorous violation.

Kellacun suddenly opened her eyes. She glanced around the room in a confused stare for a moment, as she struggled to understand the rapid jerking motions her body was being subjected to. The assassin felt the pain in her wrists, though her body weight was being supported slightly. She blinked again and everything came crashing back. The obese guard that had brought her to her cell, now stood between her legs violating her. She could smell his filthy stench and felt his cold clammy sweat as it dripped on her bare legs. Though she was repulsed at the disgusting creature that was pleasuring himself on her, she almost grinned at her luck. She had endured much worse in order to get close enough to a victim she meant to assassinate, and now she would endure this in order to escape. Men were easy prey to her and she had no doubt how to use the fat jailor's lust to her advantage. She thought quickly, because she suspected the plump man did not have interludes often and he would rapidly satisfy himself.

Kellacun began moaning, feigning pleasure. "Lick me, you ox."

The fat guard seemed oblivious to her speaking.

The assassin said it again, but more loudly, though she was careful not to alert anyone that might be standing outside the cell door.

The portly jailor stopped and looked at the woman

in disbelief. "What did you say?" He asked as he wiped his glistening forehead with his greasy forearm.

Kellacun wrapped her legs around the fat guards waist and wiggled her hips in anticipation. " Lick me, you ox, I want this to last as long as it can. If you lick me, I'll be sure to take care of you in the same way." she whispered with a vixen's voice.

The fat guard's eyes went wide as he stuttered. "Uh....like...you mean..."

"That is exactly what I mean. What harm can I cause you? I am shackled and have no weapons. I am to be executed in the morning. I would like to have one night of pleasure before I leave the world of the living." she said as she nibbled at the fat mans lip. The assassin held her breath as not to take in the repulsive odor that erupted from his rotten mouth.

The fat guard pulled away from her and roughly hoisted her up by her buttocks. He placed her right leg over his left shoulder and her left leg over his right shoulder. Scooting her hips toward his face, he began to pleasure her orally. Kellacun ignored the burning pain in her wrists caused by the shackles. She could feel warm sticky blood dripping down her forearms, but she kept telling herself she would soon be free.

The guard spent a few minutes, pleasuring her and lifted his head. "Now me. It is time for you to do it to me." he said eagerly.

Kellacun bobbed her tongue sensuously and bit her bottom lip. "I can't wait to taste you. But I can't do it chained up here."

The guard glared. "I can't let you out. " the fat man said angrily. "What do think..."

Kellacun interrupted him. "You don't have to release me, you silly ox, just let me down from this perch."

Before she could finish her sentence she watched as the guards pale white buttocks jiggled and bounced as he ran to the chain he had secured on the iron hook that held her aloft. He unfastened the heavy chain and she roughly slid down the wall and landed on her bottom. The guard ran back over and put his hands on his hips expectantly. Kellacun scooted over and took him in her mouth. She struggled to perform mediocre and almost vomited several times due to the stench of his unclean body. The fat guard seemed oblivious to her disgust and tightly gripped a handful of her sleek black hair. Kellacun deftly ran her hand into his pocket and withdrew a shiny steel ring with several brass keys attached to it. She took her time, careful not to clink the keys together, and placed the ring in her armpit under her loose fitting prison tunic. She finished a few minutes later and kissed and caressed the guards legs. " How was it?" She asked as she shifted the keys from her armpit to her hand while she held them under her breeches she picked them up from the floor. She slipped on the oversized prison breeches, as she waited for the fat guard to respond.

"I have had much better." he said as he roughly grabbed the rusted chain attached to her shackles. The fat guard didn't bother putting his pants back on as he drug the chain over to the hook to hoist her up a second time. Kellacun backed against the wall as he lifted her up and secured the chain on the iron hook. Kellacun winced in pain as she dangled with her body weight on her shackled wrists again. She didn't worry about real injury, she was a wererat and could only be really harmed by magical or silver weapons. Her shackles were neither. Though she bled, her wounds healed almost as quickly as they were formed. Had she not been beat with that silver gauntlet, her eye would not be swollen either.

The corpulent guard fumbled with his pants as Kellacun quietly shuffled in the dark room with the lock of her shackles. She tried several times until she found the key that slid into the lock. The fat guard walked over to the locked cell door and tried to open it. He cursed and reached into his pocket for his keys to unlock the door. When he searched one pocket and found it empty, he checked the other. When he didn't find the keys he turned around and began looking on the floor of the cell. He kicked at piles of excrement with his leather boot in the dim light, turning over the disgusting mounds of debris, but didn't find anything.

"Where in the hell are my damned keys?" he said under his breath as he heard a familiar click. He jerked his head up toward Kellacun in time to see her scampering up the thick chain that had held her shackles.

Kellacun smiled as she felt the tumblers turn and heard the click of the lock. The shackles opened and she grabbed the chain with both of her hands and began climbing up. Her bare toes slipped into the smallest crevices in the smooth prison wall, and with the aid of the chain, she scampered up the wall easily.

"You'll never get out of those bars, bitch!" the fat guard yelled as he opened the wooden cell door and slammed it shut. Kellacun could hear him screaming for more guards on the other side. Once she reached the top of the chain she climbed onto the window sill. The ledge was about eight inches wide and the iron bars were thick, but the stone around them was worn and weathered. Kellacun grabbed the bars and sucked in a deep breath. She exhaled long and softly, pulling with all her strength but the bars would not budge. She sighed, and closed her dark dangerous eyes, loosing the primal rage within her that she continuously kept at bay. She growled deeply as her arms shook and trembled, while long dark hair replaced the fine angelic wisps that covered her arms and her delicate face became twisted and a long snout erupted from her nose. Her ears became pointed and the hair on her head shifted and erupted from her body. In moments the transformation was complete and the once beautiful assassin was replaced by a half woman, half rat looking beast. She glared at the bars that were before her with red vibrant eyes. She grabbed them with her now muscular fur and claw covered hands, pulling with all her might, but even in her hybrid form, the bars were securely anchored in the stone. She glanced back at the door and could hear men rushing down the hall. She knew she didn't have much time.

    *   *   *

  Kalen sat in his easy chair and studied his many spells he had been trying to learn. He grew weary of not having the luxury of casting them on live persons, and Spencer hadn't came by in days. The gray elf slammed his book shut and sighed. He leaned back in his soft velvety chair and propped his head up with his hand as he leaned on the plush arm rest, drumming his fingers silently on the soft blue felt fabric that was sewn around the expensive piece of furniture. Kalen twirled his long silver hair in his hand, smiling suddenly when an idea crossed his mind. He hadn't heard from the thieves guild since it was sacked, but he could try scrying on the assassin, Kellacun. He wasn't too familiar with her, but he had seen her on a couple of occasions.

  The gray elf jumped from his chair with new vigor and selected a book from the expansive oak shelves that lined his study from floor to ceiling. He took the thick tome over to the polished white ash table that served as his workbench and opened it. After a few minutes of drumming through pages, he stopped and clapped his hands. " Ah-ha. Found it." The elf mumbled to himself with an evil grin.

  Kalen studied the spell for a few hours, stopping only to take a drink of wine from the golden goblet he had left over from lunch. He walked over to the scrying mirror and chanted softly. In a few moments, the cloudy mirror began to take shape. The image came so dark had Kalen not had infravision he would not have seen much, but to his surprise he found the assassin barely clothed and chained up. She had no pants on and there was a fat man between her thighs having his way with her. The assassin appeared to be unconscious or oblivious to what was going on. Kalen, disgusted, started to end the scry, but the assassin came around and feigned to be interested in the fat guard. He kind of chuckled at the events as they unfolded, sitting back down in his plush chair to enjoy the show.

"Don't be a fool, you corpulent slob. She has as much interest in you as she has in staying in those chains." Kalen chuckled as he watched. "Surely he doesn't believe..." Kalen was cut off by the man as he hoisted the assassin to a more comfortable position.

"Now why on earth would the fat idiot do that? " Kalen asked himself aloud. " He has no need to...ohhhh" Kalen said as the portly guard let the assassin down from the perch so she could accommodate him in the same manner he just accommodated her.

"You stupid fool, I hope she kills you slowly." Kalen said to the guard as he watched the events unfold.

The gray elf sipped his wine and watched in pure amusement as Kellacun lifted the keys to her shackles from the guards pockets as she finished accommodating him. The guard then searched for his keys while she escaped her shackles and climbed to the window sill. The fat guard screamed something Kalen couldn't understand and he tried to rush out of the room while the assassin climbed the chain but could not get the bars from the window to give. The gray elf sighed and began chanting. He had never cast through a scry before, but he had watched Hector perform it and it did not seem that difficult. He just modified the weaves and merely projected, rather than wove them. Kalen watched as the guards burst into the room as the assassin stepped into a shining blue portal that quickly closed once she had stepped through.

A bright blue dot appeared in the Kalen's chambers. The magical energy expanded from a small spot to a long horizontal line. That line then stretched and grew until it created a large oval portal. It was not long before a frantic woman stepped through. She had long sleek black hair that hung down around her. She wore a dirty light brown prison tunic that was much too big for her. One of her naked shoulders poked out of the neck as the shirt hung from her shoulders awkwardly. The light brown breeches she wore, were also too big for her and were clung to her waist loosely by a thin piece of brown twine that acted like a crude belt. Her face was swollen and she had many small bruises around her left eye.

Kellacun franticly scanned the room. It was a small round room with a tall ceiling. There were bookshelves on each wall that were loaded with thousands of books and tomes. On a polished white ashen desk sat an open book with no doubt arcane writings, and sitting in front of her in a dark blue silk cloak was a thin, yet nimble looking gray elf. He had long straight silver hair, though it was not as long as hers, and bright blue eyes. He sat imposingly in a felt chair with his thin arms crossed under his chest.

"Who are you?" Kellacun asked as she kept one eye on the mage and one eye around the room. She struggled to understand why she was in human form again, but she figured it had something to do with the portal.

"I am your employer's employer." Kalen responded surreptitiously. "And it seems you are now out of work."

"How so?" Kellacun asked as she glanced to the ceiling, trying in vain to locate a door to this cursed room.

Kalen paused and a disgusted look crept onto his face. "Please look around, you act as a rat trapped in a stew pot, but I assure you the only door out of here lies with me, so be a good little vermin, and I will let you get back to your work."

Kellacun reluctantly stopped looking for an exit and

gave her full attention to the elf that sat before her, but she glowered menacingly at him, though she could not tell if he even noticed her expression.

"I would have sent you a portal earlier, but it seemed you were rather enjoying yourself." Kalen said with a chuckle."

"Pray elf, that no one hires me to see you dead. I am an efficient killer." Kellacun retorted as anger flared through her at the elf's mockeries.

Kalen nodded and smiled. "I see that you are, but I thought you were hired to kill the Ecnal, not roll in the hay with fat disgusting guards."

Kellacun fumed. She could feel the need to release the rage, to release the beast that was within her and drink the blood of this miscreant that sat before her.

Kalen sensed her anger and continued. "Tell me, did he taste as yummy as he looked?" Kalen taunted.

Kellacun snarled and in a flash she transformed into her hybrid form. She leapt over the table, her claws and teeth bared, but before she could sink her teeth into the elf's soft flesh, ten tiny blue specks of light formed in front of her. The lights flashed and the specks encircled her leaving her held immobile by the powerful magical rings.

"Temper, temper." Kalen taunted as he got up from his chair and circled the magically held wererat that was on top of his desk. "You transformed pretty fast. I suspect if you are injured or angry it is easy for you, yes?" Kalen asked, knowing the assassin could not reply. "Cat got your tongue?" he asked again, laughing out loud at his own wit. "As I was saying before your pitiful outburst, your old employer is no more. His guild has been wiped out and every one of his members have been killed. So that means you now work for me, or I kill you. I assume you will choose the first. Any objections?" Kalen asked again and chuckled knowing Kellacun could not respond. "Good. As you may know, and perhaps you do not, the man you were being paid to kill is named Lance Ecnal. I know not how he managed to escape the orphan killings ten years ago, but the fact remains you are as sloppy now, as you were then. I am more than displeased at your pitiful attempts at assassinating him. Perhaps you should seek another profession. One that employs your better talents." Kalen said, pausing briefly while rubbing his smooth chin in mock thought. "A harlot's dress would suit you nicely after witnessing your performance with your jailer. I am sure he has fewer complaints about your job performance than I." Kalen mused.

Kellacun struggled against the magic that held her. Anger flared through her veins as she imagined ripping Kalen's throat out and feasting on his blood. But try as she might, the magic held her as easily as the sky held the clouds.

"Strain all you wish, fool. You are to stupid to slip through the spell that binds you. If I were you, I would hope the spell holds, for I hunger for a reason to kill you. But alas, I need that orphan slain. If I were not so busy here, I might do it myself, perhaps if you fail a second time, I might seek out this troublesome youth." Kalen said as he stood up slowly from his old chair and wandered to his book shelf. He pressed his narrow finger on his bottom lip as his eyes darted among the vast volumes of knowledge that rested on the old oaken shelves. Finally he came across an old book that was bound with four golden rings. Kalen carefully took the tome and placed it on his desk in front of Kellacun. The cover was made of wood and had many demonic symbols and arcane runes about it. He slowly lifted the cover, sliding it gracefully on the thick golden rings, revealing the first page of three that were also made of wood, save it was much thinner than the cover, but thick enough that it remained rigid when lifted. This page also had many strange symbols and writings on it. Kalen paused and rubbed his manicured finger over the engravings as he read aloud.

"*A day shall come to pass when the mother of mercy shall bear child. This child will be like no other, for gods and men alike will seek to vanquish him. The hate from the hells dwells within his mind, as compassion for the meek guides his heart. If allowed to live, this child will bear the false testimony of the gods, as he ascends the throne of righteousness, while working the magic of evil. The good and evils of the realms will oppose him, but they will be crushed asunder as the scorpion under an anvil or fire, for he shall command both of them alike unto his ascension...*" Kalen finished reading and turned to the magically held Kellacun.

"Do you know how long it has taken me and the scholars to decipher this text?" the gray elf asked. Kellacun, still held by the powerful holding spell could not respond. Kalen did not seem to notice her lack of response as he ran his fingers worshipfully along the wooden carvings on the ancient page. "It has taken me well over thirty years. It may seem a long time to yourself human, but in fact, it is an amazing feat of wizardry and intelligence. Deciphering a single word should take decades of study in the meaning of the old tongue, yet we did an entire page in thirty years!" The elf gloated. "The elders of Minok covet these writings insomuch that none may even glimpse the magically sealed scroll case that holds them, let alone lay their eyes on the tome itself, but I have a copy. I'll not tell you how I have come across such a coveted treasure, just know that I have. Know that if I can steal that which has been kept safe since the dawn of time, I can easily claim your life should you disappoint me." Kalen said as he shook his fingers in an odd display of movements. In moments the blue rings of magical energy that held Kellacun tight, began to glow brighter until the glimmering bonds enveloped the wererat and then she was gone.

Kalen leaned back in his velvety chair and stared longingly at the pages that were before him. He tapped his index finger against his thin bottom lip as he whispered to himself.

"Hector has his own agenda, and is confident that the child of mercy can be found and slain, saving himself and his reign. Still, I fear time has run out for us. I know the child is not merely the executioner of Nalir. I know from teachings that even as a child he is much more than that. Indeed, the Abyss Walker has been born, and his time of mourning comes to a rapid end."

*   *   *

"A storm is coming." the raspy voice of the elven ancient known as Eucladower Strongbow announced. The venerable elf sat on the giant root of an Ililander tree, the largest and oldest trees in all the realms. The gnarled twisted roots of the great tree weaved in and out of the lush forest floor as they snaked down a gentle slope that ended at the base of a shimmering pond. Orantal Proudarrow, lord ranger of the Darayal Legion, said nothing as he gazed at his ancient friend. Eucladower was clothed in a green silk robe that hung loosely on his weak frame. His thin silver mustache trailed down his face and blended with his long, straight, sleek beard that hung past his knees. His perky elven ears protruded from his silver hair that was laid back revealing a deep widows peak hairline. The tips of his silk robe were embossed with a shimmering golden hue that seemed to sparkle in the few beams of sunlight that managed to jut through the dense forest canopy. The elder leaned on a long wooden staff with a gnarled head that seemed too heavy for Eucladower's frail body, yet the ancient elder lifted it easily. The tip of the gnarled oak staff resembled an eagle that was perched atop the staff, yet it bore no profound features.

Orantal gazed out across the shimmering lake that was at the foot of the Ililander tree, pausing a moment to see if his longtime friend was going to say anything more. He had grown accustomed to the Eucladower's labored speech and it saddened him to know the elder's natural life was soon at an end. The ranger lord sat down on the giant gnarled root, next to his ancient friend, and smoothed the silk breeches that were under his thin mail. He glanced at the armor he had bore through countless trials and tribulations. The thin chain shirt hung lightly from his green and silk tunic. Great spider webs of yellow danced across the chest of his garb and almost appeared as the rays of a setting or rising sun. He wore a single shoulder plate that was strapped to his left shoulder tightly. The plate was also green with the splash of the yellow spider pattern. Orantal's blonde hair was pulled back in a ponytail that was held by a long green ribbon that hung between his shoulder blades with the end of his hair. His long pointed ears, though not near as long as Eucladower's, poked from under his sleek thin hair. And his twin narrow swords hung tightly at his sides. The ranger lord sighed and looked at Eucladower. The ancient elf began to speak again in his old raspy voice.

"Yes, a storm *is* coming, Orantal. I see the damned shall have their voice on our world, but first, the storm comes to us." the old elder said.

Orantal shot to his feet and scanned the forest around him clutching his twin sword hilts as if the enemy may be near. "What do you mean, elder? What storm? Are we in danger?"

The elder groaned as he leaned on his gnarled staff to help him stand. "Yes, my friend. We are in danger. Help as we might, try as we must, their is no stopping the Abyss Walker. He has been born and now he comes to us."

Orantal nearly stumbled forward in shock as he hopped down from the Illilander root. He and all the elves were taught about the Abyss Walker as children, though they knew not much more than he could bring the end of the world.

"How can this be? There have been none of the signs? At least none of the ones that I know of." The ranger lord proclaimed. He knew only two of the signs, like the dead that defy Rha-Cordan, and he shall come of mourning that knows not why he mourns. There were many more, but Orantal was not on the elder council and he knew of at least two other signs, though he knew not what they were.

"We may not see all the signs my young champion. But they will come to pass nonetheless. We must remain vigilant. The signs will come soon, if they have not already, but I cannot deny the Abyss Walker comes. I can feel his wrath in my soul." Eucladower said in a low raspy whisper as he slowly walked from the tree aided by his gnarled staff. Orantal merely walked alongside the elder elf and nodded with his hands grasped behind his back.

The pair plodded down from the majestic slope pausing briefly for the elder to rest. The sounds of the virgin forest seemed more loudly to the ranger lord, knowing that they could very well be a wasteland soon. It was said that the Abyss Walker would bring about a blight to the land.

Orantal and Eucladower walked from the base of the hill and entered a thick vale. The vale bore no under brush and the trees were large and perfectly straight. They showed no scars, no ill branches and animals roamed nearby, uncaring about the many elves that milled about. The Minok Vale was one of the largest elven cities in the realms. To any but an elf, the Vale merely appeared to be a group of perfect trees that were exceptionally tall and blotted out the sun. Though few humans had ever been to the Vale that could see it for what it was. Each tree bore the markings of many thin doors that were all but concealed to the untrained eye. Each tree housed an elven family that had as many as fifty members each. Some noble families were known to have many trees, but they were often found at the heart of the Vale, not on the edges. At the top of each tree, there were sentries posted that were hidden so well that many birds that perched among the branches did not know they were their. The sentries were armed with deadly bows of the finest craftsmanship. The elven weapons were superior to the humans in every way, from beauty to balance. It was not uncommon for an elven weapon smith to spend a hundred years forging a sword. Where humans spent months at best.

Many elves milled about their daily routines. Some paused to offer a bow of respect to the elder, and others offered a quick, but respectful dip, as they hurried past in their own tasks.

Eucladower turned to Orantal as he breathed heavily from the short, but tiring walk.

"Go, lord ranger. Round up the Darayal Legion. Though we cannot stop that which already will be, we can help preserve that which we might lose."

Orantal bowed low. "As you command, Elder Eucladower." Orantal said as he hurried off into the forest beyond the Vale.

Eucladower slowly strode through the vast elven city. The old elder smiled at the children that ran through the bottoms and then he grimaced at the thought of what the Abyss Walker might do. Certainly the Vale would oppose him, but the elder knew it would be futile. He had not broken the prophetic seal, but Eucladower knew that it foretold a horrible reckoning that the dark one would bring about the land. He hoped that the storm he felt was not the true Abyss Walker, but merely an agent of the damned, trying to earn favor of his dark lords. They had faced a few of those over the centuries, but he had never felt the powerful presence before that he now felt. He could usually feel the taint of lesser evils from a few miles away, but he knew that this taint came from hundreds of miles away.

"At least we have time." Eucladower mumbled to himself as he pushed his way into the elder chamber that was located at the base of the largest tree in Minok Vale.

"Time for what, Elder Eucladower?" he asked.

Eucladower glanced up and noticed he had walked into the chamber of the wise without knowing. He was planning on going there anyway, yet he was so deep in thought he must have wandered in. Cursing his old mind, he regarded the man that had spoke to him. King Christopher Calamon Overmoon sat in his polished oaken chair wearing his golden crown. The crown bore eight thin horns that represented each of the eight vales that dwelled under his rule. At the base of each horn was a jewel that bore the symbol of the perspective nations. The magnificent crown of Minok rested on King Overmoon's blonde hair that was now more silver than blonde. His deep blue eyes bore the wisdom of nearly eight hundred years of rule. He wore a bright blue robe that was streaked with silver elven runes and a bright silver shawl that ran around his neck and down the front of him that also bore ancient cobalt runes. His fingers were encrusted with many rings, though he wore them out of symbolism rather than out of vanity. The room the king sat in was more long than it was wide and had a beautifully polished red wood table shaped the same as the room was where the entire council of wise, save for Eucladower, now sat. The venerable elf slowly made his way to his seat, resting his gnarled staff against the table and folding his knobby hands before he answered.

"Time to prepare, time to flee, or time to fight." Eucladower said in his raspy voice through labored breaths from his long walk.

" Why would we do these things, Elder Eucladower? Has another claiming to be the dark one come close to our vale?" The king asked. " We will merely crush this one as we have the others in centuries past."

Other elders murmured amongst themselves in the room, but none spoke aloud.

"This one cannot be slain, my king. I fear he is the true Abyss Walker, and he is undoubtedly coming." Eucladower announced.

The council of wise murmured amongst themselves more loudly.

"How can you be certain, Elder Eucladower?" one of the other elders asked. "Many feel the Abyss Walker is more legend than truth, created to scare small children into behaving.

"Yes, how can you be certain." King Overmoon said as he rubbed his head under his crown.

Eucladower took a deep breath. "I know the same way I know when water falls from the sky it is rain, even if I cannot see the clouds. I know, for when a breeze blows against my face, it is the wind, even if I cannot see it. I know these things because he is over a hundred miles away, yet I see every feature of his face."

The room gasped at that announcement.

"What does he look like, Elder Eucladower?" one of the other elders asked wearing a red robe that was adorned with yellow runes.

"Yes, tell us of him." another shouted.

Eucladower took a deep breath and began again. "He comes as a storm, violent and deadly. I can hear the voices of the damned crying out from him as if he carries their tormented existence in his pocket and their cries for mercy on his breath. He is but a babe, a human babe, but his soul is that of the gods." Eucladower proclaimed.

The other Elders relaxed and murmured to themselves.

"We, cannot abandon the Vale on Eucladower's visions, my king." an older elf in a blue and yellow robe pleaded as he rubbed his creased forehead.

"Yet we can not stay, nor can we risk doing nothing." another elder put in. All the elders seemed to nod their heads in agreement.

Eucladower took a deep breath before he spoke. "I ask for a reading, my king. The ancients will attest to my sight."

The room gasped again and became completely silent. No one stirred, no one seemed to breath, save for King Overmoon.

"We can do no such thing, Elder Eucladower." the king said. "There are four signs the Abyss Walker is coming. All of them, we, as children of the forest, would experience first hand. We have not had a single one. Elder Humas, would kindly recite the first passing of the Abyss Walker.

The elder with red and yellow robe stood up, straightened his collar, and cleared his throat. "The son of a Vale, not by blood, will turn his back on his brethren and embrace the shadow." Humas recited.

"Elder Eucladower, the ancient tongue referred to the son of the crown as the son of the Vale. As you know I have been married twice. My first wife, Surelda Al-Kalidius, a gray elf, was slain, Leska bless her soul, before she bore me any children. And now, my wife, *your queen*, has bared only a daughter that is as we speak, traveling with the human paladin, Apollisian, as she learns the ways of Justice." the King said confidently.

" What of her son, Kalen?" Eucladower asked.

The elders whispered amongst themselves.

"How do you know of Kalen?" The King asked with an elevated tone, on the edge of anger. He leaned forward and arched his eyebrows with more than passing interest.

Eucladower settled back in his soft chair and folded his ancient knobby hands. "My king, you forget I am almost two thousand years old. There is much I have seen. I remember Surelda well. She was quite beautiful and wise, my King. She complimented you tenderly."

The king sat back in his throne, more relaxed. "It is true she had a son, though he was not of my blood, therefore he could not be a son of the Vale."

"Elder Humas." Eucladower spoke with his raspy voice. "Could you kindly recite the passing a second time."

Elder Humas cleared his throat again and recited the passing more slowly than he had the first time. "The son of a Vale, not by blood, will turn his back on his brethren and embrace the shadow."

When Elder Humas finished, the entire room was buzzing with whispered talk. The king rubbed his head under his crown. "This may appear as if the passing could be satisfied, but Kalen is no longer a son of the Vale, even under the old code. Even if he were to embrace the shadow, which I would wager my crown he has not, he cannot be named a son of the Vale."

Elder Humas spoke. "We as Elders of the Vale must vote on the passing. It is my contention that this passing is plausible."

"Agreed." the other Elders said in solemn unison.

The king leaned back in his polished oaken chair and rested his head against his hand.

"Elder Bartoke, would you kindly recite the second passing." the king asked wearily.

An elf rose in a blue and yellow robe and did not look much younger than Elder Eucladower. "A babe, half not of this earth, and half damned by the gods themselves, and feared by the children of the forest, will carry his own proclamation naming him not for who he is, but for who he will become."

"A babe is what I have seen, my King. I can hear the damned crying out for mercy when his vision comes to me. He is a human boy, though I know not of this proclamation the passing speaks of." Eucladower said.

"The Elders of the Vale must vote on the passing. It is my contention that this passing is plausible." Elder Bartoke said as he sat back in his chair.

" Agreed." the other Elders said in solemn unison.

King Overmoon, seeing the elders were serious about the readings, relaxed, but exhaled deeply. "Elder Varmintan, could you kindly recite the third passing."

An elder stood that was wearing a violet robe that bore many green runes in it, much similar to the king's robe, but not nearly as ornate. "He who walks with wrath, shall stride into the vale as a guest wearing the Cadacka, though he knows not why he mourns. If the children of the forest do nothing, they will surely perish." Varmintan recited slowly.

"I guess we will know soon enough if the false bringer wears a Cadacka." Humas said gravely. "And what are we to do if he is wearing a Cadacka? How is it possible a human babe could come across one?"

"The Elders of the Vale must vote on the passing. It is my contention that this passing is plausible." Varmintan said solemnly.

The other elders spoke amongst themselves for some time though no conclusions were reached. Finally they elected to discuss those options should the bringer prove to be true.

The king removed his crown and set it on the polished oak table. He stared for a moment at reflection in the mirror like surface of the table. Each jewel seemed to shine at him, mocking him, challenging his wisdom, his strength. He sighed and ran his fingers through his sleek hair, exhaled and straightened his posture. "Elder Darmond could you kindly recite the fourth passing."

The elder wearing a red robe with a blue sash that crossed from shoulder to hip leaned forward. His hair was uncharacteristically dark for an elf and his bright green eyes shined in the dim light of the council room.

"Woe to the children of the world, for after he who walks with wrath stands among the mothers without children, he will slay that which is already dead. He will shed his mourning and walk among them saying; I know you fools, now you shall perish." Elder Darmond recited.

There was a long silence in the room. The elders weighed the passing and contemplated it. It had been nearly fifty years since they had last been recited and the elders tried to take all possible meanings in.

Finally Elder Darmond broke the silence after almost an hour.

"The Elders of the Vale must vote on the passing. It is my contention that this passing is plausible."

The king nodded slowly. "Since the passings are contended plausible; I, King Christopher Calamon Overmoon, High King of Minok Vale, submit to you, Elders of the Vale, to read the prophecy that our great forefathers, in their wisdom, did graft for us in that when the day of the Abyss Walker is at hand, we could be prepared."

"So be it." the Elders said in unison.

"Ancient Elder Eucladower." Elder Humas said. "Would you honor us with a reading of the great prophecy."

Elder Eucladower slowly pushed back from the table and leaned on his gnarled staff to rise. He stepped awkwardly toward the king who produced a small ivory scroll case that looked fragile and old. It was about a foot long, round, and covered in ancient runes that were hundreds of times older than Eucladower himself. The venerable elf staggered back to his chair but he did not sit in it. He rested his gnarled oaken staff against the polished table and opened the ivory case. With his knobby old fingers he lightly pulled three parchments out that appeared to be written on some kind of leather. He unrolled the parchment and cleared his throat. All the other Elders and the King sat tight lipped when the ancient elf began to recite the prophecy with his old raspy voice.

"A day shall come to pass when the mother of mercy shall bear child. This child will be like no other, for gods and men alike will seek to vanquish him. The hate

from the hells dwells within his mind, as compassion for the meek guides his heart. If allowed to live, this child will bear the false testimony of the gods, as he ascends the throne of righteousness, while working the magic of evil. The good and evils of the realms will oppose him, but they will be crushed asunder as the scorpion under an anvil or fire, for he shall command both of them alike unto his ascension..."

    Eucladower took a deep breath and dabbed his forehead with the sleeve of his green silk robe. His labored breaths slowed as he carefully passed the fragile parchment to the elders. Each one read the parchment and handed to the next until it reached the king. King Overmoon read the parchment then placed it on the table in front of him.

    "Do read the second passage, Elder Eucladower." The King said in an almost whisper. The entire room sat in awe as the ancient elf began again.

    ...Let it be known to all who have wisdom that this child, the Abyss Walker, will have the knowledge and power of a thousand lifetimes, though his mortal body will be younger than the trees he walks among. He will be betrayed by blood, that is his own, when he fights that which cannot be fought. He shall defeat that which cannot be defeated and he will ascend that which hath no ascension. He will rise up for forty two cycles, the last eight will bring about a plague on the land that has never been seen before, nor will be

    seen again. His emerald eyes will bear the pain of an eternity of damned souls that only the children of the forest may see. His mouth will shed forth such fire that any opposing him will be charred to dust from which they were created..."

    Again Eucladower passed the parchment to the closet elder to read. When he had finished reading it he passed the parchment along until it reached the king. King Overmoon did with the second parchment as he had done with the first.

"Do read the third and final passage, Elder Eucladower."

Eucladower nodded and began reading the final parchment with his old raspy voice.

"... He shall wear the cloak of mourning until his forty second cycle. When he mourns no longer, the world will begin it's mourning, for his wrath will be unleashed on all the world. When his fury is sedated, the kings of the Abyss will bow to his feet and call him lord, though he will reject them saying; " You bow to me out of fear. That is all you know, therefore you are not worthy to kiss the bottom of my feet." The Abyss Walker will then turn to the heavens and all mortals dwelling in Yahna will tremble for they know he is coming, and his wrath is renewed. That will be known as his true ascension..."

" Destiny. A simple seven letter word. Simple to pronounce, yet profound in meaning. Many pay a life's wages to learn their destiny and then destroy their lives trying to avoid it. Most people seek it out, but the wise fear it, and the brave accept it. But does destiny really exist? Often lovers say if we were destined to be, we will be. In a way I believe this to be true. But I argue this; someday you will die, is that destiny? Some say yes, it is a form of it. But what if you drank some poison today, would you then die, regardless of when you would have died if you did not? Of course you would die today. Did I then change destiny by drinking the poison? In a way. The end result of destiny is the same, but the means to it did not occur like it was thought to come to pass.

I say be wary of those who claim they are destined for anything. They are most likely fools merely trying to convince others of their own greatness, when in fact they have none. I was told my destiny many times, though in a way I fulfilled it, but mostly I did as I pleased, forcing destiny to bend around me, not me around it. But as always the end result was the same. But as mortal men, we all will die. Many men learn of their destinies, it is just the wise ones that depict which path they will take to get there."

-Lancalion Levendis Lampara-

Chapter Five
And so he shall be bound...

Deep yellow sulfuric clouds raged in a dark black sky that hung over a barren rocky waste. There were no plants, no animals, no water. Just miles and miles of endless jagged onyx rocks and artic cold. This is the deep abyss. A place to house the ultimate evils and the souls they damn. Dark silhouettes of sinister winged creatures dotted the infinite sky and screams of pain and torment occasionally echoed across the barren landscape. Lightning flashed across the sulfuric atmosphere and the black clouds violently rolled and tumbled. The tumultuous scene was highlighted by the silhouette of a single man as he ran barefoot over the jagged terrain. His feet bled profusely and his eyes were wild with terror. The man was completely naked and bore many wounds on his soft pale skin. He was about thirty years old and his oily brown hair bounced stiffly in great greasy strings as he ran. His dirty hair was stiff and frozen and his body was covered in blisters from the abyssal cold, yet he did not have frost bite anywhere. No, in the abyss, nothing would inflict the damned that numbed any pain they might have. The only definite in the Abyss, was pain itself.

The man was well muscled and easily scampered up small rocky embankments, ignoring the ripped skin on his knees and hands from climbing the razor sharp rocks. His eyes watered and his lungs burned from the sulfuric air of the abyss as an occasional bolt of lightning flashed showing a narrow path for the naked man to follow. He had no idea where he was running to, yet he ran. There was no place, really, for him to run. Everywhere he looked there were endless miles of rocky waste that was littered with the foulest beasts and demons the mind could comprehend.

The naked man stumbled and fell face first, sliding on the rough rocks that made up the ground beneath him. Stone debris scattered across the ground making grating noises from his fall. The naked man did not cry out in pain as his soft flesh was torn and cut. Blood ran from his fresh wounds and pooled on the rock-strewn wasteland beneath him. He merely started to get up when his eyes saw three shadowy black twelve inch claws that dug into the hard stone. The claws were attached to a dark red foot that was more reptilian than human. Hard bony scales rose from the bottom of the shin to a knee that had a dark black horn protruding from it.

The man's eyes drifted higher up the beast and fear riddled him. He muttered a half curse half cry at the sight of the fiend that stood before him. The demon had flames that danced and flickered across his massive muscular chest and down his thick arms and legs. His head was shaped like that of a man, but he lacked any hair and deep black goat horns protruded from his head and curved down toward his back. The demon's great bat wings were outstretched behind him. His eyes were set afire with an amber aura that extended horizontally past his thick muscled face that possessed such a penetrating gaze that anyone who met it, cowered in fear. The great demon chuckled as the human hung his head low and cried.

"Where were you going, Trinidy?" the great demon asked as he towered some fifteen feet high over the frail naked man. He did not respond other than uncontrollable weeping.

"Did you think you might escape? You have been

here, oh, say ten mortal years or more. Yet, in your foolishness, you have not learned that there is no escaping my grasp. Your god has abandoned you, paladin. Why else would you be here?" The demon taunted.

"NO!" Trinidy screamed as he leaped up and threw a punch at the demon's abdomen. The demon's mighty hand caught and smothered Trinidy's tiny fist and hoisted him in the air. With one powerful arm, he shifted momentum and sent the naked man head first back into the ground. There was a sickening crack as Trinidy's neck and skull collapsed from the force of the fall. Blood spurted from the fresh wound and splattered across the barren land. Small six legged insect like creatures erupted from the tiny cracks and began feasting on the fresh blood. Trinidy moaned in pain and sat up. He struggled to see out of his eyes as blood and tissue dripped into them. His head hung limp to the side from his broken neck and horrible pain ripped through his body. He tried to ignore it. He had learned that the body cannot be killed, or destroyed in the abyss. His wounds could easily be healed by any lesser demon so they could be re-inflicted again. That was part of the torture they reserved for the damned. Trinidy has seen Panoleen, his son, and everyone he has held dear, come to him and betray him in the abyss. They hated him, mocked him, tortured him, laughed at him, though he knew it was not them at all, but merely demons in disguise trying to hurt him beyond his body, but the champion paladin resisted. The demon's were masters of lies and deceit, he had learned that quickly. Trinidy knew that as long as he held on to who he was, the demons could not break his soul. That was all he had left. If he lost that, there was no path for redemption. The paladin had no idea why the demon Bykalicus had gained control over him when he had died. Trinidy followed and worshipped Dicermadon, the god of magic and knowledge often referred to as the god of gods. He knew he was in good favor with his god at the time of his death, yet he awakened here, in the foulest place in existence. Trinidy imagined it had to be a test from Dicermadon, his god, before he was allowed to ascend with him. Trinidy had stayed true, despite the horrible trials he endured, yet his god never came for him. Trinidy knew that the demons were trying to break him for some reason, trying to crush his spirit. He had seen those that had been broken. They were never healed and often crawled about the abyss missing their lower torso with their entrails dragging behind them, or some were merely heads that were often chewed on by larger demons or kicked about by the smaller ones. They kept him whole for some large plan, he surmised. If he could discover why, he knew he could break free of their control and return to his god.

"Again, tell me where you were to run, mighty paladin?" Bykalicus mocked, knowing that calling the weak helpless Trinidy-mighty, was a great stab at his soul, for the paladin had once been mighty.

"Away, stupid dog, is it not obvious? I was running away." Trinidy retorted through his crushed skull and broken neck.

Bykalicus outstretched his arms and roared such a roar that every demon that was within eyesight fled in terror at the rumble from the abyssal king. The flames that flickered across his body erupted in a jet of violent flames that emitted such a cold that Trinidy could feel his skin freeze and crack right off of his face. Bykalicus shot out his hand, jabbing his clawed finger into Trinidy's chest. The paladin went wide eyed as the demon's finger pierced his body. Bykalicus hoisted the paladin up to inches from his face. Blood dripped from the wound and froze before it hit the stone ground making a tapping sound as the frozen pebbles of blood bounced on the hard gray slate. Trinidy could smell the acrid odor of Bykalicus's breath, despite his crushed skull and broken neck.

"Do you still pray, paladin?" Bykalicus bellowed. Acidic spit from the demon hit Trinidy's face and sizzled the already frozen flesh. The wound in his chest screamed at his mind as he felt his internal organs tear and pull from his body weight hanging against the wound.

"Can your god hear you, fool? Pray to him. I dare you. I will prove once and for all, that he has abandoned you, champion." the demon king taunted.

Trinidy's mind raced. Was he really going to be allowed to pray? Every time he had tried in the past, mind numbing pain ripped through his head, rendering him either too stunned to think, or unconscious. He has tried to pray every day, or at least what resembled days in the cold dark abyss, until he lost count of the time he had been there. And then the forsaken paladin still tried to establish that link with his god with no avail. Every now and then, despite his perpetual failure, Trinidy thought he felt something, perhaps a link or sensation, but he often disregarded it. Thinking he was fooling himself or it had been a demon's trick. He had learned how atrocious there tricks could be.

"Do not mock me, Bykalicus. I will not be tricked. I know you are planning something."

Trinidy struggled to say through the broken neck. The paladin knew that if he had been on the mortal realm, his wounds would have easily killed him, but here, in the abyss, nothing could kill you. Wounds were merely another form of torture.

Bykalicus rocked his head back in a deep bellowing laugh. He folded his thick red arms and peered down at the broken paladin with his intense raging yellow eyes.

"You make me laugh, fool. How long will you be here before you break? You cling to something, some false hope perhaps, that you will be saved. No one will save you. You are mine. If I wish to devour you, it will be done. If I wish to throw you in a deep crevice and allow the gweits feast on you, it will be done. But believe it or not mighty paladin, your god has offered me a hefty sum to speak with you. I had hoped to have you do the disgusting task through prayer, then I could say I lived up to my side of the bargain, and gain his offer. I know not why he has bothered with a fool like you, but alas it has been done. Perhaps you are stronger than I had thought."

Trinidy tried to lift himself upright. The paladin took the demon's compliment as an acknowledgement to his perseverance, lost in the mention of his god. Trinidy failed to recall that in his entire time in the abyss, the demon had never so much offered a word of weakness about himself, let alone offer the paladin a statement telling of his own strength. The demon had done nothing except try to break him down. The paladin's head hung low on his chin and hot sticky blood froze to his naked body as it drained from the ghastly wound in his chest were he had been impaled by the demon king's finger. Behind Bykalicus, Trinidy could see countless shapes of lesser demons looming in the shadows, hungering for him, no doubt smelling his wounds.

"You lie again demon." Trinidy said with a haggard voice. "If my god had a single inclination of my whereabouts, he would come here and smite you and your kind. You would beg him for mercy, but he would not..." Trinidy struggled to speak louder as Bykalicus bellowed in hideous laughter. "...even give you a passing thought as he destroyed you."

"Your god has no power here, fool." Bykalicus mocked. enjoying how well he had baited the hook. The paladin had been a worthy opponent for some time. Bykalicus could only count on his hand the number that had lasted as long as the paladin did before falling prey to his trickeries. But the demon knew that eventually he would. They always did. "If I chose to pull your god apart it would be so. The fool stays where it is safe. He has no real power here."

Rage ripped through Trinidy. He felt no pain, no fear. The mere mention of his god, Dicermadon, had lifted his spirits to unimaginable heights. The lack of despair lifted him and fed his strength. Bykalicus was pleased to see the paladin fighting back. "Pride." the demon king thought to himself. *The fool still has pride.* "Come my pets." Bykalicus said as he waved his hands at the dark shapes that were looming in the shadows around them. "Come and feast on the blood of my slave. He is wrong in his thoughts and must be punished."

Trinidy tried to look around, but his injuries kept him from seeing very well, but he knew he demons were there. He could feel them coming, feel their lust for his flesh. The paladin felt fear, but pushed it aside as he done when he had battled evil in the flesh. " Come on sons of the dark. I will kill the first that approaches. I know you can die here, so come, that I may end the world of your evil."

Bykalicus struggled to keep from a smile. The cowering, fleeing paladin of days past, now stood defiant in the face of a horde of demons while he was naked, weaponless, and broken, yet he decides to battle them. The demon king had spun his web well. The fly lay trapped before him and now it was time to spin him up.

"What in the cursed name of Leska is going on!" Bykalicus roared.

Trinidy felt warm trickles of magic surge through his body. Bright white tendrils of energy whipped around his arms and legs as the gaping hole in his chest closed and the muscles in his neck strengthened, lifting his head upright. The white tendrils heated the air around him forming the metal armor he wore when he walked the earth. The armor was polished and clean, bright like it was the day it was forged. On the chest of the great suit of full plate mail, bore the symbol of the god of magic and knowledge, Dicermadon. Trinidy felt his heavy blue cape dangling down his back and fluttering in the wind. The tendrils twisted and roamed their way down his arm and warmed his hand as they shot out past it, forming a white hot blazing sword that cackled and popped in the frigid air of the abyss. Trinidy's being glowed a blistering white light that forced the horde of demons back and they shielded their eyes and ran away hissing. Though he could not see their faces, Trinidy knew the demons were afraid, he could sense it. Trinidy looked at his feet as he felt the power surge through him. Hundreds of gweits twisted and rolled on the rocky barren ground at his feet in the troughs of death. The tiny abyssal insects, some a foot long, sizzled and smoked in the searing heat of righteousness that beamed from him. The paladin raised his sword in the air and the rammed it into the rocky ground at his feet. The glowing blade sunk into the rocky floor of the abyss as if it had been stuck into soft mud. Trinidy kneeled at the blade. Bykalicus' eyes went wide, then narrowed as a booming voice permeated the abyss.

"Rise, my child. Do not ever touch your knee to the abyss. It is not of the earth and it's taint should only defile your bottom of you boots." the deep booming voice echoed. Bykalicus raised his elbows up as to shield his face from it.

"He is mine, god of gods!" Bykalicus screamed at the dark sulfurous clouds in defiance.

"No, you have stolen him." the voice corrected. "Trinidy, my warrior, my faithful, my son, why have you remained here with the foul company of this lord of deceit. Why have you not called out to me?"

"I have, my lord, but you could not hear me. Every day I cried out to you, but the foul demon's..." Trinidy responded as tears of joy streamed down his face.

"You must release him, Bykalicus, or face my wrath." the voice commanded.

"You have no power here, god of gods. He has been mine for some time, and mine he shall stay. I do not..." Bykalicus clutched his chest and roared in pain. Flashes of dark black erupted from the flames that danced across the demon's dark red skin. The demon lord fell to his knees growling in pain.

"Damn you, Dicermadon! He cannot leave the abyss without my invitation. Rip at my insides forever, he will not accept anything from me." Bykalicus chuckled through clenched teeth.

"Make the offer, demon or I will make good your request for an eternity." the voice boomed.

Bykalicus' chest heaved as he breathed in ragged gasps while he looked Trinidy into his stern steel eyes. "I offer you to return to the mortal realm, *paladin*. To right that which is wrong, but pray your god does not forget you again. My god hungers for your eternal soul." Bykalicus said as he spit at the feet of the paladin. The spittle sizzled and burned the rocks it lay on.

"Quiet dog!" the voice screamed. You shall never inflict your tainted voice to his ears again, and if you or yours ever again take one of mine, I shall come here with my angels and destroy this cursed place."

"I accept your offer, beast." Trinidy said as he straightened his shoulders.

"Dnuob eb llahs uoy os dna." Bykalicus said with an evil grin as he rose to his feet.

The armor Trinidy wore turned black and shriveled into sable wisps of impermeable tendrils that swirled around him. Terror tore through Trinidy as he tried to shake the black snake like tendrils from his arms and legs, but the spindly wisps whipped around ducking and weaving as they were alive. He felt the horrible cold burn his bare skin and his lungs burned from the sulfuric air again as his sword and armor melted away and left him naked before the demon lord. Trinidy stumbled to the jagged rocks and looked at his bare arms and legs where his magnificent armor was a few moments earlier. The paladin gazed up from his hands and knees at the mocking demonic face that stood before him. Then suddenly he felt himself breaking apart. His skin bubbled and tore, tumbling away into a thousand tiny black pebbles. The abyss melted away from his eyes and he was warm again.

Trinidy could see the barren landscape as it fell under him and he rose to the air. He could see the ever shrinking demon as he gazed upward toward him. Trinidy's fear evaporated as he felt himself leaving the abyss.

"Thank you." he prayed to Dicermadon as the abyss fell away into nothingness and was replaced by calm darkness. "Thank you."

*   *   *

Hector walked determinedly down the polished marble corridor of his dark expansive castle. His thick blue velvet cloak flowed in the breeze from his resolute walk as the leather under his heavy metal plate armor creaked as he walked. The halls of the corridor were littered with great tapestries that hung from golden rods that were affixed to the tops of the stone wall. Servants and guardsmen dropped whatever they were doing and fell to their hands and knees as he walked by. If Hector noticed them, he didn't show it. The evil king wore a grim visage of determination and vigor. His priests had summoned him in his chambers and Kalen had surprisingly discovered the name of the child in the prophecies and located him in Beykla. The gray elf still wasn't sure who the mother of mercy was, but he was rapidly narrowing it down. It seemed whenever the elven mage was certain he had discovered the identity of the woman, the priest would point out a discrepancy and they were back to the beginning. Hector hoped the dark priests had discovered something instead of the same report he had received in the past few weeks. The king was ready to begin executions for failure, but he didn't want to kill any of the priests. Not because he held any attachment to them, but because they were quite useful and it would take a long time to replace any of them. If they had nothing of value to report he might just execute a servant or something. Spencer had been lagging in his duties.

Perhaps he would slay the pitiful wretch.

Hector rounded the corner of the corridor and paused at the ornate double doors to the church of Rha-Cordan that was inside of his great castle. The flamboyant doors to the god of death's house were made of thick oak, that was varnished to the point of being black and they were re-enforced with huge iron plates that stretched across them horizontally. At the end of the plates, where the doors met each other, two huge iron rings hung down that were used to pull the doors open. Two royal guards stood watch in front of the church and they were garbed in the deep black chain mail and leather tunics and breeches that bore Rha-Cordan's symbol, not the symbol of Nalir. The guards were tall and thin, wielding long bec-de-corbans, a long pole arm with a spear tip and a hook on one side that resembled a small axe, that they crossed in front of each other to prohibit the passing of unintended guests. Hector paused as the guards slowly and ceremonially lifted the weapons to a vertical position. They did not drop to their knees or even bow. The king did not expect them to. He had learned long ago they considered their god their only king, and the Hector was merely their employer. Hector tolerated them as he often tolerated the church. A small means to get to his ends. He knew he could have them executed at any time he wished. He was sure they knew that fact too, but they were devoted to their beliefs. Hector found that trait almost admirable, but he believed it more foolish than anything.

Hector tossed the edges of his blue velvety cloak over his shoulders and pushed the two great wooden doors open and walked inside to the worship chamber. The chamber was about ninety feet long and forty feet wide. The walls were covered in dark tapestries depicting the god of death sitting on a throne of bones and in a few other positions. There were many candles sitting on ledges at each thick wooden beam that lined the walls. The beams were fifty feet high that led to a circular dome in the center of the room. The dome was covered in divine symbols and carvings made of gold and other precious metals. At the far end of the chamber four priests, including Resin Darkhand, the high priest, and Kalen, sat in chairs at a small table that had been placed in front of the alter for this apparent meeting. When Hector strode forward, they all stood and bowed deeply. Resin started to speak but Hector cut him off.

" Be quick with this report. The body of the Ecnal's father has been located in a mass grave near the Nalir-Vidorian border. We have over four hundred skeletal remains to search through and I need you priests to go speak with the departed souls and find which bones belong to who." Hector demanded coldly.

"My master..." Kalen began with an exaggerated bow and deep sinister smile. "...we have much to..." again Hector cut in. "I care not for what you have to say to me, fool elf. You have my manservant, Spencer, so rattled his heart is not into living most of the time. I will deal with your torture tactics after this meeting is adjourned." Hector said with an evil glare.

Kalen merely smiled and bowed as he whispered to himself. "I grow weary of you, master. Soon you will be old and feeble. I shall teach you then, the cusps of my torture tactics." Kalen whispered to himself.

"What do you have to report, Resin?" Hector asked.

Resin straightened his robes nervously. "We have discovered much once we began to study with apprentice Kalen."

Hector raised an eye at his elf apprentice. The gray elf merely smiled and nodded his head submissively. "Go on." Hector commanded.

"We found the DeNaucght that the demon spoke of. It is not a ritual that we can perform. In fact, it is a ritual that angers Rha-Cordan more than commanding the undead to rise and walk from their graves. The DeNaucght is a ritualistic spell that requires three powerful goodly priests in order to cast it. It will summon the soul back to the body it came from and allow the person to live again as though he never died. If it is cast on a child, he will awake as the child he was when he died. If it is cast on a old man that was on his death bed, he will awake as the same old man, and would surely die again soon. We know not what the demon meant, but surely we could not use Rha-Cordan's divinity on such a spell. It would surely not function as it was intended to." Resin stated flatly.

    Hector frowned and rubbed his chin. " Perhaps the demon knows that it will not function the same."

    "We had anticipated that, my lord, but we searched through every archive from every priests in the nation and we found nothing ever mentioning the ritual being performed by priests of our order." Resin offered.

    Hector sat down in the soft plush chair that was placed at the head of the small table.

    "You heal sometimes Resin, but is that not against the order." Hector asked.

    "Yes, but if it is to further the goals of our god, it is overlooked." the dark priest responded.

    "Good, it is settled. Their is no other kingdom in the realms that has followed and maintained the principles of the god of death, than Nalir under my rule. You and your priest will perform DeNaucght as soon as we sort out the skeletal remains. Surely you cannot argue that furthering the kingdom goes against the wishes of Rha-Cordan." Hector asked.

    "We cannot argue it at all, my king. Your rule is a bright beacon in the eyes of Rha-Cordan, but there is information that Kalen needs to speak of that relate to the prophecy and the Ecnal." Resin said.

    Hector looked at the thin gray elf in his blue robes and long silver hair. "What do you have to say, elf?" Hector asked angrily.

    "There are two other pages to the prophecy that we

have not been able to decipher yet, and will probably not be able to in many years to come, but there are four semi prophetic passages of elven culture that coincide with the prophesies themselves." Kalen said.

Hector didn't reply. He just folded his arms impatiently at the priests and opened an ink bottle while unrolling a parchment to scribe the words the elf spoke.

"The son of a Vale, not by blood, will turn his back on his brethren and embrace the shadow. I believe that passing refers to me. The self righteous elven culture believes that

Rha-Cordan is evil. As you know I was the step son of King Christopher Calamon Overmoon for a short time. That would make me son a Vale, but not by blood."

"What is a Vale, and what does it have to do with the Ecnal?" Hector asked impatiently.

"The Ecnal you seek is also known as the Abyss Walker in elven prophecy. He is foretold to bring plagues and other horrific things to the world. A Vale is a great elven city, but elven cities are hidden among the trees insomuch that if you walked in one, you would not even know you were there. These passages refer to Ecnal, which also is the son of the mother of mercy." Kalen explained.

"Go on with the other three." Hector commanded.

"A babe, half not of this earth, and half damned by the gods themselves, feared by the children of the forest, will carry his own proclamation naming him for who he is not, but for who he will become."

"What in Rha's underworld does that mean?" Hector asked angrily.

Kalen shrugged his shoulders. "It makes no sense as far as we are concerned, but I would suspect it will be meaningful to the Vales."

"Perhaps it has something to do with giving himself a title." Resin chided in.

"Perhaps. What are the others?" Hector asked.

"He who walks with wrath, shall stride into the vale as a guest wearing the Cadacka, though he knows not why he mourns. If the children of the forest do nothing, they will surely perish." Kalen recited slowly.

"Another one that means nothing to us. What is a Cadacka?" Hector asked.

Kalen frowned impatiently. "It is a cloak worn by those who are in mourning."

Hector merely made a puzzled look and shook his head as Kalen recited the fourth passing.

"I do not know the fourth passing Hec..." Kalen corrected himself. "...King De Scoran. But I have agents working on getting it as we speak. These are elven secrets that are guarded more heavily than an arch-mage's tower. But fear not, my king, I will learn them."

"Believe me elf, It is not I who should fear your failure." Hector threatened then turned to the priests. "Do you have anything else?"

"Yes, my king. We believe the Ecnal's father's name is Trinidy. You had the family ordered murdered for worshipping another god other than Rha-Cordan. He was a paladin of the great god Dicermadon. His wife's name was Panoleen, but she did not worship Dicermadon. She was slain for blasphemy. The records show she spoke of a goddess of mercy." Resin said as he dabbed the sweat on his forehead with the sleeve of his robe.

"Why is his mother's name important? Was she some kind of merciful person, or is the Ecnal the mercy one?" Hector asked.

Resin shrugged his shoulders. "I do not know, my king, but I suspect that because the Ecnal's mother worshiped this false goddess, she might be the mother of mercy."

Hector sat up in his chair. "Is their a goddess of mercy?" Hector asked.

"If there is, I know not of it." Resin admitted.

Hector turned and looked at Kalen. Kalen shrugged

his shoulders. "I have never read anything that refers to a goddess of mercy, but there are passages in the elven scrolls that refer to a forgotten goddess, and in the ancient scrolls there are missing sentences and some even half pages that seemed as they were magically erased somehow. It could be that these missing areas contained information about her. I do not understand how the same passages could have been erased world wide, but they are in every ancient scroll that I have read." Kalen chided. " What is the most surprising, is that many scrolls I memorized word for word, have changed."

"Changed? How?" Hector asked inquisitively.

Kalen shrugged. "I do not know, but the name Panoleen just recently re-appeared. Still massive amounts of information are missing, but now the name Panoleen seems to be quite predominate, when before, it did not exist."

"No matter." Hector said as he stood up from the small table in the chamber room. "I will take my leave. Praise to you for your efforts. We shall be rewarded. I will have the excavators deliver the bones from the grave here. I want them sorted out as soon as they arrive. Be diligent, priests. Do not incur my wrath."

"We will complete your task as soon as possible in Rha-Cordan's name." Resin said to Hector's back as the king walked from the chamber room.

"Be mindful of your loyalties, priests ." Kalen said as he rose from his chair when Hector had left the room. "You might be surprised when they might be called upon."

Resin and the others looked at each other in confusion, but did not respond. It was no secret among the clergy that Kalen held no love for the king. But neither did they, save for he demanded the masses to embrace the will of their God. That was the only loyalty they would acknowledge. The only loyalty that mattered.

*   *   *

    Large wisps of dust and dirt blew like tiny storms across the barren plains. Gentle rolling hills of brown grass that were almost as high as a man, littered the ground like small patches on a pair of breeches. There were little or no trees, save for an occasional bush that had grown large enough to provide shade. Had it been summer, the plains would have been unbearably hot, but now with the embrace of autumn in full swing, the cool breeze was a friendly kiss under the hot sun. The land hadn't see rain in weeks, but so was the way with the Serrin plains. It rained seldom here, though no one knew why. Some said it was a curse from the gods, others claimed it had something to do with the wind currents from the Balfour sea, north of Beykla. Regardless, the plains were intolerably hot in the summer and endurable in the fall and spring. In the winter, the snows would all but seal off the road from the great drifts that would rise from the never ending winds. But now, in early autumn, small animals scampered around in the safe grass and some zipped across the trail. The horses were spooked at the tiny animals always darting in front of them, but after the second day, they seemed to accept the furry little monsters as harmless, though they still would tense when one scampered across.
    Lance enjoyed the slow paced ride. They had been on the trail for nearly a week. The paladin was paying them each day at nightfall and the elf did all the hunting. The Ecnal had studied his spells every night before he had went to bed inside his small one man tent that Apollisian had provided for Jude and him. Jude had declined to use his, saying that a tent kept him from seeing his enemies and allowed them to see him easily. But Lance had enjoyed the seclusion from the prying eyes. After the first week, Lance had just about learned every spell in the Necromidus. The collection of necromancy spells were

complex at first, but the basis for all of the spells were the same. After Lance had worked out the first few, he had learned the pattern to the others and mastered the book in no time. Lance shuddered at some of the descriptions of the spells and what weaving certain patterns did. Most of the dweamors resulted in the painful death of the target, and a few worse, ripped at the enemies souls. There was a spell that caused nearby dead creatures to rise up and walk on the command of the caster. Why anyone would want to make the dead walk was beyond him. There was even one that allowed the caster to drain the life force of the victim and heal his own wounds from that energy. That was the closest to a healing spell that was in the book.

They rode for most of the day and made camp on a small hill at the base of a much larger one that was a few hundred feet from the trail. Apollisian and Jude began digging a fire pit and Lance would set up his tent and tend to the horses while Alexis grabbed her bow and went on a hunt. Once the fire was set and the horse were attended to, they mulled around the camp while their supper cooked.

Lance sat around the camp fire on the cool autumn night. He held his cloak tightly around him and scooted his feet close to the fire. The once cool breeze that blew by, had turned into a cold wind that chilled the young mage to the bone. Alexis had done well in hunting and the smell of the cooking rabbit made Lance's stomach growl. Apollisian sat on a log away from the fire with Jude. The pair had seldom talked, but they sharpened their swords at the same time each night. Alexis always asked Lance a lot questions, mostly about his parents and where he was from, but she always stayed far away when she spoke. If Lance tried to come closer, she would get quiet and look away. Lance had asked her similar questions and learned a great deal about her culture in doing so.

Alexis sat down on a small rock that was next to the fire and warmed her hands and feet, occasionally turning the rabbit that roasted on the fire. She seemed distant tonight and often glanced into the darkness as if she were expecting something to emerge from it and attack them.

"You expecting company?" Lance asked sarcastically as he rubbed his socked feet together near the fire.

Alexis looked around again, as if Lance had reminded her that something was out there. After a short look, she turned back to him and stared at the ground when she spoke. She seemed to always stare at the ground. " We are in the Serrin plains. There are many creatures that call this place home. Many of which do not take kindly to trespassers, and others that like trespassers, thinking they taste good. Either way, if we meet some of them, it will not be a pleasant encounter."

Lance looked around himself nervously, suddenly more aware of the dark than he had been a few moments before. "Like what kind of creatures? Like orcs?"

Alexis turned the rabbit again and stirred the fire with a small stick. Bright burning pieces of ash erupted into the air and rose above he fire, burning out after rising a few feet. "There are a few orc tribes that live in here. The plains are vast, but they stay away from the trails and live in seclusion for the most part. Our main concern are the hill giants."

Lance blinked in astonishment. In Bureland, long before Lance had come to live there, a hill giant attacked the town. The townsfolk said it killed twenty militiamen and ten royal guardsmen before it died. It is said that it's club is the main beam that holds up the roof in the Aldon inn. Lance had often rubbed the gnarled beam, doubting the stories, thinking drunkards had concocted it to attract patrons. Lance tried to imagine what a hill giant looked like, and how a man could even fight a beast like that.

"How do they live?" Lance asked. Alexis gave him a puzzled look. Lance frowned. "I mean, what do they eat? There aren't many game animals in the plains, and I don't think they could live off of rabbits and squirrels."

Alexis smiled nervously. "Why, they eat travelers like us, orcs, whatever they can get their hands on. Sometimes, they probably eat each other."

Lance felt queasy at the thought of being eaten and his own hunger subsided a little.

"Shouldn't we put out he fire or something like that?" Lance asked as he looked out into the darkness again.

"No, they do not hunt at night. Their vision is too poor to compete with the animals so they only hunt during the day."

Lance nodded his head and curled up by the fire. Alexis got up and took the rabbit down and cut it into four pieces. She handed Apollisian and Jude a piece and then walked over and handed Lance one. As soon as Lance took the meat from her hand, she reached back quickly and sat down on the other side of the fire. Lance shrugged his shoulders and ate the juicy meat. It was not seasoned like he was accustomed too, but it was cooked on an open fire, which always seemed to make the meat taste better to him. His adoptive father often cooked out on an open fire with him when he was a boy. As he ate, Lance wondered if the letter he wrote Davohn had gotten to him yet. He hated to make the woodcutter worry, but he knew he had to investigate his parent's deaths. It was if something pulled at him to do it.

Lance finished the rabbit and tossed the bones in the fire. He licked the greasy juice from his fingers and laid back on the ground folding his hands behind his head. He gazed at the thousands of stars and wondered if Davohn were on his roof top star gazing like he used to do.

"Where did you get your robe?" Alexis asked bluntly as she chewed. Lance looked down and grabbed the front of his black and silver robe.

"What? This?" Lance asked pointing to his chest. "My mother gave it to me when I was very young. She said I should wear it when I got older. She said it would save my life. I never really gave it much thought. I kept it in a pack that was stored in a chest on the back porch of our home. When the men came and murdered my parents, I grabbed it when I fled. I didn't remember it was in there, I just kept a knife and some other stuff I had as a boy. It is a strange robe, I have never seen one like it before. I think some of these symbols are elven, I am not sure."

  Alexis stared at the black and silver Cadacka. She felt her cheeks flush with anger, though she held it in, trying to keep her tone soft. " Why do you think the runes are elven?" she asked, knowing the runes were indeed elven, though she could not read them. She had studied a few scripts in the ancients writing, but she had no idea what the complex symbols on Lance's Cadacka meant. Usually runes were designed for each individual, telling the story of why they mourn.

  Lance sat up and shrugged his slender shoulders. "I don't really know, I have these writings that I thought were Nalirian, but a sage told me they were elven. Some of the markings on my robe are the same as the ones in the parchments."

  Alexis eye's lit up and she scooted closer to Lance, though still keeping a safe distance. "You mean you have some elven writing?" she asked hoping it would shed some light on why the human was wearing a Cadacka that he knew nothing about. Perhaps his mother was the thief, or his father. Regardless, Alexis figured the explanation was in those papers. "Perhaps I could see them, maybe read them for you?" she asked with a wry smile that put Lance on edge. Lance indeed wanted the pages read for him. Kaisha, was supposed to read them, but she was a long way away. Lance reluctantly reached for his pack and pulled out the leather pouch. He stared at it uneasily for a few seconds. It was in good order, though a little dusty from the trail. It was as if he almost feared what it might say. He had grown accustomed to not knowing what it said, and now, when faced with the chance to know, he had second thoughts.

"Perhaps we should read it another time. It is late and..." Lance was cut off when Alexis reached over and snatched the case from his hands. He surprised himself when he did not try to stop her.

Jude walked over with a piece of the rabbit in his mouth. He was trying to eat every small morsel of meat from its bones. His hands shined in the fire light with grease and his face glistened also. He studied the portion for a few moments and decided there was nothing left worth picking at and tossed the bones into the fire. He wiped his mouth with his sleeve and glanced down at the elf opening the parchment. The large swordsman quickly glanced at Lance and then back to the parchment. His friend did not look to be upset so he sat down and crossed his legs in the dirt.

"She's gonna read it for you, huh?" Jude asked as he licked his fingers clean.

Lance nodded nervously. Alexis didn't seem to notice the big man's presence, she was intent on the package. With nimble fingers she drew the parchments out from the case and stared at them. She said nothing, only stared stunned at the pages.

Apollisian came over with a piece of his plate armor in his hand and a polishing rag.

"What's so interesting?" Apollisian asked.

Jude leaned over and whispered softly. " The elf is going to read some papers that my friend has been trying to understand for a long time. Those parchments are the whole reason that we left our happy little town on this fool adventure."

Apollisian backed away a few steps and whispered back to Jude. He covered his mouth with his hand in attempt to muffle his voice. " What is so special about them? Do they explain his cloak"

Jude frowned in puzzlement. "His cloak? No, he

hired a thief a while back to steal these papers from a politician in Nalir."

Apollisian's eyes arched up at the mention of thievery. "He hired a thief, huh? Why would he do that?"

"Because he thinks the Nalirian government had his parents killed. He hoped the papers were some kind of murder order or something like that, but it turns out that they are written in elven. A very strange turn of events I must say." Jude said. "Why did you ask about his cloak. He has had that since he was a boy. I assure you it is not stolen. He says his mother left it for him."

Apollisian shifted his feet. "The runes on the cloak and the colors are very similar to an elven robe of ceremony. Overmoon thinks that it means something."

"Like what?" Jude asked, looking back at the elf reading sitting on the small rock. Apollisian shrugged his shoulders and continued to polish his armor.

"Beats me. Some silly elven thing, they are fickle creatures." Apollisian said as he wondered back over to his horse.

Jude stood and watched for a moment longer then returned to his new friend to sharpen their swords. Jude liked the paladin. He didn't agree with they way the paladin solved his problems. It seemed as if the man made them more difficult than they actually were, but Jude could tell he was a good man nonetheless.

Alexis examined each parchment carefully. "I cannot make much of these out." she said with a defeated tone. "They are in elven, but the text is so old I cannot understand it. I know of a few village elders that might be able to read this. I know my father can."

Lance sighed and slumped his shoulders. "Do you think they mention my mother's or father's name? My mother is Panoleen and my father is Trinidy."

Alexis shook her head. "There are not special symbols for names, they are written the same as if they were in present day writings. I am sorry, but I see nothing that mentions any names."

Lance moaned and got up from the fire and gradually wandered to his tent. Alexis watched as he slowly climbed inside and laid down. She stood looking at the writings confused. Shaking her head she placed them back into the leather case and then put them in her pack.

"We are turning in, Overmoon. You still want first watch?" Apollisian asked.

She nodded back and drew her finely crafted bow. Notching a bright white arrow with the green fletching, she headed up the base of the large hill. She moved silently as the wind, not even rustling the tall brown grass, and quickly ascended the small peak. With the moon bright in the sky, she could watch the camp and the surrounding areas much better than on other nights. Apollisian climbed into his bedroll and Jude sat up a while longer sharpening his sword, then he too, turned in an drifted to sleep. Alexis sat on the hilltop listening to the sounds of the night. Crickets chirped their songs and an occasional wolf howled at the moon in the distance. She smiled to herself and thanked Leska for the beautiful night. She had spent enough time in the human cities to last her a lifetime. She was finally going home.

* * *

"My Guidance..." the acolyte said as he bowed low to Resin. The high priest looked up from the edge of the great book. His deep violet robe hung over his face and his dark sinister eyes peered from under the hood and just above the ancient tome.

"Yes, Pockweln? What is it. I hope it is important."

Pockweln dipped low, his blonde hair fell down over his eyes and he quickly wiped it away. "We have discovered what bones are Trinidy's. We did as the DeNaucght requires and set his agreement for resurrection."

Resin stared at the young priest for a few moments before answering. "I suspect that you did as I commanded and disguise yourself as his god?"

Pockweln nodded. "He did as you said he would, and their was another voice, we could not drown it out, or prevent it's speech. It was as if he had more power than we did combined. We tried many times to silence him, but we could not, though he didn't interfere. It almost seemed as if he helped in someway. There were things happening that we could not see. I could tell from the fluctuations in the paladin's voice."

"There was much going on that you could see, my apprentice. You could not silence the voice in a hundred years. It has more power than you ever will. Even I could not muffle him, even if I studied for ten lifetimes." Resin said flatly as he glanced back down at the pages of the tome he had been reading. "I had made an arrangement with Bykalicus that need not be discussed. You and the others did not hear his voice, nor was he present. Do I make myself clear?"

Pockweln visibly stiffened at the mention of the arch demon. "My mentor, I hope you have the power of Lukerey with you when you make such deals with the denizens of the deep abyss."

Resin chuckled to himself at the mention of the god of luck and mischief, but did not look up from his reading. "My faithful apprentice, I do need his power on my side, though using caution is an understatement when dealing with his kind. A wise man understands that luck is when preparedness meets opportunity. And my good apprentice, I am very opportunistic." the high priest said, as his thick tome hid his wide grin. "Was there any thing else to report?"

"Only one other, my mentor. There is one set of remains that gives us difficulty. They are from a female, human we suspect, but we are unable to make contact with the soul."

Resin arched an eyebrow and set down the tome. He did not expect that response. He rubbed his chin and stepped away from the dark polished podium. " What do you mean, you can't make contact with the soul. No soul is forbidden to Rha-Cordan when the body is possessed. Are you merely weary? Perhaps you should try in the morrow." Resin suggested as he walked over to a small table that was set against the wall. The high priest opened a flask of fine red wine and poured it into a silver goblet. The red fluid sloshed up around the brim and the dark priest slowed his pouring when the goblet filled. He raised the silver chalice to his lips and sipped.

"High priest. I know that I, and the others, are not weary. It is as if the remains have no soul. Is it possible for a soul to be destroyed?" Pockweln asked.

Resin took a long sip and placed the goblet back down onto the table. The sound of the hard silver hitting the wooden table seemed to echo in the high priest's chamber. "No, it is not possible. Take me to the bones and I shall see for myself. For your sake, I hope that there is something prohibiting the casting, for if it is your ineptness, you shall be punished."

Pockweln bowed and led Resin to the large examination room. If the young priest had fear, he did not show it, though that was the way of their order. They did not fear death. They knew that in their demise, they would be rewarded by Rha-Cordan, and he would shelter them from the dark abyss. They believed that no other deity had the power to control the after life like he did. And in truth, they were somewhat correct.

The priests walked into the bone chamber. The room was over a hundred by a hundred feet and there were many large tables that were littered with bones and small parchments with names and other material written on them. Pockweln led Resin to a small table in the back that contained a single set of female remains. The skeleton was not complete, but the skull and most of the torso was intact. Resin took down his robe's hood and began chanting. He began with rhythmic movements of his hands and his aging voice rose and fell in a methodic tune that seemed to enchant and inspire. Weaves of wispy black magical energies swirled around the dark priest's old knobby hands and fell around the remains that laid on the table. Resin moved his arms as if in a dance, dipping and twisting around in front of him, while he softly chanted the words of his spell. The aging priest's voice was harsh, but not yet raspy. He had somewhat of an angry expression on his face that poked out from under his long hair. His acolytes had been ordered to cast a few simple spells that allowed them to speak with the souls that had once belonged to the bones. After a few weeks they had identified all but this last set. They appeared to belong to a young woman, perhaps Trinidy's wife. Her name was Panoleen. Such an unusual name. Resin doubted he had ever heard the name in his entire life, or any other with it. His acolytes had difficulty speaking to her soul from beyond the grave. It was a relatively easy task. He surmised that perhaps they were tired from the taxing duties of summoning all the other souls.

 The high priest finished his casting, but nothing happened. Resin frowned in frustration. He knew he had performed the spell correctly, yet he did not even sense the soul that belonged to the bones, let alone make contact for speech. He took a deep breath and exhaled slowly. Rubbing the beads of sweat from his creased forehead, he began chanting again. The sable cusps of magical energy whipped around him, just like before. His voice was louder, more focused, more angry, yet after a few minutes of focused casting, he achieved nothing. Anger flashed in the composed priest's eyes. He looked down at the remains that laid out before him. The bones were indeed real. They had not been fabricated, or cast. Yet he could not summon the soul that once dwelled within them.

 Pockweln adjusted the front of his smock, and

wiped his greasy hair back from his face. "Did you make contact, my savior?" the young priest asked.

Resin seemed not to notice being called savior. It was the highest accolade to give to a leader of the church that followed the god of death. To be called savior meant that the person was responsible for saving their soul and that without him or her, they would have been lost. Yet the praise fell on deaf ears. "Get out!" Resin shouted as he hastily removed his dark violet robes and tossed it on the table that was next to him. The high priest didn't even look to his acolytes as they bowed and started for the door. Resin wiped the sweat from his forehead and began chanting a third time. Pockweln motioned to the others and they quickly departed the room. When he heard the heavy door shut, Resin took a deep breath and began casting a third time. Refusing to accept the possibility that the carcass had no soul. Even those who sold their souls to the gods, could be summoned from their remains, yet this set of bones denied him.

He tried again and again, each time he failed. A small candle was lit and set on the edge of the old table. Sweat ran down the side of his face and down his back. His violet robes had long since been removed and laid on the table crumpled in a ball. He had the sleeves of his white silt tunic that he wore underneath rolled up to his elbows and unbuttoned to the bottom of his chest. Resin placed his hands on the edge of table and leaned over the bones. Sweat dripped from his chin and he breathed heavily. The high priest stared at the remains and the lifeless skull stared back, mocking him. Resin grabbed the dark brown cranium with both of his hands and drew it near his face. His hands shook with anger and his eyes flared with fury. "How do you deny me!" he shouted, his voice echoing across the large chamber. The skull only stared back in silence. Shaking his head, Resin placed the skull gently back down on the table and sat back in one of the many hard wooden chairs. He picked up a plain wooden goblet and waved his hand over the top. With a brief chant, the goblet filled with sparkling clear water that was chilled as if it ran from a mountain stream. Resin gulped the refreshing water down and wiped his mouth, letting his weary head fall back against the stone wall. The high priest rolled his head to one side, facing the chamber door when he heard it creak open. He started to protest in anger, thinking one of his acolytes had entered the chamber without his permission, but his anger subsided when he watched the nimble gray elf, known as Kalen, stroll in.

Kalen turned and slowly shut the door, careful not to make too much noise. He was dressed in a dark gray sleeping tunic and baggy brown breeches. His silver hair was tidy and pulled back against his head. His brown furred slippers glided across the stone floor of the chamber. Resin watched as he approached. Kalen scooted some of the bones over on the table that was next to Resin and hopped up, sitting while his feet dangled off.

"Having some difficulties, priest?" Kalen asked with an evil grin. Resin turned and regarded the mage. His face bore a sinister look that made Kalen lean back slightly.

" I am not in the mood, mage, for you, or for yours. I am trying a task that you could never perform." Resin said as he stood up stretching and leaned back against the cold stone wall.

Kalen regarded the haggard priest with mild amusement. A thin wry smile crept on the gray elf's face. He sat on the small wooden table with an air of pompous authority that enraged the dark priest to near violence. If Kalen noticed the priest's angry glare, he ignored it. " Why is it so important to speak with these remains? We have Trinidy. That is what is important. In the morning you will perform the DeNaucght, just as the king wishes and all will be well. You can return to this chamber and question the bones till you wither and die." Kalen said with a mocking tone.

Resin shot forward and pointed his finger a few inches from Kalen's face. "I will perform that in which is necessary to further the need of Rha-Cordan. I will do nothing more. I am no puppet that dances on the strings of some king!" Resin shouted angrily.

Kalen smiled, ignoring the shaking finger that was a few inches from his face. Resin had become angry before, but Kalen knew the human priest was more than intimidated by his power. Kalen feigned a mock yawn and slowly patted the palm of his hand over his mouth. "So you say, priest. I need not see the wind to know it blows, and I need not see the strings that make you dance like an adolescent jester, to know they are being pulled."

Resin backed away and flexed his fists. He glanced around the room and took a deep breath before turning back to the gray elf that sat before him. "You will not weave me in your webs, Kalen. It is no mystery that you knit plots and schemes better than a jealous mistress."

Kalen did not lose his smile, though his face flushed with anger at Resin's comparison between him and a woman. The gray elf paused to regain his composure when Resin cut him off.

"Now, mage, you will leave my chambers immediately for I am finished with this verbal tirade. If you do not, I shall bring the wrath of Rha-Cordan down upon you." Resin commanded.

Kalen glanced around the room involuntarily, making frequent looks to the ceiling as if the priests were going to make good his claim. Kalen hopped down from the table and walked toward the door timidly, half expecting the priest to retaliate in some fashion, yet he reached the ornate wooden door without any incident. The gray elf turned and spoke to Resin before he ducked out the chamber door. "Know your place, priest. You never know when the toes you stomp today, will be connected to the ass you will kiss tomorrow." Kalen said wryly as he turned and confidently walked from the chamber. There was no stir of air in the stale room, but his robe seemed to flow around him when he walked as if his own private breeze seemed to follow him about.

Resin wanted to reply, to fire a few parting remarks, but by the time any had come to his mind, the gray elf had left. The priest jabbed his fist into his hand. Kalen was the one that needed to know his place. He was merely a foolish mage, caught in an epic plight that involved the very gods themselves. Resin didn't know how deep this plight ran, but the more he learned of it, the more he decided that the King was in over his head. There was something much deeper here than was let on.

Resin straightened the bones that Kalen had scooted aside and prepped them for yet another spell. He would not try casting it tonight. He was exhausted from the many previous attempts and he didn't know of anything to do differently than he had already tried. Resin sat alone in the chamber for many minutes in the darkness staring at the remains. It confounded him how these bones resisted his attempts. Never in his life had he even heard of that happening, let alone experience it himself. Yet there they lay before him on the old wooden table, mocking him. The dark priest slowly shook his head, pulled his robe close around his neck, and casually walked from the room. The morrow was certainly going to be interesting.

Kalen strode down the dark marbled corridors of Hector's dark sinister keep. There were a few sconces aflame, but the mounted torches bore little light as they were close to being burned out. The long dark velvety tapestries that hung down from the polished stone walls seemed to stare down eerily at the gray elf as he strolled by. Kalen ignored the thick hanging rugs he had walked by them thousands of times. He casually turned down a south corridor that was lit even more dimly than the one he just walked down. He walked slowly, scooting his furred slippers across the marbled floor, alerting the two guards that he was approaching. He could easily see the two humans that stood watch outside the king's sleeping chambers. They were large for humans, and were no doubt accomplished fighters. They wore polished plate mail armor and long blue silk capes. There gauntleted hands gripped their halberds tightly as they stood in full attention straining their inferior eyes to catch a glimpse of the man who was scuffing his feet, but they could not see the gray elf. Kalen chuckled to himself at how deplorable humans were. They could not even see in the dark. He could have been an assassin and the pitiful whelps would not even know he had been there until he gutted them both.

  The guards relaxed their stern glares when they recognized the gray elf. They said nothing to Kalen, it was not uncommon for him to call on the king at late hours. The pair stood rigidly and raised their halberds up in a saluting position and stepped to the side to allow the elf entry. Kalen shook his head in disappointment. He could have been a rival mage magically disguised or some clever thief. The stupid oafs would never know until they found their king dead in the morning. Kalen silently made a mental note of their lack of attention to detail, hoping it would come to use in the future.

  The gray elf stepped through the thick wooden double doors and entered the room. It was a massive room, but small in comparisons to the other chambers that the king often held. The ceilings were almost twenty feet tall, and tapestries and ornate carvings and statues littered the room. Large green plants from strange lands sat on thick marbled stands and the king lay on the bed, propped up by thick pillows, reading some parchments. The bed was made of thick wood from the Vidorian forest. It was covered with silk sheets and the plethora of silk and satin pillows that seemed to engulf him. He placed the parchments aside and took a sip of wine from a jeweled chalice. He gulped down several large swallows and set the cup back down on the bed tray with a resounding clink.

"Kalen, what pleasure do I have with this meeting? It has been a busy week, has it not?" Hector asked sitting up in the bed and shifting his feet so that they hung from the side of the bed.

Kalen bowed low. His long sliver hair, that was combed back behind his narrow head, tumbled down in front of him. The gray elf raised his chin and forced his lengthy thin silver hair behind his long narrow ears with his delicate fingers. "It has, my lord, it has. We are very close to creating a being of power to hunt out this Ecnal and eradicate him like a mouse in a burrow. Soon, he shall trouble you no longer." the gray elf said with a evil tone.

Hector got up from the bed and stretched. He was getting older and the long days performing the duties as a king seemed to become more and more taxing. He rubbed his sore shoulder muscles and walked over to a large, ornate oaken dresser. "I agree, soon the orphan will be no more, but is he really the son of the mother of mercy? We have used a lot of resources and time, I hate to waste them on some boy that is of no use to me." Hector said as he removed his tunic and placed it on the top of the desk. He glanced down at his own arms and looked at his reflection in the mirror. His once powerful body was withering with age. Though still muscular, his skin sagged and his muscles had weakened. What a waste, Hector thought to himself. For a man to work so hard and to achieve so much, to loose it all in death.

Kalen leaned against the bed and folded his arms. "My king, I assure you that the Ecnal is the son of the mother of mercy. The fact she worshiped a goddess of mercy is proof alone. If we...you, slay him, you will void the prophecy against you and ensure the propagation of our kingdom."

Hector removed his breeches and tossed them on top of the dresser. He opened the bottom drawer and removed a silk sleeping suit and unfolded it. Carefully placing the soft tunic and breeches on, he turned and regarded the elf. "What are your stakes, elf? Surely you know I will not pass the kingdom on to you."

Kalen sarcastically feigned injury. "I would never think such a thing. You have no son, or heir, I know Spencer would undoubtedly rule after your death."

Hector's face flushed red with anger and he started to argue when he noticed the thin smile on the elf's face. He relaxed and changed his tone knowing the elf was mocking him in a friendly way. "You are lucky I appreciate your humor, elf, or you would sing at the gallows for a comment like that. Anyway, I may have an heir after all. It shows how much information you get from bedding the serving wenches."

Now it was Kalen's turn to flush. He had bedded many of the serving wenches that worked directly in the king's working areas, trying to get information on his routines, in case he felt the need to remove the aging human from power. If Hector knew of him bedding the women, what else did he know?

Kalen stammered. "My... king, I uh,...needed to sew my oats so to speak. Surely you do not..." Hector cut of the stammering elf. "Worry not, Kalen. I am not angered by your promiscuous nature, though I have seen some of the kitchen help. I guess the elven culture like women on the plump side, or is that merely your personal fancy?" Hector chided with a deep laugh.

Kalen relaxed a little. "Well my lord, a little ale and I,... well, lets just say I become less particular than I usually would be."

Hector straightened his bed suit and climbed onto the bed. "Well, my elf friend, one of my concubines is expecting. I usually have the seed rooted out you see, but I have gotten rather fond of the little vixen, so I have decided to let her have it. If it is a boy, I shall keep it. If not, well, I will have her and it thrown to the rocks. Normally I would just dispose of the babe myself, but I have learned in the past that women tend to make a big deal of that sort of thing. It is a wonder how that kingdom, Aten, gets by with only women. Sorceresses or no."

  Kalen nodded. Half listening to the king and half thinking of some excuse of getting out of the chamber. The king knowing of his exploits had unnerved him. "Well, my king, I came to state that if you need my services during the DeNaucght, I would be available." Kalen said hoping the Hector did not detect any quiver in his voice. The elf hated being off balance and unsure of himself around Hector. He was confident that if they came to battle at this moment he would win. But the gray elf never left anything to chance. He needed to know everything and cover all angles so that when he decided to claim victory there was no way anyone could snatch it away from him.

  Hector waived the elf away in dismissal. "I will call on you if needed elf. Now be gone. I am weary and have a busy day tomorrow."

  Kalen bowed and backed out of the chamber, closing the door. He hurried down the halls in relief. He had to start being more careful.

  Hector knew he had to keep an eye on the elf. Every wench he bedded, thin or thick, was directly involved with his daily activities one way or the other. Hector knew the elf was not to be trusted, but it seemed the thin little pest was becoming dangerous. He would have to deal with him soon. Hector imagined a hundred plots to erase the elf before he managed to drift off into a deep sleep.

    *   *   *

  Trinidy opened his eyes. They burned and stung

horribly, but he felt no cold, though he felt no heat either. The paladin quickly realized he was laying on his back, his vision was blurry and dark. He could hear many loud heart beats from around him and he could...smell them, smell their... life. It bothered him, though he knew not why. He tried to rise up, but he could not. His body seemed stiff and rigid. He could make out a stone ceiling that was about fifteen feet above him and thick wooden rafters supported it. He tried to inhale and smell of the room, but he couldn't force any air into his lungs. He expected fear to rip through him, but it did not. It was as if it were natural for him not to be breathing. This was strange to the paladin. Even in the abyss, he breathed, but here, wherever he was, he could not. Trinidy could hear faint sounds that he thought perhaps were muffled voices, but he could not make them out. The paladin wondered where his god had summoned him. Trinidy tried to move his head, but his neck was stiff, yet it did not matter to him. He was not in the abyss, and Bykalicus was not around. That was all that mattered.

 Trinidy could see the faint outline of his nose. It was dark, not pale like his skin normally was. He guessed it was bruised or he had dirt from his trials still smeared about his face. As Trinidy tried to speak, he quickly noticed he could not force any air out of his lungs, but he could make a guttural sound with his throat. He wasn't sure how intelligible it was, but it was better than lying on his back paralyzed. He couldn't make out what the people around him where saying, but they were rushing about. He could taste the fear in the air, and it tasted good. It made him desire more.

 "Rise."

 It was a simple command that echoed in his ear. To his surprise he sat up easily. He saw three men standing before him. They were dressed in robes and bore a holy symbol that hung loosely from their necks. Trinidy's poor vision prevented him from seeing what symbol it was, but he knew it was not the symbol of Dicermadon. These priests wore dark colored robes. Priests of Dicermadon did not.

Trinidy glanced around the room, trying to turn his head again, but his muscles didn't seem to obey him. The paladin soon realized he was wearing the armor he wore before his death, though it was horribly rusted and in bad repair. In fact, his arms and legs were covered in dirt and soot. It looked as if he had been taking a bath in a freshly tilled garden. It was strange, but he couldn't smell anything, or really hear anything except the blood that was pumping through the priests veins in front of him. He could hear their damnable hearts beating loudly and the sound almost seemed to hurt his ears, yet he didn't really feel pain. It was more like the sensation of fingernails grating against an instruction slate. Trinidy could tell the priests were speaking, but he could not make out what they were saying, Their words seemed to be drowned out by the indecent thumping of their hearts. The smell of their life seemed to cause him to hunger, it... mocked him somehow. Trinidy endured it patiently. Waiting for this new environment to unfold.

*   *   *

The priest all gasped aloud, Resin probably the loudest. He, Pockweln, and Dorcastig had spent most of the day chanting and reciting the ceremonious spell known as the DeNaucght. Resin had prayed for a divine sign that he should perform the rites and received it in the form of a dream. It showed the paladin's body walking around in a state of undeath, carrying out his wishes. The beast had unbelievable power and it led an army against the enemies of Nalir. Why the king did not lead the armies himself, Resin didn't know, but sometimes dreams just didn't make sense. When Resin awoke, he knew he and his acolytes had Rha-Cordan's blessing in the rite, but the vision of the undead knight, and the reality that laid before him where two different things. The beast wreaked of rotting flesh that had appeared out of no where and covered the skeleton when the spell was being woven. The wooden table that the skeletal remains had laid on had rotted and crumbled under the remains and when the other three acolytes tried to pick it up and place it on the stone slab it now rests on, their skin was badly burned with cold and they clutched their insides and screamed, falling unconscious. Resin wasn't sure if it was due to the spell being incomplete or the nature of the undead being that laid before them. Regardless of the cause, the high priest knew that there would be many more revelations from this being of uncharted magic.

"Can you command it?" Dorcastig asked. The tall dark haired, dark skinned priest seemed the most unnerved of them all, but each were more than displaced by the vile creation.

"I know not." Resin said softly. "I am not sure if it is a being of own volition or it has to be commanded. Ready your spells, in case it turns violent. I'll not have us injured or slain by a mockery of Rha-Cordan, even if he blessed it's creation."

The others nodded slowly and began chanting a number of protection spells and other spells that did damage to undead and other creatures that were linked to the negative energy plane. Though priests of Rha-Cordan never created or controlled undead beings, they often battled them, seeing them as a mockery of their god. Only the god of death had power over souls. Undead beings were souls that were trapped in the rotting twisted bodies of their former selves. Beings that the priests of Rha-Cordan took upon themselves to destroy whenever possible. Yet sitting on the stone table before them was an undead being of unimaginable power that they created. The thought of what they had done unnerved them.

"Rise." Resin commanded.

The three priests jumped back and readied their spells when the creation sat up and stared at them. They felt magical energy whipping around their protective barriers they had placed around their minds, yet they could feel it prying, trying to loose the shields and wards.

The undead creation had red, glowing eyes that seemed sunken into it's skull. The creation's face had tight blackened skin that was drawn across it, barely making it more than a simple skull that was housed in a rusted great helm. It's lips were stretched and tight, exposing thick long teeth that were imbedded in a gum less jaw. Hundreds of tiny stinging insects rolled around in the creation's mouth, occasionally crawling out and reentering through the ear or nose holes. The three priests stared at the monstrosity for minutes when Hector entered the bone chamber. He gasped aloud at the hellish creation that sat on the stone slab. It was as if a dead rotting corpse had been dressed in a rusting suit of armor and propped up on the stone table. The king glanced at the rotted, pile of crumbled wood that had been the previous table and walked up next to Resin.

"Is this what was supposed to happen, Resin?" Hector asked uneasily.

Resin didn't take his eyes from the hellish nightmare when he responded. " I know not, my king, but it seems as if it is under my command." Resin answered.

Hector looked around the room at the other Acolytes. Dorcastig, the Kai-Harkian priest, seemed the most terrified, but held his fear in check. He glanced back at Resin. " Tell it to kill Lance Ecnal."

Resin took his eyes from the monstrosity for the first time since it's creation. " Should we tell it where he is?" Resin asked.

Hector shrugged his shoulders. "I know not, priest. This a creation of you and yours. You command it. Besides, Kalen is out in the hall. He has readied a teleportation spell to send the rotting heap to task if need be."

Resin slowly turned to the undead beast. The high priest hesitated before he spoke.

"You are to go find Lance Ecnal and slay him."

Trinidy heard the perfect words echo in his head. He could not understand anything else they had said until then. He could not move on his own accord, or even speak, yet it felt as if his bounds were loosed. He tried to stand up, and was amazed when his muscles did what he asked. He stood up slowly and gazed down at his arms. They were his again, fresh and new, just like when he was alive. He seemed oblivious to the men that stood before him. He could hear sounds, smell odors. His brain was flooded with hundreds of sensations, but the most predominant one was the sound of the men's beating hearts that stood before him. Smells assailed his nose, but the smell of their coppery blood stood out like a rose in a field of rocks. The men seemed to mock him, yet they said nothing. They seemed to fear him in some way, even the armored man that stood with an air of superiority. Trinidy guessed him to be a king or lord. They often stood that way he remembered. Trinidy frowned at his command. He was a champion of law and order. A paladin of the great god Dicermadon himself. He was no assassin, or bounty hunter

"Who is this Ecnal, and what has he done, that he needs slain." Trinidy asked, but he could already feel something compelling him toward the double wooden doors of the chamber.

Resin glanced at Hector who put his hand on his sword and backed away slowly. The other priests backed away too and seemed to be getting ready to defend themselves. Trinidy wasn't overly concerned with them for the moment. He did not understand why they seemed so afraid of him. He had not made one threatening movement and they didn't strike him as vile men.

Resin loosened the neck to his robe and wiped away

sweat that was beading up on his forehead. "Because I command you to." Resin replied with mock bravery.

Trinidy chuckled, though the door pulled at him more strongly now. " I kill no man, save he has done evil."

Resin quickly backed up against the wall and looked at the other priests in surprise. It seemed as if the once mighty paladin, did not realize that he was nothing more than an undead beast." I think something has gone array."

The other priest nodded and began chanting protective divinations. Resin straightened his back and stepped forward, remembering his conversation with the demon lord.

"Trinidy, you are to right that which is wrong." Resin said as his voice cracked and wavered.

Hector said nothing, he just watched the exchange with interest, though he too felt the magical fear aura that tugged at his mind.

The undead paladin turned and regarded the priest again. "Yes. I am to right that which is wrong. I remember that. I pledged that oath when Dicermadon rescued me from the abyss." Trinidy said as he glanced back at the door. It pulled at him violently.

Resin spoke again, seeing Trinidy was being pulled by some unseen force. He was certain now that the paladin did not know what had happened to him. Resin did not understand how he was oblivious to the state of his own body, but he guessed it had something to do with the way the DeNaucght was performed. It normally restored the man to his natural form just before he died. The high priest pulled his robe down and straightened it. "Lance Ecnal is the wrong. He must be slain for the wrong to be right."

Trinidy did not waiver, despite the visible struggle he was having against the magic that was compelling him to the door. "What wrong has he done?" Trinidy asked. His voice cracked from the strain of resisting the tremendous magic that pulled at him to leave.

Resin swallowed and stepped up, gaining confidence in what Bykalicus had told him.

"He is the son of a goddess that was banished from the heavens. It is forbidden by Dicermadon, your god, the god of gods, for a Breedikai to reproduce. It normally is impossible, but the goddess of mercy was banished to live her life as a mortal. That way when she died, she would cease to exist for Breedikai's have no soul. The goddess married a paladin of Dicermadon to mock him. They had a son named Lance Ecnal."

Trinidy struggled with what the priest was saying. He knew almost every paladin of Dicermadon, or at least he thought he did. He was the only one that he knew of that chose a wife.

Resin noticed Trinidy was deep in thought. He continued. "The paladin was used by the goddess of mercy. She choose him out of spite, not love. Her name was Panoleen." Trinidy was roused from his thoughts. The pull from the magic's at the door had no strength against the love Trinidy had for his lost wife. He ignored the ripping magic and took three strides toward the priest. He drew his sword and leveled it at Resin, forcing the high priest back against the wall. The blade was dark black and it radiated such a deep cold that Resin's face stung and his robes stiffened and froze. Black tendrils whipped around the blade randomly like tiny circling dragons made of smoke. Frost whipped through the air around the sword from it's abyssal cold.

"She used you, Trinidy." Resin said softly. "She used you to destroy your god." Resin said as he turned his head to try to get away from the cold of the evil blade.

Hector narrowed his eyes at the proclamation Resin was making. He didn't know who the dark priest had learned this information from, but he was going to find out after this creation was sent to task. And Hector doubted Resin was going to appreciate his interviewing methods much at all.

Trinidy narrowed his eyes. Their red glow intensified. " How do you know these things?"

Resin swallowed as he still tried to maneuver away from the stinging blade of absolute evil with it's frost biting into his skin, raising many small blisters. "I think you have been tricked Trinidy." Resin whispered.

"And so you shall be bound." echoed in the paladin's head. The pull for the door became too great. "You are the one that has been fooled priest. It is true I married a woman named Panoleen. And it is true we had a son, but his name is not Lance Ecnal, and she loved me with all of her soul. I'll not believe she would betray me or my god." the undead creation proclaimed. Trinidy let the sword down and he sheathed the evil blade. The air popped and sizzled until the entire blade was housed in it's case. Trinidy turned and strode toward the door. The paladin did not look back as he spoke. "This is not over priest. I will return." the wooden door twisted, crumbled, and cracked as the undead paladin walked past. The stone on the wall turned white and flaked away and the tiles under his feet blackened wherever his feet fell.

The priests ran to the doorway and watched as Trinidy strode down the chamber toward the wide double doors that went to the courtyard near the portcullis that lead out of the keep. The large iron portcullis was locked high in place to allow free movement in and out of the keep, but Hector had placed guards at the front gates of the courtyard to keep unwanted visitors. The king knew the magnitude of this day, and he did not want to be disturbed by anything.

As Trinidy passed, the stone in the floor blackened like the stone in the chamber had when he passed. The walls crumbled when he walked by and the tapestries that were fastened on the walls rotted as they hung. The priests could see a rippling haze of corruption that danced around Trinidy as he walked. They all watched as a soft blue light erupted in front of undead paladin, forming a small portal. Trinidy, undaunted, stepped through the azure door, the portal closed, and then he was gone.

Hector shook his head as Kalen stepped from the other side of the crumbled double doors, near where Trinidy had stepped into the portal. The gray elf strolled up in his quizzical way. He scrunched his delicate nose at the foul odor of rotting flesh that followed the undead knight.

"He is on his way, my lord." Kalen said with an exaggerated bow. " I have sent him to the Serrin Plains just outside of Central City so he is unlikely to be detected. I doubt the creation will be easily defeated, but Beykla does employ powerful wizards. Now if you people would be so kind as to tell me what that was?"

Resin cleared his throat. "That was a champion of Rha-Cordan. A champion of death."

Hector turned to Resin angrily. "You have been keeping secrets from me, priest. We will address your lack of loyalty another time. But for your sake, I hope your champion of death, your... *Death Knight*, succeeds. Your life may depend on it." Hector said as he turned and angrily stomped down the corridor with Kalen smiling mockingly over his shoulder. When they had rounded the corner, Resin slumped down against the wall and wiped the sweat from his forehead and exhaled deeply. "If the death knight fails Hector, It will not be I who must fear. Because the wrath of a half-god will be evoked, and Rha-Cordan does not hold you in the regards you might think." Resin said to himself with a relieved chuckle. "No, your soul is not well kept, my king. Not well kept at all."

" Past. Everyone has one. Some cannot remember their past, others would just as soon forget. It seems though, that it creeps up on you and rears it's ugly head when it is least desired. Even if a Kai-Harkian knows not his past, he knows what race he is by the look of his own reflection. He is usually a short, thick chested man with bronze skin and thick black hair. They are natural swordsman and are immune to most every kind of ingested poison. The mountains the Kai-Harkians call home are native to extremely poisonous plants.

The same recognition goes for the Andorians, though they are next to extinct. The Andorians are generally tall fair skinned men that have long powerful arms that are used to wielding a heavy sword in each hand without difficulty.

Men of all races, such as Kai-Harkians, or elves, or any other kind of humanoid, learn of their heritage and embrace it. But what if a man does not know his heritage when he is born, and does not learn of it until he was a man? Will he have difficulty accepting who he is if he did not know until he was grown? I say yes. A man develops his image as he ages. Call it a sense of self. It cannot be undone or changed because of an unknown truth. Really there are two truths. The truth of his heritage and the truth of who he is. Yet on the inside, all men bleed red. From orcs to Beyklans, they cannot change who they have grown to be.

I could have no sooner sprouted wings and flew than I could have fathomed what men claimed I was. My name was Lance Ecnal. I lost my parents that I loved dearly. They were stolen from me by a vile and evil man that feared what I was to become, instead of what I was. Strange, how that man single handedly created exactly who he hoped to kill. Had my past been shaped by those who loved me, rather than by those who hated me, would my life have turned out the same? I will never know. But of all the souls that were ever lost, I pity his *least of all."*

-Lancalion Levendis Lampara-

Chapter Six
Proclamation of Doctrine.

*A*lexis sat on an old rotten log and nervously watched Lance as he slept soundly in his tightly wrapped bed roll. Jude was reining the horses and getting them ready for the day's ride while Apollisian started cooking breakfast. Lance had last watch with Jude, and now he slept while the bright morning sun started ascent into the sky. It was still very much dark, but the eastern sky was aflame with the morning glow as it fought to erase the black of night. Crickets were chirping in the tall grass and a few birds started their morning songs while Apollisian sat on a large rock at the base of the hill next to the warm fire that they were cooking breakfast on. The paladin stirred a large iron pot with a thick wooden spoon that was cracked on the ends from years of use. The pot was filled with stew from a rabbit Alexis had caught in the night while on watch. It bubbled from the fire and warm wisps of steam rose into the cool morning air. Apollisian watched Alexis reach into her pack and pull out a few of her tightly woven bowstrings. She moved from the old log to the ground, sitting with her legs folded, waxing the string of her long bow. She kept the string well waxed to prevent it from rotting and to increase it's strength. Her long blonde hair hung over head as she rubbed the yellow block up and down the taught twine, covering it with a thick coat. Apollisian watched her intently soaking in her beauty. Neither he, nor Alexis, had mentioned the day they had in Central City just before the king arrived. It was an awkward moment for them both, and he knew there could not ever be anything between them. She was an elf. She would live a hundred of his lifetimes. While he grew old and feeble, she would remain young and full of vigor. He wouldn't curse her with the burden of loving him, though, he knew he could not change the fact that he was indeed falling in love with her. She was such an amazing woman. Her long blonde hair glistened from the red flickers of the camp fire. She would wax her bow string for a while, then she would stare at the Ecnal intently for a few seconds, then return to her waxing. Occasionally she would catch the smitten paladin looking at her. Alexis would smile and glance back down at her work, but she kept her eyes on him for a second after. The smile would remain on her face until she happened to look back at the sleeping Ecnal.

Apollisian too, looked at Lance, but all he saw only a sleeping boy that was barely a man. Though he surely had a powerful look to his boyish eyes, the paladin doubted he was this monster Alexis had made him out to be. He imagined that she too, was having second thoughts. Other than being self absorbed in his journey, the boy was quite thoughtful and considerate. Not exactly the traits of a vicious killer that was supposed to murder hundreds of thousands like she said was prophesized.

Apollisian glanced over at Jude who was still tending to the horses. Apollisian admired how well the man seemed to take care of the animals. He seemed to have some form of affinity with them. Once the paladin was certain the large man was occupied, he moved to sit next to Alexis. He inhaled deeply when her perfumed scent wafted over him. She looked surprised, but smiled, touching her knee to his when he sat down. Apollisian accepted the ginger touch and leaned over speaking softly enough Jude could not hear.

"I don't know, Overmoon. I know you have said he is this Abyss Walker, but he seems every bit the average boy to me. In fact, his heart has not even the twinge of evil to it. I have checked every night since we have left Central City. Are you sure he is this beast you claim he is?"

Alexis frowned and stopped waxing her bow string. She stared at the taught waxed line for a moment in thought, before looking up and meeting the handsome paladin's strong, blue eyed gaze. "I too, have my reservations about him. He seems very innocent, but I cannot deny what I see every time I look into those wicked green eyes of his. There is an evil lurking there greater than I can describe. It is as if every damned soul screams out to me for mercy when I meet his gaze. I can hear their voices so loudly I want to cower and cry." Alexis said as her voice cracked. She paused and glanced over at Jude. The swordsman was gathering grain from the packs and tending to the animals. The horses were calm and whined softly at the anticipation of the treat he was bringing. Once satisfied he was not listening, she continued. "I cannot determine if he is who he seems to be, but the elders can. That is why I must take him there. As a prisoner, or guest, it makes no difference."

Apollisian shook his head. "I cannot allow it any way, other than as a guest. It is unjust to imprison a man on mere suspicion alone, let alone suspicion of deeds he has not, nor might not ever commit."

Alexis stared deep into his steel blue eyes. She became lost in an azure sea of euphoric bliss. She had to force herself to keep from wrapping her arms around the handsome man, though she quickly regained composure and spoke with an eerie calm. "Apollisian, you are my mentor and beloved friend, but I will deliver this man to the council of elders in Minok Vale. Any who try to stop me, will be seen as enemies to the elven nation and will be treated as such."

Apollisian was taken aback by her half threat. How dare she threaten him. He was a champion of justice. Few that breathed air, had the wisdom to recognize true justice, and she knew he was sworn to uphold it. Yet, she sat before him, spouting idiocies as if he were a child to be spooked. Apollisian renewed his strong visage and stood up, forcing her to look up at him, adding to his presence. His thick metal armor creaked and popped from the quick movement. "I am sworn to uphold justice. That young man shall not fall to the unjust while I'm still breathing, and mind you elf, I am not slain easily. If he is taken from my care by deceit or trickery, I will hunt down the kidnappers, regardless of race, religion, or creed, and send them to their maker. This I swear by the long hand of Stephanis, and so it shall be fulfilled." He stated loudly.

Apollisian stormed over to the fire, jerking up the stew pot and slammed it down forcefully on the large rock. Some of the stew splashed up from the side and splattered out. "Soup's done." he said coldly as he walked past a confused Jude to his horse and began cinching up the saddle.

Jude looked over and frowned trying to understand the angry exchange between the two. They had been like flirting lovers most of the trip, before this proclamation. He didn't hear all of fit, something about swearing and being fulfilled. Jude guessed it was some sort of lovers spat, but he was sure it was directed to Lance. He decided to keep a closer eye on those two, if they moved against his friend, they would find his sword equally deadly.

Alexis glared at the paladin's back as he stomped off. Her face was flush with anger and she stood up wiping the dust from her pants. Lance opened his eyes, yawned and stretched.

"Everything alright?" He asked lazily, stretching his arms as he finished his yawn. Alexis turned to him. Her frown had softened, but was still readily apparent across her face.

" Everything is fine. That bull-headed paladin just needs to watch his tongue."

Lance looked over at Apollisian as he angrily packed up his things, and then back at Alexis as she started to do the same. Lance looked over at Jude, who mouthed " Lover's spat."

Lance nodded his head in recognition as he slowly climbed out of his bedroll and started gathering his belongings in the cool morning. Getting in the middle of a lover's spat was the last thing he wanted to do. When the young mage finished gathering his belongings, he poured himself and Jude bowl of soup.

Jude sat down next to him and they ate while Alexis and Apollisian finished picking up camp in utter silence.

"I think they are up to something that involves you." Jude whispered to Lance.

Lance stopped chewing and took a swig from his wine skin. He finished the long draw and wiped his mouth. " Yea, I figured as much. I think she might know what the elven parchments I carry are. It's ok. I have a spell that will turn them into ordinary pieces of paper whenever I wish. If it is some crime to carry them, her people will be none the wiser until we are long gone. If I can't get them read there, I will go some place else. With all the gold we are earning on this journey, it should prove to be an easy task to pay a scribe to decipher them."

Jude nodded and took another big bite of stew. Breakfast was the only warm meal they got to eat on the trail, and they enjoyed it dearly.

The four were in the saddle before the sun rose from the eastern sky. Lance was becoming accustomed to riding everyday, in fact his horse had become spooked several times during the trip and he was getting used to getting it under control himself without aid from Apollisian or Jude. Alexis never offered him aid, but always seemed interested in what he said or did. Lance thought perhaps that was the way elves were, but he suspected it was something deeper than that. Especially after the spat between her and Apollisian.

The sun was near the middle of the sky when Apollisian called for them to stop. Lance reined his horse in tight, while the paladin dismounted and began examining the ground. Alexis was off hunting from horse back, so Jude rode up and dismounted also. The leather from his saddle creaked when his weight was placed in one stirrup and the horse shifted slightly when the large man fully stepped to the ground. He noticed Apollisian was kneeling down at a patch of flattened grass that was probably three feet wide and about five feet long.

"What is it?" Jude asked.

Apollisian said nothing. He moved about twenty feet to the east in the tall grass where he located another patch of flattened grass.

Jude frowned and rubbed his head.

"What are you looking at, Apollisian? Is this flattened area caused by deer?"

The paladin shook his head slowly and tested the dirt around the grass. He pulled up the grass stalk and noticed the browning grass still had moisture near the break. " This does not bode well for us."

Jude frowned. " What does not bode well for us?"

"These tracks are fresh." Apollisian said.

Jude rubbed his head and mounted his horse. The beast lurched to the side from his weight until he was fully in the saddle. The leather moaned and complained from the heavy swordsman. "Isn't that a good thing? The deer can't be far off." Jude asked.

Apollisian mounted his horse and shook his head. "We need to keep our voices low from here on out. The grass was not broken by bedding deer. Those are footprints."

Jude's eyes went wide with astonishment. He started to reply but he heard hoof prints pounding from the east, over the side of the hill. Apollisian too, heard the galloping horse and turned his gaze to the east. All he could see was the tip of the hill, the bright blue sky beyond and a few white clouds that floated overhead. The wind blew the dry grass in small waves across the land.

"Overmoon must have found the same prints we have." Apollisian said calmly.

Jude glanced back down at the huge tracks. They were the largest tracks the swordsman had ever seen. What was more surprising is that it appeared the beast that made them wore some kind of boot. " What makes footprints that big?" Jude asked in disbelief.

Apollisian started to answer, but turned his gaze to the hilltop. He put his hand to his sword when he saw Alexis come charging over the hill. Her eyes were wide with fear and her horse was wet with lather. She was leaning over the front of the saddle, and her legs were flailing wildly into the side of her mount, immediately urging the horse to run faster, though it seemed the beast needed no encouragement for that. Large clods of dirt flew up behind her horse as it's heavy hooves thundered against the dry ground.

"RUN!" she screamed as she ran by. Apollisian and Jude watched her ride toward Lance, then they looked back over the hill in disbelief. A large giant broke the horizon of the hill. It was almost twelve feet tall. It's skin was a dirty bronze and it wore many dozen animal hides that were crudely woven together to make a loin cloth. It's had very muscular arms that seemed too long for it's frame. It had thick stooped shoulders and a prominent brow line with a low forehead. The giant's long brown greasy hair bounced across face and shoulders as it ran. It held a massive club in it's right hand that looked like the trunk of a small tree. The ground shook and thundered as it stomped toward them with it's monstrous strides.

Apollisian and Jude turned and spurred their horses down the base of the hill to the road. Lance and Alexis were a few hundred feet ahead of them riding in a fury away from the hill while Alexis was riding smoothly and glancing back at Apollisian and Jude, and Lance seemed to bounce roughly about his horse's back, barely able to cling to the saddle.

"We can't outrun it!" Apollisian cried, drawing his long sword." Split up and circle. We must wound it, then try to flee!"

Jude glanced back at the horrible creature. It had a great brass colored nose ring and it smiled a rotten yellow toothed grin as it gained on his horse. The giant knew it was going to over run him. Jude jerked up on the thick reins of his horse. The leather reins creaked and popped under the strain of the horses thick neck, and Jude's powerful arms, but they did not break as the terrified horse jerked it's head back twice before coming to a complete stop. Jude ripped the reins around the horses neck, turned it in a tight circle and faced the beast. If he could not outrun it, he would fight. Running was not Jude's way.

The swordsman drew his great sword from it's scabbard. The large blade glinted in the bright sunlight like a jewel under lantern light. He held the sword high in the air, spurring his reluctant horse toward the thundering beast. After he quickly wrapped the reins of his horse around the saddle horn, Jude waved the heavy blade two-handed over his head in a circular motion, cutting the air, making the blade whistle as he neared the thundering hill giant. As he closed on the giant, Jude's horse resisted the charge and reared up on hind quarters. The swordsman fell from the back of the mount as the beast ran off, rider less. Jude hit the ground hard on his right shoulder but rolled with the fall and came up to his feet quickly. The pain seemed to ignite something deep within the large man. Given the tense situation, he barely sensed it, pushing the deep sensation back down inside of him.

"Run, coward!" Jude screamed at his horse as the

ground shook from the giant's nearing footsteps.

Alexis, noticing the giant was squaring off with Jude, stopped her horse and drew her bow hastily. The white ash bow, made of masterwork quality, creaked and bent as she notched an arrow and let it fly. The green fletched missile whizzed through the air. Before it even neared mark, she drew and loosed another with rapid precision. Her horse remained perfectly still, as if knew she it needed a steady platform to shoot from.

Apollisian too turned his horse and charged the giant, eager to smite the evil beast, and to aid the foolish swordsman.

Lance stopped his horse and turned to battle at hand. Jude had fallen from his horse and the giant would be on him soon. He envisioned a spell in his mind. He pictured the magical energies that flowed around the air of the giant. Lance could see, even from the few hundred feet away he was from the beast, the bright yellow magical weaves that erupted from the air around it, nearly engulfing the creature's thick wooden club. Lance struggled with the magic to create an invisible barrier that would force the club from the giant's hand. Lance called the unique dweamor, Lance's prevention. There was no real name for the spell. He had developed it as a child to play pranks, but as he aged he found it had practical uses as well.

Jude winced as the giant brought his huge club over it's brown greasy head in an overhand slam. He could see every crack, every old blood stain on the deadly trunk as it came crashing down. The swordsman realized his error when it was too late. The giant could hit Jude when he was about fifteen feet away, long before he was able to get in close enough with his great sword. Just as the deadly club rocketed toward Jude, an arrow with bright green fletching, embedded itself into the beast's head. The giant roared in pain and thick red, syrupy blood shot out from the hole in the beast's forehead. The arrow strike forced the club high, as Jude ducked low. The giant great club hit Jude's great sword and tore the heavy weapon from his grasp. Pain erupted from Jude's wrists and he tumbled to the ground and landed roughly on his back, knocking the air out of his chest. A second arrow hit the creature just above it's knee. The giant howled in pain and lost it's grip on the great club just as the mighty weapon passed over the top of Jude. The club twirled end over end through the air and landed in the tall grass hundreds of feet from where the giant stood. The giant held his knee gingerly with one hand and his forehead with the other. Jude sat up from his back and struggled to regain his breath. He could see his great sword a few feet away so he began to crawl to it. His wrists were numb from the weapon being violently torn from his grasp and he was a little dizzy, but if he reached the weapon, he could still hold it weakly. Just as Jude grabbed his sword, he felt a strong arm hook him under his shoulder and he was hoisted to the back of Apollisian's charging mount. The paladin's spotted horse ran faster than any horse Jude had ever been on. They both watched as the giant howled in pain and clutched at the arrow that was sticking out of it's thick forehead. Long streams of blood poured from the wound and dripped off of the giant's chin. Two more arrows struck the beast in the right leg, just above the second arrow that hit. The giant howled in pain and backed away from the elf and her stinging arrows. Alexis notched a fifth arrow, but the discouraged giant hurriedly limped away muttering curses in it's native tongue. Jude sheathed his great sword and clung to the paladin's waist until he reached the others. Lance hung his head low and pushed his thumbs against his temples.

"Thank you." Jude said softy as he continued to rub his sprained wrists.

"It is ok." Apollisian replied. "But, you should heed our warnings, Jude of Bureland. We have traveled this path many times. It is deadly to face a hill giant in melee.

They can hit you with their long clubs before you can get in with your sword. It is best to wound them from a distance, then flee. If we had fought it, one of us would most likely be seriously injured or dead, even though the clumsy beast dropped his club."

    Jude ignored the paladin's reference of where he was from. He no doubt understood the man was trying to belittle him by speaking of his home town. Jude looked to Alexis to see what the elf's opinion was. She sat on her horse confidently with another arrow notched, looking past him into the vast grasslands. He knew she was a skilled archer, but he did not fathom the depth of her talent until today. She had hit the giant with near precision at almost two hundred feet away, while the beast was in combat with him. Never in his life, had Jude seen such marksmanship. He wondered how far her talents went with the bow. She fired twice as many arrows he could fire, in the same time span. The elf surely was a force to be reckoned with.

    Jude looked back at Apollisian while he waited for his horse to trot back to him. The horse had fled from the battle and was expectedly afraid to run back to the group. Jude felt uneasy with the way the paladin chastised him. He was no fool, but his ego was wounded.

    Jude cleared his throat and fired back at Apollisian. "It was no accident the beast dropped it's club." Jude said as he pointed to Lance while the young mage pinched his fingers at the bridge of his nose, grimacing in pain. "My friend has many talents. Do you think he gets random headaches from nothing? Between his magic and my sword, we can fell most enemies, though I'll be sure to heed your warnings in the future."

    Jude walked over, grabbed the reins of his horse and calmed the beast by gently patting it's neck. The small speech helped soothe his wounded ego, but he didn't look and see if the elf or paladin took him seriously. He knew what he said to be true, to a degree.

Apollisian said nothing in return. He understood the reason for the large man's claim, but he felt there was some truth to what he had said.

Jude took his terrified horse by the reins and unwrapped them from the saddle horn. The horse was panting and frothing from the attack and was quite nervous. Jude gently stroked the horse and spoke some soothing words before mounting.

Apollisian and Alexis turned and eyed Lance suspiciously. They both looked at him in a new, dangerous light. They guessed he was some kind of mage, but neither of the two had ever heard of a spell that could do such things. At least not so specifically. He had not demonstrated any great power, but the fact the spell was unknown surely did not sit well with them. Apollisian was familiar and trained in the arcane arts. Though he could not weave arcane magic, he could recognize a spell if he saw it being cast, so could Alexis. What bothered the paladin, was that he did not see any gestures made by the young mage, and by the look on the elf's face, neither had she. Only the most powerful spell weavers had the ability to create dweamors, but none could cast them without verbal or somatic components.

Alexis looked back at Apollisian in an; *I told you so tone* before turning her horse up the trail. "We need to get moving before that beast finds his club and decides my arrows didn't sting that bad." the blonde haired elf said as she turned and started to ride back up trail.

Apollisian didn't respond. He watched his friend ride onward as the soft wind from the plains gently blew her long hair about her. He gently urged his horse onward. The Vendaigehn stallion pranced and eagerly and followed the elf's horse.

Neither Jude, nor Lance, said anything in response. They just galloped their horses up the dirt path toward the ever expanding horizon line with the endless waves of flowing grasslands beyond. Each hoping this journey would come to an end soon.

*   *   *

He stepped from the flashing blue portal into the blinding sunlight. The brightness of the sun in contrast to the darkness of the portal he came from was as night and day. The dark, calm portal gateway was serene and safe. This atrocious light of day seemed to assault him at every level of his consciousness. The glaring sun burned and singed his dark decaying skin.

Trinidy raised his shield over his head to shadow the light. Never had the sun had such an adverse effect on him. It beat down on him like soft clay in a baker's oven. Trinidy looked around, wondering where in the realms he was. There was nothing but great rolling hills that were covered by endless waves of tall amber grass. The sky was a light parched blue, with thin white wispy clouds that seemed to be frozen in place. As far as his eyes could see, there were no trees to be found. The tall grass seemed to blanket the land from horizon to horizon. The light brown dirt that laid beneath his armored feet was cracked, dusty, and littered with small insects and bugs that seemed to scramble from under his boots. The insects were coal black and of every stinging type he could think of. He thought he saw a few scorpion's and many spiders. There were larger than the other sable creatures that spawned under him, some as large as the palm of his hand. He started to lift his feet in fear of being stung, but the creatures didn't seem to pay him any heed. They darted from under his boots into the expansive grass. Trinidy shook his head as he ignored the bugs and continued to glance around the desolate land. How insects of that order survived in these harsh temperatures was beyond him.

Trinidy was not standing still more than few minutes when he felt the arduous draw again. He could feel the pull, the voracious call of the same magic he felt in the keep. It was pulling him, calling him onward over the next rise, to the north. Trinidy turned and looked behind himself again, and his ancient armor creaked and popped as he turned. The death knight saw nothing different than what was in front of him, save for the magical pull. He shrugged his shoulders and stepped toward the hill, toward the magic that lead him like a dog on a leash. Trinidy despised the mysterious call, but at least he was no longer in the abyss. He would tolerate chains in the dungeon of any king, over that unforgiving torturous hell. He was finally back in the world of the living. Back to do the works of his great god. Back to right that which was wrong. " To right that which is wrong. " The thought echoed in his head over and over again like a chorus of a favorite song.

    The death knight plodded forward, over each hill, only to cross yet another. The brown scorched grass turned back and died about thirty feet around him as he walked, leaving a black trail of rotting grass. Trinidy seemed oblivious to the foliage's change. Once he past by, the grass crumbled to dust, leaving a long path of decay in his wake. The death knight held his shield above his head, protecting himself from the despicable sun. It seemed to mock him with brightness and scorch his skin whenever his arm or leg accidentally stepped form the shadow of his large steel shield.

    "Curse this damnable sun!" he barked with a guttural growl, surprising himself with the utterance. Almost immediately as he barked the curse, he was shrouded in a dark bliss. He could not see, yet he knew where he was walking and he did not stumble on the earth, nor trip over a rock or rise. And when the ground seemed to ascend to another hill to cross, it did not surprise him, as though he knew the hill was there. Trinidy lowered his shield arm as he walked in the sable paradise. His shoulder did not ache as it should have for holding the heavy steel shield above his head for so long. The shield was made of a thick steel that could stop a charging lance, it was surely heavy. Trinidy moved his arm up and down, testing to see if his muscles were indeed stiff. But to his surprise, they were not. He felt as if he could easily hold the metal shield up for hours more if need be.

    Trinidy wasn't sure how long he had walked. At least several hours, but not more than ten he guessed. His mind seemed to wander and he frequently lost track of time. His legs were not fatigued and his feet didn't ache as they should have from walking long distances in his full plate armor. He decided to stop and rest, though he wasn't the least bit exhausted, he did not want to have fatigue creep up on him. Trinidy sat down in the grass, and was surprised when he didn't feel any of the dry brown foliage around him. His shield dropped to the earth and he removed his gauntlet from his hand. The death knight felt the grass, but all that remained were the ashes of the decayed undergrowth. He struggled to look around, but the impenetrable darkness still shrouded him. It wasn't normal darkness, he couldn't see an inch in front of his face. It blocked every ounce of light, or maybe it enveloped the light, regardless of how, there was none to be found around him. Before he could wish the darkness away, it was gone as abruptly as it appeared. Trinidy realized he was sitting in a burnt clearing atop a small hill. The grass around him was gone, replaced by crumbled grassland that had been all but turned to ash. There were hundreds of stinging insects crawling around him on the ground again. They were all coal black and seemed to reflect the red sun of the autumn twilight on their glossy shells. Trinidy ignored the bugs and glanced to the rapidly setting sun. It would soon be below the horizon. The crimson orb was cut in half by the darkening skyline. The heavens were aflame with reds and yellows, as the thin wispy clouds bore a violet hue from the setting sun.

Trinidy had always loved the sunset in the past, but now he seemed more relieved of passing than enjoying the sight. In fact he felt himself becoming angry at the sun for not going down more quickly than it was. The fading bulb seemed to mock him by going down slowly, though at least it did not sting his eyes or his skin, like it had when it was in midday.

Trinidy felt the breeze that rolled over the darkening plains. He could not feel if it was a warm or cool breeze, he just felt the breeze. He felt the wind blowing his thin stringy hair and the resistance it made on his face. That lack of sensation puzzled him, but he did not dwell on it. He had not sat for more than a few moments, when the magical pull tugged at him once again. He tried to fight it but he soon found himself on his feet and plodding north, into the night. Answering the invisible beckoning from the unknown that seemed to lay just over the next hill.

Trinidy walked for many more hours into the darkness of the night. He liked the night. It was not that it was cooler, or the fact the sun was set, though he did not miss the stinging glowing orb, it just seemed more comfortable to him. More friendly in a strange way. There were no stars, it was a cloudy night, with an occasional flash of lightning from a far away storm, but he could see well in the dark. It didn't really bother him that he could see as well in the night than as in the day. It was somehow second nature to him.

Trinidy came to a small dirt trail that lead north and south. The pull from the magic, urged him to go north. He looked south though, his bright red eyes glowing with wonder at what lay in that direction. He almost wanted to turn that way to defy the insatiable call, but he did not. Trinidy did not see a reason to battle the unyielding urge just yet. No sense in wasting energy fighting the unseen leash. There would undoubtedly be a time for fighting, and now was not then. He slowly started up the dirt trail that lead north. Placing one foot in front of the other in his steady amenable trek.

He walked for the rest of the night and well into the next day, surprising himself that he was not tired, nor hungry. His feet did not hurt, nor did his muscles ache. He couldn't remember eating since he awoke on the table in that keep, nor drinking a single drop of water for that matter. He guessed he had been blessed by some sort of spell to aid him in his long journey. Trinidy decided that he would eat when he was hungry and not before. The sooner he answered the call, the sooner he would be loosed to pursue other interest.

The sun was high in the sky on the second day, stinging his arms and legs just as it had done in the first. He held his shield above his head again, wishing he had that dark shroud for a second time. He wasn't sure how he had summoned it the day before, if he had indeed summoned it at all. Yet he plodded on, often pausing perplexed at how the sun seemed to mock him. It seemed to taunt, and ridicule him as it held itself aloft in the great perch in the sky. He glared at it, that damned yellow orb. Why did it taunt him so? Trinidy shook an angry fist at the sun. He stared at it while it burned his eyes and scorched his skin, but he continued to stare. The bright globe did not seem to burn his eyes despite the fact he stared at it directly.

"Why do you mock me, sun? How dare you? Do you not know who I am? I am the will of goodness. I bring the sword of righteousness to the evils that hide under the rocks and in crevices to avoid you, yet you mock me!" Trinidy screamed. He drew his long sword from sheath and held aloft. The sword made a shrill ringing sound as it was drawn and the air cracked an popped from the intense cold that wafted from the wicked onyx blade. Great wisps of frost and steam coiled around the sword as he held it high overhead. The cold cascaded down the sword and onto Trinidy's arm and over his head and shoulders. The death knight felt a wash of coolness over his entire body. It was not cool as he remembered, but more of a calm, an inner serenity that had escaped him without his knowing.

Trinidy's tirade was interrupted by a new taunting. It came from over the next hill. He could hear it's ignescent pounding. Thump-thump, thump-thump. The sound was like grating fingernails over a raw slate. Thump-thump, thump-thump. Mocking him, laughing at him. Rage washed through the death knight. Rage like he had never felt before. It felt good. It was as refreshing as cold crystal clear spring water in the middle of the Great Desert of Tyrine. The pull of the magic called him away from the sound, but he easily ignored the insatiable pull. The rage was with him. Thump-thump, thump-thump.

Trinidy stalked over the hill, his wicked long sword in hand. Thump-thump, thump-thump. There it was, the object of the unremitting reverberation. Kneeling over a slain gazelle was a large brown skinned hill giant. Trinidy knew the beast to be inherently evil, but he didn't lust to kill it because of it's racial trends. It was the relentless pounding of it's despicable heart that drove him onward.

The giant wore a blood soaked bandage on his forehead and one around it's right knee. The dark furs from the grassland animals it had slain in the past acted as the coverings for it's wounds. Dark, crusted blood still clung to the giant's tan skinned leg, that the stupid creature had not yet wiped off. The beast seemed about twelve feet tall when it stood erect, though now it knelt over the felled gazelle chewing on the deer's hide. Trinidy calmly walked toward the creature. The burning sun no longer seemed a hindrance to the death knight. The grass turned dark brown as the death knight passed and then turned to black ash, crumbling, leaving a wake of destruction behind him. Trinidy walked as silent as death then stopped just behind the beast. The giant shivered visibly and rubbed it's arms from the abyssal cold that wafted from the death knight.

"Stand and arm yourself, beast." Trinidy said as he held his wicked blade horizontally in front of himself.

The giant leaped to it's feet, whirling around to face the voice that had somehow snuck up on him. The giant could feel the tendrils of fear ripping around his puny brain at the sight of the new enemy. It was a humanoid of some kind, dressed in dirty black plate mail armor. The armor bore many ornate skulls about it. At the knees, on the chest plate, the shoulders, and other areas. The man wore a tattered black cape that draped down his back that flowed softly in the breeze. He held a sword in front of him that smoked, sizzled and popped, though it was as puny as the swords the elves used. But it was the face of the creature that gave the giant pause. He had long black hair that was thin and stringy. The top of his head was near bald revealing pale white flesh underneath. The skin on the man's face was taught and skeletal like, with no eyes, save for a small beady red glow. His lips were narrow and tight, unable to cover it's dull gray teeth, giving the man a seemingly permanent smile. And the stench! The man smelled as if he had been dead for months. Large black bugs crawled from his mouth, into his nose and out again. It surely looked like any corpse the giant had seen before, yet there it stood before him, speaking in some language the giant did not understand. The giant beast studied the man for a brief moment before picking up his hefty wooden club. When the giant picked up his tree trunk of a club it seemed to hurl the diminutive enemy into a fury.

Trinidy rushed forward hurling himself abidingly at the giant, ducking a great sweep of the creature's club that would have surely killed any man. The death knight launched in with a barrage of attacks, slicing the beast's hamstring, then cleaving a horrific slice up the inside of it's thigh, severing the femoral artery. The death knight's sword popped and sizzled, burning the wound of the giant with it's abyssal cold. Warm blood erupted from the arterial wound and spurted the ground red. The giant howled in pain and smashed his club down at the death knight in great overhand strikes. Trinidy avoided each strike as it hit the hard earth, sending vast showers of dirt and debris into the air with the mighty blows. Trinidy backed away and stood staring at the giant. The beast panted and sweated, holding it's severely wounded leg as it's precious life blood spurted into the earth. The giant looked behind himself looking for a way to flee from this hellish enemy that stood three spans away from it.

    Trinidy watched the giant as it stood there gasping from fatigue. He could hear it's heart growing fainter with each passing second as the giant bled the ground red. Thump-thump, thump-thump. Yet the heart still mocked him. Hate tore through the death knight. How dare this beast try to live. It was dead already, it just didn't know it. Trinidy opened his mouth and roared a roar of defiance against the damnable thumping of the giant's heart. When he did, hundreds of black beetles and other insects shot from Trinidy's mouth, swarming around the giant's wounded leg. The hill giant swatted at the tiny insects as the stinging creatures bore into the giant. The hill giant roared in pain and fright as the insects burrowed under his skin making hundreds of fast moving bumps up the inside of his leg. The giant pounded his fist at his leg, dropping his club and howling in terror and pain.

    Trinidy watched on in utter satisfaction. He wasn't sure where the insects came from, but he felt a certain kinship with them. A brotherhood so to speak. He was pleased when he could hear their buzzing and the chomping of their wicked little jaws as they burrowed toward the giant's heart.

    The hill giant dropped to the ground and began thrashing about, howling and screaming. Then as abruptly as it started, it stopped. Trinidy stared in wonder at the giant as it lay still on back. He could not detect the rising and falling of the beast's chest as it drew breath, he couldn't see any movement in it's limbs, and best of all, that beating heart was stopped. It would mock him no longer.

    The death knight approached the body of the giant. It lay still back. It's face was contorted with pain in the grimace of death. It's eye's were frozen wide with horror and fear. A single beetle crawled from the giant's mouth and disappeared into the grass. Then another, and another. Soon the entire swarm erupted from the giant's mouth and vanished into the underbrush as if they were never there. Trinidy kneeled down next to the dead giant and looked at the gazelle. It was partially eaten, but it's skeleton was intact. The death knight reached down and gently stoked the gazelle's bloody cheek. He felt a flash of cold that was not cold, then the beast opened it's eyes. It blinked several times and awkwardly stood on it's own. To Trinidy it seemed as if the beast was healed. It bore no wounds that he could see and acted submissive to him, nuzzling it's soft cheek under his arm. Trinidy gently stroked the gazelle and spoke to it soothingly.

    "You are alive again, my friend. Go! roam among the grasslands as you once did."

    The gazelle reluctantly bounded off to the north, until it vanished over the hill side. Trinidy turned and searched the giant for any signs he may have belonged to raiding clan. He would not tolerate such evils roaming free to prey on those that were weak. But after a brief search he found nothing, save for three large boulders, that the giant no doubt used to throw at unwary victims. He started to track where the beast came from, when the pull from the magic became too strong. He reluctantly turned north and began his slow, but steady trek across the plains. He enveloped himself in the shroud of darkness a second time as he disappeared over the rise of the hill, leaving a wake of burned and crumbling grass that was infested with black stinging insects.

    To the north, a gazelle with it's insides trailing

behind it, and it's hide mostly ripped from it's body, left a bloody trail as it bounded lifelessly across the grassy plains.

To the south a hill giant opened his lifeless eyes. He had no heart beat nor did he take any breaths. His skin was a pale white, instead of the light brown it had once been, and he stood in a pool of his own curdling blood. Maggots festered in a grievous wound on the inside of his leg, but he seemed oblivious to the larva as they devoured his flesh. He did not blink, nor move. He just waited for his master that had created him to return and give a command. Until then he would wait.

" Can a god be killed? Surely a difficult query. I am positive it's answer lies within the depths of the question. What does someone mean by killed. Do they refer to death as a mortal imagines death. If so, then I answer no. Not exactly. If a god, or goddess for that matter, takes the mortal form, after having been shielded from his or her own innate abilities, then yes. Their new mortal forms can be destroyed, and without their godly abilities to restore the body they will cease to exist. You see Breedikai, or original gods, have no soul. They have no inner being that rests at their core. They are, and always will be, what the shell that surrounds them. That is why Panoleen, my mother, was destroyed. When she was shielded from her innate magical abilities and was made into mortal form, she still lacked a soul. When her body ceased to exist, she ceased to exist. But that is the only way I have ever learned to destroy a god. Usually the way gods and goddess eliminate one another is to shield them in their native plane, or shield them an make them serve in Merioulus as slaves, though this is never permanent and rarely has ever happened.

  I learned that Breedikai feared the " Risers." The risers are men and women who, through arcane means, have rose to such power that they tried to be accepted to Merioulus. They somehow managed to live for hundreds or thousands of years with the aid of spells and dweamors, but they were always denied acceptance. Even with the power these risers possessed, they could not match the power of the weakest god. Some in their pride attempted to battle the gods, trying to force them to let them enter the great city of the gods, but they were all defeated and destroyed. Their souls were always given to Rha-Cordon for punishment. Rha-Cordon, the god of death, hated those who lived unnaturally long lives and he punished them so. The reason that the Breedikai feared the risers, was that the risers had a soul. They could not be disposed of, shielded, or destroyed. Their soul would always exist. Rha-Cordon had control of a soul when it passed, and he did not belong, participate, nor even agree, with the laws of Merioulus. And though not since the beginning of time had Rha-Cordon ever fully released a soul to it's own devices, he would not vow to the Breedikai that he would not. Who would have ever thought that a riser could be more powerful in death than they ever were alive. The Breedikai did, a fear of theirs I would one day learn for myself.

-Lancalion Levendis Lampara-

Chapter Seven
Wrath of the gods.

*L*eska marched purposely through the garden that was littered with large rows of green bushes carved into depictions of heroes and heroines. There were great marble statues of monsters and men alike carved with lifelike perfection unseen to the mortal world. Small ornate walls of stone, a few feet high, surrounded each fertile green bush like a thin shroud. Bright flowers of every kind and shape grew plentifully in this magnificent garden. Animals of every kind bounded from her path, sensing her anger, but following curiously once she had past. The goddess's velvety green dress, clung to her angelic body revealing enough to show her femininity, but covering enough to prevent wandering eyes. Her dress was long and flowing from her waist, with light browns and yellows intertwined with the greens, though with each passing day, the browns and yellows became more predominate. She wore her hair braided back from her head and the soft tail bounced and waved as she marched with her delicate hands clenched into a fist. Her bright green eyes radiated a flash of dangerousness that she seldom showed, and the rocks under her feet seemed to growl and shudder as she passed over them. Leska, the earth mother goddess, was not happy.

  She had been overseeing the growing of a great vale in the southern reaches of Vidora, when she sensed the DeNaucght. A secret ritual that a few good sects of mortals knew about, and even fewer knew how to perform. The chant was reserved for the more powerful mortals so that they might allow a hero, or champion of righteousness, to rise from the grave, and right that which is wrong. But the sacred ritual had been perverted into some despicable act, drawing the soul back into a rotting decaying body, binding it with magic and filling a once righteous man with a taint of evil that he would eventually succumb to. It was true, Leska had no love for this mortal. In her eyes, and most of the eyes of the Breedikai, when he was alive, he had broken the oath of celibacy and married. This violation did not go unpunished, the mortal lost the powers his god had bestowed upon him, but the fool seemed relieved. Love. Pah! Leska said to herself as she marched through the great garden. That witch, Panoleen, knew nothing of love. She did not marry the poor, foolish, soul out of love. She wanted to get back at the Breedikai for banishing her from the heavens. Goddess of mercy indeed. She merely used her station to work her own sinister plots, but no longer. Dicermadon was hers now, but Leska was angry with the god of magic and knowledge. She knew of his silent workings. There was no other way for men of Rha-Cordan's sect to learn the DeNaucght than if Dicermadon, the god of magic and knowledge, had intervened. She had learned he was speaking with the arch demon, Bykalicus, but she overlooked the outlawed deed. She believed that his station often required him to operate outside of the laws from time to time, but once this sacred knowledge had been dispersed, the god king had gone too far.

  Leska stormed from her garden ignoring the questioning eyes of the other gods and goddesses as she stalked toward the god king's chambers. The very stone that lay under her feet growled and rumbled as she reached the door of Dicermadon's chamber. The great double wooden barrier was well over twenty feet tall and each half was well over ten feet wide, with every single inch of the wood touched by a master craftsman's hand. Leska pushed on the great door but it would not give. She felt the god king's magic holding the wooden portal fast.

"Open this door!" Leska demanded though she received no response. She noticed out of the corner of her eye, many of the gods had began massing around the chamber sensing the confrontation between the earth mother and the god king.

"Be gone, Leska. I have matters that are more important to tend to." Dicermadon's voice boomed like a thunder clap from the other of the great door.

Leska's face bore a deep scowl. She outstretched her arms, closed her beautiful green eyes of fury, and tilted her head back. It started as a dull rumble in the very stone of the temple that steadily grew into a loud roar. The temple shook and vibrated as the pieces of mortar and plaster fell from the ceiling. Great waves of power rippled through the air around her like a heat wave. The ripples grew and grew, becoming more rapid and narrower. She stretched her fingers out from her hands as if in pain and her body shuddered violently. The thunderous rumbling of the stone ceased abruptly. The waves of power dissipated, but Leska held her pose. Nothing stirred for moments, then suddenly there was a great eruption. A violent shock wave tore through the hall like an immense explosion, but without sound. There was no wind, no force, yet all the gods standing outside the chamber felt the powerful flow of magic rip by them. The doors of the chamber that Dicermadon had sealed, burst into hundreds of pieces. Large chunks of wood and debris shot out from the door way and scattered over the great chamber's polished marbled floor.

Dicermadon stood with his back to Leska. He was garbed in heavy gray robes and his wavy silver hair was unkempt. There were flecks of ice that clung to his collar and littered the floor. She could smell the strong stench of the abyss that hung in the air like a thick fog. She noticed a bright red flash of magical energy that vanished in front of the god king. Leska ignored the odor and the magic. " I'm no child to be kept from the cupboard, Dicermadon." She growled.

The god king turned slowly. His face was riddled with anger and hate and his steel blue eyes glowed with fury, while his wild silver hair began to dance from his power. " You dare interrupt me, woman. I ordered you to wait outside. You will soon see why it is unwise to command my attention when I do not wish to give it." Dicermadon shouted angrily.

The other gods that had assembled in the hall outside the god king's chamber, coughed and covered their mouths as the stench of the abyss floated into the corridors. Some muttered angry curses. Others mentioned fetching the more powerful gods that sat on the council. Something was amiss in Merioulus.

A blast of force shot out from the god king, ripping pieces of the stone floor loose, striking Panoleen and sending her sprawling back into the hallway. She skidded to a halt at the far wall and jumped to her feet, just as Dicermadon was walking to the shattered doorway. He stood defiantly with one of his massive hands clenched in a fist at his hips, the other pointed a shaking index finger at Leska. He glared with hate at the interfering Earth Mother.

"Go away, witch, and I shall forget your trespasses here. As you see, it takes more than a childish trick with a door to harm me." Dicermadon taunted.

Leska stood up quickly. She wasn't hurt by the blast, but his power had surprised her. She had not battled another god in millenniums, let alone one as powerful as Dicermadon, but the Earth Mother knew that the god king was making deals with devils and demons. This could not, would not, be tolerated.

"You shall be still until the council decides what to do with you. Making oaths with devils and demons is a serious crime." Leska shouted as she rose to her shaky feet. The other gods that had given the pair a wide berth, gasped at the charges Leska leveled at the god king.

Dicermadon laughed in response. "The council are fools. They have no power, save for that in which I give them. I am Dicermadon, god of gods, lord of lords, king of kings. I have to explain nothing to you feeble Breedikai's. I am the first and I shall be the last. My breath is the beginning and the ending. My dealings with demon's are none of you pitiful wretch's concern!" Dicermadon gloated.

The other gods gasped in horror. Most fled down the corridor to alarm the other gods, though they feared that even combined, they could do nothing to harm him.

Leska stiffened her shoulders and narrowed her eyes bravely. "I will do nothing that you command. You are out of order, and surely mad. You have broken the sacred law and you will be held accountable."

Dicermadon chuckled and folded his muscled arms. "Mad? Sacred law? Fool woman, who do you think made that law? I can unmake laws as easy as I make them. Do you not realize I am the king kings, lord of lords, god of gods? There is no hand above my own. My eyes, my words, my very thoughts are pure manifestations of the will I deem to impose on the world, on the realms, on you."

Leska took a brave step forward in the face of the god king's wrath. "Panoleen was right about you. I should..."

"Panoleen? PANOLEEN! You dare speak her name in my presence! She is dirt under the heel of an ass. She is no more, as you soon will become!" Dicermadon screamed as he flung his arm at Leska, hurling a bright blue force of magical energy. The deadly sphere cackled and popped as it rocketed toward the earth mother. Leska ducked low and took a deep breath, sucking the iron from the very stones that she stood upon, making a large wall of wrought iron erupt from the ground in-between her and the sphere. The powerful ball hit the iron wall in an explosion of magical energy. Great sparks showered around the earth mother singeing her hair and putting small burn marks in her dress. She quickly released the hold on the stone and the iron melded again into the floor.

"I control all that which is of the earth, Dicermadon. Enchanted iron is impenetrable to energy spheres. I expected more a fight from you." Leska taunted, though she truthfully doubted how long she could last against his immense power.

Dicermadon summoned a great blue shield of glowing energy and a sword to match. the godly weapons cackled and popped in the air as he rushed to cut the earth mother down. He charged in and let out a fitful roar as he quickly closed the distance to Leska. The Earth Mother hummed softly as the raging god king bore down on her. The stone floor in front of the her came alive as two creatures formed from the floor. They were made of solid stone and stood about twenty feet high. They were covered in great rocks that formed spikes that protruded from mace like appendages.

Dicermadon paused to weigh his new adversaries. "Elementals, and Elder ones at that." Dicermadon chuckled as he deflected a powerful strike from one of the creatures. It's massive fist pounded the stone floor sending up a shower of rocky splintered debris. "It will be a pleasure to destroy these ancient beasts." the god king taunted.

Leska jumped to her feet. She did not doubt the elementals would perish at the hands of the god king. The elementals could easily destroy entire kingdoms if she so set them upon the task, but they were nothing in comparison to Dicermadon's power. She regretted summoning the apparitions to merely die in such a way, but they would buy her time until she could rush to her garden. There she was the most powerful. Leska winced in sorrow as she ran when she felt both of the noble creatures being cut down.

Dicermadon started past the elementals to catch Leska before she could reach her garden. He knew she could summon more power there than she could anywhere else in Merioulus. Suddenly a giant fist of stone and sharp rocks struck him in the shoulder, knocking him to the side. He hit the thick stone wall roughly as it cracked and splintered from the force of his iron body. Large pieces of rock and mortar from the bricks popped and crumbled, falling at his feet. The god king wiped his long silver hair from his face, revealing a strong square jaw that grinded in angry determination. His steel eyes locked onto the two apparitions that dashed toward him, unaware of who they were battling. They knew only that their goddess had called them to slay the creature, and that they would do. Dicermadon, the lord of magic and knowledge, knew that the elementals were creatures of magic. Their bodies were made of earth and stone, but the life force that coursed through the creatures was raw magical energy. Dicermadon, the lord of magic, outstretched his hand with his palm open. He closed his steel blue eyes and hummed, focusing on the magic that dwelt inside the beasts. The elementals rose their huge spiked stone fists into the air. They had no eyes, no mouth, but they fought with the tenacity of a man defending his true love. Yet, as soon as the giant fists came streaking down for the god kings head, he drew the magic into himself. Cloudy white tendrils of a thick milky glow erupted from the great elementals. They stood, motionless as the weaves of energy that held their life force, was pulled from their rocky earthen bodies. Dicermadon took a deep breath of satisfaction as he basked in the magical weaves that enveloped him. He inhaled the white milky tendrils that danced around his body, ignoring the shock of the other on looking deities. In moments, the great elementals, that had the fury to topple mortal kingdoms, shuddered and shook, then collapsed into themselves. There was a great shower of rocks and earth until only a large pile of earthen debris remained. Dicermadon flexed his powerful arms and shook with power. His sleek silver hair shuddered as his muscles strained and great veins in his neck protruded as he flexed. The very halls of Merioulus shook verdantly as the lesser deities backed away from the god king. Many had already left the battled ridden corridors, but many yet remained. Dicermadon shook out his arms and rolled his head around to loosen his tight corded muscles. He weaved a flow of magical energy around himself forming a great suit of plate armor that had hundreds of glittering diamonds and other precious gems embedded into it. There was the mortal sign of his followers on his chest, a great moon, overcast by two towering pillars. He created a giant tower shield that was made of what appeared to be a white jade. The shield glistened in the pale light of the corridor and it too bore his symbol. Dicermadon raised his right arm into the air as white milky tendrils twisted down his arm and past it forming a great sword that was as long as he was tall. The blade was ridiculously wide, shimmering like polished chrome, and had a razor sharp edge on each side. The hilt and pommel was made of polished platinum. The pommel bore a great protruding azurite spike, and at the end of the spike was a serrated edge that glistened with a dark black fluid that clung to the wicked end like a thick syrup.

    Leska gasped for breath as she sprinted through the long corridors of Merioulus. Lesser deities stopped what they were doing and watched in confusion as the earth mother darted in and around the complex corners of the great city of the gods. While she was running she had shifted her clothing to a dark green that was mottled with brown. It had a high neckline that consisted of bright white lace that was decorated with many brilliantly shining jewels that were interwoven. The silk like outfit seemed to cling to her figure, revealing a perfectly chiseled body that would make any mortal stand and gaze in wonderment at her stature. Leska bounded out of the main doors of Dicermadon's great palace in a dazed rush. The frantic earth mother ignored the many confused looks and stares she received from the other gods that happened to be about. She did not have time to explain, and she doubted she would gain any allies in doing so. Few of the Breedikai could stand to Dicermadon's power for a short period of time, let alone a pitched battle. The earth elementals would not last long against the might of the god king. They just had too occupy him long enough for her to reach her garden.

She took the small steps of the palace doors in a great leap and landed gracefully without missing stride. Magnificent birds leapt to take flight to avoid the earth mother as she sprinted by confused onlookers.

In the wide meandering streets of Merioulus a few lesser gods watched with interest at why Leska was sprinting so. Her soft leather like moccasins padded down the polished cobblestone streets. She moved her arms up and down in sync with her churning legs of the fluid run. She strained to force her legs faster, to draw more ground between her and Dicermadon. She would have simply created a gate to cross through, but the streets had been sealed from those kind of spells since the fall of Panoleen.

Some of the gods that walked the streets called out to her, but she did not respond. They muttered to themselves in nervous excitement at the terrified, yet determined look, that shone on the earth mother's face.

Dicermadon burst through the wooden doors of the great palace. His magnificent armor shined like a great beacon in the night. The great sword sizzled with power and his long silver hair waved about his head like a thousand tiny snakes writhing in anticipation. Dicermadon noticed the many gods that stood in the street in puzzlement. He thought about ordering them to aid in the capture of Leska, but the god king knew that they would capture her, and she would be heard. She was one of the most powerful Breedikai. Only Surshy, the goddess of water and oceans, Whisten, the god of air and storms, and Flunt, the god of fire, were her equal. He did not want her captured. He wanted her destroyed. The little witch would cease to exist. How dare she try to order him about? She and all of the gods were under him. They would do well to remember that.

Dicermadon soon realized he would not catch her before she reached her garden, so he elected to march confidently to her. Let her prepare whatever defenses she thought might help her. Her strength was pale in comparison to his and it had been too long since he crushed an enemy. He would savor the battle.

The god king's chamber sat silent. The heavy stench of the abyss hung in the air, seemingly clinging to the thick furnishings that decorated the magnificent quarters. There was a flash of white energy that lit up the room. Wisps of bright light flickered from the corner of the god king's chamber near the bed. The light twisted and turned over itself until the image of a man began to form. He was taller than most, and thin, wearing a thick gray robe that cascaded around his lanky body. He wore silver sandals that poked out from under the edges of his robe and a bright platinum chain with a giant pearl mounted on the end of it, hung from his neck. His eyes gleamed a bright blue and his hair was pale white. Whisten, the god of air, stepped from the magical weave he had woven around himself and dismissed the energy. Making himself invisible was one of the many uses he had learned from Sha-Shor'Nai, the goddess of the sun. She taught the elemental god how to bend light, using a form of his abilities with air, to allow the light to pass through him, making him seemingly invisible. He had never imagined when the ability would be useful to him, until he had learned of the god king's double dealings. Dicermadon, had he not been so arrogant could have detected his weave, despite how well he tried to disguise it, but the god king was too full of himself to even check for such things. Whisten knew that a fool's pride had brought down many a mortal king, why not the king of the Breedikai?

Whisten channeled a stiff stream of wind, locking the stench of the abyss in the god king's chamber, and wrapping the rapidly fading residue of the portal to the abyss. It was an easy task for him to wield the magical energy of wind in that way, though he doubted Dicermadon himself, could have done it as well. After a few moments of casting, he whispered a message and left it hang into another flow he made. The energy floated in front of him as he duplicated it several times. When he was finished, Whisten sent his spoken words along a line of wind to the gods he wanted to hear him. He was sure Leska did not have much time.

An endless ocean of magma slowly shifted and bubbled. When the bubbles burst, it sent a great shower of molten rock cascading through the air. Small islands of dull rocky mountains floated in the magmatic seas in the distance. These volatile mountains were home to some of the creatures that dwelled naturally in the plane of elemental fire. The sky was hues of bright orange to deep reds, that held thick clouds of steam that would boil the skin from any normal creature. In fact the general temperature of this plane would kill any normal being in seconds, causing their fragile bodies to burst into flame and burn as soon as they arrived.

Flunt stood at the edge of the great sea of magma, gazing out into the fiery paradise. His great cape of molten lava hung to his thick and powerful body. His eyes, that were afire with a bright yellow flame that danced along his face, narrowed as he sensed the approach of a magical energy that entered his home plane. It was traveling to him at remarkable speed. Flunt, the god of fire, started to form a shield of magical energy when he recognized the particular weave. It was undoubtedly from Whisten, and the god of fire expected that it had something to do with Dicermadon. The god king reined supreme in Merioulus, but here, in his native plane, the god king had no power, well little power, Flunt thought to himself.

"I have your proof, come to me, but make haste. Time is not a luxury." the deep raspy voice of Whisten said flatly when the message hit the god of fire.

Flunt sighed heavily. He never seemed to get much time in this fiery paradise. The god of fire took his finger and placed it into the air even with his head, and slowly drew it down toward his feet. As he moved his hand, the air seemed to open up, creating a gateway into the god king's chamber. Flunt stepped through the portal, and into what he knew could be the beginning to an end of an era.

She swam through the endless blue of the perpetual ocean. There was no surface, no floor, just an endless sea of infinite water. Her long blue hair waved and glided behind her as she swam in the aquatic paradise. There was no sun to light the waters, but they remained a pale blue, that emitted a soft light, though many of the creatures here did not seem to need to light to see. Surshy swam slowly, elegantly flowing through the watery vastness of the aquatic pane. Her soft blue skin seemed to shimmer as she swam. She wore no clothing. There was no need for it. There were no intelligent creatures that dwelled in the plane of water that wore clothing either. Truth be known she despised wearing clothing even when she was not in the elemental plane of water. She usually garbed herself in a thin watery shawl that clung to her every feature, often gaining her disapproving looks and stares when she was in Merioulus, though she wore her shawl more thickly when in the presence of Dicermadon. Not that she felt as if she owed the god king some measure of respect. She merely disliked the way his eyes seemed to soak up her form. Surshy was definitely the most free spirited of the elemental gods. Though she herself admitted that Lukerey, the god of luck and mischief, was the most free spirited of all the Breedikai.

Surshy twisted and turned, rolling over herself as she swam in acrobatic arcs. She paused and pursed her thin azure lips as she detected a disturbance in the plane. A powerful magic had entered and was streaking toward her. She immediately wove a shield and readied herself. There were few in the plane that had the ability to cast underwater, but she could tell this weave was not cast here. It had a small shield around itself and weaving's were too intricate to be a mortals. As the energy neared at immeasurable speed, Surshy lowered her shields. She recognized the trace of it and allowed the dweamor to approach.

"I have your proof, come to me, but make haste. Time is not a luxury." Whisten's deep raspy voice murmured in the watery plane.

Surshy frowned and looked around at her aquatic paradise. Had she been anywhere else the tears that welled up in her big green eyes would have rolled down her cheeks. She knew she might never get to swim here ever again. Her heart pounded and fear trickled through her veins. It had been along time since she felt fear. Surshy bravely pushed the thought aside and readied herself. The goddess of water knew what lay ahead, though she knew nothing of what outcome lay in store for her, or the Breedikai. She took some flows of water and twisted them to a small shield, creating an immeasurably miniature void in the plane where no water could touch. She opened a portal to the chambers of Dicermadon, the god of gods. Taking a deep breath she stepped into the chamber of the god king, and stepped into the unknown.

Whisten wove a thick stream of air around the door of the god king's chambers. It would take Dicermadon long to disrupt the hold of the door, but it would give them enough time to leap through a portal. The god of air placed his arms in the sleeves of his thick robe as portals began to open in the room.

    Flunt slowly stepped through the first portal that appeared. His dark red and black molten cape immediately began to distort the air around him from the volcanic heat that wafted from it. Flunt's eyes flickered nervously and his narrow pointed nose twitched as he inhaled the wicked stench of the abyss that hung in the air of the god king's chambers. Both Flunt and Whisten turned to regard Surshy as she stepped through the portal she had summoned. Her bright blues skin seemed a stark contrast to the bright red's and whites of the room. She wore a thin shawl of water that barely covered her voluptuous body. The shawl seemed to flow about her person like a tiny stream that was cloudy enough to distort the shape it covered. Her dazzling blue hair clung to the contour of her head in a perpetual wetness.

    Surshy glanced around the chambers with her beautiful emerald eyes that shined of anger and fear. "The foul stench of the deep abyss looms here." she said cautiously as she began to weave many protective dweamors about her.

    Whisten raised a calming hand in reassurance. "There is nothing to fear here now. The demon is long gone. Dicermadon's dealings were interrupted by Leska, some moments ago." the god of air said, noticing that Flunt also had cast some protective barriers around himself too.

    Surshy fixed her cold eyes on him. Whisten had always been trustworthy since the beginning of time, but the elemental goddess had seen many gods that were thought to be trustworthy stab others in the back since the beginning of time. She stared at his unreadable face. He could match Durion's cold rocky stare easily, in fact, she was not sure the god of air could not harden his face even more than the dwarven mountain god.

    "What happened when Leska interrupted

his...meeting?" Surshy asked with a barbed tone. It was no mystery that the earth mother was smitten by the god king, despite him being open and vocal about using her as mere entertainment only.

Whisten looked at Flunt who was waiting patiently for the reply, looked back to Surshy.

"Believe what you will brother and sister, but he attacked her. They battled, and she summoned two elder elementals to hold him off while she fled."

"Battled?" Flunt asked incredulously. "I thought the pair twined as lovers?"

Surshy chuckled and scoffed. "Even the god of fire is a thick headed as any man. To quote a mortal, marriage is made in the heavens, but so is thunder and lightening."

Flunt glared at Surshy. The fire that flickered around his face brightened and quickened as he narrowed his eyes. "I apologize, sister." Flunt said with a sarcastic bow. "But we men, are not as knowledgeable about deceit and trickery as women." The god of fire said as a thin smile crept on his face.

Surshy started to respond when Whisten cut them off. "Come now, this is not time for sibling rivalries."

Both Flunt and Surshy turned a hard eye his way.

Whisten ignored them and continued. "I believe Leska was fleeing to her garden."

Flunt nodded slowly. "Yes, she would be the strongest there."

Surshy nodded as did Whisten before he started again. "I was shielded with a powerful weave from air. He could not see me unless he strained to see the magical energy. A risky endeavor I know, but I am past lecturing at this point. The truth is, I witnessed him making a deal with an arch demon named Bykalicus. The demon is quite powerful and I speculate he has been around since the beginning of the abyss. I could not detect all that was said, but I know he gave the demon the knowledge of how to cast the DeNaucght."

Surshy frowned. "What is the DeNaucght?"

Before Whisten could answer, Flunt spoke. "The DeNaucght is a divine ritual that Leska allows only her most coveted priests perform. It usually gets her an intense argument from Rha-Cordan, but she sometimes allows it anyway. He really can't do anything about it since he left Merioulus." Flunt said with a satisfied smile.

"What does it do?" the goddess of water asked, turning away from Flunt and facing Whisten in aggravation

"Whisten sighed. Even at this hour of need his siblings could not keep from picking at one another. "The DeNaucght allows he who performs the ritual to summon the soul of a mortal who has past, back into it's body."

Flunt stepped forward and explained to Surshy. "He means it will raise the dead."

Surshy clenched her fists and stepped toward the god of fire angrily. "Continue to mock me, brother, and perhaps Whisten and Leska will have need of this DeNaucght for you."

"Enough!" Whisten yelled. "We need to make haste to the garden. Leska is surely about to, if not now, battling Dicermadon. He is in violation of sacred law. He has confided with demons and given away secrets. Panoleen did the latter and look what he did to her. I have sent messages to the other gods. We will converge on him and take him there. The proof is trapped here with flows of air, though I am sure, in his own superciliousness, Dicermadon will volunteer the needed evidence. You know how arrogant he has become since the birth of Lancalion."

Surshy narrowed her beautiful green eyes. She donned a frown of grim determination that is seldom seen on her carefree face. "I agree we must make haste. I will summon the others and meet you at Leska's garden."

Whisten looked at Flunt. The two usually worked well together during typical duties or projects. Though

Whisten disagreed with Leska as much as Surshy battled Flunt, when times called for the four to work together, they banded like a close knit family.

The god of air, and the god of fire, hurried out of Dicermadon's temple, and through golden streets of Merioulus, toward Leska's garden.

*   *   *

Fehzban opened his tired stinging eyes. He stared dumbly at endless blackness that was capped by indistinguishable flickers of light. The flickers danced and twirled around the corner of his dull blinded eyes. When he tried to look at the flashes directly, they would vanish as quickly as they appeared. Perhaps he was not really seeing the flashes at all. Perhaps the flashes were remnants of the burning hot pokers that Fraitizu had seared his eyes out with. Perhaps they were tiny angels that were trying to communicate with him somehow. Perhaps... Fehzban tried to silence the rapid thoughts that bombarded his mind incoherently. It seemed as time went on, he had more trouble keeping his mind focused. He found himself entertaining outrageous ideas and other nonsense. Fehzban knew these ideas and thoughts were surly false, but for some reason he still found them creeping into his head when he least expected them. The tormented dwarf pushed the thoughts away and focused on the sequence of the shrine that held the Heart of the Rock. He was one of the four keepers that held the combination to the magical lock that sealed the enchanted stone door. Fehzban ran the sequence over and over in his head again, repeating it and repeating it again. The dwarf had done this for hours upon hours as he tried to fight the thoughts that welled up in his tortured mind. The intense pain and torture he had suffered at the hands of Fraitizu had severe effects on his brain. Fehzban knew his thought process was different than it had been. Though conscious of the distinct change as he was, he could no more correct it, than a man falling, could sprout wings. Fehzban linked his sanity to the combination of the sealed chamber.

He would find himself chanting the combination until he would drift back into unconsciousness. He tried to droll himself to sleep once more, but he could not find the dark bliss he had been able to in the past. The constant squeaking and rolling of whatever he was laying on, seemed to prod his mind into perpetual consciousness. Fehzban tried to move his arms and legs, only to discover he was held fast by a thick rope, though in his weak state, it could have been twine. He could hear the squeak of wagon's axels as the hard wooden wheels bounced over the tough rocky terrain they were riding over. The hard wooden board he laid on was undoubtedly the wagon bed. Though uncertain if he was fastened to the floor directly, he could smell the thin, cold mountain air, and feel the crisp wind on his bare face. He surprised himself that the image of his bare chin did not shame him as he thought it might. Perhaps that he did not have to face the image in the mirror, saved him the humility.

Fehzban lost track of time on how long he rode on the back of the wagon. Hunger, nor thirst seemed to assail him with any vigor and darkness came and went several times before the wagon finally came to a rest. Fehzban listened intently as two men from the wagon, obviously dwarves by the height of the sounds they emitted, lowered the back wooden gate of the wagon and drug him out. They roughly pulled him out by the ropes that bound his feet. Without bothering to grab his upper body as they drug him out, Fehzban plopped onto the hard frozen rocky ground. He felt the hot stinging sensation surge up his arms and back from striking the hard earth. He smiled and mumbled something as the two dwarves cut the ropes that bound his hands. They then quickly ran to the wagon and rode off, leaving his feet bound.

Fehzban lay quietly on the frozen road, wearing

barely enough furs to keep him alive in the frigid temperature. At first the cold snow seemed to burn his hard calloused skin, but after a few moments the stinging turned to a pleasant numb. His perfect ears listened as the wagon hurriedly squeaked and bounced back down the mountain pass they had just come from. Part of Fehzban wanted to feel sadness at the wagon leaving. It was the last remaining morsel of his former self. Though in truth, he felt little more than gratitude for the wagon's departure. The intense cold seemed to affect him little as he lay there in the middle of the rocky trail.

    Fehzban rested motionless in the frozen rocky path for the rest of the day, though he could not see the sun directly, he could feel heat on his face and skin. Being blind, he was at a severe disadvantage during the day. He would wait for nightfall before trying to find shelter. Fehzban twisted and turned until his exposed skin was covered from the snow. The pain didn't bother him at all, but he new that if he were to get frostbite, he would have more of a difficult journey than it was already going to be. Journey. He said that word over and over in is mind. What journey? Where would he go? He couldn't see, his hands were next to useless and he could not even speak to ask for help if he heard someone nearby. Had he not gone over these questions in the long weeks he was in Fraitizu's chamber, the hopelessness would have overwhelmed him, but now, he merely closed his useless eyes and laid his head back in the cold snow.

    Fehzban drifted back into unconsciousness while he lay on the rocky trail. He dreamed of the battle at Central City. Amerix came back from the human surge at the east bridge and lead a second charge that proved to turn the tide against the humans. He and the army returned to Mountain Heart with a heroes welcome. The king rewarded him and Amerix for their bravery and the humans, fearing the dwarves might attack again, asked for unconditional peace. The Clan was saved, and he went rushing to the awaiting arms of his beloved wife. He could smell her sweet perfume he had bought her from the Andorian merchant that she had dabbed on her neck for him to nuzzle in. He pictured her beautiful face but it seemed to fade from him. What was her name? Slowly Fehzban struggled to remember the simplest detail of her. He loved her more than life itself, why could he not remember her name? His son, what was his face like? He stared at the pair, seeing their faces but not being able to recognize them. He knew who they were, yet he did not. Suddenly he was snatched around the neck. His family drifted off into the background to be replaced by the dirty grease stained walls of Fraitizu's chamber. The stench of dried stale blood assailed him as Fraitizu's wicked laugh echoed in his ears...

Fehzban shot up to a sitting position and lashed out at the darkness. His mangled fingers failed to make a fist as he tried to strike the nightmares in front of him. He screamed out an unintelligible yell at the night. After sitting for a moment to calm himself, Fehzban frowned and reached into his mouth to feel his horrible, mutilated, tongue. He faintly recalled the day Fraitizu had cut it to pieces. He did not recall the pain, more of a recollection of the loss to himself, knowing that he would never speak again.

The banished dwarf climbed to his weary feet. He could not feel the warm kiss of the sun, and the air was cool and crisp. All around him the dark mountainous forest loomed over. The forest consisted of thick dark colored coniferous trees. They were spaced far apart and there were many thick bushes and rocky juts protruding from the thick white snowy blanket that covered the ground.

Fehzban plodded on into the night climbing higher and higher into the mountains, sometimes scaling fifty foot cliffs. It was slow going, he had to feel for each hand hold instead of seeing it ahead of time. His mangled hands were next to useless which acted more like hooks than hands. He climbed until he eventually found a large rocky over hang. The overhang was on the edge of a large shelf on the side of a mountain. The shelf was almost a square mile covered with trees and snow. Climbing inside to escape the frigid wind, he laid down, exhausted. The underside of the outcropping was deep and offered good protection from the elements. Fehzban knew he would have to wait until morning to find which direction it faced, but he had good direction sense and was sure it faced east. Most all storms came from the west, so this shelter should be sufficient. This was going to have to be his new home for a while, he thought to himself as he closed his weary eyes. He wondered why he even opened them since he could not see. It seemed natural to him he guessed. Fehzban curled his knees into his chest to conserve heat in the mountain air and drifted off into sleep.

*   *   *

    Men garbed in fine silks and linens busied themselves about the polished marble floors of the Central City great hall. Servants rushed back and forth from offices carrying letters, orders and sometimes even refreshments. The great hall had been busy from sunup to sundown since the king removed Duke Dolin Blackhawk from power. He was still noble and was allowed to keep his estates, but he would no longer head the council at Central City. Since then, every viable noble with the remotest claim to the office had busied their houses with the preparations needed to request the title. Oddly enough, House Ganover, the house directly responsible for the king ousting House Blackhawk, had prepared quite a strong bid for the title. With the paladin, Apollisian, gone from the city, King Theobold held no notions as to humor him and his ways of Justice. In truth the king despised

Stephanis and all of his foolish followers. The problem was that the overwhelming majority of the masses embraced the god of Justice, leaving the king no recourse but to don his facade whenever a warrior of the church was near. Fortunately for the king, few politicians embraced Stephanis and the foolish few who did, seemed to have untimely accidents that ended their tenures rather quickly. King Thortan Theobold believed that Justice had no business within politics. However, Thortan was no fool. Despite wearing the crown of Beykla, the masses still held a considerable amount of power. Power that was rapidly dwindling, and a power that he hoped would be completely diminished when he handed the crown to his son, Darious.

Thortan chuckled and rubbed his clean-shaven chin as he gazed down at the reports that sat on his desk in his make shift office in the great hall of Central City. Send a treaty of peace to the dwarves indeed. " Not likely." He mused to himself. The only foreseeable event that could lead him to such a spineless treaty would be if the southern portion of the kingdom seceded. Then he would have no choice but to make peace with the dwarves to keep his nation intact. But as soon as the south was secure once again, he would wipe his royal bottom with the treaty and make the foolhardy dwarves pay for their attacks. Beykla had never been defeated in any war or conflict since time was recorded and he was not about to the first ruler to allow it. Even if he did lose some land temporarily with the treaty with the dwarves, Adoria seemed to be on the cusp of winning their civil war and their lands would be poorly defended, ripe for the taking. His western army alone, led by General Erik Stromson, the well known warrior of the orc wars, could easily take and hold the weak Adorian lands. All he had to do was secure the southern portion of the kingdom. He was close to succeeding until those damnable dwarves sacked the Torrent and then hit Central City. Thortan wondered if the fool bearded folk had a political agenda? He doubted it. Probably just dumb luck they attacked when they did. The difficulty with understanding the dwarves perspective targets were that he could not plant any spies among them. The entire clan was like some small family unit. Close knit and unyielding, the offer of coin for betrayal of any sort always failed. In fact most of his agents that attempted to hire one of the little folk to do such spindly tasks, were usually slain. It did not take long for the underground network to get wind of the dwarves reactions and soon no one would take such jobs. But Thortan didn't dwell on the things he could not change, he opted to seek out the positive of every event. In this affair, the dwarves had drew first blood, giving the green light to eradicate them from the ore rich Pyberian Mountains. Second, the dwarves had rooted out the wererat guild that dwelled under the city, something that the local magistrate had been unable to do since they were discovered some thirty years ago. The true challenge was going to be getting the masses to embrace wiping out clan Stoneheart. The south was certainty sympathetic to the bearded folk's plight and it was unlikely that the dwarves would ever be able to strike any cities there. Thortan did not have any villain or counter attack to strike the fervor of battle here in the north and had learned of the general Amerix from some of his advisors. They said he was the leader of the attack and was the dwarven king's most trusted alley, yet reports hinted the dwarven general was slain in the battle at the bridge.

    Thortan ran his calloused hands through his long brown hair. He sipped cider from a golden goblet that bore carvings of dragons and knights while he pondered the problem in his head. Perhaps the dwarf was not slain at all. He could set a hundred rumors that the great general that had the Beyklans hiding in fear at the mention of dwarves, was running like a fox, no, a like wounded rabbit, and that it was only a matter of time before he was brought to Justice. He would set an insurmountable reward to excite the people to hunt for him, and he would set a great posse to capture or kill the renegade. He would tell no one that the dwarf was actually dead. After sometime, preferably a lengthy time, a dwarf would be supplanted in the dead general's stead. The captured dwarf would be tried and sentenced for his crimes against the people as the renegade Amerix. The people would feel a great victory at the dwarf's capture. Thortan would then make peace with clan Stoneheart for the time being, thus securing the south. He would seem sympathetic to the south for sparing the dwarven nation and he would appear a great protector to the north for capturing the wicked general that mercilessly slain so many innocents. After the south was secured, Thortan would dispatch agents to remove and break up the current noble house that held such influence that was sympathetic with the dwarves and slowly plant nobles of his own that were eager to quell resistance as he started the campaign against the bearded folk.

Thortan sipped his cider again slowly, draining the goblet as he pondered his devious plans. It would take a great deal of work to plant the rumors of the dwarven general, and he had little time left here in Central City. He could delay naming the new Duke only so long before the nobles began to become suspicious. If he were going to enact this new plan he would have to begin immediately.

Thortan pulled his heavy fur cloak about himself and began scribing orders of the day. He dabbed the gray goose feather quill into the small dark colored ink vial several times and scribed a several more lines on the thick parchment. He paused for a moment then looked up, mulling over his thoughts when a rap at his door broke his concentration. Thortan looked up at the servant that poked his head inside. Edgar was not a young man by any means, but he was far from the autumn of his life, and more importantly, he certainly was no servant. Edgar had been the king's advisor for almost fifteen years and was the closest thing to a friend that Thortan had. Edgar was born of Motivas, a relatively large community in the southern portion of the kingdom. He spent a large portion of his life fulfilling the will of the church and participating in the ever revolving political field there. He quickly rose through the ranks of the locals and eventually came to be employed at the king's castle just east of Central City. Soon after Thortan was named to the crown. After the king's passing, during the orc wars, Edgar made himself readily available to the young king. Edgar had a fine grasp on the south's politics and their nobles, helping Thortan hold together an already decaying field of trust.

"Edgar, my trusted advisor, how fares the city?" Thortan asked as he stood up from his desk and extended his hand.

Edgar took it warmly and grasped his other hand to cover both of theirs, shaking them lightly while staring into the king's eyes. Edgar had taken the king for a foolish prince when he was first crowned, but since then, the cleric had learned the man had a fair head about his shoulders, and was ruthless in dealing with those he saw as an enemy.

"It fares as can be expected, my lordship, but the nobles grow eager to learn of the naming for the new duke. I have seen packs of ravenous wolves that were more receptive than that bunch." Edgar said, smoothing his dark blue robes with a red frill around the cuffs and cowl, marking him as Beyklan.

Thortan nodded as he spoke. "I agree that I need to name a duke soon, if for nothing else, to get me back on track of dealing with the foul dwarves and quelling the rebellion in the south."

Edgar crossed his legs tentatively and leaned forward, interested in what new insight Thortan must have gained. The man's wisdom for scheming seemed to grow with each passing day. "I had thought you planned on sending an emissary to make peace with the bearded folk." Edgar asked honestly.

Thortan nodded his head in agreement. "I certainly plan to, the south is very sympathetic to the little people's plight. Making peace with them will certainly take some of the fuel from the rebellious nobles fires."

Edgar smiled and leaned back. The hard wooden bench made his rump sore. He was used to much finer seating and hoped the king would solve the dilemma fast, so he could return to his posh living in Dawson or the king's castle. "I agree, my lord. That it will. But, will it not also fail to placate the northerners here, that spilled the blood of their fathers, their brothers, and their sons, fighting the bearded demons?"

Thortan grinned, leaned back in his chair and placed his heavy leather booted feet on the desk in front of him. He cleared his throat and intertwined his fingers as he spoke. " Tis true, Edgar, they will be angered by the treaty." Thortan paused waiting for the cleric to respond.

Edgar, sensing he was supposed to question the king's statement, sighed before he spoke in a sarcastic tone, waving his hands in a circle. "So what do you plan to do about the northerners and their thirst for vengeance."

Thortan frowned and leaned forward in his chair, placing his boots on the floor and angrily planting his hands on the edges of his thick desk. "Do not mock me, Edgar!" Thortan shouted before softening his tone and relaxing a bit. "We have been friends long, but know I am your king."

Edgar leaned forward submissively. "I am sorry, my lord, but I do grow weary. I am no novice to politics."

Thortan nodded slowly and sat back down in his chair. "We will give them an object to hate. The masses will be told the mastermind behind the dwarven attack was the general Amerix. My reports tell me the general was slain when he was thrown from the bridge on the east side of the city, near the Dawson River."

Edgar interrupted. "But was the dwarven general slain? Some reports stated that he was seen floating down river."

Thortan frowned, annoyed at the interruption, but continued. "Truth is what we make of it. When we are finished, this Amerix will be able to slay a hundred giants by himself and is running in fear of my might. I will make an incredible reward for his capture, or proof of his death, inspiring the masses to pick up swords and hunt the foul creature. No doubt the mobs will slay any dwarf they see hoping it is Amerix, but of course it will not be."

"Not until you decide it needs to be." Edgar put in.

Thortan smiled and placed his feet back on his desk and relaxed once again. "And when I decide that the dwarf has been captured, he will be slain and his body will be put on display for all to see. Making the north worship me as a hero, and the south will be happy with the treaty. In the mean time, my...under workers so to speak, will be rapidly removing southern nobles who are not in favor with my policies. After a short spell, I will renew the war with the dwarves, conquering them, and what is left of the Andorian lands. Thus carving out a place for me in history as one of the greatest Beyklan kings." Thortan boasted.

Edgar merely smiled. His longtime friend, and king was really beginning to understand the ways of being a king. "Now, my lord, all we have to do is begin planting the rumors about the dwarven general escaping alive."

Thortan grinned lightly and rubbed his clean-shaven chin, staring down at the parchments that lay on his desk before him. "Yes, I agree, my friend and advisor. That is why I have taken the liberty of drawing up these wanted petitions. I will have them hung in every inn, tavern, and shop from the northern reaches of Dawson to the lands we hold south of Motivas. I was careful to keep Amerix's description vague, other than he is large for a dwarf."

Edgar nodded, reached over and examined the petition of arrest. He scanned it up and down for a few moments before speaking. "What of the few men that have actually seen Amerix? What if they decide to answer the petition?"

Thortan grinned as he stood up from his chair and pushed his arms through the sleeves of his heavy cloak. "All the better if the real Amerix is found and brought to me, though it makes no difference. Once any dwarf is brought before the masses, they will scream it is the renegade general. They will lust at want of his capture."

Edgar nodded in agreement and picked up the small stack of parchments. " I will see that these are dispatched immediately." The cleric said as he stepped from the king's make shift office with a thin smile of satisfaction. He held no favor toward the dwarves and in fact would enjoy seeing the expansion of Beykla. Since the taming of the world, there was little land left to be gained by exploration, save for the wild lands to the far south west, but the terrain was so rough, it hardly seemed worth the trouble to anyone. Yes, if Thortan's plan worked he most likely would be the last king ever to add lands to the great Beyklan nation. Edgar was saddened by the thought. Surely they were seeing an end to a great age. As he walked down the great hall in Central City, arrest petitions in hand, Edgar wondered what achievements the next age would bring.

" Unselfish acts. Do they exist? Men claim that when they're in love they do unselfish acts. Mothers and fathers claim the same. But I challenge their way of thinking. Are their acts indeed, unselfish? I say that no man can perform an unselfish act, save for one. Many argue they have done many unselfish acts on a multitude of occasions throughout the year. But I defy each of these supposed acts, and expose them for the true underlying selfishness that dwells.

A man gives a gift to women he is courting. Why is he courting her? Is he doing it for her. No, he is courting her because she makes him feel good, maybe even loved. If she did not create this sensation within him when he was around her, you can bet he would be off courting another.

Gifts on birthdays and holidays, are they unselfish? Does not the giver receive a pleasant feeling when they distribute the gifts? Of course they do. If they did not, they would certainly not give the present. A man would never give a gift to another man he hated. This selfishness in gift giving goes as far to make the giver angry sometimes, when he or she is not thanked for the gift in which they gave. Plus, they sometimes feel inadequate if the gift they gave is placed lower in comparison to another's gift. In a way, basing their own self worth in their gift. Self worth, in a gift? Very selfish.

How often in a man's life has this simple wisdom eluded him? These are some examples of why man can never rise above his mortal self. His mind is flawed. He cannot see the world past what lies on the surface. Even the wisest scholars cannot admit this, and many other facts. They are too afraid to face the weakness of their race.

Strange though, that true compassion comes from this selfishness. Love. It seems to permeate and fill someone with such euphoric proportions that the soul cannot contain it any longer, so it begins to leak out.

This, and only this, is when a mortal man can begin to perform an act totally unselfishly.

Giving ones life to save another. There is no definite reward. Hypothesized rewards, depending on the god who is followed, but no concrete evidence that the sacrifice wont be for naught. It is usually performed out of a great empathy that extends beyond ones ability to recognize. Yet again, only in death, can a man achieve something he could never, while he was alive. Strange. The human race is a collection of good and evil beings that all fall short of the strength and wisdom of the gods they scorn, or sometimes worship. But what is stranger yet, is that I am often proud to call myself one."

-Lancalion Levendis Lampara-

Chapter Eight
Those who are Hunted

*M*yson Strongbow and Eulic Overmoon camped in a tall thicket of grass, south east of the Minok Vale. The two Darayal Legionnaires bundled their gear into small thin backpacks, which were light to say the least. These elves were more adapted to living in the wilderness than their brothers, who at best, are described as being one with the forest. The Darayal legion consists of one hundred of the top elven rangers of the Minok Vale. They travel the Vales seeking out evil denizens of the forest, such as orcs, ogres, and giants. Since the orc wars, the only time in history that have been recorded where elf and man has fought side by side, there have been little of the evil races left for them to hunt. Never-the-less, the legion has remained vigilant in their patrols, endlessly searching for evil to root out. The lands of the Minok Vale were vast and still many orc tribes remained, though in truth, the orcs warred with one another more frequently than they warred with others. The humans the elves fought beside were long since aged, most were now into the winter of their lives, where Myson and Eulic themselves remember some of the brave human champions as if they had shared the same fires in recent moons.

    Myson circled the perimeter of the small camp checking his snares. He had netted two large rabbits that would serve as their lunch and super later on the trail. Myson was young for a Legionnaire, as was Eulic, but

Eulic was near royalty, being a first cousin to the Overmoon family, even bearing their name. They had been raised from the brotherhood of the sword just before the orc wars when King Kalliman Theobold led his men in the crusade to wipe out the green skinned beasts from the face of his kingdom. Kalliman was a good man as far as the elves were concerned, unlike his scheming son. The elves did not think him evil so to speak, just selfish and calculating.

    Myson hung the rabbits by their feet from his thick leather belt. His long blond hair was braided in many hundreds of thin narrow strands that bounced along his head as he walked. The legion called it a varmin. They had worn the braids since their creation some millennia ago. The soft leather beads, or symas, that were fastened at the end of some braids represented lives he has saved during his tenure. Few legionnaires wore any silver rings, they marked selfless heroism, and even fewer yet bore gold. Usually the event that earned you a gold syma was fastened to your hair at your funeral.

    It was the smell of rotting flesh that drew the legionaries attention. They were in the Serrin plains, the most deadly lands left in the northern Minok region. Rotting flesh could mean the remnants of an attack, some orcs, or a giant battle. Myson drew his finely crafted scimitar and his masterwork short sword. The scimitar blade was magically enchanted giving the blade an unnatural balance that could never have been crafted from mortal hands, and the edge was so keen that it could slice into heavy mail that normal swords could not pierce. The scimitar's pommel was round polished brass and the hilt bore two winged horses, one on each side. His short sword was no less ornate, but lacked the magical enchantment the scimitar had.

    Stalking over the hill, Myson witnessed a large deer that was walking toward him. At first glance he was not alarmed and lowered his weapons, taking an easier stance.

But as the deer closed, he could clearly see it was a walking carcass. It bore a deep maggot infested wound on neck and in it's side. Rotting festering entrails drug the ground behind the beast and eyes were dull, glossy, and lifeless.

Myson moved slowly away from the animal. But as he moved, it moved. The deer laid ears back and lowered head, much like it might treat a threat from a wolf or other predator. Myson tried to back away again in another direction, but the deer again moved to intercept him.

"You desire a fight, then beast?" Myson called out as he approached the undead deer. "You are not a natural thing. I shall rid..."

Myson was cut off as the deer lunged at him. The ranger dropped to one knee and raised his scimitar up to catch the antlers and keep them from impaling him. Spinning, he slashed with his short sword behind his back, cleaving off the front legs of the animal. The deer stumbled and fell forward. Myson stood, turned and faced the deer anew. He had never seen undead before, but he had surely heard the tales. The deer acted as if it felt no pain, and was oblivious to it's own missing front legs. It crawled and lunged at him, trying to kill him. Myson doubted the beast could see out of eyes, it just seemed to sense him wherever he moved. With a clean swipe, Myson beheaded the deer. The rotting head hit the grassy earth with a dull thud. The body still quivered and twitched as black curdled blood slowly seeped from the wound. Wiping the gore from his sword onto the grass, Myson turned and hurried back to where he and Eulic had been camped.

Eulic saw Myson sprinting into camp with a worried look on his face. "What is the matter, brother?" Eulic asked. The long brown braids of his varmin bounced around his face as he turned.

Myson paused to catch his breath. "I encountered an undead deer in the plains. At least I think it was undead...No, I am certain it was. The beast actually attacked me."

Eulic frowned and looked around as if to see more undead descending down around them. When he did not see any he relaxed visibly. "Is it still there?"

Myson turned back the way he came. "I think it is. I cut off it's front legs and then it's head. If it is not there I do not think it could have gone far."

Eulic nodded and the pair hurried toward the area where Myson had battled it. Soon they came to the rise where he met the deer. Sure enough, the beast lay like it had been dead for many days. head was severed and lay a few feet from it's body. The front legs had been cut off, and maggots and other festering insects crawled in and over the body. The stench of rotting flesh hung in the air making the two elves cover their nose and mouths with their light brown cloaks.

Eulic peered around the area of the ground until he located the animal's tracks. Myson scanned the area for any more undead creatures that might be approaching.

"How do you suppose it...you know, came to be?" Myson asked uneasily as he scanned the horizon.

Eulic did not look up as he answered. "I do not know, brother. It is said that a mage or priest, powerful in their magic, can command the dead to rise and walk. Certainly they must be dark of heart to do such a thing, and I know of no such evils intelligent enough to do these things in the Serrin plains."

Myson nodded as he looked around. "Perhaps a dark mage or priest has made a home of our vast grasslands?"

"Perhaps." Eulic responded. "Look." the elf said as he walked along pointing at the tracks in the grassy ground with his nimble finger. "The beast came from the due south. No wandering, no zigzagging. A perfect straight line."

"No deer travels like that." Myson replied as he followed Eulic tracking the animal.

Eulic stood up and stared south into the rolling plains tapping his lower lip. "Indeed." perhaps we should back track this beast, dear brother. Mayhap we will run into the evil that spawned such a horrific abomination.

"What of the legion? Should we not report out findings to Master Orantal?" Myson asked reluctantly. He wanted to hunt the malevolence as much, if nor more than Eulic did, but such a finding was important to report.

Eulic did not respond. The ranger could sense his friend's desire to hunt down the vile mage or cleric as much as he did.

Myson met Eulic's gaze squarely. "We will advance to the south. If the fiend has established some sort of living quarters, then we will report." Myson proclaimed.

Eulic smiled and drew his long and short sword. "Agreed brother. Shall we?" he said as he motioned to the south and began walking. Myson smiled, drawing his two wicked blades and started south, stride for stride, with his companion.

* * *

Amerix wandered through the dense forest for many days. He sustained himself on mushrooms and some roots from what few plants he could recognize. A few of the berries he had eaten had left him somewhat ill, and he was feeling weak.

As the venerable dwarf wandered further south, he noticed that the forest became thicker and more lush. The normally deciduous forest gave way to a thicker and more jungle like terrain. Though the trees remained deciduous, the underbrush was much thicker making traveling through it more difficult. There were many broad vines that sprouted from the ground and entwined themselves in the thick canopy. Sounds of ground animals and birds that Amerix had never heard before seemed to echo around him, making him more nervous with each passing second.

The ancient general had felled hundreds of enemies, but dark denizens of the upper world he had never faced. He had no idea what mysterious powers they held, or how big they might be. Amerix had faced most of the monsters of the underdark in his long life, but he had never ventured far in the surface. It was not like he was one of his dark dwarves who had trouble seeing in the bright surface light, but he had spent most of his surface life in the cold mountains.

As Amerix ducked under a thick vine that hung from the top of two trees, the long sword he had strapped to his back began to make the shrill hum. Amerix paused and took the sword from his back. The old dwarf held the blade in front of his face and gazed down at the finely crafted sword. The shrill hum did not seem to annoy him like it had done in the past. It seemed somehow foreboding to him.

Amerix studied the strange weapon for a few moments. The long sword was surely eleven crafted. It bore many elven runes down the side a blade that reflected the thin rays of sunlight that poked through the thick treetops like a beacon of light in total darkness. The craftsmanship was so magnificent, the sword seemed to tantalize him where he stood. Amerix wondered why he had never noticed the beauty of the sword before now. He had carried the foul weapon since defeating the paladin at the Torrent Manor, yet it never struck him as beautiful until today.

Amerix was roused from his inattentiveness by a crunching sound in the distance. Ducking down the best he could, the renegade general waited for whatever it was to come closer. Squinting his old wrinkly eyes, Amerix spied a green skinned humanoid running recklessly through the woods. It had thick yellow tusks that protruded from lower law that extended well past it's upper lip. The creature was wearing some kind of sleeveless hide jerkin that exposed it's thick muscular arms. The creature's long tangled hair that clung to tiny pieces of branches and leaves, hung wildly in it's face. The thing would stop occasionally and turn, yelling something in a deep guttural language.

"Orcs." Amerix muttered under his breath. He hated orc's, as did almost everyone and everything. They were a horrible and vicious race that loved war, killing, and maiming. Plus, the green skinned monsters were remarkably good at it.

Amerix watched the orc curiously as it neared. It seemed to be leading something along at a hurried pace. It frequently stopped and turned, motioning for it catch up. Amerix decided to wait until the green skinned demon got a little closer before he erupted from the under brush and cut it down. Just as the orc got close enough that Amerix could have charged out and ran it down, he noticed the young orc seemed to be leading something along.

The orc whelp was almost as tall as he was, and seemed to be quite muscular. It whimpered and whined as it pitifully tried to push thorny branches and vines from it's path. The adult orc, that Amerix decided must be female, looked about nervously as if the pair were being pursued. Her eyes darted around as she impatiently tugged at the younger whelp. She would pick him up for and carry him briefly, but he was obviously to big for her to carry long.

Suddenly Amerix heard a loud deep horn sound from the west. The female orc let out a guttural cry and scooped up the whelp, running as fast as she could, while branches and vines smacked her in the face. She ignored them and hurried past Amerix, often stumbling to the ground. Seconds later crunching underbrush and the sound of many heavy footfalls pounded the earth. Amerix heard the sword again, or rather felt it. It's shrill hum echoed in his mind, warning him of the approaching pursuers.

The renegade general glanced to his left to see the

female orc slowly making her way, despite the obvious efforts of haste she was making. The pursuers burst into the dwarves view moments later. He counted thirteen of the green skinned monsters. They were about six feet tall, and extremely muscular. Their long black hair was worn in many different styles and it bounced along their head and shoulders as they charged wildly ahead. Some held wicked axes that were oversized for their bodies with nicked rusted blades, while others held clubs with giant metal spikes drove into them to act as some kind of pick axe, and others yet held rusted swords with equally nicked and scarred blades. Their bodies were covered in thick hide armor, though a few wore patched metal plates that seemed to be strapped to them with no apparent thought about protecting vital areas. The heavy metal plates hung loosely from worn leather bindings that clanged and bounced as they ran. When they saw the female orc running west, they began to hoop and holler in their guttural language, fanning out to over take her on all sides.

    Amerix waited. Though he despised orc's he was not here to fight thirteen of the powerful creatures. Orc's were warriors by blood, and even half of their numbers would give the most seasoned dwarf some pause. Amerix slowly moved closer to the confrontation. In truth he was more curious than anything, figuring they could not hear him while he walked casually through the under brush with all the yelling they were doing.

    The female realized she was not going to escape. Amerix watched as she transformed from scared and fleeing, to angry and vengeful. She stopped, grabbed a small sapling and snapped the bottom of it off with her foot. She pulled the string bark away with a roar and hastily ripped away the upper braches, making a crude club. If the other orcs were taken aback by her strength or repose, they showed no signs that Amerix noticed.

    The orc's surrounded the female and the pair called

out back and forth in their guttural language, all the while she held the young orc behind her, trying to keep the horde in front of her. Suddenly they all rushed in. The female ducked the first overhand attack of a wicked rusted axe and brought her thin club across the monster's neck. The force of the blow would have shattered any dwarf or human's neck, but the orc merely howled and dropped to the ground, rolling around grabbing his throat, gasping for air. The second attack came from her left as a rusted sword thrust at her unprotected midsection. She partially deflected the strike, but the blade dug deep into her thigh. She ignored the wound as another and another attack rained down on her. Amerix watched as the female fell under the attackers. The orc's giggled as they hacked and chopped the female into an unrecognizable pile of flesh. The young orc howled and screamed as he was restrained by two of the other beasts. Once the attack was finished, the orcs fanned out and began gathering wood they found along the forest floor. They quickly started a fire, occasionally punching the young orc in the face when he would not stop crying. Amerix watched with slight anger at the treatment of the whelp, but more out of curiosity. He had never know orc's had the ability to sense loss. The fact that a female orc, even a mother, if that was what she was, would give her life defending a young, perplexed the renegade general. Orc's did not care for their young when the whelps were old enough to walk and talk. If the whelp died, it was because he was weak.

 Amerix watched the orcs for a few hours. They managed to start a fire by rubbing two sticks together and then promptly ate the female orc they had just slain. They frequently fought each other, especially when they started feeding, all the while the whelp cried incoherently. Amerix had managed to ignore the swords constant humming, but it seemed to irritate him now.

 "A fine time to start bothering me, sword." he thought to himself while anger seemed to creep into him, a deep longing for the destruction of the foul green skinned beasts. The thought surprised him. He shouldn't care whether or not they killed and ate every one of each other, yet there he sat, on the edge of the underbrush fighting the urge to foolishly charge out from the thicket and slay all of them. Amerix found his mind wandering at what the young whelp was thinking. He remembered when he was a young dwarf, not a child, but not much older than one. He recalled when the shimmering white dragon, who would have been beautiful under different circumstances, attacked his home city. There were a thousand score of dark dwarves that followed the dragon as they invaded his home. Hacking and slicing, the dark dwarves carved their way into the heart of the city, while the dragon burned the outskirts with his unearthly arctic breath. No, arctic did not describe the coldness of the beast's breath attack. Amerix puzzled it in his mind for a few moments as he reflected. There was nothing cold enough to accurately compare to the dragon's breath.

    The shrill hum of the sword grew louder and more intense, waking Amerix from his daydream. The renegade dwarf had surmised the ringing was in his head now, but before others had clearly heard it. Amerix watched the orcs as night approached. The dark blue sky hung overhead and the cold chill of mid autumn sent his breath out in front of him in light frosty wisps.

    One of the orcs reached over and grabbed the terrified whelp by the hair and roughly drug him kicking and screaming to a large stick they had broken free from one of the larger tree branches around their camp. They roughly lashed the whelp to the branch and carried him toward the fire. Amerix had had all he could stand. Though he cared little for the orc whelp, it was all the excuse he needed to charge in an cut the green skinned beasts down. The renegade general hoped for death in battle, and every passing day, he became further from that possibility. Griping the sword handle tightly and adjusting the rusty chain mail that hung about his shoulders, he took a few deep breaths and broke from the underbrush in a mad rage, yelling an unintelligible battle chant that sounded more like a deep snarl than anything else.

    The orcs stood confused and startled for a fraction of a second. They were battle hardened creatures, fighting and dieing was their way of life, but the hesitation was all that Amerix needed. With an overhead slice with the long sword, he cut a cavernous wound down the shoulder and deep into the chest of the first orc. It roared and clutched the gash, falling to the ground in disbelief at it's inedible death. Steam rose from the fresh wound in the cold night as the beast gasped for breath. Amerix turned without hesitation, kneeled low, and sliced another of the green monster's legs in two, just above the knee. The magnificent long sword cut into the green beasts like a warm spoon into fresh dolgo nut pie. The second orc dropped his crude, rusted, sword and grabbed his severed leg with both hands letting out a blood curdling howl that pierced the calm night.

    One of the orcs with an over sized axe swung it at the short dwarven hellion that attacked them. The wicked weapon came streaking down toward Amerix's exposed ribs. The renegade general shifted his feet to one side, moving closer to the orc, and away from the fulcrum of the swing, halving the blow's power. He reached out his old, but muscled hand, and caught the shaft of the rusted blade. Even with the orc's blow at half strength, Amerix nearly toppled from the force. His shoulder ached and he was knocked off balance from the beast's monstrous strength. Amerix spun, hipped into the orc, using his shorter stature as leverage, and heaved the green skinned beast over his shoulder. The orc, refusing to let go of his axe, and left a clear kill shot as it lay on back, stunned from the throw. But Amerix was forced to release the crude weapon and deflect a strike from another orc that lunged in. As Amerix parried the rough rusted blade with the fine long sword, he side stepped toward the prone monster as it tried to regain it's footing. The renegade dwarf plunged the keen elven blade into the downed orc, then stomped on the dieing beast's head while wrenching the fine blade free from the monster's chest.

The orcs squared off against the renegade dwarf, showing more respect for their new adversary, but they quickly surrounded him, allowing no avenue for escape either. Orc's were stupid, but they were not cowards.

Amerix stood over the body of the orc he had just slain. He said nothing and glared menacingly at the, now ten, green skinned beasts that attacked him. The dwarf's hot breath erupted from his mouth as he exhaled forcefully from the exertion he had just performed. Two hundred years ago, he could have fought for hours without breaking a sweat, but not now. Amerix felt a sting in his shoulder and warm sticky blood dripping down his left arm. He did not have time to inspect the wound, but he doubted it was serious. That last attack he had side stepped must have still landed, though he didn't feel it at the time. *Must protect me axe arm.* he thought to himself. Amerix chuckled when he remembered he carried a sword. A sword. If anyone would have told him when he was over four hundred fifty years old, he would be fighting more than ten orcs to save an orc whelp with a long sword instead of his family's axe, he would have called the dwarf a plain fool. Yet there he stood in a dense forest in late autumn, wearing rusted chain mail and wielding a long sword. He guessed he probably wasn't even using it right.

Amerix kept flowing in a tight semi-circle while surrounded by the orcs. It made it difficult for them to tighten the trap, and kept them indecisive on who would charge in. The renegade general figured only five, maybe six could come at him at once, and was glancing around at the orc's looking for the biggest one to kill. The largest was usually the leader and if he slain him, it would not take long for the others to lose interest in the battle. It would take them a good while to fight out a new leader, perhaps even killing a couple more in the process.

     *   *   *

  The orc's bright yellow eyes studied the dwarf nervously. Their Kar, or war party leader, had went down under the dwarf's fist strike. They didn't understand why the dwarf had attacked them, especially alone. They were near no mountains, and in fact a few of the younger orcs hadn't even see a dwarf in the flesh before. Yet, the orcs were still more than confident they could kill the grizzled old dwarf that stood before them even though he did display a good sense of skill in battle. Their hesitation was more of a desire to be the new Kar. The first one that rushed in would no doubt fall to the stocky demon's sword, but while he was slaying the first, another could get in a good strike and kill the dwarf, making a strong claim for Kar. The orcs were happy to have a successful hunt capturing and killing the witch Valga. She had claimed that clan chief Slargcar had fathered her whelp. That actually was more than likely true, though no one cared. It was that Valga spat at clan chief's feet and called him a weakling. Any normal orc would have been slain on the spot, attacking clan chief's strength, but Valga was the clan shaman. She had dark powers that many orc's feared. It wasn't until clan chief Slargcar declared her traitor and elf friend that she fled with her son, Vlargcar. Orc's hated elves most of all, and being declared elf friend was about as low as you go as an orc. Plus the witch's son, Vlargcar had been born with blue eyes! No pure blood had blues eyes, let alone blood of a clan chief. It had to be more of her dark magic. Though it was all and done with. They had killed the witch Valga and nullified her powers by consuming her body. All they had to do was kill this wretched dwarf and then sacrifice the whelp spawn to Drunda, the orc god, and all would be right. But before one of the orcs could get the courage to attack, the dwarf chose for them and rushed in.

*   *   *

Amerix waited impatiently for the orcs to attack. He guessed that one would eventually close, but none of them seemed to want to be the first. They probably wanted to be the second hoping they could sneak in a lucky shot and claim the killing blow for themselves. Orcs were essentially cowards. While they stood glancing nervously back and forth to one another and then back at him, Amerix chuckled. He would be here all night if the orcs were trying to think up a plan of attack. Orcs thinking. The very notion lifted his spirits as nearly laughed aloud.

Amerix shifted his tight grip on the long sword and he lunged at the orc, that seemed the largest. The green skinned beast was quite surprised that the short bearded creature would dare attack them, but Amerix made the surprise more apparent as he drove the sword home into the creature's chest. The orc stared wide eyed and merely gurgled in response at the keen blade that was already wrenched free and set about some of his other comrades.

Amerix ducked low and brought the razor-sharp blade around his body and up the groin the nearest orc. The sword slashed the beast deep from it's groin to it's chest. Clutching the grievous wound, the orc fell to the ground howling pain as tears filled it's eyes and it's bright red blood spilled onto the leaf covered forest floor.

The orcs seemed to recover from the shock of the dwarf attacking them when the bearded foe was surrounded and they quickly redoubled their efforts in new attacks. Amerix continued to stay low to the ground as he ducked and spun, carving a swath of death among his green skinned enemies.

The battle raged on. The orc's fought with renewed

fury each time the scored a hit. Amerix bled from many wounds though, none were crippling or life threatening, they were beginning to slow him down. He had slain, or crippled eight of the thirteen orcs, but the remaining five seemed to attack with a structured unison. They had created a flow, one attacking, then parrying allowing another to attack immediately after, giving them balanced flow of attacks and feints. It gave Amerix little time to counter strike each attack as he had to deflect or duck the next one. The orc's reveled in the notion they had outsmarted the dwarf and were going to wear him down. Yet, Amerix was no fool when it came to battle. Blood soaked from many different wounds, the had dwarf spent more hours in the heat of battle than these orc's had spent breathing. An intelligent enemy would shift the attacks so that the next was never predictable. Though the shift might confuse it's comrades and leave a small time when there was no attack, it was more likely to confuse the enemy more. Second, by performing the attacks in the same order, it taught Amerix where the next attack was going to come from after the first. Grinning with a blood soaked beard from a thin slice across his forehead, Amerix spun, cleaving the hand off that held one of the orc's great rusted axes. The heavy weapon skittered into the thick leaves that lined the forest floor while the orc stood in shock holding his bloody nub, where a powerful hand that griped his axe had been.   The next attack was an over hand slice, which the renegade general rolled under and sliced the razor sharp blade across the midsection of the unsuspecting orc. The beast howled as the keen blade smoothly sliced into ribs, severing them, thus spilling it's entrails out onto the ground before it. The remaining three orc's turned and fled. They had enough of the demon dwarf.

    Amerix plopped down against the tree as his chest rose and fall in great heaves. His breath seemed to send out a steady fog into the cold twilight air. Around him on the ground, some of the mortally crippled orc's mumbled to themselves and tried to crawl away but they would not go far before death claimed them. The renegade general dabbed the warm blood from his forehead, careful not to tear open the thin cut any more than it was. After applying a thin dirty cloth as a bandage to his several wounds, Amerix let his weary head fall back against the tree. The cool bark felt soothing against his sweaty head. Glancing over at the whelp that was tied to the stake, Amerix noticed something peculiar about the little beast. Every orc he had ever faced in his four hundred fifty odd years of life had bright yellow eyes. That was always a sure way to mark an orc in the darkness, by their sinister eyes, yet the whelp that sat bound to the wooden stake stared at him intently with crystal blue orbs. The renegade general had seen many strange things in his long life and paid the blue eyed orc little attention. The dwarf focused more on the horizon, wondering if the green skinned beasts might return with friends. He was in no mood to fight any more of the potent monsters, and in truth, doubted he could last long against any further attacks. Each incredibly strong strike he deflected seemed to suck his strength from him.

Amerix rose from the tree and adjusted the rusted mail that hung from his old body. Despite all he just endured, at least the damned sword was not making that cursed shrill noise again. His head hurt enough as it was. Walking over the whelp, Amerix leaned down and cut the thing free. He hated to let an orc loose, but it seemed foolish to risk his life battling it's captures, only to leave it bound up for more to return and kill him later. If the whelp was afraid or surprised, it showed neither. It merely continued to stare at Amerix with those steel blue eyes of his.

"What a ye lookin at ye green skinned freak? Think I'm gonna eat ye, like yer pals?" Amerix asked rhetorically.

The orc didn't respond, it merely stood up slowly

and rubbed it's wrists. Amerix gazed at the green skinned whelp wearily. The orc stood almost as tall as he and was very muscular despite it's young face, though the dwarf knew little of telling how old an orc really was.

"Loke-tah." the orc stated in a deep guttural voice.

Amerix stared at it with a confused face. The orc frowned in what appeared confusion. It tilted head to the side and bared bright yellow teeth. Two large tusks protruded from the creature's massive under bite and it's long black hair hung about it's thick neck.

"Loke-tah." the orc repeated, but more forcefully this time.

Amerix shrugged his shoulders, staring intently at the whelp that stood before him.

"What in bloody Durion's name do..."

That was all Amerix managed to get out from his mouth when the orc lashed out a quick powerful punch that caught the renegade general square in the chin. Bright stars erupted in the dwarf's mind as he staggered back trying to regain his balance. His feet were wobbly and anger flooded into him. He started for his sword when he realized that the orc still stood there before him looking more puzzled than before.

Amerix had difficulty controlling his fury. "Loke-bah to ye too, freak!" the dwarf shouted as he slammed a bone crunching fist into the orc whelp's face. Amerix felt the incredible hardness of the beast's skull against his knuckles. The orc fell back onto the ground, landing roughly on it's rump. bright blue eyes crossed with dizziness and it held it's head in it's hands. Amerix looked down at his bloody knuckles in amazement. The creatures skull was so hard, it split the skin on his hand as if he had punched stone. Yet, the whelp merely sat stunned on the ground. The renegade general placed his hand on his long sword as the whelp slowly stood up.

"Punch me again ye green skinned baby, and I'll run ye trough like I did yer cousins." Amerix stated flatly, never releasing his hold from the sword's hilt.

The orc seemed unfazed by the threat, and walked over and retrieved one of the crude axes that had been dropped by it's felled captures. The whelp picked up the over sized axe that seemed too heavy for him to wield effectively and hefted it over his shoulder. The axe was as long as the whelp was tall. The head was thick and rusted, with hundreds of nicks and chips in the blade. It was obviously poorly balanced, yet the orcs seemed to use them with great proficiency.

Amerix tensed and started to cut the beast down when a unexpected rush of serenity swept over him. There was a strange voice in his head that simply said; " Hold."

Amerix paused as the strange sensation slowly passed. The whelp stood with a calm, non-threatening posture, looking around with it's bright blue eyes. Shaking his head, the dwarf started walking south into the night, occasionally turning to try to run off the unwanted follower. But to his frustration, the orc seemed unwilling to leave him. Amerix muttered something under his breath about the next time he was at the bottom of a great river, he was going to stay there. The orc did not understand the dwarven tongue and only followed in silence.

*   *   *

Eulic and Myson followed the tracks of the undead deer diligently. They paused to rest little and their trek took them most the day and well into the dark hours of the evening. The thick grass plains waved softly in the cold autumn night under a bright starry sky. The two legionnaires relaxed sprawled out on a large hilltop, enjoyed the rabbits they had caught earlier in the day. They had cooked their dinner before the sun had set, and now ate without fear of any attacks from the denizens that roamed the Serrin Plains. Myson roughly pulled the last bits of charred meat from the leg he was eating and stuffed it into his mouth. He chewed for a bit then tossed the bones to the side.

"Ya know, I was thinking." Myson said, wiping the grease that was at the corner of his mouth with his sleeve. "Perhaps we don't find the source of this zombie deer tomorrow. Then what?"

Eulic finished chewing the bite that was in his mouth giving Myson a look of disgust at his eating habits. Eulic cleared his throat. "I suppose that we head back to the Vale and report our findings."

Myson nodded reluctantly and roughly tore another large chunk of meat from his rabbit and crudely stuffed it into his mouth. "I suppose you are right." Myson said, rolling the chunk of meat in his mouth from one side or the other when he spoke. " But it sure would be nice to present the Vale with the necromancer's head."

Eulic nodded, then shook his head in disgust. "Have you no manners?"

Myson shrugged. "Who am I to offend. We are deep into the plains. We are not before the council or at some public function."

Eulic started to reply when Myson cut in. "Besides, I rather enjoy your hundred and one faces of contempt at my eating habits. Just when I think I have seen them all, a different one pops up." Myson said, trailing off at the end from laughter.

Eulic growled and stood up. "I'm going to set snares for tomorrow's food. Do get some rest."

Myson grinned and finished eating his meal. He occasionally smacked his lips, or licked his fingers loudly enough to get a revolting groan from the darkness. After he finished eating, Myson leaned back in the soft grass, crossing his arms behind his head. He stared up into the twinkling stars that hung bright overhead and soon, he drifted to sleep.

Eulic took his time wandering around the base of

the hill setting snares for rabbits and other small ground animals. He hoped he dallied long enough that Myson would be asleep, or at least finished eating. The elf was as uncouth as a dwarf sometimes.

*   *   *

Trinidy wandered into the night. He was unsure how long he been following the strong magical pull that lead him almost due north through these thick plains. Strange enough he had seen little wildlife, though he noticed fresh tracks and even fresh droppings. It was almost as if the animals sensed his coming and fled. He was glad he no longer needed to eat or drink on this journey. Something that had to be tied with the quest, though he didn't specifically recall the blessing being cast on him. The fact he did not need sleep did not sit well with him though. He knew of spells that sustained a man so he did not need food or water, but he was unaware of any magic that made sleep entirely unnecessary. Even the strongest spells required the target to get at least a few hours of sleep a day, yet he been well over four days without sleep, maybe more, and he did not feel the least bit fatigued. Trinidy would have spent more time pondering the fact but he had difficulty thinking clearly and the tug from the magic was so strong it often disrupted the easiest of thought process. Trinidy feared what would happen if he needed to cast some protection spells to help an innocent or some healing. Surely this great evil he had been summoned from beyond the grave to destroy would have persecuted thousands that would now need aid.

The death knight marched well into the night. He crossed over hill after hill, never losing sight of the forever expanding northern horizon. Ever obeying the pull that lead him on. It was almost daybreak when he sensed it. The sky was a dark blue and the stars were beginning to melt away from the sky. The eastern atmosphere held a crimson glow from the sun that seemed to grow brighter with each passing moment. The death knight stopped in his tracks, ignoring the pull that commanded him to march forward. He could sense two separate evils over the next rise. One was moving slightly to the west, were the other lay still. He could not see the evil, but he surely felt it. Trinidy frowned. He had never sensed evil before with out actively pausing and meditating to find it. Either the evil was very powerful, or his senses had been enhanced. By the way he had sensations about the evil hill giant, he surmised his sense were somehow improved by the spell. The death knight drew his sword. The dark azure blade emitted a thick frost that wisped around it, cascading down the blade and enveloping the hilt and Trinidy's hand. Dark and sinister runes glowed bright blue on the blade near the hilt that was comprised of hundreds of tiny skulls. His shield, that held a giant skull affixed to the outside of it, emitted a similar frost and the eyes of the shield began to secrete the deep azure hue.

    Trinidy stalked forward. His rotten twisted face formed an impossibly distorted frown and the many dark stinging insects that normally roamed from one empty eye socket to the next, now skittered across his visage as if they were disturbed. As he crested the horizon he paused in confusion. An elf kneeled at the base of the hill pulling a rabbit from a snare. The elf was no dark elf, the only elves that Trinidy knew were evil. He wore finely crafted chain armor that clung to his slender form. His light blonde hair was braided into hundreds of tight weaves that dangled about his neck and shoulders, some of the weaves containing leather hoops at the end. He wore a finely crafted scimitar at one hip and a similar crafted short sword at the other. He had a dark green flowing cloak that was thick, but seemed malleable as it hung loosely at his back. Though in every outward appearance the elf seemed to be a goodly elf, but Trinidy knew different. He could feel the animal's great evil that emitted from it. The dark notion was so great it to took vast restraint from the death knight not to rush out and slay the elf where he stood. How dare the evil elf, disguise itself as one of the goodly races. Then the horrific sound of mockery started coming from the elf. Thump-thump. Thump-thump. He remembered the same sound coming from the hill giant. The sound seemed to mock him then, it seemed to insult him somehow, but this sound went beyond that. The very fact that the elf sat there taking breath seemed the greatest attack on humanity that Trinidy could every remember.

  The death knight took the first step toward the elf. Then another. It took all of his composure to march to the elf instead of slaying it. He did not retain his paladin statue when he was alive the first time by rushing in against evil. He always made sure they were evil before he slew them. Just as he would ensure this elf was evil. Despite how strong the magic screamed the elf was, despite how strong the pull ordered him to ignore the elves and continued to move forward. There was no magic that would keep him from evil. None.

     *   *   *

  Myson kneeled before the last trap Eulic had sat before he went to bed. Only the south traps had animals in them, and it was a large amount of those southern traps. Myson had gathered enough rabbits that they would not have to hunt for a week. It seemed as if something had herded the rabbits from the south, to the north, into their snares. Surely he would have to wake Eulic and see what he thought of the strange events.

  Myson took the last rabbit from the snare and affixed it to his belt. He tied the two rear feet, just as he had done the others, and as he hooked it to the leather strap that hung down when he felt a cold wave come over him. Myson shuddered. It was strange for a wave of cold like that that hit him when it didn't seem to travel on the wind. It was autumn after all, but the wave didn't move his hair, it didn't hit his skin, it was more of a sensation. There was movement to his left from the hill to the south. He turned and froze. The most ghastly seen he had ever witnessed in his life walked toward him. It was a man, or least had been a man. It was well over six foot tall, indicating to the legionnaire that it had been human, but it's face wore a glare that was unnaturally exaggerated. The frown creases started high on the forehead and the under turned mouth extended well into the jaw line, exposing two rows of rotten, decaying teeth that were either dark yellow or light gray. Hundreds of large black insects erupted from mouth and crawled to it's eye sockets or to it's ears like an ant hill that had been roused. It's eyes lacked anything but a deep empty socket that had a blue supernatural glow. It's hair hung down in thin black streaks across it's face that was devoid of muscle as if it were tight decaying skin drawn across it. The apparition wore thick rusted plate armor that bore twisted religious symbols and hundreds of tiny skulls. The armor bore hundreds of scars from countless battles and seemed as if it would crumble off of the undead beast at any moment. The thing held a great blade that was described as sinister at best. It's blade had an azure glow that radiated thin wisps of frost that cascaded down the sword, enveloping the monster's gauntleted hand. It carried a shield in the other hand that bore many twisted religious runes. It had a great skull of some unnamed beast affixed to it that had empty sockets that glowed as cerulean as the sword did.

    Myson wanted to scream, he wanted to run, he wanted to draw his blade and attack, all at the same time. The undead monster emitted an essence of such absolute evil, that the legionnaire had difficulty forcing breath from his lungs to shout at Eulic.

    "Brother, two arms!" Myson shouted hoarsely as he

slowly backed up the hill toward camp.

Eulic rushed over the rise wearing his dark green cloak and his bedding clothes, long sword and short sword in each hand. He cursed himself for not sleeping in his armor, but the chain was uncomfortable and was difficult to maintain if it was slept in.

"Do I have time to..." Eulic voice trailed off as he gasped in horror at the creation that stalked up the hill toward a backpedaling Myson. The beast seemed to leave a wake of decaying grass with each horrible step it made. The apparition stopped at the sight of the two elves at the top of hill. It stuck it's wicked blade into the dirt and pointed at them with it's gauntleted hand.

"Yhw od uoy edih dniheb eht esiug fo yldoog sevles."

Myson glanced over at Eulic nervously. "Do toss on your armor, brother. I suppose this is our necromancer."

Eulic nodded stabbed his blades into the earth, reaching down to his bed site and picking up the lightweight smooth set of glimmering elven chain.

*   *   *

Trinidy neared the elf that was kneeling near the trap. The creature seemed to sense him as he approached. He cursed to himself silently. The beast must have a method to detect goodly beings. The elf seemed horrified at his sight. Good, evil always did run and cower when confronted by good.

Trinidy followed the elf as he slowly backed up the hill calling something out in a foul dark language he did not understand. The death knight glowered his deep blue eyes. They were certainly evil now, he had heard the tongue of damned escape from their lips. It was almost certain he would have to slay them now, though he would give the elf one chance to spare his life. Trinidy started to speak when a second elf came from over the rise wielding a long sword in one hand and a short sword in the other. It too had a similar haircut to the first elf. Trinidy figured they were part of some kind of cult, though he knew of no cults that wore such styles. The two elves conversed in the sinister tongue from the abyss. He had heard it spoken when he spent those years under the enslavement from the arch demon, Bykalicus. The mere thought of the demon seemed to send Trinidy into a murderous rage, but he fought to suppress it. The elves emitted that horrible taunting; thump-thump, thump-thump, that nearly drove him mad, but he clung to his disciplined mind. He would not slay them out of hate, regardless of how evil they were. He offered them one chance to save their lives. He pointed his gauntleted finger at the pair.

"Why do you hide behind the guise of goodly elves?" He asked.

The elves did not respond right away. They just stood defensively and watched him. Then the blonde haired elf with the rabbits tied to his waist spoke something in the abyssal tongue. The other stuck his swords in the ground and donned some chain mail. Trinidy smiled. The fools wanted to fight. That was fine with him. He needed and excuse to slay these children of night so he could get on with his quest for his god. The magical pull commanding him north was growing stronger and more difficult to ignore with each passing moment. When the dark haired elf finished donning his chain armor, Trinidy gave them one final chance for salvation.

"Throw down your swords and I shall let you live." Trinidy said calmly. The two elves looked at each other, then the blonde haired one drew his swords and stalked to Trinidy's left flank. The brown haired elf drew his swords from the ground and stalked right. Trinidy smiled and prepared to rid the world of the evil vermin. Finally he was going to get to do something worth while.

* * *

Eulic quickly donned his chain armor. Just as he fastened the side straps with his nimble fingers, the undead apparition spoke again. The monster's voice seemed to echo within itself in a deep demonic sound.

"Worht nwod ruoy sdrows dna I llahs eraps ruoy sevil."

The elves shivered. The thing appeared to have once been human, but it was obvious to the legionnaires that any remnant of humanity left in the magically animated corpse, was long since lost.

Myson drew his scimitar and short sword, circling the foul creation, while Eulic pulled his blades free from the hard clay earth and circled the opposite side. The two elves decided to fight in a flanking nature, in case this creation had some skill with a blade. The two legionnaires doubted the thing carried the wicked sword for prosperity.

Myson flashed in with a feint from his short sword and low slashing attack with his enchanted scimitar. Eulic lunged in with his short sword showing a low attack, then twisted, striking high with his long sword. The two moved as one, striking just where the other was feinting. The calculated attack would have felled most any opponent, few were skilled with blades in all the realms as a Darayal Legionnaire, let alone a pair of them set upon a single opponent. But to the legionnaires' surprise, their attacks were deflected. The feints were ignored as what they were and the low strike from Myson was deflected with a crushing down stroke from the heavy broad sword Trinidy wielded. Eulic's feint was also ignored and his high strike was deflected to the side with a powerful sweeping motion from the dark and sinister shield.

Pain shot up Myson's arm from the bone rattling block. His scimitar shook from the horrific strike that he was sure would have shattered any normal weapon. He watched in disbelief as Eulic's strike was deflected easily by the apparition's shield, sending the brown-haired legionnaire's arm wide, exposing his underside. Trinidy spun his heavy broad sword around his back, cutting into Eulic's chain shirt, laying a neat slice under his arm. Eulic winced in pain as the abyssal cold from the weapon sucked his breath and shot stinging magical energies into his flesh. Though the wound was far from fatal, far from crippling for that matter, the elf could feel the dark magical energies swirling into his body.

As Trinidy spun to strike Eulic with his broad sword, he brought his heavy shield around striking Myson in the head and shoulder as he stood low after his strike was deflected. A blast of blue energy blasted out from the mounted skull that was on the shield, and hit Myson, knocking him backwards into the tall grass. He landed with a hard thud, knocking the wind from his lungs. He had managed to hold onto his blades, though as he started to rise, he realized he had been knocked back a dozen feet.

Eulic clutched the wound in his side for a brief moment before resetting himself. He knew the wound was not fatal, little more than a scratch, but he could feel his strength waning from the wound. It burned cold and the legionnaire could feel his side going numb. He had little time to react as he was put on the defensive from a barrage of attacks from the undead creature. Eulic worked his blades in a magnificent dance, blocking and ducking the corpse's wicked attacks. The elf was amazed at how quickly the creature moved. It was impossible to move the way he did in the heavy plate armor, impossible to wield such a heavy sword that was designed to cut through plate armor, not fence with any precision, yet the legionnaire used every ounce of energy, ever ounce of skill he possessed, to keep the deadly blade from striking him. The corpse attacked with such perfect flow, he had no opportunity to mount any kind of attack of his own. It seemed as if he were merely delaying the end. Never had he faced a foe so skilled with a blade. Fear began to well up inside him. It was not fear of death, not fear of injury. The Darayal Legionnaires had long ago given up fear of those things. The things a Darayal Legionnaire feared were failure. Eulic feared he might fail his kinsmen or worse yet, the Vale.

Myson flipped to his feet, swords in hand. He rushed forward slashing and stabbing.

Trinidy deflected each strike, though it was obvious the pair attacking him strained his abilities. The elves ducked and struck with uncanny precision. Trinidy danced among them, though now his armor rang from an occasional elven strike.

Deep crimson blood, streamed down Eulic's side from the wound that ran across his ribs. This apparition was dangerous indeed.

*   *   *

Trinidy deflected each strike with harrowing precision. He marveled at well he moved with his armor on, and how light his heavy broad sword felt. Normally the elves, with their lighter weapons and thinner armor, would have been somewhat difficult for him, but he seemed to match them stroke for stroke. He felt himself taker a few hits, but strange enough, he didn't feel any pain. He knew he had hit the elves. The brown haired one with the long sword and short sword bled from his side from a thin slice he had managed to lay just under the elf's arm. They were good, deflecting most of the death knight's attacks, but Trinidy could plainly see the elves could not hold out forever. He laughed aloud as he fought.

"You, fool elves. Did you really think evil would triumph over good?" Trinidy bellowed.

The elves responded in the twisted abyssal tongue that infuriated Trinidy. How dare they speak their blasphemous language to him.

Trinidy growled and focused his attack on the brown haired elf. The death knight could see the wound in his side was weakening him, causing to him to lessen his guard with that weapon arm. The battle would soon be at an end.

     *   *   *

Steel rang on steel across the early morning plains. The elves danced swords in a game of death among a circle of black dead and decaying grass, that rotted with each passing moment. Eulic and Myson fought for their lives. Their thin braided hair bounced about them as they twirled and ducked low. Large beads of sweat had formed on their brows from the great exertion of the battle, despite the frosted cold air of mid-autumn. The two elves were vaguely aware of the rapidly dieing and decaying grass that encircled them like a small battle arena. Myson could tell that Eulic was growing weak from the wound in his side and he was losing a lot of blood. Myson could tell the corpse they battled also detected a decline in Eulic's ability to defend himself, because he suddenly shifted his tactics and focused on his wounded brother. Anger welled up inside Myson. This necromancers pet was not going to slay his kin. He was not! Myson renewed the ferocity of his attack. He pressed harder, faster, whirling his blades like a court jester might whirl a baton. He ducked and struck, each time coming closer to hitting home on the apparition. He had score a dozen hits against the thing, but it seemed impervious to minor blows. It bled only a little from the wounds, and it was not really even blood. A thick black substance trickled out that had the density of pine tar on a cold day.

Eulic was tired and hurting. The pain in side grew more intense. The wound itself was very cold and numb, but great tendrils of white hot pain erupted from the edges of the wound and shot into his arms and down his legs, making it difficult for him to move with great precision. The corpse seemed to detect his weakness and it pressed harder. Eulic tried to circle, to keep the power stroke away from his weak side, giving Myson a greater line of attack. Eulic doubted the corpse was as skilled in life with his sword as he was now, in undeath.

    The death knight pressed harder and faster. Each sword stroke from the wicked sinister blade that the death knight wielded came closer to hitting home, yet Eulic fought on. Eulic felt a sharp sting on his leg as he backed away from the death knight in a defensive dance of death. He glanced down to see many small dark black stinging insects crawling on his leather breeches trying to bite and sting him. The ground seemed to be alive with hundreds of the tiny bugs.

    Myson pressed harder. He struck faster and with more meticulousness than he ever had before. Narrowing his grim determined eyes, he saw an opening and took it. He slammed his scimitar home into the thick armored plate that covered the death knights back. The enchanted blade easily sliced through the rusted mail and rammed to it's hilt. The death knight raised his hands up into the air and arched his back as if in great pain. He dropped the wicked broad sword and his shield arm went slack. The sinister blade clanged to the cold hard earth. Eulic paused to begin clearing his breeches from the many scorpions and spiders that had crawled up them. Myson tried to wrench his word free, but it was held fast in the thick armored plate that covered the death knight. The corpse turned with a look of shock on it's twisted rotted face. cold blue eyes stilled glowed, but it appeared as if the battle was soon over.

    *   *   *

    Trinidy pressed the attack. He knew the elf behind him was pressing his, but he needed to finish of the weak one before the damnable elves got in a lucky strike. Despite them being evil, they were remarkable swordsmen. Trinidy had to focus all of his attention to battling this pair. It was a pity these blade artist had to be slain. Their skill was surely dizzying. The death knight noticed, however, that while he fought these two denizens, the magical pull that seemed to almost force him to go north, had subsided completely. Perhaps these two were what he needed to slay. Maybe they were this great wrong that needed righted. That seemed to easy, but he had performed other tasks in his past, that were thought to be impossible, that were just as simple. The one thing that still clouded his mind was that cursed thump-thump that echoed in his head. There were clearly two separate thumping sounds, though now they reverberated much faster and blended together, but Trinidy was sure the sounds were the markings of evil. They had to be the way he despised it so.

  Trinidy had pressed the wounded elf to circling, making his attacks one dimensional and easily predictable. He started to focus more of defending the elf that struck at his back. That one's strikes were getting to close. That was when he knew he had erred. Trinidy felt the tip of the elf's sword pierce the plate armor that covered his back and he watched in horror as a sharp scimitar blade erupted from his chest. He arched his back and he dropped his sword and shield in anticipation of the incredible pain that was sure to follow. How could die like this? How could he fail his god? Would he be sent back to the abyss? The thought of Bykalicus' hideous laugh and the cold sulfuric air of the great underworld launched him into a fury. If he was going to die, he was not going to die until these two elves were long since dead! He turned and faced the blonde haired elf that had just stabbed him in the back. A definite sign of the evil elf's cowardice.

  Trinidy angrily reached out with his gauntleted

hand. The rusted fingers outstretched, the old armor creaked. Trinidy felt a great rumbled from inside of him, like a hunger, but not. It seemed to be some kind of force that dwelled within him. A force that cried out to be sated. It felt as if it bulged and grew inside him, like an ever growing bubble about to burst. The elf stood wide eyed and stepped back.

"Necropium Nectues." Trinidy said. The words seemed to crawl out from deep inside him, almost as if someone else had said them. He did not know exactly what they meant, nor what language they were. They were more a culmination of each language at the same time, separate in their uttering, but united. As if a thousand condemned voices cried out, rather than the deep growling voice of Trinidy. He had never cast any spell in that manner, nor commanded the wrath of his god, without first grasping his holy symbol. He did neither, yet the flash of dark black and blue swirling weaves erupted from his finger and shot into the blonde elf's body.

The wispy tendrils poured themselves effortlessly into the elf, like wind might blow through the leaves of the tree. Myson gasped and grabbed at his chest, writhing on the ground. Twisting and rolling in the decayed ash that had once been tall grass while hundreds of stinging scorpions and venomous spiders swarmed his body.

Trinidy turned and faced the wounded elf. He did not know how much longer he had before the sword sticking into him took his life, but he had only one more to slay. One more evil one to vanquish to fulfill his quest. As Trinidy started toward the elf, he marveled at how his wound did not hurt. He could feel the sword protruding from his body, he could feel it's weight in him, but he did not feel weaker, and there was no pain. No pain at all. How much time did he have? Probably not much. The lack of pain in a mortal wound was always a bad sign.

     *   *   *

Myson backed away wide eyed as the creature did not even cry out when he impaled it. He could see the tip of his enchanted sword sticking out of the creature's front breastplate, dripping a thick black ooze that seemed to sizzle when it hit the ground. Tightening his grip on his short sword, he prepared to either finish the undead denizen, or it finish him. Eulic was safe for the time being, though he seemed to be slapping his legs for some reason.

    Myson pushed his blonde braids back behind his ear with his free hand. Griping his short sword tightly he decided to try to draw the apparition away from Eulic until his friend could right himself. It was then that the undead extended his hand. His rotting fingers covered by the creaking gauntlet pointed at him. The black insects rocketed in and out of his eyes and his nose, some even going in his ears as if they were more excited than they had been moments ago.

    "Necropium Nectues." the death knight said in a dark low growl that seemed to echo in Myson's ears. Suddenly Myson felt stabbing pains in his chest, as if something were being ripped out of it. His body shook with pain and unimaginable cold rocked his muscles, causing them to tighten and curl up. He fought to stay conscious, but the pain increased. He wanted to cry out, to scream, but the legionnaire could not make his throat utter a single sound. His lungs held his breath and his very thoughts seemed to become sluggish. He was barely aware that he was lying on the ash-covered earth when he lost consciousness, oblivious to hundreds of tiny black scorpions and spiders that swarmed his paralyzed body.

    *   *   *

    Eulic swatted the pests away quickly. The wound in his side seemed to level off for the moment, though his right side still was a little sluggish and cold, at least the shooting pains had subsided. He scrambled out of the ashen ring that seemed to follow the death knight wherever he walked. The thing seemed to cause the plant life around him to die and turn to ash whenever he came near. The great many stinging and biting insects seemed to stay within a close proximity to the creature also.

    Eulic watched as Myson ran the creature through. The thing seemed to arch it's back and drop it's weapon. A rush of triumph washed over Eulic. He hoped beyond hope that the wound would finish the beast, but in the back of his mind, he was certain it would not. To his horror the beast righted itself, pointed a single finger at Myson. It said something, perhaps it was some kind of chant or command, Eulic could not tell, but he watched Myson suddenly fall to the earth. Eulic hefted his swords and charged the undead apparition. He had taken a few steps when he skidded to a stop. Myson's body was instantly covered with hundreds and thousands of scorpions, spiders, centipedes, and other insects that stung him countless times. The little beasts crawled into his mouth and burrowed under his skin. Eulic cried out, half in terror and half in rage, as he charged into battle. This evil would die today.

    *   *   *

    Trinidy turned as the elf fell to the ground. He did not know what he had done, only that he knew it was fatal and the evil elf would soon be dead. Instead he turned and faced the other elf that was standing few dozen feet away watching the scene. The brown haired elf screamed in a twisted rage and charged. Good. If the elf had decided to run, Trinidy wasn't sure he would live long enough to pursue him, but now, he would either complete the quest his god set him on by killing these two evil elves, or he would die trying.

*   *   *

    The two met in a shower of sparks, swords hitting swords, swords hitting mail. Eulic's finely crafted blade hit home gain and again. Great gouts of sticky black fluid erupted from the death knight's wounds. Some landed on the ground and some landed on Eulic's hands or breeches, but the elf ignored either, despite the stinging pain he felt as the acidic fluid burned him. Each strike did not seem to slow the corpse. Though Eulic felt himself slowing, he had taken many nicks from that sinister blade. Though the wounds were superficial at best, he could feel the evil magic boring into his flesh from even the tiniest of scratches. If the blade had even touched his skin, a festering wound would rapidly grow.

    The death knight pressed the attack, it's blade coming closer and closer to hitting home. On the rare occasions Eulic managed to strike at an exposed area of the corpse, the ominous shield seemed to shift faster than comprehension, deflecting his strike. It was becoming apparent that he could not defeat this monster by himself. Glancing over the undead monster's shoulder, Eulic could see Myson's body laying still. His face was covered with hundreds of purple welts that dripped yellowish fluid from the bites and stings, and his chest did not rise and fall with any breath. Muttering a curse Eulic broke away from the fight, turned, and ran. He hated leaving his kin's body, but he needed to warn the Vale. This monster was beyond any Darayal Legionnaire. It would take the elders and the wise ones to defeat it. Eulic did not know if the creation held a keep or commanded an army, but he doubted it. He turned to see the creature following him at a slow pace. The grass around it quickly died, decayed and turned to ash with each of it's steps. Sheathing his swords, Eulic darted as fast as he could to the north. His wounds screamed at him in protest, but they did not feel as if they were getting worse. It seems once he disengaged from combat with the monster, they stopped and leveled off.

The legionnaire had a fair journey ahead of him, though he did not pause, nor did he hear the hellish ball of fire that was rapidly descending on him.

    *   *   *

Trinidy turned and strode toward the other evil elf. The brown haired elf's wounds had weakened him, but Trinidy knew he was still a threat.

Amazed that the sword that was rammed through him did not cause him any pain or discomfort, Trinidy pushed on. Could it be by the grace of Dicermadon, that the sword missed any of his vitals? If that were true, why did he not feel any pain. He didn't even feel weaker. He should have at least been weaker. The death knight didn't have much time to ponder the wound as the elf attacked. The elf fought ferociously though his attacks were labored and his defense was poor. Trinidy managed to score a few minor hits as they battled. Why didn't the elf run? Evil was always weak when faced with adversity, and they would rarely risk themselves to save another. Perhaps the elves feared failing their evil master more than they feared dieing by his blade. It did not matter to Trinidy. He would slay him soon. Just as the elf's defenses weakened to where Trinidy planned to make the killing strike, it ran. How dare the despicable little beast run? Trinidy started after him, but quickly realized he was not suited for running in his heavy plate. He watched helplessly as the elf bounded up and over the rise on the hill. That was when it started again. The incessant pounding that echoed in his ears. Thump-thump, thump-thump. It was louder and faster than it had been before, but as the elf moved farther away, the fainter it grew.

Anger welled up inside Trinidy that he had never

experienced. How dare that evil beast think of running away and spoiling his victory. It was then he felt it. Another bulge inside of him. Like a great hunger that grew rapidly. It burned hot and demanded release. The death knight raised his hands in the air. Great weaves of magical flows erupted from his hands and shot into the sky. They swirled and twisted, drawing in great amounts of energy from the sun, swirling and twisting, intensifying rapidly until a great sphere of flames hung high over head. Trinidy gazed to the north and stared at the hill. He could feel the great sphere hanging over head. He could feel the link from it to his mind, like a leash to a hound. When the elf rose to the top of the next hill, he released it. No, it was more like a launch. The great flaming sphere plummeted from the sky and crashed into the elf. A great flash erupted form the explosion and the ground shook. Great chunks of dirt and ash erupted into the sky, slowly cascading back down to earth as the sphere died out on the hills peak.

    Trinidy casually walked to the area where he fire ball had hit the ground. There was a large hole a dozen or so feet in diameter. It was about four feet deep at the center, and there was no remains of the elf. At the bottom of the crater, Trinidy could see pieces of red hot melted metal pooled up at he bottom and a bit of chunky ash. Thin wisps of smoke slowly ascended into the cold morning air. Trinidy smiled. The damnable thumping was gone and he felt the magical pull to the north again. Pulling the blade from his back and tossing it on the ground, he was oblivious to the wave of maggots and other larvae that spilled from the open wound and wiggled around on the ground as he strode away. Creating the veil of complete darkness to protect him from the sun, the death knight continued on to the north, answering the never ending pull that drug him onward.

" Prejudice. Such a horrible thing, or is it? Is it merely a product of a human's ability to protect itself. Why do humans fear orcs, ogres, and others of the evil races? They fear them because they are prejudice. The preemptive dislike or hate, comes from the basic emotion that all creatures despise. Fear. No creature that has a mind at any level likes to be afraid. Fear crushes the strong willed, it stupefies the intelligent, and enfeebles the wise. It can override any basic emotion in any intelligent being. Few human emotions are as strong, or overpower sense as quickly.

A man who had never seen nor had heard of an orc, might not be terrified of them, he might not be even afraid. But a man, who had heard the tales of the wicked beasts, or witnessed their malice first hand, will surely hate them as much as he fears them. The hate derives from the fear. No one enjoys being afraid, so they in turn, become angry. I cannot fault anyone for being prejudice, though it surely is not a position that should be taken by the wise. Though, prejudice is still an important tool. It is important when it becomes an overlying issue of hate and persecution that it is transformed into a hindrance. Some may argue that imprudence based off of prejudice is the real cause. The inability to be cautious. I say nay, for even then, if discriminatory nature over rides thought, then much is missed, and much evil is done. It is dangerous for any man to try to give every orc the benefit of doubt when the beasts are encountered, but if the man is in no danger from the orc, I say; why not. Much could be gained, and much could be lost.

Thousands of years before my birth, the elves have had visions of me, of what I was, of what I would become. But in their ignorance, they never tried to understand why I became what I was prophesized to be. Surely that was no fate anyone would choose. Had the elves been as wise as they had claimed to be, they would have searched to understand the factors that drove me to what I would become. Instead, they feared me and feared the title that was given to me thousands of years before my birth. A title that had no meaning to me, nor a title that I was even aware of. My name was Lance. I was an orphan. I loved my parents dearly before their death's and I loved my adoptive father, despite how much we differed in views. It was the men who feared what I was to become and what I was prophesized to do, that actually set my feet upon the very path to become what they sought to vanquish. Strange, but through their attempts to prevent what was prophesied to be, they actually created what they sought to defeat. Prejudice, a gift only to those with wisdom to understand it's true meaning."

-Lancalion Levendis Lampara-

Chapter Nine
A Prisoner's Welcome

*T*he bright glaring sun was set high in the barren sky. No clouds floated by, and the heavens were bare save for a few white wisps that more resembled thin feathers, than clouds. At first glance, the day might appear to be a bright, warm summer day, but the cold autumn air stilled the atmosphere. Long blades of tall brown grass bore many ice crystals, despite the noon sun and a cold chilling wind swept across the endless plains. Lance sat lightly in his saddle as his horse plodded on to the north. The inside of his legs hurt constantly from the long hours in the saddle each day, and despite his growing tolerance, he doubted he would ever get used to it, despite what Apollisian, Overmoon, or Jude said. He was just not built to ride. Lance pulled his thick heavy cloak around himself to try to keep the chilling wind from his skin. They had awoke before the sun rise, and Lance thought there was little worse than climbing out of his warm bed roll to move around in the cold morning air. But they had camped in the valley of a fair sized hill. Now the chilling wind was much worse, and his cursed horse made his legs and but hurt. He was sure he had sores on the crowns of his rump and he probably wouldn't sit right for weeks. Reaching up and pulling the hood of his shimmering black cloak, known as a Cadacka, Lance lowered his head and tried to recapture some of his lost sleep.

Jude rode on comfortably. He inhaled the chilly morning air deeply and exhaled. There was nothing like the air on the open plains. He was a little chilly, but some good riding and the rising sun, would take the bite out of an otherwise good day. He glanced over at Lance and chuckled at the miserable sight. The poor mage was riding with his head nearly completely covered by that shimmering cloak with the strange runes. He would slowly lean more and more forward, until he was just about to fall from the saddle, then jerk upright, muttering a few curses under his breath and adjusting his cloak, then he would start the process again.

The battle with the hill giant had given the party a little cohesiveness, but Jude still noticed that Apollisian and the elf, kept to themselves. Jude was a little distrustful of them, more of the elf, but Apollisian was a paladin, and Jude knew them to die before breaking their word. Readjusting the thick leather jerkin that rested under his chain armor, Jude rode on silently, humming a tune to himself as he enjoyed the calm autumn air.

Apollisian rode silently. As they neared the Vale he became more uneasy with what the elves would do with young Lance. The boy had done no wrong as far as he could tell, and he knew next to nothing about this so called "Abyss Walker." Alexis did not speak highly of the title. Apollisian was torn between loyalty to the elves, and the fact that Alexis had an ulterior motive to get Lance and Jude to accompany them. The elf asked for the pair to be escorts, and she paid for their services, thus making the statement true, but her underlying motive was to get Lance to the Vale to go before the elders. It was the underlying issue that upset Apollisian. True, She spoke nothing false, but the paladin found it difficult not stating what was omitted. It was like lying without actually being mendacious. Certainly there would be a trial for his inner character. Though after many days of pondering, he decided that Alexis hadn't committed any untruth's, though he would scrutinize the treatment of the boy, and his large friend, personally. If the elves meant to treat him unfairly, he would step in and prevent them. If the elves thought to take the boy by force, they would have to do the same to him. Apollisian doubted the elves, regardless of how wicked they perceived the boy, would dare disrespect a champion of Stephanis.

The paladin looked over at Alexis as she rode quietly next to him. Her long blonde hair hung down from behind her in a single thick tight braid. She wore a dark green cloak that hung over her back and draped over the rump of her horse. Her quiver of arrows jutted out from a thin pocket in the back of the cloak, and her bright green fletching stood out in the plains over the never ending brown. She kept her white ash bow strapped behind the saddle, unstrung, next to her tightly packed bed roll and bouncing waterskins. What a magnificent woman she was. Blushing, Apollisian looked away. She was not a woman. She was an elf. She was his charge, as a friend to the crown of the Vale, not some lady in waiting that he could court at his leisure. Cursing himself for being foolish, he looked back at her. Was there a chance? No, how could there be? She would live ten of his lifetimes. He would grow old and feeble, where she would remain spry and young. How could he condemn her to love someone that would grow and die before her very eyes? Chastising himself for such foolish thoughts, Apollisian scanned the horizon. He would have much to explain if enemies managed to lay an ambush because he rode smitten eyed at Alexis like some love sick child. Tightening the reins to his war horse, he jaunted ahead a few paces, his eagle like visage ever bound to the horizon.

Alexis rode on into the day lost in thought. She fought herself to keep from daydreaming about her encounter with Apollisian at the city hall in central City. Had she really almost kissed him? The fool man probably didn't even notice. Men were more than inept at noticing things like that. She had been alive for over two hundred sixty years and she was yet to kiss a man. She wondered if Apollisian counted as a man. He wasn't elven after all. So he wasn't much in her society's eyes. But his eyes, and his...Alexis blushed under her cloak. She had tried thinking less of the fool human and more of her task at hand. She had the Abyss Walker traveling with her for Leska's sake. She should keep her mind on that.

  Alexis peered over to her right at Apollisian from the corner of her eye, just around the edge of her bright green hood. He rode looking straight ahead, scanning the horizon. His long blonde hair bounced around his face as his horse plodded the ground. The thick headed man probably didn't even look her way once since they left Central City.

  Alexis was startled by Jude's deep voice to her left. " How far do you suppose we have to go. I have been seeing a few more birds in the air of late and I suspect that there are trees up ahead. I doubt there is much area left in these plains." Jude asked as he rode, keeping both of his hands in front of him gripping the thick reins that held his horse's head.

  Alexis tried to hide her flinch when he spoke. She had been so caught up in thought of the fool paladin, she hadn't noticed the large swordsman approach from behind her. Muttering a silent curse under her breath that was meant for her own ears she turned. By the expression on Jude's face, her curses must have been a little too loud. Blushing again she placed her hand across the front of her cloak, just above her breasts. " Perceptive swordsman." She said turning and facing forward lifting her chin in a regal pose. " We are indeed approaching some forest, but we will have a day or two ride yet once within. Do not worry, when we arrive a the Minok Vale I will tell you."

  Jude frowned and looked forward, straining to see what she was looking at. After a quick scan and seeing nothing, he glanced back at her, more annoyed than before. " That will be worthless. Once we are there, I am sure I will know." Jude said condescendingly.

Alexis turned her body to face the swordsman as she rode. Her pompous face, turned to wrought anger. Her bright green eyes, flashed to a cold glare that would have given the most menacing men pause. " You are sure you will know?" She asked angrily. " I bet your pathetic human eyes couldn't see a single elf if you stood in the center of the clearing, you big lummox."

"Pathetic human eyes?" Jude asked incredulously. "I do not have to tolerate such speech. Woman, where I come from..." Alexis cut him off.

"I don't care where you come from, you stupid oaf. Wherever that back woods hamlet is, it is not here. You are in the Serrin Plains, just at the foot of my Vale. You will do as you are told, or you will face the laws that govern all creatures here, and the elven nation does not take kindly to any humans, let alone, loud mouthed fools such as yourself."

Jude merely sat flabbergasted at the woman's barbed tongue. His jaw hung open at a loss for words. Seeing the swordsman's unevenness, she continued. " Now fall back and do as you are told. You have been paid to do a service and I intend to hold you to that."

Jude slowed his horse astounded. He had never been spoken to like that by any man, let alone a woman. Had he not been so close to the elven lands, he might have wrenched the fool wench from her saddle and paddled her bottom, like she obviously needed.

Jude glanced over at the paladin. He wore an angry face, but he said nothing, not did he look at either of them. Jude did not like the situation one bit. As soon as Lance got his script deciphered, they were going to head back home as fast as possible. These fool elves were pompous enough for ten kings! Jude glimpsed over at Lance. The mage sat slumped over the front of his horse in his perpetual slouch, then jerking upright motions. Shaking his head, Jude chuckled despite his confrontation with Alexis. Lance maybe a refined city lad, but he could sleep just about anywhere. Jude remembered once back in Bureland, Davohn had Lance cutting wood most of the night to fill an order he had from the mayor for the Freedom Festival. The Freedom Festival was a celebration for the victory over the orc horde in a war that lasted almost twenty years, though most of the vicious fighting took place in the first five. Lance had split a whole wagon load by himself trying to cut more wood than Davohn had. No one thought he could have beaten the seasoned wood cutter, but come morning Lance had almost as much and a half again as Davohn. When Jude and Davohn went to congratulate Lance on his hard work, he was no where to be found. It wasn't until later in the after noon when old Morilla went to fetch some water from the well out back of her shop, when she found Lance asleep on top of a second pile of wood that he had cut, but did not have the time to pile it up in the wagon. Jude chuckled softly to himself as he recalled Lance walking gingerly for the rest of the week from splinters in his behind from the split wood.

"Something funny, swordsman?" Lance asked, peering out from under the hood of his thick sable cloak.

Jude jumped, not thinking his friend was awake, but quickly regained his composure. "I was just thinking back to the freedom festival when you fell asleep on the wood pile and got all those splinters in your behind." Jude said with a brazen grin.

Lance grimaced and slowly shook his head from side to side, pulling down his heavy hood and sitting up right in his saddle. "That was a horrible day." He said rubbing his behind as if it hurt. "And then, old lady Morilla and Davohn held me down while that accursed Sespie Twinner pulled out all those splinters. I don't know what was more red, my face or my bottom. She would jump at any chance to torment me."

Jude smiled warmly. Despite the tragedies they had witnessed since leaving Bureland, they could still joke about their childhood, though Jude was a few years older than Lance. "You know she practically begged to help old Morilla pull them out of you, don't you?" Jude asked as his smile grew to cover his entire face.

Lance gave him an incredulous look, then faced forward on the trail a moment before turning back to Jude with his hands on his hips. " What do you mean, she practically begged?" Lance asked.

Jude chuckled, shaking his head in disbelief. "You would sooner know how to swordfight than you would know a girl's interest."

Lance frowned. What was that supposed to mean. Who ever knew what a girl thought.

They seldom made sense, and if you seemed to have an idea of what they meant, they would change their own meaning in mid sentence, just to keep you from thinking you knew what the heck they were talking about. " No one knows what girls think." Lance said angrily.

Jude seemed to chuckle again. "I know she may have been a few years older than you, but she could not have chased you harder or made it more obvious without being the scandal of Bureland."

Lance seemed to loose his smile. It slowly faded and was replaced by a serious scowl that seemed deeper than the mere expression on his face. "I suppose I spent to much time studying. It is just like; I knew one day I was going to find my parents killers and bring them to justice."

"Whoa, whoa, whoa." Jude said as he put his hands up in the air. "We set out on a journey to decipher these papers of yours, not put our necks in a noose. Lets find the identity of the killers and let the local magistrates deal with the dogs. They are better equipped to handle such things. You are a beginner mage, despite what you say, I think some of the things you do surprises you as much as it does me. Sometimes I think you need to go study under a real wizard before you hurt yourself."

Lance lowered his voice. "I know you are concerned, Jude, but I do things that wizards cannot. It is hard to explain. Wizards take pre-existing magical energies that dwell around them. By moving their hands, or chanting a few words, they have learned how to manipulate those energies. I can do that too, but Jude..." Lance trailed of nervously.

"Not only can I weave those energies, I do not have chant or move anything. It is like I look at them and command them with thought. It is hard to explain. Just imagine that you could draw your sword and swing it with your mind, where other swordsman still have to use their hands. To make things stranger, I feel the same magical energy inside of me sometimes. Like a hungry feeling, or a worry feeling. It seems like I can channel that energy out of me, or I use it to manipulate the natural flows around me without using my hands. I'm not sure what that means, but I am afraid that if I went to a wizard, he would find out I do it differently."

Jude said nothing. He just rode forward staring at Lance's pleading face, listening.

Lance continued. "Jude, you know how those wizard guilds are. You have to join a guild just to follow their order to learn their schools of magic, and people seem to disappear from those schools all the time. I think that finding about my parents will shed some light on why I can do what I do. Jude, I think that is why they were killed. Maybe they could do the things that I do."

Jude nodded slowly. "You had better not mention that to anyone else but me, Lance. I agree, someone might try to do something to you. I don't know what, but as soon as we get those papers deciphered, lets go far away from elves. I have had my bloody fill of the one we are traveling with, let alone a whole city of them."

Lance nodded and rode next to Jude quietly.

Jude sighed deeply to himself. It must be tough being a mage he thought. Lance always seemed tired, and what was that elf up to? She acted like she had a separate agenda than the paladin, and Jude could detect a stress between them, though he knew not of what.

Though, if he had to ride with the pompous elf, he would have more than a little unmentioned stress between them, she would have been turned over his knee long ago. Let that cursed pair watch their own backs, gold or no gold, he was going to look after his only friend, and it seemed Lance had a strong need for watching.

Alexis glared at the hulking oaf of a human as he trotted his horse away. She figured given the chance, the fool might try to remove her from her steed and make good his threat. Human women were so weak. They were nothing like elven maidens. Elven maidens were strong and fierce, bright and wise, where human females were submissive and foolish, led by emotions rather than by intelligence and logic. It probably had much to do with the pitiful creature's short life spans. Alexis couldn't imagine living such a short life. How would anyone get anything done? A good suit of elven chain would take almost twenty years to create, a human would be near quarter dead by the time it was finished. Why the gods ever created the weaker race was beyond her. What made matters worse, her father seemed to have a soft spot for their plights. True, Alexis didn't judge every human the same, she still had a good general idea of what and how they acted. " Brazen and foolish." She mumbled under her breath.

"What was that?" Apollisian asked turning his head as he easily swayed in his thick leather saddle. His Vendaigehn mount from Central City seemed much more agile than a normal horse, it's thin slender legs seemed to flow across the land rather than walk.

Alexis felt her face flush. "Nothing." she said, as she became lost in his deep blue eyes. How could a human man have such perfect eyes? Set in such a stern gaze that seemed inviting to friends and deadly to enemies.

    Apollisian narrowed his eyes and firmed his jaw. "I was sure you had referred to Jude as Brazen and foolish."

    Alexis's flush of embarrassment turned to hot anger. "Of course, aren't all human males?" Alexis cringed before she finished speaking. In her haste and anger, she had forgotten Apollisian was a human male. But he never acted like one, he acted more elven than a lot of elves, cool and calm in the face of danger, always thinking of the greater good, than was at risk for the moment.

    If the paladin was angry, he didn't show it. Smiling he slowly shook his head from side to side. "I can think of a friend elf that acts that way sometimes. Especially when she is in defense of her friends."

    Alexis frowned and pondered the thought, then turned back to look at Jude. He was riding side by side to Lance, and seemed to be offering some words of encouragement, though elves were known for expert hearing, she could only pick out small parts of the conversation. She turned back and glowered a glare of near hate, in-so-much, Apollisian swallowed hard and leaned away as if the glare would lash out at him. "A friend to Abyss Walker is merely a pawn to be cast aside when his usefulness has run out."

    The paladin gathered himself, leaning forward, to match her glare. "You may not judge a man for crimes he has not yet committed. Stephanis does not allow it." He paused then quickly added in; "I will not allow it."

    Alexis growled, had she not felt a deep kinship to the man, she probably would have crossed blades with him just then. "It is not my place to judge anyone." she added furiously. "Nor is it your place to question the elders. Justice comes in many guises, human. You'd be best to learn that." she said, riding ahead angrily.

    Apollisian ground his teeth together. The nerve of that fool woman. She dared to think she could lecture him on justice? Only a fool believes it has more than one meaning. Justice is justice, it is nothing else. Too many times, people think they are getting justice, when they are in fact getting revenge, but the paladin was at a loss for this event. How anyone could think of trying a man for a crime they think he might commit, regardless of how heinous.

Apollisian started to work himself in a fervor, then he calmed himself. King Overmoon was a wise man, he had been alive longer than some countries historians can remember. He surely would not make such a grievous error in judgment. In fact, he would go to the king with the boy and plead his case if necessary. Apollisian could detect evil hearts and though the boy surely had many dark emotions sometimes swirling about him, he was, without a doubt, not evil. Setting the plan clearly in his mind Apollisian let his apprehensions slide away about the Minok encounter. He was revered by the Vale, and his word was a strong as some law. He would voice his objection, and he would be heard.

Jude moved his horse away as the group continued north into the early afternoon sun. The wind was soft, though cold, and the air was crisp. The waves of dark brown grass that covered the plains seemed to move slowly with the wind, like many waves on they open sea. All the bugs had surely died or burrowed deep into the ground yet his horse swished it's tail occasionally out of habit. A few light wisps of clouds were frozen in the bright blue sky that seemed to streak from horizon to horizon. The air had a definite autumn smell to it.

"That seemed to go well." Lance chuckled. "You have such a way with women."

Jude gave him an angry glare. "That fool elf needs her bottom paddled."

"That one is worse than a pit of vipers, I'd say. As soon as we get theses parchments deciphered, we will leave her. I like the paladin enough, but the elf seems to look at me as if to kill me one moment, then as if she pities me the next."

Jude nodded. "I don't know about the pitying, but she surely holds you in some kind of contempt. Perhaps we should return the gold and head back. She does not seem to like you wearing that cloak much, maybe she plans to punish you or something like that."

Lance shook his head stubbornly. "And where do you suppose I would get the translation from? The wandering elf travelers that seek to decipher their own sacred guarded language for a fool human?" Lance asked sarcastically.

Jude narrowed his eyes angrily. "There is no need to take that tone with me Lance, save it for the tavern wenches. I am just saying you might rethink the importance of the translation. If we are dead, there is no point in them." Jude said trailing off.

The pair rode on in silence. Lance seemed to be weighing his words. Jude spoke up again. "Besides, if need be I would ride all the way into Ladathon if you liked. Hell, I would ride next to you into Kingsford City."

Lance gaped at Jude. Ladathon was hundreds, no thousands, perhaps tens of thousands of miles to the south. It was south of Tyrine, the kingdom just south of Beykla. The fact that Jude even mentioned Kingsford City amazed Lance. Jude disliked large cities. He didn't even like Central City, and you could fit over a hundred of Central City in Kingsford, or so it is said. Lance paused and then swallowed hard before speaking.

"Thank you, my friend. But let us just go to this Vale and then head home for a while. I am sure Davohn is worried about me, though I suspect they will know you are missing too. That should put his mind at a little ease."

Jude nodded his head in agreement when he felt his horse step lightly under him. There was loud pop of something breaking. Jude quickly moved his horse to the right and peered down.

Lance stopped his horse and scanned the ground

also. "What did you step on.?"

Jude leaned over the side of his saddle staring at a large bleached white bone. It was slightly pitted from exposure from elements, and seemed brittle enough to have a fair level of age to it. " It looks like a bone of some kind, and an old one I would say by how easy it snapped under my horse."

"A bone?" Lance asked. "Good, I was worried that you may have injured your horse."

Jude didn't respond. He dismounted carefully and checked his horse's foot. Tapping the animal on the front leg, it raised it, letting the Jude look at the under side as if he were going to clean it's feet. "No, the horse is ok." Jude said as he picked the bone up from the ground and held it in his hand. It was shaped like an upper arm bone from a human, but it was twice as thick. It was too small to be a femur and too large to be any other kind of bone.

Lance motioned his horse around to Jude's side. "What kind of bone is it?" Lance asked.

"It's not human, at least I don't think it is." Jude said, as he examined the bleached white bone.

"It's orc." came a honeyed voice from behind them.

Jude whipped around quickly and Lance glared at the elf who sat imposing on her horse, looking down at the two humans as if they were children who she was supervising.

Alexis smiled at their frustration as she sat on her horse a few paces away. " We are reaching the Quigen. Best to be mindful of where your horse steps for the next ten miles or so. Those bones could cause a horse to come up lame if they wedge themselves into their hooves." Alexis said before she trotted her horse off to catch back up to the paladin.

Lance frowned. Quigen? That seemed familiar to him from his days as a boy in school.

Jude tossed the bone onto the ground with a disgusted look on his face and turned to Lance as he swung his heavy leg over the saddle. "The Quigen was the greatest battle of the orc wars. The elves were weak and fleeing north back to the Vale. The orc horde was right on their heels. They were numbered over a thousand score, where the elves were maybe five thousands in number. They had their famed legionnaires, but even their skilled blades were no match against so many foes. King Theobold dispatched his entire northern army from the Dawson Stronghold to meet the orcs head on to give the elves some time to retreat. They met here." Jude said motioning around them. "The Beyklans were only fifteen thousand strong, outnumbered nearly four to one. But the army led by general Laricin West, charged on, knowing they were surely to die. I am not sure how many weeks the battle lasted, but some say a season came and went while Laricin and his men fought to the last. The orc's were not defeated but it was known as; 'The Breaking.'

After the battle the orc leaders were crushed and the horde was broken. The remaining clans fought amongst themselves on who would lead for the remainder of the war, keeping themselves from becoming organized again. The elves focused their remaining armies and scattered the orc clans across the plains. Too weak to hunt them all down, the elves left the orc's to the plains. Most of the tribes moved south, but a few remained."

Lance looked at Jude as if seeing him for the first time, his emerald eyes staring in astonishment. "How do you know all this?"

"It was part of your history lesson's in school, had you paid attention as a child, you might have remembered better than me." Jude answered, resting both of his large gloved hands on the horn of his saddle.

"I seem to remember a certain swordsman getting paddled for trying to kiss Sally Mae in the back of the class." Lance retorted.

Jude frowned. "How do you remember that? We were not in the same grade. I am older than you, you would have still been learning your alphabet back then."

Lance smiled a knowing smile. "The whole town knew about that, and other events you and Sally Mae partook in."

Jude felt his face flush. Sally Mae was the most beautiful girl in school. Why she ever was interested in a big lummox like himself, he wasn't sure, but he wasn't about to look a gift horse in the mouth. Jude soon became lost in the memories of beautiful Sally. He recalled slipping back by the Congarn's orchard with Sally during the fall festival and kissing her all day long. How he loved to gently touch his lips to hers. They were so...

"Hello, Jude?" Lance asked with an amused look on his face. "Did I drudge up some old memories?"

Jude ignored him. For Leska's sake, what else did everyone in the town know? He might not want to show his face there again for the mere fact that everyone seemed to know some embarrassing stories of his that he thought were private. Of course, it didn't matter now. If anyone tried to embarrass him about his past, he would pop them in the mouth. Fat lips usually spoke softer, at least that is what his father always used to say. Regaining some composure he answered Lance. "Nothing big, just thinking about being a kid again."

Lance nodded thoughtfully. Though he was barely out of his childhood as it was. He had many fond memories of years past.

Glancing around him at the vast flat area that the elf called the Quigen, Lance felt an eerie calm wash over him. He tried to envision the huge battle that raged over the land, but he could not. Armies of that magnitude were beyond his visual comprehension. " The ground must have rumbled as they charged." he said, half under his breath.

Jude nodded in agreement. "It is said that so much blood was spilled on the earth during the months that battle took place, that the grass died and the ground was stained red for years afterward."

Lance took it all in awe. He tried to imagine what it was like to have been there at the battle. The taste of fear and the smell of death. The scream of men and orcs alike as they were cut down. The bravery that the men had in face of insurmountable odds as they fell to the last man. Lance felt a great sense of loss as he gazed out across the battlefield and greater sense of pity for the last man that was standing. To die alone with his comrades, no, his brothers, laying dead around him; a terrible fate.

It took the better part of the day to cross the Quigen. Apollisian stopped briefly when it seemed to be in the middle of it and gave a prayer for the men that sacrificed their lives there. To Lance's surprise, even the elf seemed to feel a sense of lost. It was late in the evening when they stopped to camp. Apollisian was sure they were out of the Quigen before stopping. It was a typical autumn night on the plains, dark, windy and cold. They set off again at first light.

The following day Apollisian seemed to glance behind them a lot and frown frequently. Lance would turn and look, but he saw nothing except the never ending grassland horizon. He asked Jude about it, but the swordsman could proffer no ideas as to why the paladin might be looking behind him. He didn't think they were being followed, surely the dwarves were all but defeated. Jude decided to keep a eye on the south, just in case. If something was bothering the paladin, Jude figured it was worthy of taking notice about.

    *   *   *

He trudged on into the cold night and then into the morning. The obvious shift in the temperature didn't seem to affect him at all. In fact, he couldn't even detect that there was temperature. He was neither hot nor cold, ever. And as strange as that was, he became quite skilled at summoning that globe of complete blackness that surrounded him during the day, and found he could move in it just as easily as he could with sunlight. He couldn't see the terrain in front of him, it was as if he sensed it. All theses new revelations were bizarre developments for the death knight. He was beginning to wonder about his new powers and how they were applied to him. It was weeks since he had been rose from he dead and he was yet to eat a scrap of food since he was raised from the dead, sleep a wink, or become tired. He knew there were no spells that could provide such comfort, even magic had limits. Trinidy guessed that it had to have something to do with Dicermadon's power, but exactly what or how didn't seem to bother him. It was foolish to take the unexplained for fact and it was a fool that followed the unexplained blindly. He would piece it out eventually, though often enough he had trouble clearing his thoughts. Whenever he would try to concentrate on something, that magical pull at the back of his mind that drove him forever north, seemed to pop up and disrupt him.

    Trinidy marched into a clear flat area. He could hear thousands of voices at the edge of his mind, calling out to him. He stopped and glanced around. As far as he could see, the ground was flat, from horizon to horizon. Trinidy couldn't see anyone or anything. It was as if the voices beckoned from the recesses of his mind, yet projected from the earth around him. He could not understand what they were saying, only that they were saying it. Standing motionless in the glaring sun, protected by his globe of darkness he stopped. The magical pull was still there, he could still feel it, but it was much weaker. Then it happened. Trinidy raised his hands to the heavens and began chanting. He did not know what the words were that he spoke, only that they sounded purely angelic to him. He witnessed great tendrils of deep black erupt from his outstretched hands and shoot out across the plains. The great tendrils thrashed about, plunging into the earth and out again, creating an ever expanding spider web of impenetrable blackness. The webs shot out as far and as fast as he could see, and in a breath they had extended past the horizon, like great porpoises somersaulting in and out of the sea, until they were suddenly gone. When the tendrils subsided, Trinidy felt tainted, foul. The magic that washed over him was different than the magic he had ever wielded. Before when he cast the will of his god, he felt cleansed, pure. But now he felt infected, soiled, and worse, he liked it. The raw sensation of the taint seemed to make him lust for it again. Trinidy fought back the urge to loose the magic that was somehow inside of him.

As the death knight struggled against the magic, the ground erupted in front of him. Hundreds of thousands of clawed skeletal hands exploded from the ground, tearing and pulling entire skeletons to the surface. Large pieces of dirt hung from their dark gray skulls and their eyeless sockets emitted a shadowy cobalt glow that bore into the death knight. Trinidy felt as if he should be frightened, as if he should draw his sword and smite the damnations of good, but he did not. The skeleton's seemed to thank him in an unseen way, as if he answered their prayers by raising them up from the earth that had claimed them.

In minutes the skeletons stood motionless in front of him as thousands more rose up every second. They were not threatening, and Trinidy could sense every last one of them as if they were extensions to his mind. It was as if Trinidy watched the events unfold from a prison cell. He knew what was happening, or at least had a good idea, but he was powerless to stop it. The sensation of wielding the necromancies were too great. The skeletons slowly and tediously dug themselves out of their earthen tombs with their bony claw like fingers. In a few minutes, the skeletal army stood before their new master awaiting his commands. Like an addict pleasing his addiction, Trinidy marched north, with an army of skeletons that trailed the stench of death far as they eye could see. Their bony frames clicked and clacked as the walked clumsily, some carrying swords and axes that were rusted to near uselessness. He would answer this call to the north, silence it, then he would address the fact he may have not been raised by his god. When he was finished with this so called wrong that needed righted, someone was going to pay.

*   *   *

Myson opened his eyes. Pain ripped through his naked body from the intense cold as he lay sprawled on his back. He choked and gagged on the sulfuric air that swirled and wafted around him. Sitting up, the legionnaire looked around himself. He sat on cold bare gray rock that seemed to expand forever into the horizon. Bright vapors of yellow billowing clouds that seemed to be filled with a dark black moisture violently shifted in the deep purple skyline. Huge beasts sailed past in the distance that lacked any fur or feathers, made up of mere skin and bone. The air was cold and stinging, but Myson adjusted quickly, hugging his naked body from the horrible cold.

The legionnaire gingerly tip toed over the sharp gray rocks to the edge of the small rise that stood before him. He stepped around small wide centipede like creatures that seemed to try to maneuver themselves under his feet. Reaching the rise, he looked over. Hundreds of small goblin looking creatures seemed to be scampering his way. They were about three feet tall and had dark blue skin. Some had horns protruding from their elbows and knees, where others had horns shooting from their heads. Some of their horns were on the side and some in front, like a unicorn. But all the horns were twisted wickedly and were jet black. The beasts had bright yellow eyes that seemed to shine like a glittering gold coin in pale fire light. They all wore wicked smiles that bared hundreds of tiny needle like teeth. Giggling and cackling, they ran at unnatural speeds toward him hurtling large rocks and small ravines as they closed like a pack of wolves coming for the kill. Myson turned and ran. He felt his bare feet being cut and sliced as he sprinted across the cold barren slate. Running back down the slope, running for his life, his stinging eyes frantically searched for a cave, or some form of shelter. He could not fight the beasts at once, but if he could force them to come on him one at a time, he might be able to do something. Exactly what he could do, he wasn't sure, but anything was better than being cut down and slaughtered. The legionnaire had seen every kind of forest denizen the realms had to offer, and he knew nothing of these beasts that pursued him. They moved at unnatural speed and it seemed that no two were exactly alike. Yet that changed nothing, he had to find some form of shelter, or wherever he was, would be his final resting place.

    Myson ran as fast as he could, ignoring the hundreds of small bloody cuts that he had endured from running and scampering across the razor sharp slate. He did not know where he was, but he knew of nothing like the land he was in. Myson ran through cause ways that led in between huge rocks that seemed to leap out at him as he ran by, making large cuts in his arms and legs. Though the wounds were not deep, they stung and burned in the cold sulfuric air, bleeding profusely, leaving a trail of thin blood across the rocky floor. Myson paused, glancing over his shoulder. He could hear the hideous laughter and giggling of the wicked beasts that pursued him. His chest heaved trying to suck in great gulps of air, but he choked and shook his head as he breathed in a toxic breath. The legionnaire turned and scampered up a small cliff face to his left. His hands and knees scraped the unnatural sharp rocks, dripping blood down the cliff's dull gray features. He could hear the disappointed protests of the little beasts under him as they tried in vain to climb the cliff face. Their thick claws dug and clawed at the rocky wall but they could not climb it. Myson placed his bloody hands on the top of the small cliff and hauled his naked body up. He turned and peered back down. His long blonde symas, made dirty with the charred black ash of the rocky slate that he had climbed, bounced around his head as he stood triumphant over the hundreds of wicked beast that bellowed below.

"You will find a legionnaire is no easy prey, foul beasts. Despite your speed, you are too stupid to catch me." Myson shouted down, shaking his bloody fist at them. The little beasts fought and climbed over each other as a single drop of blood from his hand landed down on the cold rocks below. They bit and clawed at each other, trying to lick up the globule of his blood.

"A wise huntress does not pursue her prey, she lets her prey come to her."

Myson whirled, fists tight against his side ready to lash out at any enemy. What he saw startled him. Choking on his words he stepped backwards involuntarily. Before him stood the most beautiful woman he had ever seen in his life. She was a full foot taller that he with long straight black hair. Her eyes were the brightest blue that seemed to light the air in an azure hue around her face. The blue orbs bore into him, making his mind wander to lustful areas of thought he had never dreamed before. Her skin was the palest white, like a perfectly carved alabaster statue in a king's court. She was completely naked. Her large plump breasts seemed to be in perfect proportion with one another and an auburn erect nipple crowned each one. She was well muscled from her narrow shoulders to her thick shapely legs, though her beauty stopped there, replaced by a sinister aura about her. She had two small dark black horns that protruded from under her sleek thin hair, and her two fang teeth on her upper jaw protruded from the top lip of a seductive smile. She had two large red bat wings with a small black claw at their crown that were neatly tucked behind her.

Myson swallowed hard and glanced back down at the beasts below. To his surprise they had vanished. All that remained were the claw marks in the stone where the droplet of his blood had landed. Turning back to face the strange woman that stood before him, he steadied his footing. " What manner of creature are you, and where in the realms am I?" Myson asked through clenched teeth., trying to ignore his nakedness in the presence of the female.

The woman merely chuckled and flipped her hair with a delicate finger that was tipped with a long black claw. She shifted her weight and folded her arms under her firm breasts. She smiled seductively, her large oversized fang teeth danced around her mouth as she spoke. "I am nothing you have seen before, and all that you see for eternity. As for where in the realms you are, the answer is simple; you are not."

Myson stepped toward her threateningly. He had no weapons, but she was only a woman, though as strange her appearances was, how powerful could an unarmed woman be? Shaking his finger at her, Myson roared. " Do not answer me in riddles, woman. There is a powerful necromancer threatening my Vale, and I'll not stand idly by while it ravages the land. Now, either give me some answers or step aside, that I might return from only Leska knows where, and smite the beast."

The woman chuckled, though her face scrunched in distaste when he mentioned Leska.

"You amuse me, elf, but I warn you, do not mention that bitch, Leska again in my presence, or I will abandon you to your own devices. I doubt you will survive long here in the abyss."

The abyss. The woman's words seemed to echo in his ears. No one could describe the helpless feeling that erupted from deep within the elf's body. He feebly looked around at the dark yellow sky, the bubbling black clouds of soot, and the unimaginable demons that chased him with unnatural speed, and the cold. The horrible cold. Why else would he be naked after fighting the necromancer, but how did he get here? If he was dead, why was he not with Leska in her garden. The woman seemed to understand the blank look of doubt that planted itself starkly on his face.

"You are dead, elf. You were slain by a beast that is neither alive nor is dead. I am sure you are the first of many. Fortunately for you, I am here to take you to my lair, though you will work off your debt to me." She said with a seductive smile, biting her lower lip.

Myson felt bile in his throat at the repeated insults of his goddess. "I'll go no where with you, wench. You dare mock the earth mother? No naked slut is going..."

Myson was cut off with a lightning fast punch to his jaw. The demon struck so fast he could hardly see the blow coming. Her delicate fist hit him like wrought iron sledge, driving his jaw back into his skull. His eyes popped with the resounding crunch of his jaw and he felt the frigid rocky slate rise up, striking him in the back. The cold stone floor of the abyss sliced into his bare back. Bright flashes of light exploded in his mind from the force of the blow. Looking up from his back, Myson gazed dizzily at the naked woman standing before him. Her stern face stared down at him from between her perfect breasts.

"I have powers that you cannot begin to fathom, elf. You may come with me until I grow tired of playing with you, then you will beg to stay."

Myson rubbed his throbbing jaw and sat up. He had overcome the vulnerable feeling caused by his nakedness. He noticed the she devil's eyes roaming over his body, making more than a momentary pause and licking her lips, when she reached his lower midsection.

"Now follow me, fool. The slate is not safe, even for me." the woman said as she turned her back and glanced about the skies. "We must hurry. The arch demon is about."

"Arch demon?" Myson asked hesitantly. "The plains are barren for miles. Wouldn't we see anything long before it approached us?" the elf asked, glancing around. He did not like entertaining the idea of following the wench, but his options seemed more than limited at the moment.

The woman turned and faced him. To the elf's surprise, her eyes were filed with worry.

"Things are not as you are used to, elf. Another detail to recall, fool, is that you are not alive. You are long dead. You are not here as a man. Your body is not really here, it is a creation of this realm." she said as she led him along a narrow walkway atop the barren slate.

"What do you mean?" Myson asked as he grasped her hand, being led along the cold hard rocks. He recoiled at the cold of her touch, but she kept a firm hold, pulling him along.

Without looking back, she answered him. "You cannot be killed here. No, there are far things worse than death."

Myson ran with her, ignoring the searing pain in his feet from the jagged rocks.

"Strange, I imagined more people in the abyss. Where are the damned?"

Pulling him around the corner of a large slate boulder she pressed him close, wrapping him in her enormous bat wings. She pulled him in, pressing his body close to hers. He could feel her cold breasts press against his bare chest, but the cool clammy touch of her skin, washed away and sense of the reality of being so close to someone so beautiful. She whispered to him, her acrid breath wafted over his face, making him scrunch his nose in disgust. "The lake is a good distance away. You appeared in the spawning ground. After demons and the like are done with the new arrivals, they discard their twisted and mangled bodies and toss them in the lake."

Myson cringed. The thought of being tossed into the lake did not appeal to him. Perhaps it was a dream. Maybe he would wake and be next to the camp fire with Eulic. The wicked lustful gaze of the woman in front of him, drew the legionnaire back to the bitter cold reality of where he was.

A booming voice echoed across the barren landscape. "And how many souls have you tossed into the lake, Delania."

The woman spread her bat wings away from the man and raised her arms in defense of her face. Myson squinted his eyes at the bright spectacle that stood before him. A large manlike beast with great bat wings outstretched wielding a blue fiery sword in one hand a snake like whip in the other. The end of the whip was forked and dripped molten rock. He wore a single loin cloth made of a thick dark scaled hide that covered his dark crimson skin that was ablaze with small flames that flickered across his body. He had a thick jawed head atop his fifteen foot frame that had two great ribbed goat horns that curved back over his head. He had thick black claws protruding from his scaled toes and a large black horn that jutted from his knees. His eyes were bright yellow and had an amber aura that extended horizontally past the demon's face. His large canine maw dripped acidic drool that burned and singed the stone floor. The beast's body emitted cold that paled the frigid air of the abyss.

Delania stepped back from Myson and the great beast defensively. She glanced over at Myson with sorrowful eyes and then back at the arch demon with hate. The demon roared with laughter and tossed his head backwards as his massive body heaved with each chuckle. The bright flames that danced across it's body flared up, causing Myson to shield his eyes from the brilliance. Delania clenched her fists and scowled at the arch demon. "Is it enough that you have yet again ruined my chances at a pet, let alone tell the fool my name?" The she demon snarled. "If he ever speaks to someone from the outside..."

"You will have to worry about being summoned. You are weak compared to me, Delania. Do not tempt me into punishing you further for trying to take a spawned." the arch demon warned.

"Pet?" Myson repeated incredulously. "I'll be no one's pet." he said, ignoring the blisters rising up on his soft skin from the incredible cold of the abyss.

Delania shot him a sideways glance and the arch demon roared even louder with laughter. "I love the ignorance of the newly spawned. Of course you would have been her pet, you were well on your way. You would have leapt head first into the lake of the damned had she merely mentioned it. Tell me, did you have any lustful thoughts when you looked into her big blue eyes?"

Myson's look of shock answered the question for the arch demon. "Of course you did. Few mortal souls can resist the look of a succubus."

Myson shot his head back to Delania with a new regard for her. He stepped back warily, looking around for a place to run.

She turned to face him and her face softened. "I was trying to rescue you, really. You could have at least found some comforts in my arms. Here in the abyss, you will find nothing but endless torment." Delania pleaded.

The arch demon chuckled. "I doubt you would know what to do with him if you had taken him to your little alcove. I am sure you are the only virgin succubus in all of the abyss."

"I wouldn't be if you had not made your sick existence revolve around keeping me so." Delania sneered as she shook her tiny fist at the face of the imposing demon. Her pale face scowled with anger.

Myson slowly stepped back to the edge of the rocky slate they were standing on. Looking below were the little demons had been, he lowered his foot to climb down.

The arch demon shot out the molten whip with a flick of his thick wrists. The searing whip's tail lashed out and wrapped itself around Myson's neck with a loud crack. The powerful arch demon jerked the helpless elf through the air, and with a single stroke, he cleaved the elf's head from his body with his flaming sword. The elf's body bounced and twitched across the cold gray slate, while the demon's massive clawed hand, caught the elf's head in the air. He turned the head in his hand until it was facing him.

Myson's eyes were stark wide with terror. The arch demon loved this part. The elf was struggling not only with the fact that his head had just been severed from his body, but the fact that he was not dead. Myson could still smell the demon's acrid breath and he could feel the overwhelming pain in his neck from the wound.

"You cannot die here." the arch demon growled. " You are already dead. You will spend your eternity here as your head. Did you think that I would not recognize a Darayal Legionnaire when I see one? And don't worry about your friend." the demon said as he hoisted up Eulic's severed head with his other hand. "He is quite safe." with a toss the arch demon hurled the two heads through the thick smoky air of the abyss, and over a deep dark chasm.

Delania scowled at the arch demon. "May the great lord smite your wickedness!" she screamed with her fists and arms tight against her sides.

The arch demon merely smiled and stepped closer to her, his bright yellow eyes washed over her nakedness and basked in the sight of her lustfully. He lashed out his whip with a loud crack, but it merely passed right through where Delania had been standing.

She reappeared instantly. "I am not yours to be taken, Bykalicus!" she yelled defiantly and vanished. The arch demon roared in a anger. How dare the bitch say his name aloud. The arch demon turned to sense if any planar creatures were scrying in. If they learned of his name, he would have to answer to more of the pitiful mortals. Bykalicus knew in time, he would feast on their souls, but he hated little else more, than serving the plots of foolish men. *That whore succubus would pay for that.* The arch demon thought, but he had other matters to attend to. Soon, the death knight Trinidy, would be sending many more elves to him. The arch demon knew he needed to gather some of his henchmen to collect their heads. Their was much work to be done.

  Myson felt incredible pain as his head bounced off hard jagged rocks, coming to rest at the bottom of a deep ravine. He could see the back of Eulic's head. His long brown symas hung loosely, matted with dried blood. He started to speak, but was cut short when he saw them coming. Those strange centipede looking insect like creatures he saw before. They scurried toward them, their hundreds of legs were moving in rapid succession that seemed to crate a ripple effect from the rear of the creature to the front. Their tiny chitin legs click clacked over the slate rock as they swarmed near. The back of the creatures were made of many tiny armored plates. Each plate had a single horn atop of it with the tip pointed forward. It was then Myson began to understand the horror of an eternity in the abyss. He could hear Eulic screaming. Whether it was in pain or despair, he wasn't sure, until he saw one of the creatures erupt from the back of the legionnaires head, and then burrow back in. Myson screamed inside his head but he dared not scream aloud, in case the creatures might hear him. But to his horror, the tiny creatures bounded on him. He could feel each of their tiny razor like teeth, ripping into the flesh of face. The elf suffered each of the hundred tiny legs crawling under his skin, with that backwards horn, ripping flesh as it burrowed. He wanted to scream, his mind commanded the arms he no longer had to claw and dig at the tiny little beasts, but all he could do was endure the hellish torment.

Endure it for eternity.

*   *   *

Lance awoke from the cold night and wearily rubbed the sleep from his eyes. Yawning and stretching he sat up and pulled his bed roll tight against him. He could still see his breath in the late autumn morning, but to his delight, his companions had prepared a fire and was cooking some soup, or so it smelled, for breakfast. Dressing quickly, Lance rushed to the fire and sat down, rubbing his hands together as he tried to warm himself. Apollisian was polishing his armor and Jude seemed to be trying to do the same, though his thin chain mail, paled in comparison the grand plate the paladin wore. Lance didn't see the elf anywhere, but as he glanced around, he was startled by the fact he could see a tree line in the far distance ahead. The trees were tall and narrow, but they were tress. Lance had thought they would never get out of the god forsaken plains, with it's blowing dust and howling winds. Wiping the edge of his leather water skin with his shirt, he took a swig. The water was extremely cold, but since he was sitting so close to fire, he doubted the chill would reach his bones. The sun was not quite up yet, but the eastern sky was afire with bright yellows and pinks with a few splashes of orange here and there. There were a few light scattered clouds that hung in the west, colored dark blue by the eastern dawn.

Jude glanced up at Lance as he polished his armor, and sword. "Good morning, my friend." Jude called out to Lance when he spied him sitting next to the fire with his sleeping roll still tightly wound around him. Apollisian glanced Lance's way and offered a brief smile, then diligently returned to his work.

Lance pulled the bed roll tighter around himself and scooted a little closer to the warm fire. "I guess it is, my friend, since we can see the trees. I am more than eager to be out of this damnable plains.

Jude smiled and stirred the wooden spoon in the bubbling cauldron. " I made some soup. It has a bit of plains rabbit, if you don't mind the gamy taste to it, and a few vegetables that Overmoon rounded up before she left, but it ain't half bad." Jude said without looking up from the stew pot before abandoning it to sharpen his great sword. The rough two-handed blade sat long ways across his lap.

Lance frowned. "Where did she go? Hunting perhaps? I am sure there must be a lot of larger game in the forest."

Jude shook his head and answered without looking up. "No, she went to fetch some of her people. I guess since we are not elven, we are only allowed in at certain times, or something to that effect."

Lance shrugged and took another swig from his waterskin. Apollisian frowned, looking up from his polishing. "I do not think that is entirely it." he said hesitantly.

Jude looked at the paladin sideways in between strokes of the whetstone. "What do you mean?" Lance also turned from the fire and looked interestedly at the paladin.

Apollisian frowned and shook his head. Why was being a paladin so difficult sometimes. He just could not sit idly by, when he suspected that the elf was up to no good, despite his personal feelings for her, right was right, and wrong was wrong. Not telling this pair of what he suspected was surely wrong to him. "I suspect she thinks you are some kind of enemy to her people, Lance." he said slowly. "I had to practically restrain her from attacking you during the battle at Central City. You see, the cloak you were is called a Cadacka. It an elven ceremonial robe of mourning given by an elven family member to another when a loved one dies. They wear it until they have decided that their period of mourning is over. It is forbidden by elven law for any non-elven to even see a Cadacka, let alone wear one."

Lance jumped to his feet. "You mean, she is taking me to the elven city to try me for some crime I knew nothing about?"

Apollisian tried to speak but Lance cut him off. "This cloak was given to me by mother!" Lance shouted as he griped the fringe of the dark black cloak with silver cuffs and strange runes.

"Calm down, Lance." Apollisian said coolly. "I will prevent that from happening, though the fact that you wear elven property will be addressed, worst case scenario you will have to give it back."

"Give it back?" Lance asked incredulously.

Jude just hung his head low and shook it from side to side. He knew Lance was more protective of that cloak than he was of his own life sometimes. The cold didn't seem to bother Lance as he stood up in the gentle breeze of the plains.

"My mother gave me this. She is passed. It is all that I have of her memory. I will not relinquish it, short of it being pried from my cold dead hands!"

"That can be arranged, human." came a voice from the top of the small northern rise. Lance, Jude, and Apollisian whipped their head up and saw four elven riders atop the purest white horses. Their manes were cut short, save for every six inches or so, that was topped with bright green ribbons. The horses themselves were covered in thin sleek elven chain mail and their legs were covered in long thick hair that extended past their hooves. The horses wore green bridles that were enveloped with jewels and bits of silver and gold, making the four riders quite a spectacle. Alexis sat atop one of the steeds, wearing a bright green robe that blew in the breeze exposing a finely crafted suit of chain armor that hugged her figure well. Her long blonde hair was braided back in a single braid that danced in the wind. The beauty of her made Apollisian's jaw drop slightly, but the sternness of her gaze, sobered him just as quickly. The other three riders wore cloaks of various patterns but all were colored in shades of green and brown with bright vibrant runes that danced along the fringes, similar to the robe that Lance wore. Jude touched his hand on the hilt of his sword and Lance touched his mind of the thoughts of some dweamors.

Apollisian sensing the boiling emotions raised his hands and called out. " Halt! This nonsense is unnecessary!" His armor and polish clanged to the grass plains as he rose up.

"Do interfere Apollisian!" Alexis shouted. "This is above you."

"Above me?" he screamed, drawing his sword and tossing the scabbard to the ground. Jude drew his sword also and Lance began the makings of a spell.

It all happened in a flash. Lance barely saw the flows coming. They shot out from the middle elf and wrapped him in six green shimmering rings. The rings were made of pure magical energy. They did not hurt, though they prevented him from moving or speaking. All he could do was watch helplessly as the rings revolved around him spinning. They didn't seem to have a beginning, or an end, but they were spinning. He could clearly see that.

"Lance, what is wrong?" Jude asked nervously while he widened his stance and swayed back and forth, awaiting the moment to strike. "Lance?" suddenly Lance watched a single flow of energy come from the elf from the right and surround Jude, just as it had him, though the green ring was thinner and it rotated much more slowly. Lance thought he could see a section of it, like it was where the beginning and end met. Anger ripped through the young mage, though he could do nothing. He was as helpless as a babe. Lance needed to move his arms to cast the necromancies he had learned from the Necromidus, but he didn't need to move to cast any of his own spells, yet the minor dweamors seemed fruitless right now.

Jude stepped forward. The large swordsman didn't see anything, and he was suddenly held fast and could not move or speak. He could still hear and see but he could do little else. Jude could not see what held him, though he was certain it was the same thing that held Lance.

"Stand down, Apollisian." the middle elf said calmly. "There is a reason we brought three wizards with us this morning."

Apollisian looked at Alexis angrily. She avoided his eye contact. He turned his attention from her and regarded the three mages that sat before him. "I will not stand down. This is unjust. I demand that you release them this instant."

"I am afraid that cannot be, my good paladin. They are under arrest for crimes against the elven nation. I have the warrant issued by the king, if you wish to see it. However, I am ordered not to overlook your standings with the Vale, despite how much it may disgust me. It seems our king holds you in favor, as does his foolish daughter." the elf said as he cast a sidelong glance at Alexis. She ignored the gaze and stared down at Apollisian pleadingly. The paladin glared at her and stepped toward the elves. They seemed unaffected by Apollisian's show of force.

"We are instructed to offer you to travel along to ensure their just treatment and their just trial, if you wish. In fact, the king said you may even lobby on their behalf if you so desire, but we are enforcing the law, Apollisian. You may not agree with it, but Stephanis does recognize all forms of law. He is..."

The elf was cut off by the paladin's harsh words. "Do not lecture me on my god, elf. I am well aware of what he honors. It is too bad, your misfit posse here has no idea of justice."

The elves glared their narrow eyes at the paladin,

though he met their angry stares with a gaze of cold death. "I will indeed oversee your treatment of the boy and his friend, and so Stephanis help me, the moment you out step your laws, you will surely see the wrath of justice unfold."

"You dare threaten us?" one elf called out, turning his mount to face the paladin. The white steed jerked his head in response to the yanking of it's reins.

The middle elf waved his hand in dismissal. "Stand down, Malwinar. He may say as he wishes. It hinders our journey not."

The other two elves did not say another word, but they watched Apollisian as he donned his armor and mounted his Vendaigehn steed with virulent glares. Mounting up, he followed the elves as they led Jude and Lance, shielded by magic, north into the deep forest of the Minok Vale.

Lance struggled against his bonds, but he could not budge them neither physically nor mentally. The rings were twice as thick as the one that was wove around Jude. Lance watched the section that seemed to connect the band that was around Jude as it slowly circled him. Staring down at weaves that bound him, he searched for a similar section, but the rings were too thick and swirled around him at great speeds. The magical energy seemed to shift and turn within itself, making it impossible for him to see the cross section, but Lance figured if there was one on Jude, he could see the one on him.

Lance wondered if the bands around him also stopped him from casting. Obviously he couldn't use any of the spells from the Necromidus, but he could cast some of his own. They took no verbal, chants, or gestures. Lance narrowed his eyes and focused on the elf that held the weaves around him. Lance watched in delight as shimmering white weaves erupted from him and encircled the elf's head. The elf turned and glared at him in disbelief just as the weaves set into him. Lance immediately started casting another.

The elf started to warn the others that Lance had been casting, but when he opened his mouth, he merely belched loudly. The other two elves gave him a disgusted look and moved their horses away.

"Good gracious, Garlibane." Malwinar said as he cocked to the side in his saddle and regarded the high mage suspiciously. Alexis gave the high mage a worried look, and Apollisian immediately glanced at Lance, narrowing his eyes.

The high mage tried to give another sound of warning, yet a deeper louder belch than before erupted from his mouth. The other two mages deepened their frowns. " What has come over you, Garlibane?"

Lance focused his thoughts and sent the silvery weaves of shiny flows into the girth of the saddle. He had used this particular dweamor on his father's axe. When Davohn hoisted the implement high into the air, it would cause the axe to repel from his grasp. Lance hoped it worked half as good with the saddle's girth strap as it did with Davohn's axe. The fine weaves settled on the strap just under the horse's belly. If he could disrupt the mage's concentration, perhaps this binding spell would weaken, allowing him to escape.

The high mage did not respond and he started to raise a finger to point at Lance when the girth of his saddle seemed to erupt from the horse. The fine leather saddle shifted under the rider's weight and the high mage spilled onto the ground. He hit with a hollow thud and yet another belch erupted from his gurgling throat.

The two mages looked at the high mage in confusion. Alexis started to dismount when she saw the paladin glancing at Lance, shaking his head from side to side slowly.

"The Abyss Walker is casting!" Alexis screamed as she drew bow and reached back for one of the white ash arrows with the green fletching that protruded from her quiver. Notching and arrow, she pulled her powerful bow back easily and leveled it at Lance.

"NO!" Apollisian screamed, leaping from his steed, catching Alexis in the shoulders. He wrapped his armored arms around her. The elf's arrow flew high and wide as they fell to the ground with a thud. Her bow landed a few feet from her, and her arrows spilled out onto the ground behind her. Apollisian grabbed Alexis by her wrists and held her to the ground.

The mages whirled their horses quickly. "He is a sorcerer as well!" Malwinar screamed as he immediately shot out magical weaves around Lance. The face of the elf contorted with pain as he struggled to form a shield between Lance and his abilities. "I need help!" Malwinar shouted. "He is powerful."

The other mage formed a similar weave around Lance, but not as strong. Lance watched as the blue weaves enveloped him, making some kind of crude wall, then they seemed to sink into his body. He suddenly felt his ability to cast, but he could not summon it's use, much like his arms and legs. He felt as if he could move them easily, but the magical rings surrounding him prevented him from doing it. He could feel the energy from each source, though he detected each was different. Fear ripped through Lance as he contemplated his helplessness. Who was this Abyss Walker? These fool elves had the wrong guy. He was nothing of the sort. He was merely an orphan from Bureland. Hopefully the paladin would help him clear himself.

"Get off me! You orc loving buffoon!" Alexis screamed.

"How dare you label me so." Apollisian said with a grimace. "And I'll not let you up until you promise not to harm either of the prisoners until the Vale's courts try them. You forget, I am a paladin of justice, and I'll not rest until it has been served."

"You forget your station, human." Malwinar said

venomously as he fought to keep his skittish horse under control. "You are but a privileged guest. She is Alexis Alexandria Overmoon. High elf of Minok Vale, daughter of King Christopher Calamon Overmoon, and daughter Heir to the throne of Minok. I suggest you either unhand her immediately or find yourself in chains next to the criminals. After all, privileges can surely be revoked."

Apollisian glared at the elf mage, then softened his look when he peered down at Alexis. She was staring at him with a face of scorn, but he detected more embarrassment. How could he have been such a fool. She was not with him on the trail anymore. She was an elven noble. Her father had warned him of that. Shaking his head and pulling her up he started to apologize, but she cut him off. Her words dripped venom and spite.

"If you ever place a hand on me again, Apollisian Bargoe of Westvon, regardless of what good you think you might be performing, you will find that hand roasting on the picket of some witchdoctor. Do I make myself clear?"

Apollisian did not miss the formality in which she referred to him. Her face held scorn but her eyes were soft and full of remorse, yet they also seemed to harbor a great deal of fear. No doubt, afraid of the boy and his swordsman. Apollisian didn't understand why anyone was afraid of him, regardless of whatever supposed power he possessed, right now he was not evil, and he was not dangerous, though their treatment of him, might surely set him on such a path. The paladin started to help Alexis pick up her arrows, when she batted his hand away.

"I will retrieve my own belongings, paladin." Alexis sneered.

Malwinar re-secured the loose items on his horse from the incident and aided Garlibane in trying to dispel the dweamor that prevented him from speaking except by belching.

Apollisian mounted his Vendaigehn steed, and

patted the stallion's neck. The horse was well trained and seemed to understand how to keep him in the saddle if his weight shifted. It was rare that a horse actually tried to keep the rider on it's back, as opposed to helping him fall from it.

Lance focused his eyes on the crude barrier that seemed to be blocking him from using the magical energy that seemed to be innate inside him. He could see the magical energy swirling around inside the milky blue barrier. It was not well made, in fact it seemed very unstable. If he pushed a little there. Suddenly the barrier shattered and he felt the flood of energy as it filled him.

"He is free! He is free! He has broken the shield!" Malwinar screamed as he began casting again. Alexis started for her bow and then slowly lowered her arm, when she saw Apollisian tensing to pounce again. She did not mean what she had said. Well not entirely, but she would have to make good her threat in the presence of Garlibane, the high mage. As much as she was furious with the paladin at the moment she would not harm him willing. She just hopped they could contain the Abyss Walker before the human's ignorance at what they dealt with killed them all.

Lance started to weave another dweamor that he set upon the first mage. It seemed incredibly effective in neutralizing the man. He had thought someone of his power would have been able to break his weave easily, but he could clearly see it, snuggly wrapped around the man's head. But before Lance could finish the weave, Malwinar shot out a wave of green sparkling dots. It was no weave he had ever seen. It was, in a way, beautiful. Suddenly Lance felt his mind faltering and his eyes closing. The last thing he heard before he fell asleep was the triumphant voice of Malwinar. "That ought to hold him until we arrive in the Vale and receive our welcome."

Some welcome. Lance thought. No welcome I had ever heard of before. Maybe a prisoner's welcome, if there was ever such a thing. With the last thought, he drifted into a deep sleep.

"A prisoner. What do you think of when you here that title. Most men think of a man in a jail cell, or dressed in gray rags working the fires of some castle or keep as a slave. Few men think of themselves, or others they may see, as such. In truth, I say a prison is never a building of stone walls, or barred windows. If you searched, you might find a few of the so called prisoners that dwelled there, were actually more free than you or I.

Is a man who is not a prisoner, free? The answer is all in perspective. My mother was forced from Merioulus and had to live a mortal's life on this plane of existence. To the gods that banished her, it was supposed to be, not only prison, but a death sentence. And the later proved true, but she was as free as you or I are as we walk among the land. The truth is no one is physically free. A man must obey the laws of the land, or he will be arrested. The local magistrate must arrest law breakers, or he will lose his job, and or be arrested also. The king who makes the laws must govern his kingdom. The vagrants that walk the streets, cannot go into many of the establishments they walk among.

Freedom. No one is truly free physically. True freedom comes from within. It is strange that the few mortals that begin to understand this revelation, have been imprisoned most of their natural lives, save for the few wise that may discover this on their own. It took me years of persecution and imprisonment for me to understand the true meaning of freedom. What is sad are the men who think they enjoy the most freedoms are most likely the most imprisoned."

-Lancalion Levendis Lampara-

Chapter Ten
Trials of Innocence

"We cannot afford to debate the issue." Elder Eucladower argued before the elven council as he sat in his grand polished oak chair with hundreds of carvings depicting trees and birds of the forest. The old elf gripped his long golden pipe with his clenched teeth.

"The passages clearly state, and I quote; ' He who walks with wrath, shall stride into the Vale as a guest wearing the Cadacka, though he knows not why he mourns. If the children of the forest do nothing, they will surely perish.' It is obvious the boy is the Abyss Walker. He was wearing a Cadacka for Leska's sake!" the room muttered silently at Eucladower's uncharacteristic curse. "We must try him!" he pleaded to the king.

King Overmoon sat on his throne in the great elven hall. He held his weary head up with his hand. He had been hearing both sides of the debate every day since Garlibane, Apollisian, Alexis, and the other two other mages returned from fetching the humans. The room was more of a chapel than a hall. It was over three hundred feet long one hundred fifty feet wide, and it's ornate carved ceiling of gold and sliver rested some two hundred feet over the polished marble floor. At the far end was king Overmoon's golden throne, set upon a small dais depicting the greatness of Leska, and the names of every Minok king before him. Every twenty feet along the walls of the hall, majestic wooden beams erupted from opulently carved wooden bases depicting unicorns and other majestic creatures of the forest. Every third beam held a shining brass sconce whose flame flickered and danced sending ripples of small shadows across the great room.

 The king shook his head slowly and exhaled leisurely before speaking. " We have been over this, Elder Eucladower. I fear his power as much as the rest, but our hands are tied. What can we charge him with, short of possession of a Cadacka. He claims his mother gave him the cloak. However remote that possibility is, we cannot disprove it."

 Garlibane sneered. "He cast a dweamor on me, my king, that was so strong I had to wait for the weaves to dissolve, rather than dispel them. He wields both types of arcane powers. He is a wizard and a sorcerer. That is unheard of! No one in the history of our world, man or elf, has done such a thing. He was carrying the Necromidus, and he carries an elven copy of the prophecy. That alone satisfies a second passing. Need I recite it again?"

 "Watch your tongue, Garlibane. I am no maiden that frequents your bed. I am your king!" King Overmoon growled as he slammed both of his hands down on the polished oak table. The heavy slap of his palm against wood silenced the chamber and echoed across the room." A babe, half not of this earth, and half damned by the gods themselves, feared by the children of the forest, will carry his own proclamation naming him for who he is not, but for whom he will become." The king recited whole heartedly. "I am aware of every passing, mage, but in your wisdom, can you tell me how the boy is half of this earth, and half damned by the gods?"

 Garlibane looked down and bowed deeply. "I am sorry, my King, I have overstepped my bounds. May your graciousness forgive me, and by Leska's light I am humbled by your words."

King Overmoon eyed the high mage suspiciously.

"My lord..." Elder Humas interrupted. "Is it necessary for every passage to be confirmed in order to convict the boy? They were written before our grandfathers' grandfathers. Surely the context of their words is lost in our pages. We cannot place the burden of absolute proof on our shoulders alone."

King Overmoon arched an eyebrow, but did not interrupt Elder Humas.

"I mean, surely there are things in which they speak that we do not understand." Elder Humas stated flatly.

King Overmoon nodded his head slowly, adjusting the jewel encrusted golden crown that rested there. Today the crown of Minok seemed heavier than it had in a long while. The king glanced at Apollisian. The paladin sat disapprovingly as he witnessed the debate. His finely crafted armor glistened in the pale lamplight of the hall, but his eyes shined with fury and contempt. The king had listened to his argument to free the boy the first two days. Elder Bartoke, Elder Varmintan and Apollisian, all had argued on the boy's behalf. Elder Humas, Elder Darmond, Elder Eucladower and High mage Garlibane, all argued against the boy. As king, he was supposed to be impartial to debates by the council, but in truth, he felt the boy possessed no threat. He surely should be guided, or at least held as a respected guest, but executed, no.

"We will recess until tomorrow. I will hear your final arguments for the execution of the boy then." King Overmoon said as he slowly rose from his throne.

"But, my king, Eucladower protested. "The sun had not set on the day, surely..." the elder trailed off as king Overmoon shot him an angry glare.

"I am tired, Elder Eucladower. The boy is shielded and held. He is not a threat. I will retire to my chambers for the evening. I shall not be disturbed."

Every one in the room stood as the king moved

from the table and strode out of the hall. No one spoke until the heavy door at the far end of the great room, boomed shut.

    Garlibane grabbed the paladin by the heavy plates that covered his arm, and turned the paladin to face him. Apollisian towered over the smaller elf, but Garlibane seemed to match his presence with intensity and hate. "Surely, fool human, the king will hear our cause and see the true wisdom of it, unlike your foolish plight. You are not elven. You do not belong..."

    Apollisian cut him off, as he easily jerked his arm away from the smaller elf. "It is forbidden by Minok law to speak of the dissension of the hall during the three days the king hears each side." Apollisian said as he turned his back and walked toward the door.

    Garlibane growled in contempt. "You dare lecture me on the laws of my people, human? I will speak..."

    Eucladower yelled above the high mage. "Garlibane! Is it not bad enough that the human must teach you our ways, but must you further insult your own intelligence as to argue with him about it? Let us retire with some dignity. We will address the issue tomorrow. Now, disperse." the Elder said as he waved his hand in dismissal.

    Garlibane sneered, but said nothing else as he strode from the chamber muttering under his breath about teaching the fool human to interfere where he did not belong.

    *   *   *

    Lance awoke in a dimly lit room with no furnishings save for a silver and pewter chamber pot that stood in the corner. There was a small glass bulb that was affixed to the ceiling. The bulb had a bright yellow weave that was simple in creation, yet Lance had never thought to create such a weave. If he could twist it differently, he could make something more practical. Lance tried to reach his inner power but he hit a murky white wall instead. This time the wall was three times as thick and consisted of a clearer white, with little swirls of energy. This one would be much more difficult to break, so he rolled onto his back and studied the roof of his room. There was a door just a few feet away, but he didn't bother trying it, until the effects of the spell wore off completely. He still felt a little groggy. The ceiling was old, but well maintained. Though, it, and the wall's olive drab color, did little for Lance's mood. His head ached from the magical sleep, so he decide to lounge awhile before trying to stand.

Lance occasionally pushed at the barrier that prevented him from reaching his power, but the barrier seemed to twist at his probing. It was not like he could actually see the barrier, it was more like something he imagined in his head. Yet, he knew it was no imagination. Pushing again he forced his thoughts around the entire wall, and learned that it was not a wall at all, but an encompassing sphere.

After a few hours of pushing and searching against the barrier, Lance decided to try to stand. His knees wobbled at first, but in minutes he needed only to lean against the wall. He felt queasy, but his head was clearer and his balance better. Taking small steps he walked his bare feet across the dirt floor to the large wooden door. It was not ornate, and lacked any lock or latch. The hinges seemed to be on the outside of the door and he could determine which way it opened. Sitting down in front of the wooden door, Lance hugged himself to keep warm. He was not cold, but the room was anything but warm. Staring down at the gray rags he wore, he immediately missed the cloak his mother had left him. The elves had mentioned something about that. Regardless of what they thought, the robe was his. His mother gave it to him with her bare hands. They would not take it from him. As soon as he escaped from here. Escape, the word echoed hopelessness in his mind. He was useless against the elf's magic. He was too weak and too inexperienced to rival them. His only hope lay with Jude, or the paladin, but the paladin seemed cowed by the elves and Jude was probably was just as stuck right now as he was. Letting his head fall back against the hard stone wall, Lance closed his eyes. He would think of something, he just needed a little time, and the moment time was all he seemed in abundance of.

*   *   *

  Jude growled inside as he recalled being tossed into this cell. The elves had the audacity to call him a guest, when he was locked in a room with no furnishings, save for a silver and pewter chamber pot and a glowing bulb at the top of the ceiling. The walls were a sickly green color and the old wooden door seemed the only thing he had seen that did not have some sort of carvings on it since he arrived in this forsaken city. Those damnable elves took everything he owned and said he would get them back in time. In time for what? In how much time? He had been here for two days now, trying to get full on small portions of meat and a few nuts they stuffed under the door. Didn't the scrawny, pointed eared hellions know he was not a small as them? He needed meat, and a lot of it. Some ale would hit the spot right now too, but he was sure the fancy little beasts had none of that.
  Jude gave up pounding the door that had no hinges, latches or knobs. It just seemed as the door was magically held in place, and after making that discovery he decide he hated magic a little more than before. He had warned that fool Lance about coming here. In fact he had warned the prissy man, no child, of ever leaving Bureland. He could be snug in his big warm bed back home chasing a few rogues that had settled in the hills, or some thief that had eluded the local magistrate. Instead, he let Lance talk

him into a fool journey. But his father always had asked him, who was the bigger the fool. The fool, or the one who followed him. Jude now was feeling very much a fool. His muscles and strength were useless here, and he hated more than anything to feel useless. Feeling a fool was bad, but his father had taught him that was a good thing now and then to remind a man to be humble. Well he didn't much feel like being humble at the moment. Jude ran through his head how he was going to repay the elf, Overmoon, or whatever her name was. Apollisian seemed to call her that, but here the elves called her Alexis something or other. He would call her bent over his knee and paddled if he ever seen her again. As for that paladin, he would see the man with a bloody lip, or his church notified of this, but Jude was not much of the institution notifying type. He quickly tossed that idea out of his head, and went back to thinking of pummeling the man. As for Lance, he imagined a hundred things to say and do to that fool for getting him locked in this hellhole. Jude hoped the pretty boy was getting no better treatment than he. Yet knowing that hoodwink wizard want a be, Jude was sure he was up to his scheming and making out like a fat rat somehow.

With a heavy sigh, Jude sat down on the dirt floor of his room and leaned against the wall. Only time would tell how this misadventure was going to go, and it seemed at the moment he had an abundance of that.

* * *

Stieny crawled through the crawl space between the ceiling and the roof of the great meeting hall of Central City. The crawl space was made of thick wooden planks that were surprisingly free of dust and other debris. He wore only a thin cloak and some small clothes, fearing any extra weight of any kind might cause him to fall through or make some of the wooden shafts creak. Either would be bad. Not only had the little halfling received a poor reception here in central City, many of the crazed folk seemed to think him a dwarf and went stark mad, screaming in the streets. He had been arrested twice and he was just now beginning to break the law. That had to be a first.

He had since learned that it was most unlikely that a dragon had the ability to capture his soul in gem, but it was a big chance to take. So the little thief elected to go ahead and fetch the dragon's information if he could. Stieny had learned that this Lance had been here in Central City, but left to the east with a paladin and an elf. Strange companions for a dragon like Darrion-Quieness to be interested in, but that was the dragon's business, not his. All Stieny wanted to do was complete the quest, get his soul back, if the dragon ever really possessed it, and get the heck out of town. Heck, out of country would be nice. There was a lot of money to be made here in Central City and it seemed for some strange reason there was no guild in town. Stieny had never seen a city this size that did not have a thieves guild. The people were wealthy in the higher class area. They wore silks, and often had full coin purses of satin, dangling from their belts. Their belts! Never had Stieny seen a city of this size where that happened. Why given a good afternoon he could make more money than he had in his lifetime. Ah, but now, he was on a mission. He needed to find as much information regarding this Lance fellow. He would send word to the dragon and be done with him. He believed dragons were noble creatures, even if this one seemed evil, he felt it would honor it's bargain, and of course, their bargain did not specifically entail that he personally deliver the message.

Stieny deftly crept further along the crawl space between the ceiling and the roof. He had passed many rooms searching for this supposed meeting about the mage, and Stieny had even passed a room where a nobleman was getting along quite well with his maid, so to speak. Had Stieny not been so disgusted with the look of naked human bodies, he might have stayed and enjoyed some of the show, but human females were, well, too stretched out. Rumors around the magistrate were that he and his swordsman, whatever the swordsman's name was, were wanted for a murder in their room a few weeks back. Stieny hadn't heard much more than that. The guards did not want to speak to a halfling, and he had difficulty sneaking about since their were little else but humans in this town. He hated Beykla. Of all the kingdoms in the realms, they were the most intolerant of other races. Nothing like Aboe, where Stieny had been born. Aboe was a coastal kingdom that was made up of a giant peninsula at the southern area of the continent. The land was mostly mountainous near the coast and it's borders, keeping it, for the most part, unconquerable. Beykla had never been conquered in it's history either as far as Stieny could recall, but who would want to have the stinking human's land anyways?

"Like I said, we have received notification from the elves that they have captured the two murderers." Stieny heard a man say. The halfling paused and slowed his breathing and tried to get comfortable on the wooden ceiling planks as the voices continued.

"By their description it had to be Lance and the swordsman, Jude. Who else would dare travel to their lands? The pair were seen leaving with the paladin and an elf, though no word was said whether either of the other two arrived with them, I say it is them." The voice continued.

Stieny strained to listen further as another voice chimed in. "What did the elves say they intend to do with the pair?"

"The letter was brief, but they stated that they were holding the mage for reasons that were their own. But they were willing to send us the swordsman for a one hundred gold crown fee."

"A high price for murder, but I suspect the swordsman will fetch twice that in revenues fighting in the arena. Make the deal. Tell them to send him through the portal at our mage tower in Kalliman castle. If they do not wish to do that, we can dispatch a group of soldiers to meet with them in the Serrin Plains and take custody of him there." the second voice said.

"As you command, my king."

King! Yipes! Stieny thought to himself. What had he gotten into? This low power mage the dragon wanted him to follow was wanted by a king! That was all Stieny needed to hear. He would hire a linkboy to deliver the message to the mountains, give a vague description of were the dragon could be found, of course, he would mention that it was colleague of his, searching for a bounty, but first he needed to make a few coin to pay the man. A trip into the mountains was not going to be cheap.

Climbing back down from the crawl space, Stieny day dreamed about making a few extra coins for himself, and leaving this forsaken country. The trip back south was going to be long one.

    *   *   *

The great elven hall sat quiet. The elders had assembled before King Overmoon at the grand glossy oak table. The table was as ornate as the rest of the room, leaving little of any space, without hundreds of carvings and depictions of elven achievements. The king has heard the second day of arguments against the human. He was now convinced that the boy was indeed the prophesized Abyss Walker, or at least he would become him. The problem the king deliberated over, was how to deal with him now. The deafening silence was broken by the gnarled voice of high mage, Garlibane. "Surely we cannot keep him here among our people, my lord. When will he grow into the power to overwhelm us? We cannot have the liability among us. The risk is too great. He must be executed."

The others frowned at Garlibane, but even the Elders who did not believe they had the right to execute the boy based off of events he was yet to achieve, they agreed he could not be kept in the Vale, it was just not safe.

"Give him to my charge, your highness." Apollisian said as he stood up from the table. His darker mirrored reflection danced across the oak slab and his creaking armor echoed across the stark chamber.

"Surely you must jest?" Eucladower said as he pointed an upraised palm at the paladin. "We respect your position and your valor, Apollisian Bargoe of Westvon, but we cannot place the entire future of the Minok Vale in the hands of..." Elder Eucladower trailed off and looked away. His hand slowly lowered to the table.

"In the hands of a human." Apollisian said with a sneer.

"That is surely not what I meant to say." Eucladower replied as he wiggled in his seat. Trying to ease the icy glare from the paladin.

"Enough! " the king announced. The bickering will end now! Apollisian is one of us, or he would not be at this table. The banter of his race will cease! He is above the normal behavior of his race, that I must say, you elders have mimicked well."

The elders mumbled amongst themselves, but they dare not interrupt the king. King Overmoon was as lenient as any elven king in speaking out of turn, but he was deep in anger, when he felt someone stepped beyond their station.

"It is agreed that something must be done, and I have heard the arguments of each side and in part, I agree with each. I will make my decision in one hour." The king said as he stood from the table, as did the elders and

Apollisian. The king turned and his long green velvet robe fluttered as he strode out of the chambers.

Unlike days past, there was no bickering between the two sides. The elders Eucladower, and crew had succeeded in convincing the king that the boy was a threat. But they had not convinced him that he should be executed. Apollisian sat alone in the flickering torch light of the chambers after everyone had departed. He sat against the wall with his knees up and his elbows rested on them. His brilliant plate mail shimmered under the wavers of the torch. His head hung low with his chin to his chest and his long blonde hair streaked down, covering his face. He ignored the sound of the great door closing. He was in no danger here, and he did not feel like speaking to anyone. He was preparing himself to draw steel in defense of the boy. If they ordered him executed, he would give his life, if need be, trying to protect him, and he knew drawing steel against the elves would surely result in in his death.

King Overmoon sat in his chair in the lounge room behind the great hall. The room was small, but ornate as any other room in the Vale. It had a lounging sofa that was covered in dark brown velvet and stuffed with goose down. He had one arm resting on the back of the brown lounging chair and his feet were propped up on a small wooden footstool as he sipped warm wine from a golden cup that was encrusted with emerald and topaz jewels.

"You see, Garlibane. He is no ordinary human. He weeps for those who are wronged, and he weeps for himself. He knows he is in a lose-lose situation and he is undoubtedly preparing himself for his death."

Garlibane turned on the king and frowned. "Why would he be preparing for his own death? He is not the one on trial. In fact with the favor your majesty holds for him, I would doubt he should fear for his life if he was on trail."

King Overmoon chuckled and shook his head as he

leaned forward and refilled his empty chalice. " He prepares for death, because he knows when he draws steel against us, we will kill him."

Garlibane turned from the small peeping hole in the wall and faced the king. His hands were tight behind his back, tucked in the bright yellow cord that kept his robe closed.

"Why in Leska's name would he draw steel against us? We surely are not his foes." Garlibane asked in confusion. The high mage stepped to the king and picked up the other jewel encrusted chalice and filled it.

The king chuckled again at the high mage's lack of wisdom. It was true what he learned. Priests had the wisdom. Wizards merely had intelligence. "You see, my good mage, Apollisian does not fight enemies that you and I might think of. His foes are those that make others suffer injustice, such as he sees us."

"Us?" Garlibane asked incredulously. " What injustice are we causing.?"

"We are trying a man over the deeds has not yet performed. That is why I cannot make my decision lightly. You see if I sentence the boy to death, I am also sentencing one of the greatest and noble humans ever to walk the earth to death also."

Garlibane nodded as his face lit up in understanding. The high mage turned and looked back out the peep hole. " It seems you are not the only one that holds the paladin in such high regards." Garlibane said with an arched eyebrow.

The king frowned, placing his chalice on the small wooden table that was at the end of sofa and stood up. "What ever do you mean?" He asked as he walked to the peeping hole next to Garlibane.

The figure that came in shuffled on padded slippers. Apollisian noticed out of the corner of his eye, that the slippers were a silky red. They paused in front of him. It was then he smelled her. She wore the strong scent of morning flowers, and fresh soap that seemed to drift from her presence, clouding his mind. He raised his head and peered deep into the worried face of Alexis. Tears streaked down his chiseled face, sticking strands of his golden hair to his cheeks. She stared down at him with worry and pity. Alexis had never seen so much emotion from the paladin. She doubted he cried for himself, but for the welfare of the boy. Pulling her robe tight behind her, she lowered herself next to him on the floor of the great hall. Apollisian merely lowered his head again. He was now sure he loved her, and she would hate him for doing what he had to do. Had to do? Did he? His heart screamed for justice, to help those who could not help themselves, but who was helping him? He was giving up more than just his life. He was giving up on love. He quickly chastised himself for thinking such thoughts. Stephanis had filled him with more love and privileges, since taking up the sword in his name. How could he be so selfish to turn his back on his god now? He was a fool to think he and Alexis had any future anyway. She was an elf, he was human. Their union was forbidden by both races, more forbidden by hers. Plus she was no ordinary elf that could forsake her race. She was the daughter of a king. Daughter heir to the Vale. She had responsibilities that took precedent over her personal wants and needs, much like he did. Plus, the way she reacted to him in the plains, she did not likely return his feelings, at least not at the level he did. But did elves even love as a man does? So many uncertainties. To big a risk, to selfish of a risk. Even after coming to the conclusion that he and she would never be, the tears did not seem to stop flowing.

    Alexis placed a warm hand on the plate armor that covered Apollisian's shoulder. It was so hard and so cold. Much like his heart must be. She could tell by the tears that the man must feel immense remorse and sadness, she had already learned that traveling with him, but to what level did he feel it now. Were the tears shed in behalf of the boy? She doubted it, but she could not be sure. With the short lives of humans, did they really love as strongly as an elf did? She doubted it. She was sure she had grown to love Apollisian on their journeys. He fought and argued with such passion. He risked his life at every turn to try to enforce justice and what he felt was right. He would spit on no man, and if spit upon, he would ask the man for an apology before moving on. Never in all the realms of her kingdom, of her world, had she met a man with those qualities. It was strange, these humans. They lived hectic erratic lives, yet one might find a jewel that would rise so far above all others of any race, only to die so young. They seemed to pack a lifetime of wisdom and knowledge in the time it took her to grow enough before she was allowed to leave the Vale by herself. Yet the human race could produce a man such Apollisian, it could also create such a vile creature that he would appear as a demon in the body of a boy. She had heard tales of men who raped and killed children, ate other men for food, and even rose to become powerful allies and slaves of the denizens from the dark planes, yet before her now sat the most noble creature she had ever met. He reminded her of a unicorn, in the body of a man. The shoulder plate she had been touching shuddered under her. Alexis scooted closer and laid her forehead on the cold unyielding steel.

"I am sorry for things I have done." she said quietly. "Though I had no choice."

Apollisian nodded his head solemnly. "I too, am sorry for things I have done." *And things I have yet to do.* "But we cannot dwell on what is already done. Those things cannot be changed. We must instead look to what can be changed, and what has to be done." He said grimly.

Alexis lifted her head and was startled to meet the paladins steel blue eyed gaze. She could peer into his soul it seemed. Her dark russet eyes locked with his cerulean stare. Did he feel the same as she? She could almost see it in his sea of blue. Or was it the realities pressure to duty that stared back at her. She was sure he thought of her as a friend, sometimes as a spoiled brat, but she wondered if he every viewed her as an equal.

Apollisian gazed back into her almond eyes. How he could become lost in them. Those russet orbs told a thousand tales and sung a thousand songs of love and devotion to him, but was it real, or simply a figment of his imagination? Did his heart create what he thought he was seeing, merely because he wanted to see it more than anything else he ever wanted? He quickly found himself leaning toward her ever so slowly. Thoughts erupted into his mind like a tidal wave of emotions. What was he doing? He was in the great hall of the elven king of Minok, about to try to kiss the daughter heir to his throne. Something that was outlawed by her race. What madness had befallen him? But wait. She seemed to lean forward. Was it his imagination? He stared at her full lips. How he longed to feel their warm embrace on his. He leaned closer, as did she. Apollisian could feel her warm breath against his cheeks. The scent of her drove him wild. They were inches apart. His steel blue eyes remained locked on hers, while her auburn orbs danced across his face with uncertainty.

"Alexis." the sound of her name being called from the distance seemed to echo in her ears. The voice was familiar to her, it warmed her heart in a different way than the current raging inferno. "Alexis!" Came the voice, louder and more impatient than before.

She jerked her head around and immediately her face flushed into a sea of red. Her father came striding out of his personal chambers with the high mage, Garlibane. She glanced back and realized that Apollisian was already to his feet, smoothing his pants, and looking quite ridiculous doing so, since his legs were not covered with breeches, but rigid armored plates. She chuckled at his uneasiness and stood up, pulling her cloak tighter around her. "Yes father?" she asked and placed an indignant smile on her face, completely contrasting the stark horror that seemed frozen on the paladin's.

The king and the high mage strode over to the pair slowly. Garlibane followed a few steps behind. He was no fool and he saw the confrontation coming, knowing it was going to be more than heated. "You may take your leave, Apollisian." the king said with a forced smile.

Apollisian bowed deeply. "My thanks, your highness."

"You too, Garlibane. I will catch up with you later." the king said without taking his angry gaze from Alexis. She matched his angry stare and placed her hands on her hips.

The high mage frowned. He had wanted to see the little brat get the chastising she deserved, but he dared not defy King Overmoon. "As you command, my liege." Garlibane replied and quickly followed the paladin out of the great chamber.

Garlibane closed both doors to the great chamber and turned to see Apollisian quickly walking down the hall. "You do our nation a great favor, paladin." Garlibane said wryly. Apollisian stopped walking, but did not reply or turn around as the high mage finished.

"Go ahead and court the girl. Doing so without the king's permission, beside the fact you are a stinking human, and you will solve the old elf's dilemma for him." the high mage said with a haughty sneer.

Apollisian wanted to turn and argue with the mage. He knew the elf lacked much wisdom and did not think it would be difficult to slip him up in a verbal tirade, but he feared his emotions. He had lost control in the chamber. Had the king not intervened, he was sure he would have given into passion and kissed Alexis.

"But who could blame you, paladin? She is beautiful is she not, her long hair, her wonderful eyes,...the way her hips sway when she walks? I mean you are only human." Garlibane taunted.

Shaking his head, Apollisian walked from the chambers. The damned mage was trying to taunt him into a fight. But the elf was right, why shouldn't he want her. It was natural, to an extent, barring the interracial issue. But he was not like other men, he was a paladin, a champion of justice. He was wed to his sword and the way of his god. If he allowed himself to love another being more than any other, he opened the door for emotion to cloud his judgment. Could he allow her to die in order to preserve justice? Even now, he knew the answer to that question was, no. No matter what would come of it, he would no sooner allow her to be harmed than he would cast aside his god and denounce him. No, he realized that if he were to choose between his god, and her safety, he would have an intense struggle. He could not allow that to occur. Stephanis came first over all mortals. His will, his ideas were greater than any one life, even his own, even...hers.

*　　　　　*　　　　　*

"What in Leska's name do you think you are doing?" King Overmoon asked, shaking an angry finger in Alexis's face.

"I was trying to comfort the friend to the elves. My friend. *Your* friend. He seemed sad to me. I wonder what struggle is going on in his head, and I wonder what is the cause of it?" she asked accusingly.

Her father shook his head. "I have not given him permission to court you, Alexis. It is forbidden. He is a human, he is..."

Alexis cut him off. "I am not being courted by anyone!" she yelled. Her fists clenched at her side. Has he bought me any trinkets? Composed any ballads in the honor of my name? Has he ever belayed an interest in me to you, or any one member of our family?" Before the king could answer her, she quipped in. "No! He has not. And if he did father, what is wrong with him? He is the noblest man I have ever met, human or elven." she stressed elven harshly.

The king opened his mouth and tried to respond, but only empty air escaped his lips as she continued.

"He is a man that you trusted my life with enough to send me out amongst the humans, amongst their vile wickedness, amongst their wars. For what? So he could be chastised and made second rate before my eyes, before our brethren. If he stands so high in your eyes, then place him up on the pedestal he so rightly deserves, or so help me father..."

"Enough!" King Overmoon shouted. He was not going to take any more of this verbal tirade from his daughter. "You were in the best care you could have been in, and learn the real ways of the humans, and the ways of Stephanis. None knows justice like Apollisian's order, and none of them knows it as he. He is a beacon of light when there is nothing but darkness, but he is not elven."

"You're right, father." Alexis said with a much quieter tone than before. "He is not elven, and for that reason alone, he has risen to such greatness."

King Overmoon felt the sting in eyes of unshed tears. He embraced his daughter and held her head close to his chest. "My poor Alexis..." he said as she began to weep. "The man will grow old and die before your very eyes. His body will fail him, while his mind and heart will still love strong. The elven bond of love lasts a lifetime for us. As does the mourning of loves lost. If you begin to love this man, in a few short decades, you will wear Cadacka black, and probably never remove it. Few ever do. Not only that daughter, but the man is wed to his god, and his sword. It would be near impossible for him to give those things up. He could easier turn his back on Stephanis than he could stop being who he is." the king said in a near whisper.

Tears streaked down Alexis's face. "Then let me don my Cadacka now, father. It is too late, I already love him."

King Overmoon wept as fiercely as his daughter did in the cold empty hall. He knew the pain of losing a loved one. He could not imagine that without the joy of the memories to placate his loss.

Alexis pulled away and looked up at the tear streaked face of her father. "I ask you as my father, not as my king, do I have your permission to wed Apollisian Bargoe of Westvon, if he will have me?"

King Overmoon's soul wailed. His poor daughter could not begin to fathom what she asked, what pain she would subject herself too. But in truth, there was not a man alive, save for the paladin, that was close to good enough for his precious Alexis. "You know not the extent of which you ask, daughter. But if your heart wishes, I consent." the king said sadly.

Alexis looked up at her father with joy and admiration, but the bells of alarm sounding and the screams of the elves outside the hall, took away her endowment. There was something that was terribly wrong.

The king hurried to his chambers. "Go to the safe house, Alexis. I will see to the disturbance." the king said as his heart raced. The alarm bells had not been sounded since the orc wars. What could have possibly happened for them to be sounded again.

Alexis rushed out of the chamber, and turned to see if her father was watching her go. Satisfied he was not, she hurried to one of her many private rooms. She needed to fetch her bow, and find Apollisian. If there was going to be danger, she would much rather face it with him.

* * *

Apollisian marched down the long corridors when

he heard the alarm bells sound. He wasn't sure exactly what they meant, but the screams and shouts from outside quickly told him trouble. Drawing his short sword, he quickly rushed outside. The scene that greeted him was something from nightmares. Thousand of skeletal monstrosities attacked and fought with the elven villagers. There were too many for the watchmen to fight. Dead and slain elven children littered the ground, as did women and unarmed civilians. Apollisian roared into a fury. He set into the skeletons, cutting a path to the center. Their yellow, and bleach white bones were difficult to cut with his sword, but he fought on anyway, easily evading their clumsy attacks. He could see great balls of fire coming from the heavens striking trees and buildings as great pieces of stone and debris erupted from the shattered structures and littered the ground.

    Apollisian heard a shriek around the side of the great hall. Turning and making his way there, he saw Alexis surrounded by a pile of broken and shattered enemies, swinging with her unstrung bow. She was surrounded and it seemed every skeleton she smashed, three more took the their place. It was as if the entire city was alive with bleach white enemies. Seeing her in danger, Apollisian outstretched his arm. Grabbing his holy symbol tightly in his clenched fist, he chanted in a thick deep voice that seemed to echo unnaturally loud.

    "By the hand of Stephanis, disperse fetid undead, and enjoy the afterlife you were so evilly ripped away from."

    When he finished, a wave of an unseen force, like a ripple in reality, shot out from him in all directions. Skeletons by the hundreds seem to explode in a shower of bone debris.

    Alexis stared wide eyed as her attackers exploded in front of her. Her face was hit by stinging fragments from the skeletal foes. She looked to her left and saw Apollisian running to her. The sight of the man was majestic in his shining armor and flowing cape as he ran to her with his face full of worry and compassion.

"Are you all right?" he asked between labored breaths.

The sight of him in front of her at last caused Alexis to momentarily forget about the horde of skeletal enemies that surrounded her, she forgot about the lives lost, and the lives that would be lost in this battle, she forgot about the confusion of how the attacks arrived, and how they would be defeated. She only knew that standing beside her man, her friend, her champion, she could defeat all evil that rose against them. In a single moment without hesitation, without fear of the unknown, she reached up and grabbed Apollisian by the sides of his face. His warm skin seemed ablaze under her touch, as she pulled his face down to hers. She reveled in the puzzled look in his blue eyes and the pleasant shock as she kissed him. The kiss lasted a fraction of a second, but to her it extended from the beginning of her existence to the present day. She did love him. She was sure of it, and if they died today in this battle, she would have at least told him. " I love you." she whispered. Without waiting for a reply, she pushed his face away and drew her short sword. She did not need a reply from him. Her heart did not rest on whether he returned her love, though she desperately wanted him to. She was content in knowing that she loved him and no matter how he felt, he would not hurt her, or take advantage of her. He was a pure man.

Apollisian stared in shock. She must have been overcome by the moment. And what did she say afterwards? He must have been confused by the battle. But what if he was not? In Stephanis' name, he would rather face ten thousand more of these skeletons, wearing only his birthday suit and wielding a wet stocking, than face the battle between his god and her, because he did not know who exactly would win.

"We need to make our way to the mage tower." Alexis said as she strung her white ash bow finally and tightened down her green cloak. "It is likely that whatever is controlling these things will strike there."

Apollisian gave her a sideways glance. "Overmoon, you do not believe that the boy has summoned these apparitions to fight for him, do you?" he asked.

Alexis shrugged her shoulders and started off toward the mass of skeletal monsters that lay ahead. "How else would you explain them?" she said. "And my name is Alexis Alexandria"

Apollisian took a deep breath and gripped his sword tighter, following after her. Why had she revealed her real name? As if he didn't know it, but she told it to him as though she wanted him to call her by that. Her first and second names were only allowed to be spoken by others of her race. Apollisian pushed the thoughts out of his head, including the image of her warm smile. It seemed he was to do battle again today, only this time with steel, not against oppressing elven elders.

*   *   *

Trinidy marched into the thick trees, he could sense that pull ever so close. Finally he would be finished with this quest. But as he neared and entered deeper into the forest, he could hear hundreds, no thousands, of those mocking drums. Thump-thump, thump-thump. Every where they mocked him, taunted him, their very being seemed to insult him to the core. Suddenly the forest was alive in front of him. Elves scurried away like roaches under bright torch light. Some ran to challenge him, while others seemed to challenge his skeletal army. "An entire city of evil elves." he thought to himself. How he would enjoy cutting these denizens down. He longed to feel their soft flesh screaming and squirming under his blade.

"Attack." he silently commanded the skeletons with a thought. And like an army of ants that were set against a foe that had disturbed their hill, the skeletons rushed into the elven ranks. They moved like rigid clockwork in perfect unison. The ghastly soldiers did not bump into one another, they did not falter or lose moral, they did not fear or grow angry. The skeletons moved and fought as pieces of a game, being wielded and commanded by their master. Every where Trinidy looked, he could see elves cutting his army of bones into rubble, but for every ten skeletons that fell, so did an elf. The death knight didn't pause to count, or do the numbers in his head to see if he was winning the battle. The battle was irrelevant. The true fight was yet to come. He would find this wrong he was to right, he could sense it close by. The feelings were incredibly strong here.

    Trinidy reached out his rusted, corroded, gauntlet covered hand toward the source of the pull that had led him north for so long. He focused his thoughts on the hunger, focused on that which called to him. His rotted and decaying eyes scanned the immaculately carved elven buildings. As they moved from one side to the other, excited black spiders and scorpions spilled out from the corners of their rotted sockets, until those shriveled eyes rested on a small squat structure that seemed to be built into the hill, with no windows that he could see. It was there. His enemy that he needed to kill was close, as was the completion of his quest.

    *   *   *

    "What in Leska's name are they doing sounding the bells?" Garlibane asked Malwinar between breaths as he rushed down the polished wooden floor of the north corridor. The young elven mage shrugged his narrow shoulders and slowed before coming to a thick wooden door.

    Garlibane stepped in front of the young elf and knocked on the door. "Isham-dorrie." he said, cutting a small flow of magical energy that he had used to lock the door from anyone but him. Hastily, Garlibane pushed the heavy door open and rushed inside. The room was large and held hundreds of strange artifacts and decorations. There was no furniture that could be seen, but wands, staff's, and other such equipment littered the walls like tombstones in graveyards.

Garlibane grabbed a staff from the wall and tossed it to Malwinar. The young elf awkwardly caught the gnarled wooden staff with both hands, holding it out in front of himself with awe. "Leska's nook?" the young mage asked, his voice dripping with uncertainty. "Shouldn't we see what the problem is, Cranetium?

Garlibane paused from rummaging through an old chest, pulling out small wands and other items. The ancient title, Cranetium, used to be used in all settings of wizardry in the Vales, now it held only a ceremonial position. The fact Malwinar referred to him as his official title gave him pause. He stuck his head back into the deep wooden chest and began to draw out more items. He pulled his upper torso from the chest and tossed the awe struck mage a string of pearls on a leather thong necklace. Malwinar flinched as the pearls landed with a hundred simultaneous sounds of the tiny beads hitting the floor. Malwinar's eyes widened at the site of the pearl necklace.

"The pearls of Matoon?" he asked with more uncertainty than he did when he caught the staff.

"We are not here for a quiz in the titles of our arcane vault. You do know how to use each, do you not?" Garlibane asked with a muffled voice from digging out more relics.

"Y-yes, but shouldn't I sign them out, or leave one..." Malwinar stammered.

Garlibane jerked up from the chest. "Damn you, fool! Do you think we have the luxury of standing about? The alarms have sounded! Get your hide outside and help with whatever is the matter! If it is some cruel prank, it is better to be prepared!"

Two more elves rushed into the room. They were dressed in their mage robes and one was bleeding from a deep gash on his right arm. Malwinar turned and regarded them, before leaping back when he saw the blood. "Whatever is the matter?" Malwinar asked.

"A legion of undead!" one of the elves panted, hands on his knees. "The Abyss Walker must have called them down on us!"

Malwinar set a determined look to his face and slipped the pearls over his head and gripped the wooden staff so tight his knuckles tuned white. Striding out the door, he became a memory to Garlibane.

"What do you mean undead? Garlibane asked in disbelief. "The Abyss Walker is nothing more than a foolish boy. He could not possibly know how to summon undead, let alone a legion of them."

"It is true, Cranetium." the other elf piped in. "We rushed here to get some tools to battle them. We did not prepare any battle spells today." the second elf said as the first shook his head in agreement.

"As did none of the mages, I suspect. Where are the others?" Garlibane asked as he hastily closed the lid to the chest. It slammed shut with a loud thump as dust wafted into the air.

"We are the only ones that managed to get by. The skeletons number in the tens of thousands, maybe more. They are led by a undead knight that summons balls of fire from the air, and surrounds himself in globe of impenetrable darkness at will. The order is fighting the apparition in front of the jail, where the Abyss Walker is being held. The undead knight must be trying to free him."

Garlibane felt his face flushing red with anger. His vision became tunneled as white hot rage surged into him. "I warned those damned fools he would bring the death of us all!" The passings said if we do nothing, we would die, now we have done nothing, and we will surely perish."

the high mage said as he slipped on a thick red robe and placed several gold rings about his fingers.

"What are you to do, Cranetium?" the mage asked, placing on the black leather gloves Garlibane handed him. "The king said that no one could harm the boy until he decided what to do about him."

Garlibane shouldered past the young mage. "I am not going to harm him, but mark my words, I'll not let us perish by the king's foolish indecisiveness. If he can summon legions of undead to free himself, then I will send him to a place more deserving of his talents and his attention."

The young mage started after Garlibane into the polished wooden hallway, clutching the deep wound in his arm. "What are you to do, Cranetium?"

Garlibane stormed down the corridor and did not turn as he answered with a taught jaw. "If the Leska be damned boy is powerful enough to break my shield, them I'll send him to the only place in the realms where their are mages and sorcerers with the talent to hold him."

Where is that, Cranetium?" the young mage asked.

Garlibane did not respond as he marched purposefully down the corridor.

     *   *   *

Dicermadon paused as he neared Leska's garden. He could sense hundreds of elaborately woven traps, wards, and glyphs set about the entrance to her lair. She would be the strongest there. Dicermadon knew he still would have no difficulty crushing the earth mother, where ever she hid, but if she had time enough to band with the other elemental gods... Dicermadon turned back and started toward his room. He would need to gather his supporters and deal with her in that fashion. Once united, the elemental gods were not a group to be trifled with.

As the god king walked back down the glittering streets of Merioulus, he saw every god and avatar standing in front of their domiciles. They no doubt knew of the earth mother's treacheries and she was surely spreading her filthy lies about the abyss. How that fool wench discovered his plot was beyond him, but that changed nothing. The boy was more dangerous than anything that had ever existed, he knew that now. Dicermadon needed the death knight to slay the boy, giving Bykalicus, lord of the night, control over his soul. Getting caught in a trap by the elemental gods would not help his plight. Killing the boy was more important than anything. More important than his own existence, though he would fight to remain in power, if need be, he would sacrifice himself to ensure the boy's demise. But avoiding that outcome was on his top priority.

Flunt, Surshy, and Whisten rushed into Leska's garden. She stood on an alter to herself in full plate armor that was brilliantly covered in emeralds and bronze. The plant life seemed alive and ready to do battle and she stood among hundreds of magically created wards, glyphs and traps. She turned to regard the others and nearly wept in delight. She started to warn them, when they informed her that Dicermadon had turned back. She fell into Whisten's arms.

"Oh brother, he has meddled with demons. What are we to do?" Leska asked with uncertainty after straightening herself and sitting on a marble bench in her garden. She dispelled her armor and the bright polished mail dissipated in a flash and fizzled into nothingness, replaced by her dark green shift that barely covered her breasts and hips.

Flunt's fiery eyes burned in anger at the attack on Leska. "He is to be disposed." he said with a blazing, cackling voice.

Whisten nodded with Flunt's dire words, as did the water face of Surshy.

"Then it has begun." Leska said solemnly. "The heavens are broken once more."

*   *   *

Trinidy forced his way toward the small hill. His legions of skeletons battled the elves back, but his army had stalled in the face of many elven wizards, sorcerers, and a few priests. They hammered at him with a barrage of spells. Most of the weaves and dweamors slid off of him without much effort. Trinidy guessed that he had a resistance to their spells. Sometimes a blue bolt of energy might hit him in the chest with a bright flash and a shower of sparks, but he was managing to force his way forward, despite their attempts to stop him. Nothing would stop him now. He was so close. Trinidy felt the pull, the drive called him to the hill. It was so close. The insects that crawled about his face became more excited, scampering from his eyeless sockets and around his head. Another and another elf fell, as Trinidy paid little heed to whether it was wizard or warrior, male or female, all he focused on was the hill. He could feel the hate building inside, bubbling to a head. The energy welled to the surface, pushing, pushing to escape. The feeling was exhilarating. The imagination of the death of this creature filled him with such ecstatic harmony, that he could hardly imagine what he would feel in moments when his desire became realty. Who could stand against him? These elves were helpless against his power.

Trinidy reached the wooden door that held what he sought. He reached for the door, then nothing. The intense pleasurable sensations vanished. Whatever he had been seeking was gone. There was no pull, no command, nothing. Rage ripped through the death knight and he turned and faced the elves. The elves had hidden what he sought. They had tried to keep him from his salvation, and now they had moved it. They would pay! He would kill every last man woman and child here. Just as he began to summon another white hot fireball, the rage vanished. It was replaced by a feint pull to the west. It was not strong, but it called to him. Trinidy recognized it. The prize would not elude him this time. The death knight took his first step to the west. His first step to redemption. Nothing would stop him now.

     *   *   *

 Lance strained his ears to the distant sounds of battle that seemed to permeate the thick walls of his room. No, after looking around at the few furnishings and the mediocre bed, not to mention the fact he could not leave and was shielded from using either type of his magical abilities, he decided that it was most definitely a prison cell. He had labored and forced his will against the barrier that held him, but the white milky wall did not have any seams, or bend to his prying. Lance marveled at the spell that held him, even if it left him helpless. He could not actually see the wall, it was just as if he sensed it was there. Like he knew it was white, and the consistency of it, yet he had never experienced it before. It was much similar to the first one that they had placed on him, though he burst through that one easily, this one was much better constructed. Lance wished he could have tutored under this Garlibane. He was sure he would learn great amounts of knowledge.

 Sighing, Lance leaned against the cold hard wall and slowly lowered himself to a squatting position. Pulling his knees into his chest, he hugged his legs and placed his chin on his forearms. The sounds of battle were getting closer. Lance figured it was some sort of elven exercise. He doubted the dwarves had any squabbles with the elves and if they did, how many hundred years would it take for them to tunnel under here? The thought of the murderous dwarves here, made him shudder. He had never encountered the little folk before, but if he never came across them again in his lifetime, he would count himself lucky.

Suddenly the heavy door to his cell burst open. Lance jumped to his feet and backed away to the far corner. He had no magical ability and no weapon. If the dwarves were attacking, he would have no way to defend himself. He wished Jude were with him. His friend was quite an accomplished hand fighter. Straining his eyes through the bright light that poured into the room from the open door, Lance saw two small short silhouettes. His heart stared to race. It was the dwarves! They had come to kill him. Tightening his fists he leaned forward and tensed his muscles. The bastard bearded folk were not going to take him without a fight, regardless of how feeble the fight may be.

The voice that came from the two shadows were soft and honeyed, nothing like the dwarven voices he had heard before. To his relief, two elves stepped into the chamber.

"Stand down, boy." came the elven voice. Elves voices were soft and honeyed, almost sounding like a woman's. "We have come to help you."

Lance narrowed his eyes. "Yea right. You idiots think I am so kind of a..." Lance was cut off by absolute silence. He grabbed his neck with both hands as he tried to talk. He could feel the vibrations coming from his throat, but no sound. In fact he could not hear any sound from anywhere. Suddenly those blue rings appeared around him again that held him in place, keeping him from moving. He didn't see the weaves as they came at him this time, but he could clearly see them around him. There were only four, unlike the six from last time, they were not as thick as before, and did not spin as fast, but he could see the section that held them together. His mind raced. If he could focus his mind and break these rings, he might be able to escape. Lance felt the wall that shielded him from casting with flows weaken, and his mind strained. He watched each ring as it spun, it's sparkling green swirls that dipped and rose inside of each ring seemed to slow. He reached out with something. Lance wasn't sure what, but he waited, waited, then in a flash he wedged the energy into the section. The ring shook and popped into a glittery nothingness.

"He is escaping!" Malwinar screamed nervously while Garlibane moved his arms and hands around as he chanted slowly.

The high mage did not respond, he remained focused on the intricate spell. Suddenly a bright orange light appeared in front of the two elves, just as the second ring shattered into a flash of green shimmering nothingness.

The orange dot of shimmering light that hovered off of the ground in front of the two elves stretched and quivered until it was a long horizontal line that was about waist high.

Lance struggled to break the rings faster. He figured the wall was weakened by Garlibane's fool attempts at casting multiple spells at the same time. Lance was sure he had memorized the weaves that made the shield. If he could get free in time...

The third ring shattered as the horizontal line in front of him grew until it was a tall shimmering doorway. Lance could see an alley way that led to a city street that was covered in hundreds of shiny rounded stones. Rain was pouring down and the alley was dark, or he would have seen more.

"Focus on the rings." Lance thought to himself. He was vaguely aware of the woman wearing a bright red robe with long flowing red hair, that was frowning as she approached the portal.

"Quickly shove him through!" Garlibane said through gritted teeth. Sweat beaded on his forehead as he spoke. "Hurry, before one of the dammed women shoves a wedge into the gate, then we are all in for some headaches!"

Malwinar grabbed Lance by the collar, just as he shattered the final ring. The elf wizard shrieked as Lance reached out and snatched the Cadacka from his hands. Malwinar tried to force the larger human through the portal, but Lance fought viciously, punching the smaller elf several times in the face with his fist. Blood poured from the elf's nose and mouth.

"Help me!" Malwinar shrieked as he tried in vain to shove Lance through the gate.

Garlibane narrowed his eyes and whispered as he took a deep breath. He was too small to physically move the larger human into the portal, and he could not allow the boy to escape, the entire Vale's safety depended on it.

"Leska, forgive me." Garlibane said as he wove a thick thread of blue energy. In moments he created a large wall of pure air and by shoving his hands out in front of him, he forced both, Malwinar and Lance, into the portal.

Lance hit the wet bricked alley hard. He rolled with the powerful force that had knocked him through the air and came to his feet quickly. Malwinar tumbled head over feet, skidding to a stop before he scrambled on his hands and knees in the pouring rain, reaching out in vain at the rapidly diminishing portal. The elf shoved his hand into the bright orange light, futilely trying to grab something and haul himself back in. As the shimmering orange light of the gate popped into nothingness, it severed the elf's hand that was reaching into it.

Lance was not prepared for the howling shriek that echoed throughout the dark, rainy alley. He hugged the robe that his mother had given him, ignoring the cold rain that soaked him, unaware of the strange woman wearing bright red robe behind him.

Malwinar rolled on the ground clutching the wrist that had once held his hand. The terrified elf, wailed and shrieked, begging for mercy from the gods. Blood poured from the wound and mixed with the rain, making the alley floor turn to a soft red.

Lance started to run down the alley when he felt thick strands of energy whipping around him. Before he could counter them, he found himself once again held by a bright green magical ring. Frustration overtook the young mage at how a spell so simple seemed to frequently ensnare him. Lance watched as three women walked past him. The hard pouring rain seemed to fall around them, but not a single drop hit their crimson robes. It was almost as if an invisible barrier shielded them from the rain. The women wore bright red cloaks that had arcane symbols covering them entirely and one stopped to eye him suspiciously. She was almost as tall as Lance and her long red hair was braided and pulled up in a bun on the top of her head. She had bright green eyes that seemed very intelligent, but her unyielding face was as cold as ice. She paused a moment and then stared into Lance's emerald orbs intently.

"Mother..." one of the other women that was dressed in red started. They were kneeling down around the quivering Malwinar. Lance could barely see them from behind the stone faced woman that stood before him, but he dared not take his eyes from her. She held his gaze like a medusa.

"This one is injured. I think he will require extensive healing." the woman called out as they held the shrieking Malwinar to the ground.

The woman standing in front Lance smiled, but did not take her eyes from his. You know what to do. Healing costs gold. We do not waste gold on men."

Lance watched in stark horror as the two women casually pulled daggers form their belts and plunged them into Malwinar. The elf struggled for a few seconds, then went limp.

"It is done, Mother." the other two red clad women said in unison.

The woman with the long red braided hair standing in front of Lance kept her wicked icecold smile. "Good. This one will make a fine slave."

.

" And woe to the world the day the son of mercy was set upon the mother's without children. They edified to him what it meant to hate, and then in turn, he edified the world."

-Ancient prophecy record kept in the great library of Kingsford City-

-author is unknown-

Glossary

Adoria- (A-door-ee-ah) Kingdom just west of Beykla. It is engaged in a bloody civil war against it's eastern half, Andoria.

Alexis Alexandria Overmoon- (a-lex-us / al-ecks-zan-dree-uh / Over moon) Daughter heir of King Christopher Calamon Overmoon, high lord of the Minok Vale. She travels with Apollisian Bargoe, the paladin of justice, trying to learn the ways of Stephanis to aid her when she becomes queen.

Amerix Alistair Stormhammer- (am-er-icks / ali-stair / storm ham-er) Dwarven general of clan Stoneheart, formerly of clan Stormhammer. His clan was wiped out when he was very young by dark dwarves and a white dragon. Amerix fled with a few survivors from his clan and was welcomed into clan Stoneheart where he excelled in the art of war.

Apollisian Bargoe- (A-paul-issi-in / bar-go) Paladin of justice that was sent from his order in Westvon keep to oversee the negotiations between the humans and the dwarves from clan Stoneheart in attempt to derail a conflict, when he was caught in the middle of the war.

Andoria- (an-door-ee-ah) Formally eastern Adoria, this kingdom's brief history came when it declared it's independence from Adoria. It waged an eight month long war with Adoria, but was eventually re-conquered.

Aten- (A-ten) Queendom to the far west that is ran solely by women. Males of any race are considered inferior and are immediately made into slaves, or killed at birth. Only a choice few males are kept alive for reproduction purposes only. The women of Aten are adept sorceress and keep a rigid society of back stabbing and political maneuvering.

Beovi- (bee-o-vi) A subterranean fish that live in the deepest freshwater caverns of the undermountians. They are a delicacy to dwarves, dark dwarves, dark elves and other subterranean races. These fish can grow to unlimited size, depending on the lake or river in which they live.

Beykla- (bay-kla) Human kingdom on the north eastern corner of Terrigan. The kingdom is wealthy, militantly powerful, and well patrolled. It has never, in it's long history been conquered.

Blue Dragon Inn- Inn in Central City that is nearest to the Dawson river and the Dawson river bridge, where Lance, Kaisha, Ryshander, and Apollisian battled the dwarven horde, until the king arrived with re-enforcements.

Bordeck- (bore-dek) Dwarven torture device that is made of iron. The device is shaped like a mask with many spikes laid on the inside of the mask. It is placed on the victim
while a thick iron bar is fastened to two long screws on each side of the Bordeck. The bar is then cranked upwards under the chin until it forces the lower jaw into the victims upper jaw very slowly, causing the teeth to pop and shatter, crushing the jaw and eventually causing death.

Bureland- (bur-land) A small hamlet in the southern part of Beykla where Lance spent most of his childhood and early adult life with his adoptive father, Davohn.

Breedikai- (bree-da-kii) Original gods, or gods that were created. They have no soul and most dwell in Merioulus.

Brother of the sword- Term given by the Darayal

Legionnaire to their Legionnaires in training.

Bykalicus- (Bye-kal-eh-kus) Powerful Arch demon that controls much of the Abyss.

Cadacka- (ka-doc-uh) Black ceremonial robe worn by elves when they have lost a love one and are mourning. Most elves never remove the cloak once it is donned.

Calours- (ka-loo-ers) Non sedimentary rocks found in the undermountian. Subterranean races, mostly species of dwarves, heat them to cook meat on.

Cerebron- (sare-eeb-ren) Human boy that Apollisian had saved from the dwarven onslaught at the Torrent Manor.

Central City- City just south of the Dawson Stronghold that is in the center of the Beyklan nation.

Christopher Calamon Overmoon- (Kris-toe-fur / Kal-a-mon / O-ver-moon) High king of the Minok Vale.

Colonel Mortan Ganover- First lieutenant of Duke Dolin Blackhawk, and acting mayor when the Duke is gone. Was widely considered responsible for the slaughter at central City by the dwarves due to his failure to act on the paladin Apollisian's recommendations.

Commander Fehzban Algor Stoneheart- (fez-ben / al-gore) Commander and loyal follower of general Amerix Stormhammer. Was tried and convicted of treason after the Torrent manor and the Central City campaigns.

Commander Kestish- (kest-ish) Commander of and loyal follower of general Amerix Stormhammer. Commander Kestish vanished after the battle of central City, and is believed dead.

Congarn's Orchard- (kon-garn) Large orchard by Bureland where Lance would often steal apples and pears as a child.

Council of wise- Consists of ten elders that sit on the governing seat at Monk Vale, though not all ten are usually present at meeting, there has to be at least six to hold a vote.

Cranetium- (krane-tee-um) Official title given to an elven high mage. The title means little to other elves, save for the wizards and sorcerers of their Vales.

Dalton Thornfist- (doll-ton) Dwarven king that died from an illness and left the clan to a young Tharxton Stoneheart.

Darayal Legion- (dar-ray-all) One hundred of the finest elite elven rangers that patrol the Minok Vale in pairs. They are skilled swordsman that wield a weapon in each hand during battle. They are as feared as they are awed.

Darious Theobold- (dare-ee-us / they-bold) Eleven year old son of king Thortan Theobold.

Dark Dwarves- Dwarves that live solely in the undermountian. They have pupil less eyes that have adapted over time to see solely in the dark by detecting heat patterns. They hate bright light as it is painful for them, and have turned to wicked and evil ways as a society.

Darrion-Quieness- (dare-ee-on / kwee-eh-ness) Great white dragon. Oldest of all white dragons and most powerful. His lair is in the mountains of Nalir, but he roams all over the realms. He often leads lesser races against their enemies, and takes the majority of the treasure after the victory. His last major campaign was in aid of a clan of dark dwarves against the dwarven clan Stormhammer.

Davohn Ecnal- (da-von) Adoptive father of Lance. He is a woodcutter that made his home in Bureland and found the boy when Lance was only six years old. He raised him as his son until Lance left when he was seventeen.

Dawson River- Largest river that runs in Terrigan. It stretches from the Sea of Balfour, north of Beykla, all the way through the southern kingdom of Aboe.

Dawson Stronghold- Capitol of Beykla and located at the northern mouth of the Dawson River.

DeNaucght- (day-nok-tuh) Ritual performed by goodly priests to raise a dead person back to life.

Dicermadon- (die-sir-ma-don) God of gods, Dicermadon plots with demons to kill the son of a goddess, drawing the wrath of the gods that he governs.

Dolgo seeds- (dole-go) A tasty mountain nut found on the steepest slopes of the highest mountains. Considered a delicacy by all dwarves and mountain people, including Kai-Harkians.

Dorcastig- (door-cast-ig) Tall muscled priest of Rha-Cordan. Follows under high priest, Resin Darkhand. One of the priests that participated in the DeNaucght.

Durion- (dur-ee-in) Dwarven Mountain god.

Duke Dolan Blackhawk- (doe-lin) Duke and general of the Beyklan central army. Was relieved of his position as Duke by king Theobold after the dwarven battle in Central City.

Dregan City- (dree-gan) Home of clan Stormhammer before it was wiped out by the dark dwarves and a white dragon.

Drunda- (drun-duh) The god the orcs follow. It is not known if he actually exists, or even if he is male.

Ecnal- (eck-null) sir name given to all orphans of Beykla before they were nearly all killed by unknown assassins.

Edgar Sorenson- (ed-ger / sore-in-son) Powerful cleric of Surshy, advisor and close friend to King Theobold.

Elder Bartoke- (bar-toke) Elder of the Minok Vale, member of the council of the wise, and Keeper of the sealed passings.

Elder Darmond- (dar-mond) Elder of the Minok Vale, member of the council of the wise, and Keeper of the sealed passings.

Elder Humas- (hue-mass) Elder of the Minok Vale, member of the council of the wise, and Keeper of the sealed passings.

Elder Varmintan- (Var-mint-ton) Elder of the Minok Vale, member of the council of wise, and Keeper of the sealed passings.

Erik Stromson- (strom-son) General of the Beyklan western army and hero of the orc wars.

Eucladower Strongbow- (you-kla-dow-er) Oldest Elder of the Minok Council of Wise and Keeper of the sealed passings.

Eulic Overmoon- (yew-lick) Darayal Legionnaire and cousin to Alexis Overmoon.

Fifvel- (fife-vul) Barkeeper and owner of the Blue Dragon Inn in Central City.

Flunt- God of fire, and one of the four elemental gods.

Freedom Festival- Holiday celebrated in Beykla to commemorate the end of the twenty year long orc wars.

Garlibane- (gar-lee-bane) High mage and Elder of the council of wise in Minok.

Glaszric- (ga-laz-er-ick) Half-orc bouncer at the

Blue Dragon Inn in Central City.

Grascon the nimble- (grass-con) Wererat thief that Lance double crossed back in Bureland. The thief bears a horrible scar from his nose to his ear that he received from an encounter that stemmed from him leaving the thieves guild in Central City.

Grinder- Main passage ways in the sewers under Central City that are used by the wererat thieves guild.

Gweits- (ga-weets) Tiny insect like demons that dwell on the rocky floor of the Abyss. They feed on flesh, and burrow under their victim's skin with their horrific claws and hooks.

Heart of the rock- A gemstone mounted on a gold ring that is said to have magical properties that can prevent the wearer from being harmed by any dragon's breath.

Hector De Scoran- (heck-tor / day-skore-an) Evil warrior wizard that is king of Nalir. Believes that Lance was prophesized to destroy his kingdom, and will stop at nothing until the boy is dead.

Illilander tree- (ill-lee-land-er) Largest trees in the realms. Over five hundred feet tall.

Inn of Aldon- The only inn that is in the hamlet of Bureland, where Lance grew up.

Jahallawa extract- (ja-hall-uh-wah) Sap from the Jahallawa plant which is extremely toxic if injected into the body. Leaves the victim paralyzed for hours, and it can take weeks for the victim to fully recover.

Jude- (Jewd) Mercenary swordsman from Bureland. He sold his services to fight brigands, polecats and other minor enemies of Bureland. He is also Lance's only friend.

Kaisha- (Kay-sha) Wererat thief guild member

from Central City.

Kai-Harkia- (Kay-Hark-ee-uh) Mountain kingdom north west from Beykla. It's people are dark skinned, dark haired, heavy chested, nomad swordsmen. They seldom form static villages, though some such villages do exist.

Kalen Al-Kalidius- (kay-lin / al-kal-id-ee-us) Grey elf ex-stepson of King Overmoon of the Minok Vale. Kalen has turned to the shadow and hungers for power, hoping to take over the throne of Nalir when Hector dies.

Kalistirsts- (kal-eh-stirsts) Underground mole people with no eyes that live in the undermountian.

Kalliman Theobold- (kall-eh-man) Deceased king of Beykla, father of current king, Thortan Theobold.

Kalliman Castle- (kall-eh-man) Castle and home of King Thortan Theobold.

Kar- Orc war party; excursion leader.

Kellacun- (kell-eh-kun) Wererat assassin that worked for the guild in central city before it was destroyed. Now she works for Kalen in attempt to kill Lance.

Kingsford City- Largest city on the continent of Terrigan and capitol of Ladathon.

Korrin Hentridge- (core-in / hint-ridge) Twelve year old son of Master David Hentridge.

Kreegan Malone- (Kree-gun) Acting duke of Central city when Dolin Blackhawk is away.

Ladathon- (lad-uh-thon) Southern country, south of Tyrine, where mysterious animals live in thick jungles. Kingsford City, the largest city in the world, is it's capitol.

Lancalion Levendis Lampara- Birth name of Lance Ecnal.

Lance Ecnal- Adopted son of Davohn Ecnal. Lance's birth name is Lancalion Levendis Lampara. His natural mother was Panoleen, the goddess of mercy. Lance is prophesized to bring plague and death on the world, though he sees himself as nothing more than an orphan trying to discover his past.

Leska- (les-kuh) The Earth Mother goddess. She rules over all living things while they are alive, including plants and animals. She is one of the four elemental gods.

Loke-tah- (loke-ta) Orc word equivalent to comrade. The orc's use this word in reference to another that he or she likes as a friend, though the orcish language does not have a single word for friend, yet it has over a dozen for enemy.

Lostos- (low-stoes) Name for the underground complex of the severed heart thieves guild of wererats in Central City.

Lukerey- (lou-kear-ee) God of luck and mischief.

Malwinar- (mal-win-are) Elven mage apprentice of Garlibane.

Master David Hentridge- (hint-ridge) Leader of small mercenaries guild that is disguised as a farm, just south of Central City. King Theobold uses them to hunt and kill orc's that he does not want the public to know exists; keeping the public unaware of the actually amount of the green skinned beasts that still live in his kingdom.

Matoon- (muh-toon) Aquatic elf city in the sea of Balfour.

Merioulus- (mare-ee-oh-you-lus) City of the gods. Set on a form of the Astral plane.

Midagord Milence Stormhammer- Amerix Stormhammer's deceased father.

Minok Vale- (my-nock) Name of the elven sovereignty that is set in Beykla.

Miranhka- (mere-aunk-uh) Wererat thief that managed to survive the dwarven assault on Central City and escape.

Morilla- (more-ill-uh) Town seamstress in Bureland. She was a good friend of Davohn and Lance.

Motivas- (moe-ta-vis) Southern most city in Beykla. City is built on a large brick foundation that is rumored to be ruins of an ancient civilization.

Mountain Heart- Home city of clan Stoneheart, located in the Pyberian Mountains.

Myson Strongbow- (mice-in) Darayal Legionnaire that faced Trinidy, the death knight. Myson was the first death in what was latter to be named the dead war.

Nalir- (nall-er) Evil southern empire that made primarily of swamps and quagmires. It is a militantly powerful nation that worships most of the evil gods, primarily Rha-Cordan.

Navlashier- (nav-luh-sheer) Elven city in Vidora.

Necromidus- (neck-rom-eh-dus) A collection of the first four tiers of necromancy spells.

Optis Midigan- (op-tis / mid-eh-gun) Young servant of Hector De Scoran and follower of Soran Songstream.

Orantal Proudarrow- (or-an-tall) Commander of the Darayal Legion and protector of the Minok Vale, friend of Elder Eucladower.

Panoleen- (pan-oh-leen) Goddess of mercy that was banished from the heavens.

Pav-co- (pahv-coe) Fat wererat guild leader in Central City.

Plains of Vendaiga- (vin-day-guh) A large grasslands in southern Aten that is home of the Vendaigehn steeds, the fasts horses on Terrigan.

Pockweln- (pahk-welln) Right hand supporter of Resin Darkhand, high priest of Rha-Cordan.

Pyberian Mountains- (pie-beer-ee-an) Mountain range in the north west corner of Beykla, near Andoria.

Quigen- (kwi-jin) Elven word for sacrifice. Most widely known as the name of the great battle field were general Laricin scattered the orcish horde by fighting until every man fell in the Serrin plains.

Raynard Cliffs- (ray-nard) Large group of cliffs that extend the entire north border of Nalir.

Resin Darkhand- (rez-in) High priest of Nalir, worshiper of Rha-Cordan and advisor to Hector De Scoran.

Rha-Cordan- (rah-kor-don) God of death and dying. Not inherently evil, he reins over the placement of souls when they enter the afterlife, though he has been known to be incredibly vengeful to those who prolong their lives through magical means.

Ryshander- (rye-shan-der) Wererat thief that left Central City with Kaisha after the dwarves destroyed their guild.

Sea of Balfour- (bal-four) Sea north of Beykla. Ancient lore tells of the sea once being dry ground and home of an ancient kingdom known as Balfour.

Serrin Plains- (sare-in) Dangerous expansive grassland just south of Minok Vale where most of the evil races that live in Beykla dwell.

Sespie Twinner- (ses-pee / twin-er) Young woman from Bureland that had been practicing medicine with Morilla, who learned her healing ability from helping injured soldiers during the or wars.

Severed Heart- Unofficial name of the wererat thieves guild that live in the sewers of Central City.

Sir Oswald Thorrin- (thor-in) Captain of the king's royal guard in Beykla.

Slargcar- (sa-larg-car) Orc tribe chief of tribe Glargcar.

Soran Songstream- (sore-in) High sage, and practicing wizard in the kingdom of Nalir.

Stahlsman- (stalls-man) City guard that works at the north gate of Central City.

Stephanis- (stuh-fawn-is) God of Justice.

Stieny Gittledorph- (stie-knee / get-tull-dorf) Halfling thief who became mixed up with the dragon Darrion-Quieness.

Surelda Al-Kalidius- (sir-el-da / al-kuh-lid-ee-us) Ex-wife of King Overmoon and mother of Kalen Al-Kalidius.

Surshy- (sir-she) Goddess of water. One of the four elemental gods.

Symas- (sim-uhs) Bead like ornaments hung from the ends of the braids of a hairstyle called Varmin. Varmin, the chosen hairstyle that is worn by the Darayal Legionnaires. Symas are given for meritorious acts of bravery ranging from leather, as the least, to gold, being the greatest.

Tamra Hentridge- Daughter of Master David Hentridge.

Terrace Folly- (ter-is / fall-ee) Small hamlet southeast of Central City.

Terrigan- (ter-eh-gun) Name of the continent that

all known civilization exists.

Tharxton Stoneheart- (tharx-ton) Young king of clan Stoneheart and political rival with Amerix Alistair Stormhammer.

Therrig Alistair Delastan- (ther-ig / al-eh-stair / del-eh-stan) One of the surviving members of clan Stormhammer.

Torrent Manor- small keep northwest of Central City that was built specifically for enforcing the trade embargo and taxation on the dwarves that dwelled in the Pyberian Mountains.

Travits- (trav-itz) Wererat thief and guild member of the severed heart guild in Central City.

Trinidy- (ttin-eh-dee) Dead paladin of Dicermadon that was raised from the dead by evil priests of Rha-Cordan.

Tyrine- (tie-reen) Kingdom southwest of Beykla.

Valga- (val-guh) Vlargcar's mother that was slain after she fled the ruthless orc village to protect her son from the rest of the tribe. The tribe believed since Vlargcar was abnormally large and his eyes were blue instead of yellow, she must have been consorting with evil gods.

Varmin- (var-men) Long braided hair style worn by Darayal legionnaires.

Vendaigehn- (vin-day-gun) Type of horse from the plains of Vendaiga. The steeds are marked with white spots n their flanks, and are taller than most horses with longer, thinner legs. Legend says that Vendaigehn steeds are the off spring of a Pegasus and a unicorn, though that has never been proven.

Victor DeVulge- (day-vul-juh) Squire of Apollisian Bargoe.

Vidora- (vie-door-uh) Wild, uncivilized, kingdom southwest of Tyrine that is mostly inhabited by elves.

Vlargcar- (va-larg-car) Orc whelp saved by Amerix when he and his mother were ordered to be killed by their tribe.

Vrescan Alistair Delastan- Therrig's father that was killed fighting side by side with Midagord Stormhammer in defense of Dregan City.

Westvon Keep- (west-van) Large keep and hamlet to Beykla's far east on the banks of the Dawson River.

Whisten- (wiss-ton) God of air, and one of the four elemental gods.

Yahna- (ya-nuh) City in the heavens where souls dwell that are blessed by their gods.